William Thomas Stead

From the Old World to the New

A Christmas Story of the Chicago Exhibition

William Thomas Stead

From the Old World to the New
A Christmas Story of the Chicago Exhibition

ISBN/EAN: 9783743435667

Printed in Europe, USA, Canada, Australia, Japan

Cover: Foto ©Andreas Hilbeck / pixelio.de

More available books at **www.hansebooks.com**

P.P. Price One Shilling.

Christmas No. 1892.

From the Old World to the New.

A
Christmas
Story
-OF-
Chicago
Exhibition,
1893.

Editorial Office: Mowbray House, Norfolk Street, London, W.C.
Publishing Office: Horace Marshall & Son, 125, Fleet Street, E.C.

THE PILGRIMAGE MOVEMENT;

OR,

What Co-operation will do for Travel.

BY REV. DR. LUNN.

General Editor of the "Review of the Churches."

In this Christmas number Mr. W. T. Stead has forecast a future for the Grindelwald Conference, which in my most sanguine moments I never looked forward to. , I have, however, myself already been greatly astonished at the rapid growth of the movement. The co-operative holidays organised by the Polytechnic were the first great step in this direction. For something less than £3 they sent over 1,000 of their members and friends to the Paris Exhibition, and gave them a week in Paris. This was a great feat, and was followed by their subsequent successful experiments with respect to Norway and America. This, however, is only one of many departments of the great work by which Mr. Quintin Hogg has done so much to help the youth of London.

When I commenced my experiment in a co-operative holiday for ministers, and took the first Reunion party to Grindelwald numbering twenty-eight, I little imagined how rapid was to be the development of the work I had taken in hand. There seemed to be something peculiarly attractive about the idea of taking a Swiss holiday for the sum of ten guineas,

CHIOPS AND THE GREAT SPHINX.

the members being free from any responsibility in looking at time tables or choosing the route, while at the same time having liberty of action never granted before in combined parties, and the right of returning any time within forty-five days. About one thousand persons availed themselves of this holiday in 1892, that number being nearly doubled in 1893.

My friend, Mr. Woolrych Perowne, undertook at the Grindelwald Conference to carry out an extension of this co-operative travel which from the tourist's standpoint has proved quite as successful as anything that has been accomplished in Switzerland.

Last year he successfully carried out for the sum of twenty guineas an Italian tour which gave the greatest pleasure to a number of persons. Under all these circumstances no one will be surprised to learn that he is intending to repeat last year's successful Pilgrimage to Rome this year, and has also arranged a similar tour to Palestine, and a tour to Spain and North Africa.

Mr. Stead has kindly allowed me to publish in the form of an appendix to his story, the programme of these several tours.

Those who intend to join the parties for the Holy Land or Rome will do well to apply early. Last spring the parties for Rome which were first announced were filled up very early.

NAPLES, CAIRO, JERUSALEM, and ATHENS for Seventy-Five Guineas.

Lectures by Archdeacon Farrar, Professor Mahaffy, Canon Tristram, and other eminent Archæologists.
Sermons by the Bishop of Worcester, and others.

I believe it was Mr. Stead himself who suggested the idea of a Reunion Pilgrimage to Jerusalem as a logical outcome of Grindelwald. I am glad to say that this Pilgrimage will leave England on February the 6th, accompanied by Mr. Woolrych Perowne (the son of the Bishop of Worcester), who will have charge of the Pilgrimage.

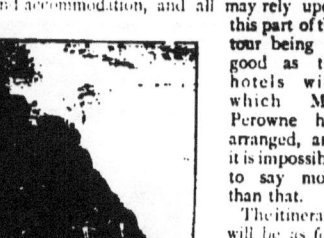

THE ACROPOLIS, ATHENS.

The whole cost for those who travel by sea the entire way will be seventy-five guineas. Those who go overland through Lucerne and Rome will pay five guineas extra. Further particulars of the prices may be found in Mr. Perowne's circular.

The journey by sea will be taken on the ss. *St. Sunnita* (one of the most famous of the Norwegian passenger steamers). This vessel is fitted with every comfort and accommodation, and all may rely upon this part of the tour being as good as the hotels with which Mr. Perowne has arranged, and it is impossible to say more than that.

The itinerary will be as follows:—

FIRST WEEK.—Tuesday, leave London and Dover for Lucerne. Wednesday, at Lucerne. Thursday, over the St. Gothard to Milan. Friday, at Milan. Saturday, Sunday and Monday, in Rome.

SECOND WEEK.—Tuesday, Wednesday and Thursday, in Naples. Friday, Saturday, Sunday, and Monday, through the Mediterranean to Alexandria.

THIRD WEEK.—Tuesday, Wednesday, Thursday, and Friday, at Cairo, visiting the Pyramids of Ghizeh, the Obelisk of Heliopolis. Saturday, by train to Alexandria, embarking for Jaffa. Sunday, arrive at Jaffa. Monday arrive at Jerusalem.

CORINTH.

FOURTH WEEK.—Tuesday, Bethlehem, and over the hills of the Wilderness of Judea, encamping in Kedron Valley. Wednesday, Jericho, encamping for the Jordan. Thursday, Bethany and the Mount of Olives. Friday, Saturday, and Sunday, at Jerusalem. Monday, return to Jaffa and embark.

FIFTH WEEK.—Tuesday and Wednesday, crossing the Mediterranean. Thursday, arrive at the Piræus, and drive to Athens. Friday, Saturday, and Sunday, in Athens, including a visit by railway to Corinth. Monday, leave the Piræus by steamer for Naples.

SIXTH WEEK.—Tuesday and Wednesday, on the Mediterranean. Thursday arrive Naples. Friday, arrive Florence. Saturday and Sunday, in Florence. Monday, leave Florence for Venice.

SEVENTH WEEK.—Tuesday, leave Venice for Lucerne, returning home direct, or staying in Lucerne, if desired.

POMPEY'S PILLAR, ALEXANDRIA.

ENTERING THE PYRAMIDS.

For further details apply to The SECRETARY, "The Review of the Churches,"
5, Endsleigh Gardens, London, N.W.

ROME, FLORENCE, MILAN, AND LUCERNE.

An Eighteen Days' Tour for Twenty Guineas.

THE FIRST PARTY WILL LEAVE LONDON ON FEBRUARY 5th or 6th.
Three Lectures in Rome by Archdeacon Farrar.

THE SECOND PARTY WILL LEAVE LONDON ON MARCH the 12th.
Easter in Rome, with Special Sermons by Leading Preachers.

THE THIRD PARTY WILL LEAVE LONDON ON APRIL the 17th.
Special after-Easter Party for Clergymen and Educationists.
Lectures by the Rev. H. R. Haweis, and others.

It is difficult to give the tour according to the days of the week when three tours are arranged in this fashion, but anyone wishing to start on any one of the

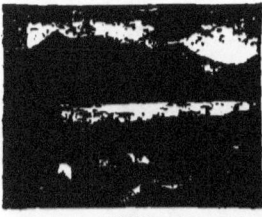

LUCERNE.

three given dates can calculate their tour with the aid of a calendar. Here the arrange-

PALAZZO VECCHIO, FLORENCE.

ments are described for the first date :—
FIRST DAY.
—Leave London, Holborn

ST. MARK'S CATHEDRAL AND THE DOGE'S PALACE, VENICE.

Viaduct, for Dover 9.55 a.m. ; leave Dover about 12.30 ; arriving at Ostend a little before 4 p.m. ; cold dinner will there be served in the Belgian carriages.

SECOND DAY.—Arrive at Basle at 6 a.m., where breakfast (café complet) will be served ; leave Basle at 10.10

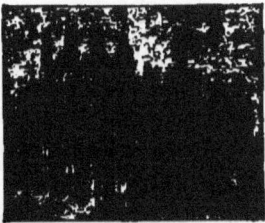

MILAN CATHEDRAL.

a.m., arriving in Lucerne at 1.37 p.m. The journey from Basle to Lucerne is through striking and pleasant scenery. Lunch, dinner, bed, and breakfast will be provided at

NAPLES AND VESUVIUS.

the Schweizerhof and the Luzernerhof, which are recognized as the best hotels in Lucerne.

For further details apply to The SECRETARY, "The Review of the Churches,"
5, Endsleigh Gardens, London, N.W.

THIRD DAY.—Leaving Lucerne at 10.20 p.m., the journey will be taken by the St. Gothard Tunnel to Milan over one of the most remarkable railways in the world, and through scenery almost unsurpassed for grandeur and beauty. Milan will be reached at 7.32 p.m., and dinner and first class accommodation will be arranged for in the Hotels Continental and De la Ville, the best in the city.

FOURTH DAY.—The day will be spent in seeing Milan, "la Grande," the capital of Lombardy, near the Ticino: the ancient *Mediolanum*. The party will leave Milan at 8.30 p.m.

FIFTH DAY.—Arrive in Rome at 10 a.m. Hotel accommodation will be provided for ten days in Rome at the following hotels (the names are given in alphabetical order) : Anglo-American Hotel, Hotel Marini, Hotel Minerva, Hotel Royale, and Hotel Russie. The first party will have the privilege of hearing Archdeacon Farrar lecture on Monday, February 12th, Tuesday, February 13th, and Wednesday, February 14th. At the conclusion of the ten days in Rome members of the party can prolong their stay in Rome, visit any other part of Italy, or break the journey at any of the principal towns on their return, at their own expense, within a period of forty-five days from leaving London. Those who return in the direct conducted party will travel as follows:

FIFTEENTH DAY.—Leave Rome at 9 a.m., arriving at Florence 5.30 p.m., dining and staying at the Hotels Cavour, Minerva, and Milano.

SIXTEENTH DAY will be spent in seeing Florence.

SEVENTEENTH DAY.—Arriving at Bâle at 7.57 p.m. Dinner, bed, breakfast, lunch, and dinner will be provided. This is giving an opportunity of thoroughly seeing this interesting city.

EIGHTEENTH DAY.—The party will leave Bâle after dinner at 9.11 p.m., arriving in London on the nineteenth day at 5 p.m.

The Rev. H. R. Haweis, in an article on last year's Easter party, wrote : " The whole thing was well done and pleasantly done. Mr. Woolrych Perowne, our special conductor, took advantage of the dinner-hour to make announcement of plans, advertise lost property, and give hints, and after delivering himself at one end of the table, he used to go to the other and *da capo*, so that all might hear.

"Mr. Arthur Perowne, his brother, was in charge of another band. At the Schweizerhof we were all taken in and done for together, but at Rome our one hundred and twenty and more were distributed by fifties and sixties in the Royale, Marini, Minerva, and elsewhere.

"Our little companies were very sociable, and made up tours and had teas in each other's rooms, and discussed each other in their own—may I say, sometimes too loudly. The bedroom doors acting as good sounding boards, in this way several of us had the opportunity of knowing what our fellow-pilgrims thought of us, which was sometimes both interesting and instructive. But as far as I know, there was very little ill-nature. . . ."

For further details apply to The SECRETARY, "The Review of the Churches, 5, Endsleigh Gardens, London, N.W."

AN EXTENSION TO VENICE FOR THREE GUINEAS.

A very delightful extension of the tour is arranged, giving another day in Florence, and two days in Venice, staying at the Hotel Britannia, Daniele, and Grand. This extension must be arranged beforehand, and is always largely availed of by the members of Mr. Perowne's party. Venice, the capital of

Venetia and a naval command, 176 miles from Milan, 181 miles from Florence, built on piles, on 3 large and 814 small islands, made by 150 narrow canals, crossed by 380 short bridges; founded upon the decline of Aquileia (after 462) in a shallow lagune of the Adriatic. Lat. of Campanile, 45° 26' N., long. 12° 20' E. Mean temperature 36° (Jan.) to 75° (July). The main island is divided into two unequal parts by the Canalazzo, or Grand Canal, which takes the form of an inverted S, 2¼ miles long, 300 feet wide, and crossed near the middle of its course by the famous Ponte di Rialto, of one spacious marble arch. Ponte Nuovo and the Iron Bridge are above and below. Two smaller islands, Giudecca and St. George, lie to the south, across the Giudecca Canal.

In the midst of the labyrinth of canals and streets there are several Piazzas (or Campi), nearly all adorned with fine churches or palaces. The principal of these is the Piazza di San Marco, an oblong area 562 feet by 232 feet, near the Mole, surrounded by elegant buildings, and containing the metropolitan Church of San Marco, a singular and richly decorated combination of the Gothic and Oriental styles, now under restoration. It was made a cathedral as late as 1807, when the patriarchal seat was removed to it from San Pietro; but was founded as early as 828 by Doge Giustiniano Participazo, to receive the relics of St. Mark from Alexandria. It has four bronze horses of Nero's time over the middle of the five bronze doors, 500 marble pillars, numerous gilt and other mosaics from eleventh century, and rich altars, one said to rest on pillars from Solomon's temple. The two crypts, now cleared of water, will be open to the public.

In the Piazza is the Campanile, 316 feet high and 42 feet square, with a pyramidal top, to which the ascent is made by an inclined plane; also, the three cedar flagstaffs for Cyprus, Candia, and the Morea; and Lombardo's Orologio, or clock tower. On the Piazzetta (or branch next the Mole) are two granite pillars from Syria (1127) with statues of St. Theodore and the Lion of St. Mark. Library of St. Mark, a noble building of two orders, Doric and Ionic, Zecca, or Mint, adjoins the library on the Mole. King's Palace, at the Procurate Nuove, has paintings by Bonifazio, Tintoretto, etc. The Doge's Palace (10 to 3, 1 lr.), 240 feet square, on the east side of the Piazza, was rebuilt 1354-5 by Doge Marino Faliero, and is highly adorned. It contains the Giant's Stairs in the Court, the Lion's Mouth in the Bussola Room, and Rooms of the Council, Senate, Scrutiny, and Council of Ten, bas-reliefs, library of MSS., Museum, and pictures by Tintoretto and P. Veronese of events in Venice history.

AN EXTENSION TO NAPLES AND POMPEII FOR FOUR GUINEAS.

Those who can afford the time and care to spend a little more money, will be well advised to take advantage of the extension which has been arranged by Mr. Perowne for Naples and Pompeii, giving four days extra at Naples, for four guineas, with a ticket to Pompeii.

THE ITALIAN LAKES FOR THREE GUINEAS.

A similar extension has been arranged for the Italian Lakes, which can be taken either after Naples and Venice, or by the members of the party who do not visit either of these cities.

The itinerary is so arranged as to give a thorough glimpse of the Italian lakes.

For further details apply to The SECRETARY, "The Review of the Churches," 5, Endsleigh Gardens, London, N.W.

A TOUR TO SPAIN AND NORTH AFRICA.

Lectures by the Rev. H. R. HAWEIS.

During the 1893 Rome tour, several members of the party suggested to Mr. Woolrych Perowne that he should organise a tour to North Africa and Spain. This has accordingly been arranged, and a party limited strictly to fifty will leave London about February the

STRASBURG CATHEDRAL.

21st by the P. and O. steamer for that date for Gibraltar. They will then cross over to Tangier, where Mr. Haweis has very considerable influence with some of those who have control over the Moorish palaces. Here travellers will have an opportunity of witnessing Oriental life. The customs of the inhabitants, the numerous bazaars, and the market places form a picture which will be long remembered. Return-

SEVILLE.

ing to Gibraltar by steamer they will visit Alhambra, the ancient palace of the Moorish Kings. The magnificent ornamentations of the Alhambra have rendered it a lasting memorial of the taste of its builders, and one of the chief objects of interest in Spain.

The next town visited will be Seville, the cathedral of which is the largest and one of the most magnificent in Spain. "The first view of the interior is one of the supreme moments of a lifetime. The glory and majesty of it are almost terrible. Nave, side aisles, and

GRANADA.

lateral chapels, all of singularly happy proportions, a vista of massive and yet graceful columns, a dim religious light, gloriously rich stained glass, and an all-prevailing notion of venerable age—such is the sum of one's first impressions."

Cordova is the next town on the programme. The cathedral is one of the most remarkable in Europe, having been built by the Moors as a mosque in 770, and still retains the chief charac-

THE ESCURIAL.

teristics of a Moorish place of worship. Countless columns of marble, porphyry, jasper, etc., brought from Carthage, Constantinople, Alexandria, Nimes, Narbonne, Tarragona, etc., support the roof, and divide the Cathedral into nineteen principal and thirty-six lesser aisles. Some

For further details apply to The SECRETARY, "The Review of the Churches,"
5, Endsleigh Gardens London, N.W.

exquisite arabesques and mosaics adorn the interior. A fine view of the town and surrounding country can be obtained from the Bell Tower. Madrid and the Escurial will next be visited. The Palace of the Escurial is justly considered one of the wonders of the world. It was erected by Philip II., in commemoration of the Battle of St. Quentin; its walls enclose a palace, a monastery, a church, and a royal mausoleum. In the palace are the rooms formerly occupied by Philip, in one of which he died. The church contains some magnificent statues, and the mausoleum contains the remains of royal princes for many generations, including the late King Alfonso and his first wife Mercedes. Burgos and St. Sebastian will

LEAP-FROG ON A P AND O. LINES.

be called at *en route* for Biarritz, one of the most charming French watering-place; passing Irun, the Spanish frontier town (near which is the hill of San Marcial, where on August 13th, 1813, 12,000 Spanish troops under General Merino repulsed 18,000 French troops commanded by General Reille), and Hendaye, where Custom-house examination takes place. The Cathedral of Burgos was founded in 1221. Its lantern tower over the transept is considered to be the finest in Europe, and the artistic richness of its interior is scarcely rivalled, even in Spain, abounding in magnificent

statues, tombs, bas reliefs, stained windows etc. The Town Hall contains a coffer with the bones of the Cid. A short distance from the town - are the Monastery of Miraflores and the Convent of Los Huelgas, containing monuments remarkable for their artistic and historic value. The coast is rugged, and the configuration of rocks and shore has been so adapted by art as to present at every step fresh aspects of natural beauty. From Biarritz the party will return home through Paris via Calais and Dover.

This tour, in consequence of the expensive character of Spanish hotels, and the fact that the Spanish Government does not yet make concessions for parties travelling together, will cost fifty-five guineas for each member.

Hotel accommodation terminates with the departure from Paris. The fare includes first-class travelling, hotel accommodation, consisting of bedroom, lights, and service, plain breakfast (bread and butter and coffee or tea), meat breakfast or lunch, dinner at table d'hôte, fees to servants, porters, and guards, omnibuses between stations and hotels, and the services of a competent courier.

The party is to be strictly limited to fifty.

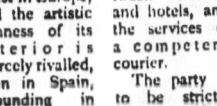

COURT OF LIONS GRANADA.

A STREET IN TANGIER.

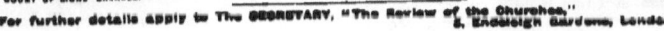

For further details apply to The SECRETARY, "The Review of the Churches," 5, Endsleigh Gardens, London, N.W.

THE
GRINDELWALD CONFERENCE, 1894.

A Twelve Days' Swiss Holiday for Ten Guineas.

The Grindelwald Conference in 1894 will be divided into five sections. The first section, lasting from June the 30th to July the 13th, will be devotional in character. The second section, from July the 14th to July the 27th, will be devoted to the discussion of Social Problems. The third section, from July the 28th to August the 10th, will be the central and most important section, and will be given up to the consideration of Reunion and Church Problems. The fourth section, from August the 11th to September the 7th, will be devoted to a series of lectures for young people. The fifth section will consist of a week's lectures on the History and Politics of Switzerland, Switzerland being considered as an object lesson in democracy for the rest of Europe. This week will terminate with a pilgrimage to the most interesting points in Swiss history, Rutli, Sempach, Morgarten, Einsiedeln, etc. Full details of this Pilgrimage will be announced later on, but they will be of the most interesting character.

The sum of ten guineas will include second-class return ticket from London to Grindelwald, with first-class on the steamer. Meals *en route*, a week's hotel accommodation at Grindelwald, a ticket over the Brunig Pass to Lucerne, and three days' hotel accommodation at Lucerne, with a return ticket to London, available any time within forty-five days.

Supplementary tours will be arranged for (1) The Italian Lakes, Milan, and Venice. (2) The Grimsel and the Furka. (3) Falls of the Rhine. (4) Zermatt for the Matterhorn, and Chamounix for Mont Blanc, and home by the Lake of Geneva.

The **booking-fee** will be **one guinea** for this tour, half of which will be returned to any who may cancel their booking up to one month of the date of starting.

As the hotel accommodation at Grindelwald is very limited compared with that of Lucerne, and as a large number of bookings were refused last year for the month of August, those who intend to visit Switzerland under these arrangements should send in their booking-fee at once, specifying the date upon which they intend to leave England. Special trains will leave London every Tuesday and Friday from June the 29th to September the 14th.

All cheques should be made payable to Henry S. Lunn, and crossed London and County Banking Co., Oxford Street Branch.

All letters and inquiries whether personal or by post, should be addressed to—

The Secretary,
The " Review of the Churches,"
5, Endsleigh Gardens,
London, N.W.

THE WETTERHORN OVERLOOKING GRINDELWALD

A Novel Scheme for the Distribution of Christmas Presents.

TO MY READERS.

Offer of One Hundred Pounds as a start.

WHEN I projected this Christmas number, I contemplated issuing a certain number of free passes to the World's Fair for distribution among my readers. On looking more closely into the matter, I found that the sum available for such prize distribution would only suffice to purchase four tickets for the round trip, even at the minimum scale of the Polytechnic, and the difficulty of apportioning those tickets on any system save that of the lottery pure and simple was almost impossible, if every subscriber was to have a chance of securing a prize. Therefore I abandoned my first suggestion to make another, which I commend to my readers, in the hope that it may meet with their approval and support.

I set apart the sum of one pound for every 1,000 copies of this Christmas number sold, for distribution as Christmas presents on an entirely new principle. As I shall publish editions of 100,000 copies, this is equivalent to the offer of one hundred pounds, to be given away according to the wishes of my readers.

I regard this £100 as the water which you pour down a pump to make it draw, and I am not without hope that this comparatively small sum may be the means of a distribution of Christmas bounty on a far more extended scale than would otherwise be possible. My idea briefly stated is as follows :—

I invite my readers to establish a Christmas Present Distribution Fund, to which I undertake to contribute £100.

At present every one is aware of the fact that while Christmas presents are exacted as a seasonable impost by many numerous classes, there are others to whom Christmas presents would be very acceptable, who never receive them. This is due to a variety of causes, the most common being a feeling of pride on one side and delicacy on the other, and the absence of any agency by which presents in money or in kind can be made without offence. At present, no public servant, excepting a postman or a philanthropist, ever receives any substantial recognition of the gratitude with which he is regarded by the public whom he serves. But there are many other deserving public servants to whom it would be both useful and just to extend some recognition of their services to the community. Unfortunately, however, there exists no method by which this sense of general indebtedness can find its natural and graceful expression.

That gap in the machinery of social beneficence I propose to endeavour to fill by the establishment of a scheme for the distribution of Christmas presents. I invite any of the readers of this Christmas number who may desire to mark his appreciation of the services of any person by making him or her a Christmas present, to forward me the sum that he desires to be handed over, specifying the person to whom it is to be given and the shape which he wishes the present to take. I will add ten per cent. to the first thousand pounds of *bona-fide* Christmas presents sent me for distribution, and hand over the total to the persons indicated by our subscribers. In all cases, unless the contrary is expressly stipulated, the source of the presents will be regarded as strictly anonymous.

A moment's reflection will indicate what a wide field of helpful effort this scheme opens up. There may be many of us who would be very glad to help to send half a dozen representative labour leaders to the World's Fair at Chicago. But as it will cost about £50 a head, this is beyond our means, and so nothing is done. If, however, ten per cent. of those who purchase our Christmas number were to send me a shilling postal order for this purpose, they could, with the added ten per cent., send eleven representatives of British labour to the World's Fair. Why should this not be done? Or if ten readers were to send £5 apiece to give an Exhibition pass to some one man or woman to whom such a trip would prove useful, the thing could be done.

That is only one form of the suggested Association for the Distribution of Christmas Gifts. It is an open secret that, not so many years ago, one of the most universally respected of our labour leaders was reduced to such straits that he absolutely fainted for want of food, when he was actually engaged in public duty. No private person could have given him money without offence, but a public subscription by anonymous donors would have been a graceful means of recognising the gratitude of the community for laborious service honestly rendered. There is no reason why this Christmas Present distribution should not become a pleasant and opportune mode whereby the public can discharge some portion of its indebtedness to those who have sacrificed much on its behalf. This is especially desirable after a General Election, when some tried and trusty servants of the people have suffered heavy losses and much personal mortification.

It is not merely because the proposed scheme supplies the necessary machinery for collection that I venture to press it upon the attention of my readers. Christmas boxes as collected now-a-days are often only nominally free-will offerings. They are levied as a tax, and paid under virtual compulsion. The dread of adding another to the long list of recipients whose customary "tip" soon hardens into a vested interest, has many times prevented the free flow of Christmas beneficence. We may be able or disposed to give this year, but we may not be able to keep up the present next year, so we abstain from giving at all. My proposed scheme obviates both these disadvantages. It is purely voluntary. I offer an opportunity for subscription. I do not press anyone to give a single cent. And as the subscriptions will be anonymous, no one who sends in a subscription this year will be expected to repeat the gift next Christmas.

England needs some simple mode of recognising by some such kindly tribute her sense of gratitude for those who have spent themselves in her service. I am not without hope that as the years roll on, this Christmas distribution system may attain wider and still wider dimensions, and that no honour will be more highly prized by those who have done their country service than the popularly subscribed Christmas gift made to those who have deserved well of their fellowmen.

Endless are the methods in which such a system could be worked for the advantage of both donor and recipient.

It offers a simple and easy method of discharging a social debt. A subscriber can send in his cheque, and order a goose or a ham or a round of beef, to be sent to every minister of religion, or elementary school teacher, or Poor Law official in the parish or town in which he has prospered. The scheme could in this way become the natural outlet of thankofferings for prosperity, it could also become a useful means of making some acknowledgment to those whom you have, if not exactly wronged, yet managed to "best" in some way or other. In such a case it would be a kind of conscience money.

As a kind of *aide memoirs*, I would remind subscribers who may be disposed to fall in with this scheme of the following categories of persons whom they may care to remember in their benefactions, naming one or more individuals of any class as the object to whom their subscription is to be paid.

(I.) THOSE WHO HAVE DESERVED WELL OF THE STATE :—
    Philanthropists, Social Reformers, Trades Unionists, Politicians, Writers.
    Soldiers, Sailors, Policemen, Firemen, Poor Law Officials, Teachers.
    Nurses, Doctors, Ministers of Religion, Public Servants, etc.

(II.) PUBLIC INSTITUTIONS :—
    (1) Society for the Prevention of Cruelty to Children.
    (2) Dr. Barnardo's and other Homes for Waifs and Strays.
    (3) The Social Scheme of the Salvation Army.
    (4) The National Vigilance Association.
    (5) The National Lifeboat Institution.
    (6) Your Local Workhouse, for pictures, books, toys, and boxes for collecting papers.

(III.) THOSE WHO HAVE BENEFITED YOU :—
    Workmen, Tradesmen, Employees, or Personal Friends.
    Localities where your money has been made.

The subscription may take any form—excepting that of intoxicating liquor, poison, and other deleterious commodities.

The cost of a ticket to Chicago and back and two months' board and lodging is £50.

Mudie's or W. H. Smith and Son's library subscription for a twelvemonth, a much-esteemed present by ministers, teachers, etc., one guinea.

Cost of sending any of the sixpenny magazines by post, eight-and-sixpence per annum.

Cost of newspaper collecting box, with glass front, and lettering, for local workhouse, ten shillings.

No._____ £____ : ____ . ____   *Received*_____

Christmas Present Distribution, 1892.

FORM OF CONTRIBUTION.

To W. T. STEAD, " REVIEW OF REVIEWS " OFFICE,

MOWBRAY HOUSE, TEMPLE, LONDON, W.C.

Please forward on my behalf as an anonymous Christmas Present*_____

_____

_____*Name* †

_____*Address*

_____

*in recognition of*_____

_____

for which I enclose the sum of   *pounds*   *shillings*

Please acknowledge receipt on postcard to

_____*Name*

_____*Address.*

_____ _____ _____

* If I must inform recipient of donor's name, strike out the word "anonymous."

† If you wish to distribute your bounty among several, write their names and addresses on the back. _____

All post-office orders, cheques, etc., to be crossed and made payable to W. T. STEAD.

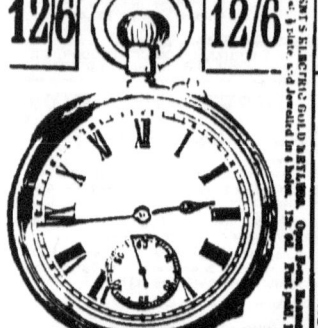

BOOKS FOR CHRISTMAS PRESENTS.

THE Christmas number of the REVIEW OF REVIEWS possesses something more than the passing interest which usually attaches to extra numbers published during the Christmas season. While possessing all the eternal interest of love, courtship, and marriage which is expected in a regulation Christmas story, there is interwoven into the romance so much actual information of a practical kind that when it is finished the reader ought to know exactly what to do if he decide to go to the World's Fair at Chicago next summer. The reader is therefore respectfully requested to recommend it to any who may be contemplating such a trip to the New World. It should be understood that it is quite distinct from the ordinary issue of the magazine, and is a story complete in itself. ..

In choosing books for presents during the festive season, we are disposed to think—however egotistical it may appear—that the purchaser could do nothing better than offer a set of volumes of the REVIEW OF REVIEWS. As a record of contemporary history, politics, and literature, these volumes occupy a unique place. They contain the essence of all that has occurred of importance during the period which they cover. Volume I. is unfortunately out of print, but Volumes II. to V. may be had immediately, handsomely bound in cloth gilt, at 5s each, or if purchased by the set, 20s, carriage paid. These volumes cover the period from July, 1890, to June, 1892.

Or, if a less pretentious present be required, it may be found in the new and cheaper edition of "Character Sketches," by W. T. Stead. This handsome quarto volume, in cloth binding, contains many of the best "Character Sketches" published in the REVIEW OF REVIEWS, and being printed on thick, expensive paper, and profusely illustrated, it is one of the very cheapest gift books in the market.

Others may wish to present literary or journalistic friends with something more useful than ornamental. To such may be recommended the "Index and Guide to the Periodicals of the World," which is universally admitted to be the best work in its line ever published. It is an absolutely indispensable work of reference for Librarians, Booksellers, Journalists, Clergymen, and all contributors to the literature or our time. It contains an accurate description of the leading magazines and reviews of the world, and a detailed index of all the articles that appeared last year in the chief English and American magazines.

Some may think that a book dealing with the Passion Play at Ober Ammergau is more appropriate to the Easter than to the Christmas season, and strictly speaking, such is the case; but, nevertheless, many may find in "The Story that Transformed the World" (cloth boards, gilt, 2s 6d.), a present peculiarly acceptable to some people, containing as it does the full text of the play (in German and English), as well as reproductions of the photographs of the play, and other pictures.

Christmas cards are still in great demand, but the Christmas Booklet is a prettier and a somewhat handsomer souvenir. A dainty specimen of this class of literature is entitled, "James Russell Lowell: His Message, and How it Helped Me," by W. T. Stead. This may be had in a 64-paged booklet, with a portrait and other illustrations, daintily bound and fastened with ribbon, and enclosed in an envelope ready for posting, 1s.

All the above may be obtained through any bookseller, or from the REVIEW OF REVIEWS, 125, Fleet Street, E.C.

CO-OPERATIVE TOURS TO
Rome & Chicago, 1893.

THE FIFTY GUINEA TOUR TO CHICAGO

Organised by Mr. Woolrych Perowne (see page viii.) will include—

First-class Return Railway Coupon London to Liverpool (30/- allowed when this is not required).

Return Saloon Liverpool to New York.

Two Days in New York. First-class Hotel.

Pullman Car to Philadelphia (Pennsylvania Railway).

Dinner in Philadelphia.

Pullman Car to Washington.

Two Days in Washington. First-class Hotel.

Pullman Car to Chicago over the Allegheny Mountains.

Five Days in Chicago. First-class Hotel.

Pullman Car to Chautauqua.

One Day at Chautauqua. First-class Hotel.

Rail to Niagara, where the party will be met by conveyance, and taken a carriage drive of fourteen miles, embracing the chief points of interest and finest views of the Niagara Falls and Whirlpool.

After dinner at the Hotel, the party will proceed to New York in Pullmans, embark on the Guion steamer and return home.

THE ENTIRE TOUR WILL OCCUPY ABOUT THIRTY-TWO DAYS, AND CAN BE PROLONGED BY ARRANGEMENT.

THE TWENTY GUINEA TOUR TO ROME

WILL INCLUDE—

Second-class Railway Ticket, *via* Dover, Ostend, Basle, Lucerne, Milan, and Genoa. First-class Ticket five guineas extra. Hotel accommodation *en route* at Lucerne, Milan, Genoa, Strasburg, and full Hotel accommodation in Rome.

The following are the Arrangements for Booking:—

1. The cost of the trip will be twenty guineas for each person. This sum will cover second-class railway fares, first-class on the steamboats, meals and accommodation as specified above on the journeys, and first-class hotel accommodation at Rome for ten days. The hotel accommodation will include bed, lights and attendance, breakfast, lunch, and dinner. Anything ordered specially beyond this must be paid for to the hotel proprietor by the person giving the order.

2. Any one wishing to travel first-class throughout the entire journey can do so by paying an extra five guineas.

3. The party will travel together on the outward journey, but on the return journey each member of the party will be at liberty to break the journey at any of the principal stations after Milan, returning at any time within forty-five days.

4. All charges for luggage, refreshments other than those named, and other incidental expenses must be paid by the member of the party by whom they are incurred.

5. The booking-fee will be two guineas, which amount should be paid at once. The balance must be paid on or before March 1st. If anything should occur to prevent any one who has booked a place from accompanying the party, the booking-fee will be returned, less 10s. 6d. for preliminary expenses, if notice be given prior to March 1st. After these dates the booking-fee cannot be returned, but the ticket can be transferred to a friend. All cheques should be made payable to J. T. Woolrych Perowne, and crossed London and County Banking Company, Limited.

CARBOLIC SMOKE BALL.

TESTIMONIALS.

FREE TRIALS AT OUR CONSULTING ROOMS

FOR INHALATION ONLY.

Colds.

The **Rev. Canon Fleming, B.D.**, writes from The Residence, York, September 7, 1892 : "Canon Fleming has pleasure in stating that he has used the Carbolic Smoke Ball with great success. Its use not only checked the progress of a heavy cold in its earlier stages, and removed it, but has prevented it from going down into the chest, and preserved his voice for his public duties."

The **Rev. H. Baugh**, Kimpston Vicarage, Bedford, writes : " I have found the Carbolic Smoke Ball very beneficial, both for the voice and preventing colds. I have recommended it to many friends. Kindly refill my Smoke Ball, and return it by first post."

Catarrh.

The **Rev. Dr. Lunn** writes from 5, Endsleigh Gardens, London, N.W., November 16, 1891 : " I have much pleasure in testifying to the great value of your Carbolic Smoke Ball. It has been used in my household with the best results in cases of bad Catarrh."

The **Rev. T. Rogers** writes from Llandrindod Wells, Radnorshire, May 21, 1891 : " Your Carbolic Smoke Ball is a most efficacious remedy. It has completely cured me of a dry nasal catarrh of very long standing."

Asthma.

Charles Moore, Esq., writes from Sunnyside, Birchington, Westgate-on-Sea, October 9, 1891 : "Your Carbolic Smoke Ball has afforded immense relief to my wife, who has suffered severely from Bronchial Asthma. When I bought the Ball she was unusually bad, and it acted like magic."

Miss Huddleston writes from Walmersley House, near Bury, Lancashire, October 15, 1891 : " Miss Huddleston is finding the Carbolic Smoke Ball a great blessing for Asthma. She is very glad to say it is doing her a great deal of good when hope had almost gone."

Bronchitis.

Dr. H. D. Darling, M.D., writes from Linden Cottage, Shepherd's Well, Kent, April 18, 1892 : " I had used the Carbolic Smoke Ball only a few times when it gave me immediate relief—although I am 83 years of age, and have suffered more than one-third of that time from Bronchitis complicated with Asthma."

General Fasken writes from 214, Cromwell Road, S.W., January 10, 1891 : " The Carbolic Smoke Ball has proved most beneficial to two members of my family, who are constant sufferers from severe colds and Bronchitis."

Deafness.

J. Hargreaves, Esq., of Manchester, writes, August 28, 1891 : " Since using the Carbolic Smoke Ball I can hear my watch tick three or four inches away, which I have not done for months."

Mrs. Kingsley writes from the High House, Woking Village, May 10, 1892 : "I am most thankful to be able to say that my hearing still continues to improve, so I am anxious not to miss using the Carbolic Smoke Ball even for a day. The Catarrh has entirely disappeared."

Sore Throat.

The **Rev. H. S. Viako Turner** writes from Potter Hanworth, near Lincoln, November 25, 1891 : " I have derived very great benefit already from the use of the Carbolic Smoke Ball for my throat."

The **Rev. Dr. Hitchens** write from 92, Gloucester Street, Belgravia, S.W., January 1, 1891 : " Your Carbolic Smoke Ball relieved the head and throat to a large extent."

One **CARBOLIC SMOKE BALL** will last a family several months, making it the cheapest remedy in the world at the price —10s., post free.

The **CARBOLIC SMOKE BALL** can be refilled, when empty, at a cost of 5s., post free.

ADDRESS:

CARBOLIC SMOKE BALL CO.,

27, Prince's Street, Hanover Square, London, W.

14, Rue de la Paix, Paris. 196, Broadway, New York. 72, Front St., Toronto, Canada.

Contents and Illustrations.

PRINTED BY HAZELL, WATSON, & VINEY, Ld.,
LONDON AND AYLESBURY.

ROSE IN ANN HATHAWAY'S ORCHARD.

FROM THE OLD WORLD TO THE NEW;

OR,

A Christmas Story of the World's Fair, 1893.

ILLUSTRATED.

BEING THE CHRISTMAS NUMBER OF THE "REVIEW OF REVIEWS."

Editorial Offices :
MOWBRAY HOUSE, TEMPLE, LONDON, W.C.
13, ASTOR PLACE, NEW YORK.
EMPIRE BUILDINGS, COLLINS STREET, MELBOURNE.

1892.

Preface.

Mowbray House, *December*, 1892.

HE World's Fair at Chicago will be the great event of 1893. All the world and his wife will be going to the Exhibition. Few questions will be more generally discussed this Christmas at family gatherings than the attraction of the Chicago trip.

Therefore the Christmas Number of the *Review of Reviews* this year is devoted, from first page to last page, to telling the British public about Chicago and its Exhibition, and the way there.

Last year our Christmas Number, dealing with the shadowy under-world, achieved for "Real Ghosts" an unprecedented success. This year we make an equally unprecedented departure from the conventionalities of journalistic Christmasery, but we deal, not with the truth about the dim, obscure world of spirit, but with the latest embodiment of the genius, the enterprise and the labour of Man in the material realms. Yet there is a living link between the two.

Chicago Exhibition, Chicago itself—which is greater than the Exhibition, and the great Republic which welcomes all nations to the great festival of nations—these are but the latest temporary materialisation and realistic development of the great idea which possessed Columbus when, four hundred years ago, he steered his tiny caravel across the Unknown Sea and re-discovered the New World. In our last Christmas Number we collected some of the shadowy fragments of evidence as to the reality and accessibility of the Invisible World, which, however incomplete and unsatisfactory, were more numerous and more conclusive than the disjointed rumours and abstract reasonings which led the Genoese navigator to take that voyage, the fourth centenary of which is being celebrated at Chicago. Last year we indicated the New World that man has still to explore. This year we record the latest results of the supreme triumph wrested by the faith and courage of a solitary adventurer from the great mystery which had been guarded for ages by the ignorance, the timidity and the superstition of mankind.

In telling the story of the voyage of a party of English tourists from Liverpool to Chicago, the writer has endeavoured to combine two somewhat incongruous elements—the love story of the Christmas annual and the information of a guide-book. Side by side with these, in the main features of "From the Old World to the New," are incorporated two other elements, viz., a more or less dramatic representation of conclusions arrived at after twelve months' experimental study of psychical phenomena; and an exposition of the immense political possibilities that are latent in this World's Fair. To deal in a Christmas number with such practical questions as the price of tickets and the choice of hotels, and at the same time to discuss the existence of the soul after death and the prospective assumption by America of the leadership of the English-speaking race, without sacrificing the human interest of a simple story of true love, is an undertaking which might well daunt the most practised story-teller. It was necessary, therefore, to entrust the task to one who had the audacity of the novice who always believes that he can do impossibilities in his first story.

Speaking critically, as editor, of the result of this bold attempt, I may at least hazard the remark that this Christmas story deserves the compliment paid by a Scotchman to the first number of the *Review of Reviews*: "It is like a haggis—there's a good deal of confused feeding in it." I would add one other remark, viz., that I have not allowed the writer, when treating of psychometry, clairvoyancy, telepathy, or automatic handwriting, to go one step beyond the limits, not merely of the possible, but of that which has actually been attained. This I have verified by experiments conducted under conditions precluding fraud or mistake.

I wish my readers, alike in the Old World and the New, a merry Christmas and a bright New Year.

WILLIAM T. STEAD.

FROM THE OLD WORLD TO THE NEW.

A Christmas Story of the World's Fair.

PROLOGUE.

ON Christmas Eve, 1892, in the library of Orchardcroft, some friends were discussing in the flickering firelight their plans for the New Year It was after dinner. The Yule log was burning brightly, the red glow of the cheery hearth streamed through the windows across the snow, making the comfortable country house a symbol of genial warmth and human kindliness in the midst of the wintry wilderness.

The company in the library was not too large for the talk that goes round and unites, which is very distinct from the conversation that breaks up a large party into groups. It was a middle-aged party, the youngest of whom had seen her thirty Christmases, while the oldest was nearer fifty than forty. But excepting that they did not propose to play Blind Man's Buff, or Puss - in - the - corner, there was no trace of age in the circle. "Young people," the Princess of Caprera used to say, "were like babies, interesting to see, but somewhat wearisome at a prolonged *tête-à-tête*." So, when she lit up Orchardcroft with the brilliance of her presence, "no one under thirty' was the rule, only relaxed for some youthful hero whose exploits had attracted the attention of the great world.

"For my part," said Sir Wilfrid Bruce, under whose roof the company had met to spend Christmas, "nothing in the Old World or the New is interesting enough to tempt me away from Westminster, the Coliseum of the British Empire. With the gladiatorial games about to begin, under the leadership of the noblest Roman of them all, positively for the last time, it would be a great temptation indeed that lured me from within driving range of the Clock Tower."

"You English," said the Princess, "take your pleasures so tragically. What is it that attracts you in the Parliamentary arena, but the great game which is played against an old man's life? It is the death's head on the dice that is the winning throw."

"You must admit," interposed Walter Wynne, a young doctor who had distinguished himself by the intrepidity and skill with which he had devoted himself to the service of cholera-stricken Hamburg, "that there is something heroic in the spectacle of Mr. Gladstone, indomitable to the last, confronting the serried ranks of his opponents with such a heterogeneous crowd at his heels."

"Heroic, yes," remarked Mrs. Nightingale, an American lady, poet and professor in the University of Chicago, with beautiful eyes, full of latent fire, and a brow on which sorrow and bereavement had left their traces, "heroic for him, but not very heroic on the part of those who are rallying for the last attack. It reminds me of that Scottish martyr-maiden, bound to a stake in the Solway, and left to be drowned by the rising tide. But her persecutors refrained from stoning their victim as a preliminary entertainment."

"Poor sport," said the Princess, "but Sir Wilfrid must ever be in at the death, whether it is that of a fox or of an administration."

"We are a long way off that yet," said Sir Wilfrid; "and the sport is in the run, not in the kill. I would back Gladstone's physique against the Gladstone Government."

"That may be," said the Princess, "and we all hope it will be so we, at least, who stand outside your party battles, and only see the stately cedar that overtops all the trees of the forest. Besides, there is not an old man—or an old woman either—in Europe but would feel as if the undertaker were nearer the door when the papers announce that Mr. Gladstone is no more. A few years ago the world was ruled by the greybeards. The reign of the old is passing with the century—the reign of the young has begun."

A momentary silence settled over the little group. Then, suddenly, from without was heard the confused murmur of many voices, the shuffling of many feet in the snow, out of which presently emerged clear and strong some rustic voices singing :—

> "Ring out the old, ring in the new,
> Ring, happy bells, across the snow,
> The year is going, let him go.
> Ring out the false, ring in the true.
>
> Ring out a slowly dying cause,
> And ancient forms of party strife;
> Ring in the nobler modes of life,
> With sweeter manners, purer laws."

When the waits tramped off on their round, Lady Wini-

ORCHARDCROFT : CHRISTMAS EVE.

fred broke the silence: "I wish they had not come, or, at least, that they had sung something else. It sounded like a voice from the grave."

"A voice from the grave that has closed over another of the famous men of old," said the Princess. "They fall fast, these goodly cedars. Our own Renan accompanied your Tennyson into the Land of Shadows."

"And our Whittier did not linger long after Whitman," said Mrs. Nightingale. "And with us, as with you, it is a race of pigmies which succeeds the giants."

"I protest," said the doctor, "really, I protest. If you must have old men, Bismarck still fulminates in Germany, and the old Pope forges his anathemas in Rome. In the British Empire, the old Lady on the throne, and the old gentleman who is her Prime Minister will outlive many of their younger contemporaries. But, Princess, if the shadow of the death's head forbids your participation in English politics, where are you going to spend next year?"

THE PRINCESS OF CAPRERA.

"As usual, in Paris, when the Parisians are in their capital; the rest of the year yachting among the Isles of Greece, where you combine the traditions of the heroic past with the primitive barbarism of the present day."

"Could we not induce you to come to Chicago?" said Mrs. Nightingale.

The Princess looked up in mild amazement. Sir Wilfrid laughed. "Why not to Pekin at once?" he asked.

"There is nothing doing at Pekin," said Mrs. Nightingale, sedately. "Why should you go to Pekin? But at Chicago we have the World's Fair, the greatest Exhibition that the world has ever seen!"

"No consideration in the world would ever induce me to go to America, that land of barbarians who have got the electric light, and therefore imagine they are civilized," said the Princess. "They are a clever people, ingenious mechanics, no doubt, with a remarkable talent for producing tinned meat and potted lobster. But I would as soon go to a candle-maker's as to Chicago."

"I entirely agree with you," said Sir Wilfrid. "The Americans are the Chinese of the English-speaking race. The Irish are our French, the Scotch our Germans, the Welsh our Portuguese, but the Americans are our Chinese. That is why I said I would as soon go to Pekin as to Chicago."

"I don't see the analogy," said Mrs. Nightingale, somewhat warmly.

"The analogy is so close," said Sir Wilfrid, "that you can hardly miss it. The Chinese, like the Americans, are an immense people, immense in numbers, immense in territory, immense in resources, but still more immense in their own conceit. Americans have not yet made the Chinese discovery that all non-Americans are barbarians and foreign devils. But they are on the road. Before long they will try to exclude foreigners as the Chinese forbade Europeans to set foot in the Middle Kingdom. Their tariff is Chinese; McKinley might have been a mandarin with a pig-tail. They are not a military people, neither are the Chinese, although both can fight on occasion, and both are beginning to have a foreign policy and a navy. They are as a people industrious, ingenious, pacific; but their civilization like their mind is vulgarly materialist, and their mediocrity is monotonously uniform. They speak English after a fashion, but as they say nothing worth listening to, they might as well speak Choctaw."

Mrs. Nightingale bit her lip, not trusting herself to speak.

Lady Winifred, seeing the storm rising, interposed. "Really, Wilfrid, you are going too far. I don't know any pleasanter company than some of our American friends, and if the Chinese are like them, I should be very glad to be a Chinese."

"And as for the World's Fair," said Dr. Wynne, "I understand it is a dream of phantasy suddenly materialised, not in marble, but in stucco or staff, and that the White City by the sea is a city of palaces the like of which neither the New World nor the Old has yet gazed upon."

"But," said Sir Wilfrid, "if there is one thing more detestable than another it is a great exhibition. Crowds are not lovely even in Europe. What they may be in America I decline even to imagine. Heat, dust, mosquitoes, general discomfort, high prices, and bad smells these are always on show at a world's fair. I would prefer to bury myself in some Italian valley with no other company than my books and my dogs, rather than swelter in the metropolis of hogs looking at the greatest dry-goods store that ever disguised itself as an exhibition."

"There I differ from you," said the Princess. "If you had gone to the Paris Exhibition, you must have felt yourself rebuked at every turn. It is possible to have an exhibition which is an embodied poem. But that is only possible in Paris. At Chicago—why you might as well try it in Berlin, which is only a little more German than Chicago!"

"German or Irish," broke in Mrs. Nightingale, "the World's Fair is American, distinctively American, and if you are good enough to visit it you will know more about America than you seem to at present. Why, you could stow away everything in your Paris Exhibition—the Eiffel Tower excepted—in a corner of Jackson Park."

"Bigger, I admit," said the Princess. "Better, I deny. It is the characteristic delusion of the American mind that mere bulk itself is an advantage. In reality it is the reverse. The art of civilisation is to reduce things to manageable compass. The savage hurled a huge crag down the hill upon his foe; the civilised man shoots him two miles off with a bullet as slender as a lead pencil. A diamond is worth more than a truck-load of coke. The greatness of a country consists not in the number of miles that intervene between its cities, it rather is to be found in the skill and resource with which the engineer and the mechanic have obliterated that yawning space."

Mrs. Nightingale for reply, opened a portfolio lying by her side, and displayed to the company illustrations of the buildings of the World's Fair. As they passed from hand to hand, the Princess pointed triumphantly to the dome of the Administration Building.

"There," said she, "look at that! There you have the crownless summit of American imagination! It is an imitation of the great dome at Paris, but they spoil what they purloin. Where is the radiant figure which crowned the Paris dome? In its place there is only a flagstaff. The great dome has no more crown than an inverted bell-glass. But," she added, with a pitying smile, "it would be too much to expect from Chicago even the homage of faithful imitation."

Mrs. Nightingale, in her own phrase, "got just a little mad." She was of a beautiful disposition and chastened temper, but the Princess in her malicious moods was more than a trifle trying even to a saint.

"Perhaps the Princess of Caprera," she said, speaking with some effort—"perhaps the Princess of Caprera would change her mind if she saw the World's Fair with her own eyes instead of trusting only to these poor photographs. Those who have seen both Paris and Chicago are much less disposed to conclude that the Old World has beaten the New. As for your gilded figure standing on one leg on the top of your Paris dome, I do not fancy that is either natural or beautiful. It may be your Old World likes to see the unnatural creature perched up there, but we like it different," said Mrs. Nightingale. "Our buildings are better and bigger and more imposing than any you had to show in Paris."

"Bigger," said Sir Wilfrid; "bigger, no doubt, but better—query?"

"Why, Sir Wilfrid, surely you have not forgotten what a fuss the Paris ans made about the size of their show," replied Mrs. Nightingale. "After the Eiffel Tower, which was the tallest shaft of iron ever thrust up into the sky, they were proudest of the Palace of Machines, and why? Solely because it was the biggest section of space ever roofed in by man. But we have beaten them hollow. We could tuck the Paris building inside our big palace, and still have ample room to spare. So far as dimensions go, we have beaten Paris hollow. And in beauty also. We have the advantage of site. Our White City of Palaces stands like modern Venice on the shores of the Adriatic of the West. Nature has done for us what Art could never do for your Paris show, which was twisted in and out of your Paris streets, and straddled across your petty Seine."

"Mrs. Nightingale is right there," said Dr. Wynne. "There is more poetry in the ocean than in anything under the starlit sky. The idea of Venice in Illinois fascinates me strangely. Between the sea—for the horizon on Lake Michigan is as the horizon on the ocean—and the prairie, on the edge of the newest millionaire city in the world, to heap up the trophies of the civilisation that has subdued the Continent is a grand idea if worthily carried out"

"But it is worthily carried out," interrupted Mrs. Nightingale. "Come and see for yourselves. We challenge comparison. Chicago cannot improvise a Pompeii, or a Coliseum. She is nowhere in antiquities. But give her a thing to be done which dollars and cents can do, and you may back Chicago against the world. Why, our American cities, who were as jealous as they could be of Chicago, are all wheeling into line behind the banner-bearing city, and owning up that she has erected Exhibition Buildings that the New World need not blush to show to the Old."

"Rather a violent transition, from pork-butchering to high art," said Sir Wilfred. "Some of these buildings are worth looking at. All Exhibition buildings are more or

lets sheds. But these are glorified sheds, it must be admitted. And not even American advertisements can vulgarise the sea even an inland sea. But if I went to Chicago I should go not to see the Fair so much as Chicago itself."

"And you would be right," said Mrs. Nightingale; "Chicago itself is the greatest exhibition at the World's Fair. She is one of the wonders of the world. She is the supreme civic monument of American enterprise. She is the embodiment of go-ahead. Other cities pride themselves upon their grey antiquity. Chicago is the city whose glory is her youth. She is her own ancestor When you were born she was little more than a country town. To-day she has a million and a half inhabitants, and is adding to them at the rate of 40,000 a year."

"No doubt," said the Princess, tartly, for she was not accustomed to the second place. "No doubt 'tis the Mammoth Mushroom of the Modern World. But a city without a history is a city without romance."

"History," interposed Dr. Wynne, "is of two kinds—

MRS. NIGHTINGALE, OF CHICAGO.

history made and history in the making. Chicago has plenty of the latter sort. It is in the centre of the roaring loom of time, and if it had existed a thousand years since we should all have found romance enough in traditions of its growing into line to attract us to the study of that marvellous outburst of human energy."

"New history, like new wine, is not for me," said the Princess, with asperity. "It is neither mellow nor clear. When the lees have settled and the rawness has gone it will be time enough to think of it. There is no repose in Chicago. It is all a vulgar, headlong stampede, as of bungry buffaloes in the mad rush for wealth. Rush, push, grab, gamble, drive, one mad struggle for the almighty dollar. No, thank you, I prefer my island rock, with its calm simplicity and evenness of life."

A PAIR OF LOVERS ON THE DECK OF AN
ATLANTIC STEAMER.

"As for us." said Mrs. Nightingale, rising—for it was near midnight—"we prefer the New to the Old. We live in the light of the coming day. Ours is the might and the energy and the restless fever of youth. We do something more in Chicago than hunt the dollar. We are building up a city out of the most varied conglomerate of humanity that ever was supplied to city builder since the days of Cadmus. There are more Germans in Chicago than Americans. But Chicago is an American city. Poles, Magyars, Bohemians, Irish, Swedes, Russians, Jews—out of this strange amalgam we have reared the Queen City of the West, and in another generation the whole population will be American. All these polyglot myriads, already impregnated with the feverish energy of Chicago, will be habituated to the atmosphere of our political institutions. Their children will speak the tongue that Shakespeare spoke, and grow up with the conviction that the world revolves on its axis every twenty-four hours subject to the Constitution of the United States. You are interested in generals who conduct compaigns against savages. Our campaign never ceases, and its victories are more lasting than those of Cæsar. You are interested in scientific discoveries. Here in this great crucible we are experimenting in the new alchemy of Humanity. We are transmuting the baser metals. We have discovered the philosopher's stone in our common school. But, my dear Princess, I must apologize for my vehemence," and then Mrs. Nightingale departed with Lady Winifred to her room.

"A fiery little lady," said Sir Wilfrid, after the door had closed behind Mrs. Nightingale; "who would have thought she could have blazed up like that, and all about that pigsailing metropolis out west?"

"The Americans are all touchy," said Dr. Wynne. "Say a word against their city or their state, and it stings them like a nettle."

"All parvenus are the same," said the Princess. "The *nouveaux riches* always stand on their dignity, and the less they have the more they assert it. But I fear we were really too hard upon her. Come, it is time we all followed her to rest."

It was midnight, and as the little group stood around the statue of Voltaire they could hear the peal of Christmas bells float down from the village spire. The fitful flames of the firelight flung, as it were, a flickering smile upon the satyr-like features of the sarcastic philosopher as he reposed upon the pedestal formed of the complete edition of his works which Sir Wilfrid had collected.

Just as they were leaving the room Dr. Wynne started slightly as his eye fell on a photograph which Mrs. Nightingale had left lying on the couch. It was a snap-shot of a pair of lovers on the deck of an Atlantic steamer. He stooped down, examined it closely, sighed, and turned away.

"What is the matter, doctor?" said his host.

"Nothing," he replied. "I only thought I recognised one of the figures in that picture. But it was a mistake," he said, somewhat bitterly. "I shall never see that face again."

"Come, cheer up!" said Sir Wilfrid; "it will never do to begin Christmas sadly. Here is your room. Good-night."

It was a pleasant room, with a great bay window for the western sun, and an extended outlook over the garden and the grounds. One side of the room was devoted to books. A great cheval glass swung near the dressing-table. Dr. Wynne stood before it for a moment,

"AND LISTENED TO THE CHRISTMAS BELLS."

and then passing to the western window opened it, and looked out. The cold air beat into the comfortably warmed room, bringing with it a great flood of melody from the Christmas bells. The night was dark, save for the glimmering whiteness of the snow. The bells ceased for a moment. In the silence he heard the merry greeting of some strayed reveller, and then all was still. Then the bells began again, not with the jubilant strain of the Hymns of the Nativity, but a plaintive, simple melody, in striking contrast to the joyous peal with which the ringers had hailed the Christmas morn.

"Her favourite hymn!" he muttered. "How strange! I have not heard it all these years."

And, regardless of the icy cold, he leaned out of the window, eagerly drinking in every note of the music, as if perchance amid the music he could catch some echo of a vanished love. As one after another the solemn notes floated down the air he seemed to hear her voice singing as in old time—

"Lead, kindly light, amid the encircling gloom
Lead thou me on!
The night is dark, and I am far from home,
Lead thou me on!
Keep thou my feet; I do not ask to see
The distant scene—one step enough for me."

At last the bells ceased, and with a sigh he closed the window and sat down before the fire. The resemblance in the photograph and then the melody of the hymn had revived memories that had not for years been so strangely stirred.

He pulled out a pocket-book which he carried in his left hand breast, and, opening it, took out a small envelope, carefully sealed. It bore the date "September 28th, in memory of 1886."

"Six years since," he said, as he read it. "Six years, and during all that time it has never left me. I have never broken the seal all these years, but now I must see it just once again."

And then, reverently, as if he were raising the lid of his mother's coffin, the doctor broke the seal, and took out the contents of the envelope, which were carefully folded in tissue paper. His hand trembled as he unfolded the paper, but at last the wrapping was removed, and there lay revealed a little white rosebud tied together with a tiny thistle by a lock of brown hair. It was a dry and withered little rose now, with a faint flush of gold and pink still visible on its shrunken leaves.

"It is just as she gave it to me," he murmured, and, bending reverently, kissed the little rose. Then, folding it up again in the tissue paper, he restored it to the envelope and replaced the book in his pocket.

In an absent-minded fashion, he set about undressing and began walking to and fro. Then he stopped.

"Oh, Rose, Rose," he cried, "where have you been all these long and lonely years? How gladly would I go to Chicago, or any

"A DRY AND WITHERED LITTLE ROSE."

where in the whole world, if I might but have the chance of meeting you once again before I grow too old and grey."

As he spoke he stood before the glass, and he looked to see if the grey was appearing in his hair. And as he did so a strange thing happened. Whether it was some hallucination, whether it was a fact, or whether it was due solely to the vivid revival of the memories of the past, and that his

"THERE WAS NO MISTAKE ABOUT IT: THERE WERE HER EYES."

eyes were heavy with unshed tears, cannot be answered here, but as he looked at the glass he saw it gradually cloud over with a milk-like mist. He was not near enough for his breath to dim the surface of the mirror. Then he noticed, as he watched with startled curiosity the gathering mist on the glass; that, to his intense amazement, in the centre of the mirror the mist began to clear away, and there, plainly visible before his astonished eyes, he saw the features he had recalled so often of her whom he had loved and lost. There was no mistake about it: there were her eyes, lovelit and lustrous, gazing at him from the heart of the mist-cloud, as from an infinite distance.

"Rose!" he cried, "Rose!" not daring to say more. Even as he spake the image dissolved, as the reflection on a lake disappears when the water is stirred; the mist came over the dark spot which seemed to have opened up a vista into infinity, and then it too cleared away, and the doctor stood gazing at the polished surface of the great mirror, in which he saw nothing but the reflection of his own face.

"It was Rose," he said. "Oh, why did she go when I called her by name?"

And then wearily, and in a kind of dull stupor, he went to his bedside, gazed for a moment on Bartolozzi's beautiful engraving of Venus refusing Love to Desire, and in a few moments was in a heavy sleep, dreaming that he was on the Atlantic on board a steamer, seeking Rose. In some strange and mysterious way, Rose and Chicago and the Atlantic steamer were all mixed up together with Bartolozzi's picture of the beautiful Venus and the Winged Love. But in his dreams he always seemed to find her, and she was his Rose, and claimed from him the token of her trust, the little white rose with the lock of hair. All night long he tossed about in troublous slumber, and when the morning came the doctor got up, knowing that, whatever happened, he must go to Chicago in the ensuing year.

ANN HATHAWAY'S COTTAGE.

CHAPTER I.—ROSE.

EVER since that Christmas Eve at Orchardcroft, Dr. Wynne had cherished the determination to go to Chicago. He said nothing about it to any one, not even to himself, but ever since he had seen her face in the mirror at Orchardcroft he had been full of a new hope. It was not so much a new hope as a revival of an old hope—a hope which for two years had buoyed up his heart amid adversity and disappointment, but which, for the last four years, had grown so faint as almost to disappear. Nothing could be more absurd than the fancy, suggested by the photograph and the face in the mirror, that he might see his long-lost Rose at Chicago, or on the way there. It was in vain that he reasoned about it, arguing to himself how utterly insane it was to imagine that he should meet a girl whom he had not seen for six years in the myriad multitude which was swarming to the World's Fair. He did not know whether she was alive or dead. He had no more reason to think she was in Chicago than in any other place on the world's surface. And then, if he did discover her, what chance was there that she had been faithful to him all these long years? To all of which excellently sound objections the doctor could make no answer beyond remarking—

"Anyhow, I will go to Chicago. The odds may be a million to one against my finding her, but until I give myself the odd chance I can never rest. Besides, it is a good thing to go to Chicago even if Rose is not there."

All the same, no one knew better than himself that not for a dozen World's Fairs would he have refused the tempting offer of Medical Superintendent in a great Indian hospital which was pressed upon him by those who had known of his heroism and skill at Hamburg. It was the kind of post of which he had dreamed from his boyhood; but now its acceptance conflicted with the other dream—the dream of his early manhood. He had a night of struggle. All his friends were unanimous in urging him to accept the post, which assured his career. For several hours he hesitated. Reason, common-sense, and the pressure of authority triumphed. He sat down and wrote a letter, formally accepting the appointment, but when he opened his pocket-book for the stamp, he saw the envelope with the little white rose. In a moment the old spell re-asserted its power; he flung the letter he had written into the fire, scribbled a hurried note formally declining the appointment, and then rushed out into the night to walk for miles and miles under the cold, clear stars until the morning light gleamed in the East, and he came home haggard and worn, but resolute to carry out his purpose.

"It is a kind of post-hypnotic suggestion, I suppose," he said to himself, lugubriously one day, when the madness of his conduct presented itself to him more forcibly than ever. "Sometimes an idea gets fixed in the mind, and you only waste your time by trying to dislodge it."

As the spring came on the longing to start for Chicago increased. He remembered as each spring flower came into bloom how he had watched for the early blossoms to gather a posy for his love. When the apple trees were white with blossom, he remembered how he had first seen her in the orchard behind Ann Hathaway's Cottage, had wondered at her grace and beauty, and had from that hour never had but one ideal of female loveliness. When the May began to bloom, and the hedgerows were fragrant with the hawthorn, it recalled the long walks they used to have through the daisy starred meadows by the sleepy Avon while the larks sang overhead and the murmurous hum of the bees was loud in the limes. But when at last the roses budded, and the buds swelled into opening flowers, he could contain himself no longer. The day on which he saw the first white rose he packed his portmanteau, and, next morning, found him at Euston en route for Liverpool. He would break the journey at Chester, where he had friends. But on Saturday he would sail for New York.

He was alone in the railway carriage, and when Willesden Junction was passed, he abandoned himself, without let or hindrance, to the memories which came up unbidden of the days that seemed long ago, but which in reality were but six years distant. Between now and then, what adventures, what trials, what baffled hopes! There seemed an abyss in which all the joy of life was buried for ever. Everything he saw reminded him of the love of a vanished past. Seldom had the old world seemed more

"THE OLD SPELL RE-ASSERTED ITS POWER."

lovely than on that June morning as the train swept through fields that were like gardens for verdure, flecked with sleek cattle, while here and there a young foal frolicked at the heels of its dam. The trees were in the fresh green glory of early summer. Everywhere there was gladness and brightness and joy. But the doctor sat moody and distraught, chewing the bitter cud of the memory of departed joy.

He retraced, in imagination, every step of the primrose path of dalliance which had so rude and abrupt an ending. Eight years before he was a young doctor, just settled in the neighbourhood of Warwick. He was of fairly good family, his parents had been, if not exactly county people, then on good terms with county people, well to do, and full of ambition for their talented son. He had gone through his studies with distinction, had taken his degree with honours, and had commenced his first practice as a man *lenms* for one of the most flourishing doctors in the country. Everything seemed promising when on one fine day in spring, in the course of a professional visit to Stratford, he called at Ann Hathaway's Cottage, and saw the lissom figure of Rose Thorne under the blossom-covered branches of the apple trees. He was dazzled by her beauty. Not without cause. She was tall, graceful, with a wealth of long brown hair hanging in profusion over her shoulders. They had been playing Queen of the May in the meadow, and she still wore the garland the children had placed on her head. The colour rose to her cheeks as she saw the

the orchard. But, with an effort of will, he dismissed the subject, and immersed himself in his pills and potions and his professional avocations.

But as 'll-luck would have it, one time when riding home from Stratford, he was hastily summoned by a policeman to help a boy who had fallen from a tree, and it was feared had broken his back. Following the constable, Wynne noticed with quickened interest that he was being carried to the cottage in the orchard behind Ann Hathaway's Cottage. As he crossed the threshold he saw with delight that he was in the presence of the startled

SHAKESPEARE'S CHURCH.
(From the "Homes and Haunts of Shakespeare.")

young doctor, who was contemplating her with unconcealed admiration, and casting down her eyes, she ran into a cottage half hidden in the orchard.

Walter Wynne was young, hardly more than two-and-twenty. He was standing in Ann Hathaway's cottage. It was the first flush of springtime ; the air was redolent with the fragrance and the music of Shakespeare's country. And now, sudden and beautiful as a startled fawn, there had flashed upon him this bewildering vision of youthful loveliness. All the way he rode home along the pleasant country road, he seemed to see her image dancing before his eyes. Was she real, or was she one of Shakespeare's women suddenly come to life?—this rustic rosebud of

fawn of the apple orchard. She was too much distressed about her brother's fate to notice anything beyond the fact that he was the doctor, and that her brother's life or death might hang upon his help. "This way, doctor, please," was all she said, but there was a dumb agony in her eyes which he never forgot. He found the boy, a lad of fourteen, had fallen from a tree on his head, and had been carried home unconscious. A moment's examination, however, sufficed to satisfy the doctor that he was only temporarily stunned, and that, so far as he could see, there was no fear of a fatal issue. Returning to the outer room, followed by the sister, who, in the absence of her parents, had charge of the house, he said,

" Don't distress yourself; there is no danger. In an hour or two he will be all right." ·

For a moment the glad light shone in the girl's eyes, and then the revulsion of feeling, the recoil as it were from the very presence of death, was too much for her. The room swam round, everything became indistinct, and before the doctor knew where he was, he had caught the swooning girl in his arms, and was carrying her to the window. She was deadly pale, the long dark-fringed eyelids were closed, she lay motionless and beautiful as the drowned Ophelia. The policeman hurried out for some water, and the doctor was alone with the girl. How his heart beat! Presently there was a faint fluttering as of a trembling bird, the girl moved slightly, and opened her eyes.

"Where am I?" she said, faintly, and then recognising who was supporting her in his arms, she murmured, "Oh, doctor!" and lay quite still for one brief moment. Then the constable came with the water and the cordial, and the doctor took his leave with a promise to come again.

He did come again, and many a time again, and that for long after the last semblance of illness in either patient called his attendance. By degrees he found out all about the family. They were cottagers; the father a stonemason by trade; the mother a superior woman, whose love for reading had been transmitted to the daughter. Her daughter Rose was but turned eighteen, but although a woman in stature and in mind, was a child in the simplicity and innocence of her soul. All her knowledge of the world was gained from books and the conversation of her mother and an occasional neighbour, whom she met on her way to or from Shakespeare's Church. There were not many books in the stonemason's cottage beside the Bible and Shakespeare, and on these two Rose had been brought up. Perhaps it was the air of Stratford or the association of Ann Hathaway's Cottage, but, whatever it was, she lived in a Shakespearian world.

Of the great hurly-burly outside, with its pomp and state, its sins and sorrows, she knew nothing. Her world was the realm which Shakespeare had peopled with the creation of his brain. Gladstone and Salisbury, Bismarck and the Czar were to her words without meaning. But she loved gentle Romeo as if she had known him from her youth up; she mourned the hapless Imogen and counted Miranda and Rosalind as her most intimate friends of her girlhood. They were real to her, while these shadowy phantoms of the dramatist's fancy were more real, almost visible and tangible as they seemed to her, than the statesmen and sovereigns of whose existence she was unaware.

From her youth up she had lived among the flowers and in the orchard, blithe as the thrush and as happy as the lark, cultured with the love of one book, and wondering sometimes, as she moved in maiden meditation fancy free, when her Romeo would arrive. She worked in the house at all times, helped sometimes in Ann Hathaway's Cottage, milked the cow in the croft, and helped to make hay with the best of them, but living all the while her life apart, feeding her soul upon the magic page. It was this ideal, hidden life, into which as with one great plunge Dr. Wynne had suddenly burst. To say that he loved her is unnecessary. He was young, romantic, and alone. She was beautiful as a poet's dream, living in a fairyland of love and romance, with no one to share that life, or even to understand that she had that life, but he who had so unexpectedly come into her existence.

The white roses were just beginning to flower when he told her of his love. They had been having a long walk by the Avon talking of love and Shakespeare's lovers, when the sun began to sink behind the clouds on the western horizon. She said but little in reply to his declaration. She had loved him from the first time she had spoken to him, and she told him so It was pleasant to hear him say he loved her, for now she might tell him how she loved him. When they parted at the cottage-door in the twilight, he plucked the first white rose in the garden and said —

"Keep that in memory of me until our wedding day."

She hid it in her bosom and went indoors, while he, walking as if in Paradise, hurried home.

For a time all went well. Then gossip with its hundred tongues began to talk about the doctor and the stonemason's daughter. Some envied the girl her good luck; others foresaw her certain destruction; but of all their surmisings the young lovers thought nothing. They were in the rapture of first love. But after a time his friends heard of it, and began to hint that it was unwise to entangle himself in an affair with a village girl. As for his marrying her, it was not even to be dreamed of. He listened to them as though he heard them not, and they indulged to his heart's content in the interchange of affection natural to two full hearts. Then his brother-in-law went to the little cottage, and told Rose that she was ruining her lover's life, disgracing him before his friends, and that it was the height of presumption in her, a mere cottager's daughter, to dare to love one so much her superior. Poor Rose turned very white, quivered a little, and then, without a word went into her room and shut herself up for a long time.

When she came out there was a hard gleam in her eye and a rigidity about her mouth no one had ever seen before. The next day she had disappeared. The evening post brought Dr. Wynne a little note, and in the note was written :—

"I return you the little white rose. It has never left my bosom night or day since you gave it me. Some day when I am in a position to be loved by you without injuring you by any law I may claim it again.

"Till then, farewell —

"ROSE."

The rose was tied up with a thistle by a lock of her brown hair and with the rose there was a page torn from a diary. The doctor rode over at once as one distracted to the cottage. Rose had gone that morning. But where? "To London," was all that she had said. "She had seemed queer like," said her brother. "She had never been asleep all night, and had gone off with her box to the station." That was all he could learn. But, incidentally, the boy mentioned that she had had a visit from his brother-in-law the previous day. It gave him the clue to her otherwise mysterious letter.

He had to hurry back to the bedside of a country gentleman who was struggling painfully back to life from the borders of the grave, but what a tempest of emotion surged through his brain. That poor girl in London, friendless, almost penniless, as innocent of the world and its ways as a child! It was maddening!

As soon as he could get a substitute he rushed off to London, but no trace of his lost Rose could he ever obtain. For two years he searched for her, subordinating all professional advancement to the quest, but it was all in vain. She had disappeared as utterly as if the earth had opened up and swallowed her. What had become of her? Who could say? Or rather, who could doubt what to say who calculated the chances coolly and dispassionately? For months Dr. Wynne walked the streets, eagerly following every tall, slim girl with brown hair, fearing horribly that each poor wanderer might be "Shakespeare's girl," as he used to call her, and always

"THROUGH THE DAISY-STARRED MEADOWS
BY THE SLEEPY AVON."

finding quite another face than that he knew so well. The little white rose never left his heart, but, alas ! it was no talisman to guide him to her. At last, hope long deferred made the heart sick. He had abandoned the hopeless quest, and never had he dreamed of renewing it until last Christmas eve.

As he thought over it all the train had passed Rugby, had left Warwickshire, and was speeding through the skirts of the Black Country. He took small note of the change in the landscape. His thoughts were with his heart, and that was far away. And as he sat and revolved endlessly the question of her fate his hand sought instinctively the pocket-book where lay the little white rose. He took it out and pressed the envelope to his lips. Then he opened another envelope, and re-read for the thousandth time the page from her diary now all yellow and creased. It was enclosed in the only letter she had ever sent him. She had written it the night after that summer day when he had first told her that he loved her. She had received his declaration so calmly, the intensity of her delight forbidding utterance, that he had no sooner left her than she hastened to pour out her soul to him in her diary, and when she went away she tore out the page and sent it him, as if to let him know what she might never have an opportunity of telling him. His eyes, dimmed with tears as he once more perused the passionate outpouring of the heart-soul of this child of nature, and remembered how tragically it had all ended.

This is what she had written in her diary :—

"Oh, Walter, my own dearest darling, how can I ever tell you of the love which glows in my heart ? I have never in my whole life felt such rapture as I did when I heard you say you loved me. Oh, Walter, I would willingly die rather than not have heard these sweet, sweet words. Oh, my own, then you really do love me—love me—love me ! These are the only words in the whole language I care to hear. Oh, my Love, how I love you ! I cannot say what I feel or how I feel, I am all in a glow of joy and peace, and of contented rapture.

"Oh, Walter, my own, and really my own. How wondrously your love has transformed life for me ! My whole soul is transfigured. I am radiant with the glow and glory of your love. Oh, Walter, I cannot speak for the throbbing and palpitating of my heart It seems all too unspeakably marvellous to be true. I used to think dreams were sweeter than life could be ; but now I know that life is sweeter, richer, and more divine.

"This night I have been in Paradise. In Heaven I could not be more full of ecstasy. Oh, Walter, you are mine, mine, mine, Love, Love, Love, mine, mine. mine—the words ring in my ears like the music of chiming bells. I am sitting on the side of my bed surrounded by your gifts, the rose-bud and your portrait, like a queen among her jewels, and I wonder and wonder and wonder again how it was that God gave me this great gift of love. Oh, Walter, you who hear the very throb and beat of my heart, I need not. I cannot tell you how I love you. But that is an old tale now ; the new, the delightfully incredible new tale is that you really do love me, and that you are mine. Love, mine ! Now, beloved, I must tear myself away until I can go to bed and dream. Oh, what a miracle that reality should be even better than the brightest dream !

"You will never cease to love me. I know that now. Oh, the bliss of your love. It is beyond my utmost dreams. I will keep the white rose till it withers all away, dear messenger of love. I have almost kissed it away !

"Oh, Walter, how good you are to me, how kind, and I to you am what ? Oh, less than nothing, but whatever I am I am yours—yours altogether, for life and death, time and eternity, body, soul and spirit. Yours now and for-evermore."

"Poor child," he said, "she is a passionate Juliet, and to think——!" And he clenched his teeth, and said no more, but his brow grew dark, and his thoughts were so sombre that when his friend met him at Chester, he was startled by his gloom, nor could he shake off the oppression for many hours.

CHAPTER II.—IDEAL AND REAL.

WHEN Dr. Wynne woke the next morning the sun was shining brightly, and there had come to him in the night a strange new hope. He was on his way to Chicago ; he had started to put his fortune to the touch, to win or lose it

THE DOCTOR.

all. At last it was to be settled one way or the other, and the conviction grew that it would be settled the right way. He had dreamed of Rose—that was nothing new. In the two years during which he had sought her vainly, his dreams were his chief consolation. She was always with him in dreamland, and it was the abiding sense of her reality in sleep that enabled him to support the misery of the day.

Since Christmas at Orchardcroft, he had dreamed of her more frequently. That night at Chester he had dreamed that he was again at Ann Hathaway's Cottage. There was the familiar thatched roof and the cottage garden, and the well-known windows, and the white rose by the door, but the surroundings seemed strangely unfamiliar. For the Hathaway Cottage seemed to be standing near the shore of a great sea, and all around it were other sounds than the murmurous working-psalm of the bees or the matin song of the lark. What the sound was he could not make out, but it was as the irregular footfall of myriads of men, and the buzz of the talk of multitudes greater than had ever trodden the Warwickshire lanes. And, before the cottage, he saw a form that seemed at first the figure of a stranger. He approached her, and something made his heart throb wildly. He came nearer still, and saw it was his long-sought-for love. And behold it was only a dream!

But the sun shone brighter for the dream, and in an irrational, superstitious kind of way, he felt as if the vision was an encouragement of his quest of Rose. So, after breakfast, he gladly agreed to his friend Tom's proposal to spend a few hours before the train left in strolling around the city.

"To tell you the truth, Tom,' said the doctor, "I came here almost as much to see Chester as to see you. When one is starting for Chicago, it is good to take a last, lingering look at a place which is everything Chicago is not."

"Yes," Tom replied, "I never understand how it is so few Americans, comparatively, come to Chester. It is the most authentic antique in the Old World, planted, almost as if for inspection, close to the very American edge of the Eastern hemisphere, and yet how few there are who deem it a duty 'to do Chester.' "

They went down Watergate Street to the city walls, and were soon looking down upon the Roodee and the winding Dee.

"From Chester to Chicago," said Walter, as he leant over the parapet, "the journey is but one of days, but it spans two thousand years."

"You had better take your fill of antiquity here," said Tom, flippantly. "You will find more history here in a single street than in all the booths of the Vanity Fair that is built on the shore of Lake Michigan."

Chester is a city whose beginnings are lost in the "purple mist of centuries and of song." The Welsh border has not yet found its Scott, or even its Wilson, to make the heroism of its past an imperishable possession for all time. But Chester was a great Border stronghold.

Round these once rugged battlements which, though patched and modernized, remain the one perfectly intact city wall in England, sentinels have for sixteen centuries been keeping watch and ward for the dominant power. The city is a microcosm of English life. The Cathedral, the Castle, the City Walls, the Towers, enclose as much English history as any spot save the sacred circle around the Abbey at Westminster. It is a kind of jewelled clasp with which History links together the first century and the nineteenth. It unites the fortunes of the centurions of the Twentieth Legion with the bishop who alone with his brethren has grappled in the spirit of a statesman with the almost insoluble problem of the tavern.

As the doctor looked down from the city walls over the Roodee, Tom said. "There is the most beautiful race-course in England—almost, if not quite—and quite the most interesting. Long centuries ago there was a famous shrine at Hawarden—Mr. Gladstone's Hawarden—where there was an image of the Virgin held in high repute of all the countryside, for Hawarden has from old been a place of pilgrimage from far and near. But, unfortunately, it fell out—I don't know exactly how—that the prayers of the worshippers were not answered. They bore it for a time, but finding that there was no improvement, they acted as the present lord of Hawarden did with the Unionism which he professed so ardently in the days when he exhausted the resources of civilisation by locking up Mr. Parnell. That is to say, they rounded on their fetich, pulled her down from her shrine, and bundled her ignominiously into the river. Down the Dee she floated, a miserable, forlorn spectacle, until the tide washed her ashore on the Roodee, which you see before you. Then there happened what has happened quite recently. The despised outcast from Hawarden became the god of Chester's idolatry, and the shrine of the Virgin rescued from the flood became the central object of the popular faith."

"Curious," mused the doctor. "But Hawarden triumphed after all. Where is the Virgin to-day? Her shrine is given over to the Bacchanals of the turf, whereas Hawarden sways the sceptre of the empire of the Queen."

"Now," said Tom, "come along to the Tower, which interests me more than all the exhibits at Chicago. It is the Phœnix Tower, at the north-east corner, right at the other extremity of the city.'

So saying, they left the walls after a last long look at the Roodee and the famous river where Egbert, first king of the English, was rowed in his barge by six tributary kings, and hurrying down Watergate Street, were soon at the central cross made by the streets running at right angles in the old Roman fashion from gate to gate of the ancient Castra.

"You will find nothing in all America like the Rows," said Tom, pointing as he spoke to the wonderful and unique arcades in the first floor, which the Chester people call the Rows. "'The like,' as old Fuller said, 'is not to be seen in all England, no, nor in Europe again.' Arcades there are in Paris, in Bologna, where they

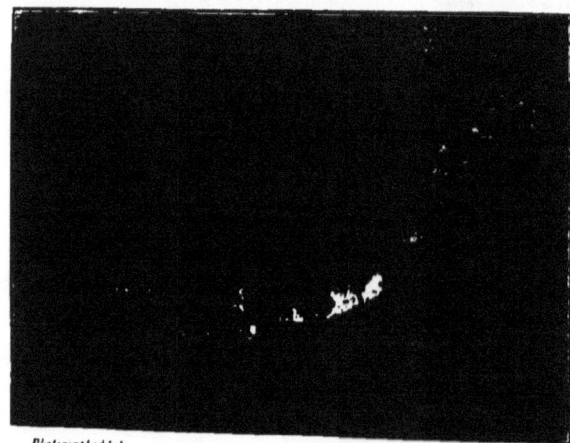

are endless, and in Berne, where they are beautiful, but it is only here where you have your arcade on the first floor."

They slowly sauntered on, admiring the quaint old masonry, the characteristic compound of timber and stone, the picturesque gables over the occasional inscription. If it were on the Continent, Cook would organise tours to visit it. As it is in England this native Nuremberg escapes attention. After a time they came out upon the walls again, and in a few minutes were at the Phœnix Tower.

"Here," said Tom, "is where I always come when I

sweep of the city walls. "And what a mine for a psychometrist! To a really gifted clairvoyant it would be difficult to go along the street for the throng of memories that are embodied in these old stones: Roman legionary; the Mercian earl who wedded great Alfred's daughter; Hugh the Wolf, who came over with William the Conqueror and was his warden of the Welsh Marches; Charles Stuart, down to Kingsley and Gladstone, he who could utilise the sixth sense that enables one to use this great phonograph of ancient stone would need no other guide to English history. But, alas! psychometrists are rare, and the most gifted might well be baffled by the palimp-

THE ROWS, CHESTER. "THE LIKE IS NOT TO BE SEEN IN ALL EUROPE."

am worried or inclined to despond and imagine myself the most miserable of men. For it was from the summit of this tower that Charles the First, hunted and driven, and ready to perish, strained his eyes to see the last cast of the dice, on which kingdom, yes, and even life, were staked. It was towards the end of September, 1645, when the Royalist cavalry under Sir Marmaduke Langdale, who had escaped alive from the hammer strokes of Cromwell's Ironsides at Naseby fight, made their last stand for the ancient monarchy on the battlefield of Rowton Moor. Imagine how he must have felt when the Cavaliers broke and fled, never to re-assemble, and the king came down from the tower to flee for his life.'

"What an old-world place it is," remarked the doctor, as he looked over to the Cathedral and followed the

sest of impressions there must be in those old streets."

"Now," said Tom Gatenby, after they had strolled through the Cathedral and visited Cæsar's Tower, "there is one thing you must do. You must really go to Eaton and see the pictures."

There would be no need to follow the doctor and his cicerone to Eaton Hall were it not that, when they were going over the drawing-room of that stately pleasure house, Tom Gatenby felt his companion grip his arm.

"Look," said the doctor, almost under his breath, "it is her face!"

Tom Gatenby looked where his companion pointed, hardly noticing the white intensity of his face.

"Yes," said he, carelessly, "it is one of my favourite

Photographed by]　　　　　　　[F. N. Eaton.
" FROM THIS TOWER CHARLES I. STRAINED HIS EYES."

pictures—very true. But what ails you, man? Come out into the fresh air," and so saying, he led the doctor into the grounds. He seemed temporarily distraught.

"It is her face! it is her face!" he muttered. "I could swear to it out of a million."

Tom Gatenby looked at him with some curiosity, not unmixed with sympathy. Like the rest of the doctor's friends, he had a more or less dim idea that Wynne had broken his career for a woman, and this picture, no doubt, had some mysterious resemblance to the lady in question. So he said nothing. After a while, the doctor regained his self possession.

"Pardon me," he said. "I felt a little upset. But let us go back to the pictures."

They went back to the drawing-room without a word. The doctor scrutinized the picture closely. It was one of the characteristic paintings of a great artist, full of suggestion, of imagination, and of beauty. But the soul of the whole composition centred in the eyes, in the mournful pathos of the eyes of the central figure.

"If she was like that," said Tom Gatenby, *sotto voce*, "she was a beauty, and no mistake."

"Not like that," said the doctor. " It is she herself."

No other word was spoken, and after carefully noting the date of the picture, they left the place.

The doctor was strangely silent. His eyes seemed to have caught some of the far-away dreamy expression of the painting. Presently he said,—

"I shall not go to Liverpool to-night. I am going to Hawarden."

It was Saturday afternoon. He was going to spend the last Sunday in the seclusion of an ideal parish. On the

Monday he would go to Liverpool, book his passage, and turn his back on the Old World. It was characteristic of the man. He would go alone, he said, when his friend proposed to accompany him. And he went. He put up at the "Glynne Arms," and, as soon as the inn was quiet, he went to bed.

But not to sleep. At last he had a clue. The year 1887, the date of the picture, was not inconsistent with his theory. The eyes were painted from no other eyes than those of his Rose. . . . He did not argue about it; he knew it. They were her eyes, just as he had seen them long ago, just as he had seen them only the previous night in the dream-vision at Chester. She must have sat to the artist as a model. He bit his lip as he thought of it. Had his Rose to come to that. And, yet, reflection told him it

Photographed by]　　　　　　　[F. ... Eaton.
" THE ENGLISH NUREMBERG."

was by no means improbable. Her graceful, slender figure, her singular beauty, would secure her constant employment. "Fool that I was," he thought, "ever to have worked that vein before." But now that he had the clue he would follow it up. He almost thought of giving up his journey to Chicago. It was only for a moment. He lay still for a time, and then he got up, lit the candle, and wrote to a friend in London, asking him to call on the artist in question, and ascertain if possible, the address of the model who sat for the central figure in the canvas of 1887. "Follow up any clue, and telegraph me 'White Star, Liverpool,' what results." He sealed it, stamped it, and then went to bed, this time to sleep.

Early on Sunday morning he posted it, and when the bells began to ring for morning service, he made his way to the parish church. The Prime Minister, fresh from a crisis of mutiny in the Commons, with a crisis of defiance in the Lords, had hurried down to Hawarden to breathe the divine air of early June, and escape for a day or two from the harassing buzz of whips and colleagues at Downing Street. It was not generally known that he was at the Castle, and there was no crowd such as is sometimes attracted by the chance of hearing the Premier at the lectern. The old church was fairly well filled with villagers and residents in the neighbourhood. The Rev. Stephen Gladstone was at the reading-desk, and Dr. Wynne saw with some satisfaction, Mr. and Mrs. Gladstone enter the church and take their seats in the chancel.

When the service began, the doctor forgot the Prime Minister, forgot everything, even forgot his own personal anxieties in the wave of emotion that passed over him. He was not dulled into indifference to the beauties and the significance of the Morning Service by constant use and wont. His profession left him little time for attendance at church, and he did not make the most of the chances he had. Hence, when on rare occasions he found himself in an English church, it appealed to him with fresh force. When the organ pealed through the nave, he seemed to hear the inarticulate voice of successive generations of the English race struggling in vain to express their aspiration after the ideal.

And as the service went on with alternate prayer and praise, and the chanting of the white-robed choir filled the church with the sweet voices of youth attuned to immortal melody, he surrendered himself utterly to the hallowed influence of the scene and place. Like a great golden shaft of divine light, this service seemed to stretch athwart dim forgotten centuries. All over England that day, and also in all the colonies, dependencies, and republics, where men spoke with the English tongue, that service had gone on. these prayers were being prayed, these psalms were being chanted, that simp'e creed was being said or sung. It was one of the great unifying elements of our world-scattered race. In the midst of lives sordid with constant care, and dark with the impending shadow of want and the darker gloom of death, this service, attuned to the note of "Our Father," made for one brief hour music and melody with gladness and joy in the hearts of miserable men.

It is the constantly renewed affirmation of "God's English-speaking men" of their faith in their Father-God; and here in Hawarden, Prime Minister and peasant knelt together equal before their Maker. For hundreds of years these solemn words had embodied all that was highest and best in the thoughts of the greatest and noblest, and for many hundred years to come, the English-speaking race will find the expression of their hopes and their aspirations, in the simple but stately words of the Book of Common Prayer.

"What is there in the New World?" thought the doctor, as he stood among the dispersing congregation, and bowed as the Old Man Eloquent passed out to resume the guidance of his country's destinies—"Where, in all the rabblement of sectaries which has sprung from the seed sown by the men of the *Mayflower*, will you find a service so harmonious, so beautiful, so true to human nature as this? They have no Church Establishment

HAWARDEN CHURCH.

perhaps. But is that dubious gain not bought with a heavy price if it makes impossible the national organisation of Christian effort along concerted lines of progress, this uniform upholding of the Christian ideal in every parish of the land?"

It was with some such thoughts as these still lingering in this brain that, the next day, he took the train for Liverpool. "There," he said, "is the American gate of our sea-girt citadel. At Hawarden we have the ideal rural parish. At Liverpool, the doorstep of the Motherland, we shall, no doubt, find as ideal a civic recognition of Christianity."

A friend met him at the station and took him to his hotel, and then undertook to show him the sights. Like every one else, he admired St. George's Hall, and, like most people, he was interested in, but not delighted with, the Nelson monument on the Exchange Flags.

"The group is striking," he said ; " but how pagan the exultation over the conquered foe, displayed in the manacled prisoners round the base of the statue! I have seen nothing like it since the Assyrian sculptors carved their bas-reliefs at Nineveh, showing the triumphant monarch marching over the prostrate bodies of their enemies."

They had left the Flags, the Cotton Bourse of the world, and were out in the street.

"What a splendid site that church occupies," he remarked to his companion, "I am glad to see that even within stone-throw of the temple of Mammon the piety of Liverpool has reared a Christian temple."

"Hum, hum!" replied his companion, "that church is doomed. It is one of the Corporation churches, the largest, the emptiest, and the most costly. Come on Sunday, and you will find a cor gregation of half-a-dozen. For some years the incumbent was always in the courts. Fortunately, the days of Corporation churches are ended, and the large, useless place is to come down."

The doctor looked at his guide to see if he were making a bad joke. Finding him serious, he asked to be taken to the Cathedral. They were not long in reaching it.

"This the Cathedral? You must have made a mistake. I don't associate the word cathedral with that abortion."

"You may or you may not; but this is our cathedral, we have no other."

Dr. Wynne's amazement was not unnatural. Liverpool, which prides itself upon being the second commercial city in the empire, and which is the first English town visited by our friends beyond the sea, has a cathedral that would disgrace the Muggletonians in the back slums of Southwark. A more hideous specimen of the architecture of the days when the beautiful oak stalls of Chester Cathedral were painted green it would be difficult to find in all England.

Dr. Wynne and his companion entered the building, which is as ugly within as without. It was Monday christening day in Liverpool. They sat down to observe the administration of the Sacrament of Baptism according to the rites of the Church of England. He had read and admired the service in the Prayer Book. It would be difficult to find a more beautiful ceremony than this of the dedication and consecration of the young life at the font. Everything was provided for. Parents were to be there to present their infants at the font, and lest they might fail in their duty a kind of understudy was to be provided in the shape of godfathers and godmothers, who were to take solemn vows upon themselves for the due upbringing of the children in the nurture and admonition of the Lord.

Dr. Wynne, who was no small enthusiast in his way, especially about subjects with which his acquaintance was so slight as to afford his imagination elbow-room, had frequently disgusted his Nonconformist friends by the vehemence with which he praised the Anglican baptismal service as the English child's Bill of Rights.

Photographed by]   [F. N. Eaton.
THE NELSON MONUMENT, LIVERPOOL.

Photographed by]   [F. N. Eaton
THE CATHEDRAL, LIVERPOOL.

"Mother Church," he used to say, "may have her abuses, but one thing at least she has done. She has compelled generation after generation of Englishmen to recognise publicly in the most solemn manner the sacred obligations of parentage, and has affirmed among the fundamental rights of every English child the claim to have not only a legal father and a legal mother, who will stand up and acknowledge their responsibility for its rearing and education, but also two supervising and supplementary foster parents, upon whom, if the original parents die or fail in their duty, will devolve the solemn obligations of training the child in the ways of Christian citizenship."

It was, therefore, with keen and sympathetic interest that he settled himself in one of the high-backed pews to watch the progress of the ceremony.

There were about a dozen mothers all in a row holding their infants. In front of them stood a surpliced clergyman reading, more or less indistinctly, something from the Prayer Book. The attention of the mothers was concentrated upon keeping their charges from crying. Behind the row of mothers stood a solitary man.

There were no fathers, and there was only this solitary substitute for the posse of twenty-four supplementary parents, the godfathers and godmothers, which were the legal right of the dozen unconscious little mannikins who squirmed and cried as the water fell upon their faces, and were named in turn by the strange man in white robes, who held them for a moment in his arm and then restored them to their mothers. It might not be legal, but the fact was there. Instead of having father and mother and godfather and godmother to take vows before high heaven for the right upbringing of the newcome morsel of humanity, each little Liverpudlian had got but the vow of one mother and the twelfth part of a single substitute for godfather and godmother. Here was a descent indeed from the lofty idealisation in which he had indulged so freely. It was with a sense almost of a personal injury that the doctor left the church.

His companion took his arm. "You are new to our ways, I see," he said, pleasantly. "What ailed you at the christening?"

"Christening!" said the doctor, bitterly. "It is no baptism, it is a farce. A sacrament forsooth! Why, I never saw a more hugger-mugger travesty of the order of service in my life. What is the Bishop about to allow it?"

"Hoity-toity, my good friend," replied his companion. "Don't be in such a pickle. Lofty ideals are all very well, but in this workaday world if you look too steadily at the stars you sometimes get landed in an uncommonly dirty ditch. Do you think one Churchman in a thousand takes godfathering seriously? I know of none. What does godfather mean in the middle-class? Practically, a tax of the cost of a silver mug which the godfather gives to his godchild. If that is so among the serious people who attend church regularly, what can you expect among the masses of the poor and uneducated?"

Dr. Wynne was silent. His companion had halted just outside the cathedral door. Three disreputable-looking creatures, standing with their back to the wall, were lighting their pipes. From where they stood caught the familiar sanguinary adjective with which low-class Englishmen variegate their vocabulary.

"Doctor," said his friend, as they moved away, "do you see those three fellows yonder?"

"Yes," said the doctor. "They are not difficult to see, or hear, or smell," he added, as the wind brought the reek of their tobacco into his face.

"Who do you take them to be?"

Dr. Wynne scrutinised them from head to foot. "One might be a broken-down clerk with a brandy nose; another a corner-boy with a black coat on; the third a dock labourer waiting to be hired."

"Just so. But you will never guess what they do for their living. Wait here a moment and you will see."

They crossed the street and took up a position from which they could observe the three worthies. Presently it became evident that there was to be a second christening service, for mothers with babies began to come up. As each neared the cathedral door one of the touts approached her with a question. Most attempts were rebuffed, but one man was fortunate. After a little parley he followed the mother and child into church.

"Now, doctor, what do you think of that?"

"I understand nothing. It was all dumb show to me."

"Well, if you had stood nearer them, as I have done many a time, you would have heard their question. It is always the same: 'Missus, do you want a godfather?' Most of them, as you see, were rebuffed. In one case an arrangement was effected, probably for the usual considera-tion——"

"Which is——"

"A shilling and a drink. That used to be the regular tariff when I was familiar with the business. These men are professional godfathers. Every Monday they used to hang round here on the chance of picking up a shilling for a christening job, with beer thrown in. The clergy, of course, discountenance all such bargains, but they cannot altogether stop them. They struck a heavy blow at professional godfathering when they allowed one man to stand sponsor wholesale, but the practice lingers, as you see."

Here was Realism displacing Idealism with a vengeance. What a descent from the lofty musings at Hawarden to the professional godfather at a shilling a head!

"Perhaps the men of the *Mayflower* were not so very far wrong after all," he said, "if this is the outcome of formalism worked like a crank machine. I wish I had not had to say good-bye to the Old World with such a disagreeable taste as this story leaves in the mouth."

"Facts are facts, doctor," said his companion. "They are not nice, no doubt. But, after all, the poor beggar made a living out of it, and no one really was very much the worse."

"I wonder," said Dr. Wynne, as he wound up his watch before going to bed that night, "If that is the net practical outcome of nineteen centuries of effort to impress the human mind with the importance of Christian baptism!"

CHAPTER III.—OFF AT LAST.

"HALLOO, Wynne, where in the name of fortune are you bound for?" was the unexpected salutation which greeted the doctor as he was entering the breakfast-room of his hotel the next morning. In a moment he had grasped the hand of his old college friend, Jack Compton.

"Dr. Wynne, let me introduce you to Professor Glogoul, one of the Faculty." The introduction over, the party of three sat down to breakfast.

Jack Compton was a swarthy, dark-bearded man in the prime of life; of middle stature, with an eye which had a strange far-away look, as if it saw into eternity, which

JACK COMPTON.

contrasted strangely with the resolute under-jaw and the humorous smile that played around his lips. He had left college six months after Walter had entered it, but, in these six months a strong attraction had drawn them together, and although they seldom corresponded, they had never entirely lost touch of each other. Compton was reputed to be enormously wealthy. He was unmarried, and money was to him merely a counter in the great game upon which he had staked his life.

His companion, Professor Glogoul, was a strange contrast in every way. He believed in protoplasm, and nothing behind it; in the social organism, and nothing before it. Man was, to him, temporarily animated matter, suspended in a fragment of space of which he knew little or nothing. Of New England stock, he inherited the philosophy of Jonathan Edwards, *minus* his theism. Believing that man, like other phenomena, could only be studied under the microscope, he spent his life in a kind of

THE PROFESSOR

moral vivisection, practised chiefly upon criminals and the insane. His great word was the "Abnormal." "Study the abnormal!" he used to say; "it holds the keys of the normal. Only by magnifying the kink a million times can you understand how the kink is formed. Everyone is a bunch of latent kinks. The criminal and the lunatic are simply the result of the exaggeration of one or the other of the kinks in your own head." He was just returning from a visit to Lombroso, with an imperishable manuscript in his wallet, explaining the physiological genesis of all the famous murders of the last ten years. Free will was to him as absurd as the philosopher's stone; moral responsibility an exploded delusion. There was no God but the Social Organism, and the experimental physiologist was his prophet. What was good for the social organism was right; what was not good for it was wrong. Of other tests he knew nothing.

Dr. Wynne felt a curious kind of attraction and repulsion in the presence of the professor. He was an enthusiast, with the stuff of a martyr in him. But like the demoniac in the gospels, his dwelling was amongst the tombs, and his eye had the steely glitter and glare of one who, having gazed into hell, has caught some reflection of its flames.

"Now, Wynne," Compton began, after helping him to coffee. "Where are you off to? Chicago, I suppose, like all the rest of us. And what is your ship?"

"I don't know yet," replied Wynne, "but I want to sail at once. What steamers are leaving to-morrow? Do you happen to know?"

The professor pricked up his ears, levelled his swivel eye at Wynne's cranium, and seemed to make a mental note of some physiologico-mental peculiarity in a new specimen.

"If that doesn't beat Banagher," said Compton, laughing. "You want to sail to-morrow, and you have not taken your berth yet?"

"Certainly not," said Wynne, feeling slightly uncomfortable. "Why should I? I only arrived yesterday, and I thought of going down and seeing about booking to-day."

"O sancta simplicitas," said Compton. "Are you not aware that this is the year of the World's Fair, and that all berths are booked three weeks, and sometimes three months in advance? When did we book our berths, professor?"

"Just six weeks since, and then we thought ourselves lucky to be in time," replied the professor.

The doctor felt very uncomfortable.

"When do you start?" he asked.

"To-morrow, on the *Majestic*, of the White Star Line, one of the best boats afloat. And she is as comfortable as she is swift. But, don't be downhearted, we must take you along with us somehow. It is a chance not to be missed."

"Yes," said the doctor, ruefully. "It ought not to be missed, indeed. But what I should have done not to miss it was not done, and now it is too late. Is there much difference between one berth and another?" asked the doctor.

"Rather," replied Compton. "The great thing to get is a berth as near the centre of the ship as possible, and as far away as possible from the entrance to the galley or a lavatory. If you get a berth in the bow, if there is much of a sea, when she pitches well forward you feel as if you were being suddenly dropped a hundred feet into the abyss. Then, if you are next to the cooking-place, you are disagreeably reminded of food at moments when the desire for it is at a minimum. But look here," he continued, producing a small plan of the *Majestic*, "these are first-class cabins, 133 of them, varying in price from £130 for a room to £18 for a berth. These below are second-class, or intermediates, costing from £8 to £12 per berth. The steerage passengers are fore and aft. They are bedded, lodged, and carried, if they bring their own bedding, cups, plates, and other utensils, at £4 a head. Our cabin is letter V. We have a cabin to ourselves. They are made up with berths for two, or berths for four. It is a great lottery whom you have to room with; sometimes you may be very unlucky, being berthed with the sea-sick, or the chatterbox, or the snorer."

"But what must I do?" said the doctor, somewhat helplessly. "Wait for three weeks, or go steerage?"

"Never say die, old chap," said Compton, encouragingly. "Come down with me to the White Star office as soon as breakfast is over, and we will see what can be done."

"You look after him," said the professor, "for I must leave you now. I have an appointment in Walton Gaol. There is a murderer in the condemned cell, who is to be hanged next Monday, and I hope to spend a few hours with him to-day. A most interesting case, with features that baffle me. One gets to be quite a connoisseur in murderers," he added, half apologetically. "Many are so commonplace I would not cross the road to see them. But this man is a jewel. It is a thousand pities he is to be hanged so soon. Of all nations I think the English make the most spendthrift waste of choice specimens of criminal pathology."

When the professor left, the doctor said,—

"What a strange fellow you have picked up in that professor! It makes one's flesh creep to hear him talk, and to see that swivel eye as if it were a telescope through which he could look right into the middle of your brain."

"Oh, the professor is a first-rate good fellow. You hear how he talks about specimens. I keep him near me as my specimen. You know we have to study the abnormal to understand the normal. He is the abnormal scientist, to which human beings are as interesting as larvæ, worthy of as much consideration and of as little. He was born good, with half-a-dozen generations of Puritan blood in him; otherwise he would be intolerable.

He is tender hearted, kind, enthusiastic, and a very pleasant companion. But, for all that, he is the type of one kind of man whom we are rearing in our schools. That is why I keep him near me. For those who would influence the generations that are to come must be constantly reminded of the streams of tendency with which they have to contend, and the nature of the strata on which they have to build."

As he spoke, Compton's eyes assumed that far-away look which gave his face the semblance of a seer. It was only for a moment, however. "Come," said he, "let us lose no time."

They went into Water Street, and walked down among the crowd of clerks and merchants making their way to their desks and counting-houses. Presently they reached the White Star office.

"When can we book for berths on the *Majestic*?" Compton asked of the booking clerk.

"July 14th Every berth booked until then. Only forty or fifty left free after then. Will you select your berth?"

"No, thank you," said Compton. "I am booked for to-morrow. But I want to take my friend with me."

"Impossible," said the clerk. "We could have booked every berth three times over."

"I know that," said Compton, somewhat impatiently. "But my friend is going on the *Majestic* all the same. Will you book him for the first berth which will be left vacant at the last moment?"

"For the first, no. We have already five booked for chance vacancies. We can let him have the sixth, if he cares to take it. But it is a very off-chance, and I doubt if he will hear of it at all until it is too late to take his luggage on board."

"Never mind that," said the doctor, "I will take my chance anyhow."

The clerk duly entered his name and the address of his hotel.

"Now," said Compton, "let us make up our minds that you will go, and act accordingly. Having secured your chance of a berth, let us fix you up comfortably. What luggage have you got?"

"None to speak of. An old campaigner marches with a minimum of impediments. All my earthly belongings are in one Gladstone bag. I prefer to buy as I go."

"But your hat-box?"

"Haven't got one, and don't mean to. I have a beaver, with flaps for the ears, in my bag, and this low-crowned thing on my head."

Compton looked at him with a half-envious admiration. "Well, so be it. But three things you must have which you have not got. A chair for the deck, which you must buy at once, and have it sent on board with the other chairs, of which you see a pile in the hall of the hotel. You can spend from 5s. to 50s. over a deck chair, but a good comfortable chair will cost you about 10s. or 15s. You can stock it at New York, or sell it, or give it away, or bring it back when you return. Then you must have a rug. And my experience is that nothing for warmth and wear beats an opossum skin rug, which you can get at any price from £2 to £8. Lastly, you want an overcoat and a light waterproof. Please yourself about the former, but, if you are wise, you will have a waterproof that is likewise cleverly ventilated at the shoulders by Byers' patent. Now, you go to get these things. I must attend to my correspondence."

Before Dr. Wynne went on to make his purchases, as he was choosing his chair, his attention was attracted by the arrival of some new comers—passengers for the *Majestic*. One was a young widow, who was apparently alone; another, whose figure made him start - it was so like that of his Rose, was an English girl of twenty-two. The features were not Rose's, but she was beautiful. She had the eye of an artist, and the indescribable poise of

IRENE VERNON.

head and shoulders that spoke of self-conscious power. Yet there was a restlessness about the eyes and mouth which boded of storm. She seemed to be alone, and as she was looking about somewhat helplessly, the doctor asked if he could do anything for her. She said she had been expecting to meet her cousin. He had not come and she must wait for him. Her name, she said, was Irene Vernon. She was on her way to Chicago.

He did not see her again until they all met at the dinner table. Irene's natural beauty, which had impressed the doctor when he saw her in her travelling wraps, was seen to much greater advantage at table. She was beautifully but simply dressed, and there peeped out from her raven hair a deep red half-opened rose. Her cousin had not even then arrived, and Dr. Wynne, as her only acquaintance, took her in to dinner. She sat between him and the professor.

That excellent member of the social organism was describing, with the keen enthusiasm of a collector of *bric-à-brac*, the wonderful specimen of the abnormal with whom he had been locked up at Walton. He could hardly attend to his dinner, so full was he of the traits he had noted in this poor wretch, who had but five days to live.

The doctor listened with shuddering horror. As for Irene, she seemed fascinated. Dr. Wynne, seeing how absorbed she was in the professor's story, interposed, saying,—

"Really, Dr. Glogoul, I am afraid you are spoiling Miss Vernon's dinner.'

But she turned round almost indignantly. "Oh, doctor, how can you say this? I am listening with both ears. It is quite a new thrill, and I would give anything for a new thrill."

The professor turned his eye upon her swift as a thrush strikes down at the new worm he spies on the lawn.

"If that is your wish, mademoiselle, I think it is fortunate we are going in the same steamer."

Then he resumed his conversation. "I call it wicked, criminal waste. From the point of view of the social organism it is more wicked to hang that choice specimen of a homicide than it was for him to kill his miserable wife. She was a poor creature, consumptive—bad stock. If she had lived, she would probably have had some rickety children. Now the race is, at least, saved their appearance. It mattered nothing to anyone whether she lived or died. But he—what a wonderful specimen! What would I not give for his skull—even his skull, which is worth nothing compared with his living form."

"And what would you do with him if he were given over to you instead of to the hangman?" asked the doctor.

The professor's eye sparkled. "Oh, what a glorious suggestion! What a gain to science, if it could but be done! What an endless field for experiment there is in his head alone!"

"What kind of experiment?" asked Irene, somewhat timidly.

"Every kind," replied the professor. "Firstly, by interviewing him, I would extract everything consciously present in his memory. Then, by hypnotising him, I would possess myself of the contents of his subliminal consciousness. Then I should proceed to vivisect him."

"Not alive, I hope?" said Irene, shuddering.

"Mademoiselle, you dissect when dead; you vivisect when alive. But I would not hurt him—at least, not at first. He might not last so long if he were made to suffer too much. I should reserve the agony until I had exhausted all other resources. I should ——"

"Professor," said Compton, authoritatively, "that is enough. The social organism imperatively asserts that

instruction in vivisection does not suit the dinner-table."

But Irene said under her breath, "You will tell me all about it, won't you, when we get on board? I should die happy if I could only see something thrilling—like an execution or a vivisection. Life seems so humdrum."

And the professor, delighted to have found a listener for the voyage, assured her that, if it could be done, she should see both.

She was really a pretty girl, with the artist developed at the expense of the judgment, the will, or the conduct of life. She was a *nevrose*, like Marie Bashkirtseff, in music what the Russian prototype was in painting, and just as liable to sudden fits of gloom or rapture. That evening, she played and sang so charmingly that Compton voted her musician for the voyage on board the *Majestic;* and she flushed with pleasure, and went to bed wondering how long the delightful period would last.

"It won't last," she thought, as she looked at the saucy eyes and rosy lips in the glass before putting out the light. "It never does. Heigho! Now up, up, up; then down, down, down. What a switchback my life is, to be sure! Only, sometimes the car sticks in a hole; otherwise it would not be so bad, after all," with which sage reflection she blew out her candle, and slept for the last time in the Old World.

In the smoking-room the doctor, the professor, Compton, and one or two others were having a hot discussion as to the best cure for sea-sickness.

"Nothing is a cure for sea-sickness," dogmatised the professor, "and I don't want to see a cure. Sea-sickness predisposes the patient to the communicative. I find a liner my best human laboratory, better even than a gaol. For in a gaol the prisoners have no sea-sickness, whereas, after a stiff gale, the most secretive of men will tell me anything."

"All very fine for your profession," said Compton, who would torture the whole human race in order to verify your theory of the biliary ducts, but we who are less scientific would prefer to be rid of sea-sickness, even if it made your laboratory less useful. I have tried many specifics, from champagne to sea-water, but to my thinking nothing beats 'Georgia Water.' It is the product of a natural spring in Georgia. I know many who, before they used Georgia Water, used to dread the Atlantic passage as only one degree less bad than death. Georgia Water is not dear. You can buy it in London at 5s. per dozen bottles. It is as palatable as the ordinary water. Miss Frances Willard was, I think, one of the worst sailors on record. After she got Georgia Water she was as free from discomfort on the water as on dry land."

"I always use 'Mattei's Scrof. Giap.' as a prophylactic," said the doctor. "It is cheap, easy to take, and it is excellent as a digestive, even if it fails to effect its immediate purpose. You take the globules dry or in solution, before going on board and whenever you feel qualmish. A patient of mine recently cured a whole shipful of sick with this anti-mal-de-mer."

"And I maintain, in spite of you both, that sea-sickness being an affection of the nerves," said the professor, "cannot be cured by water, or wine, or medicine, or anything, and it is good that it should be so. To lie flat on your back until your system adjusts itself to the pitching and rolling, and heaving and plunging—that is all that can be done. Why should you object to be occasionally unwell?"

The discussion was interrupted by the waiter, who wished to know if they had their luggage all labelled for the hold, as the tender would take it off at four in the morning. Dr. Wynne had no luggage, and he busied himself in helping Miss Vernon through her little difficulties.

"Take everything in your cabin," he said, "that you need during the voyage. When your luggage disappears into the hold, do not expect to see it again. You can take a good deal of personal luggage into your cabin, and stow it away under your berth. If the weather is bad, it will roll about, no doubt, but that will do it no harm—at least not if it is well packed."

The next morning they were up early, and about. The doctor, seeing it was bright and sunny, took Miss Vernon a long drive around the city, preserving a discreet silence, however, as they passed the cathedral concerning his disillusion. They thoroughly enjoyed themselves, and when they met their friends at lunch they were the brightest of the party. The professor was in good spirits. He had spent the morning in a lunatic asylum, and was enchanted at discovering a human specimen admirably adapted for illustrating one of his favourite themes.

"It is a poor lady," he said, "who has the horrible hallucination of being strangled by a ruffian. So vivid and realistic is her impression that she would joyfully die to escape from it. But do they let her die? Never! For fifteen years she has been guarded night and day, compelled to eat, forced to continue to live ; and why? In order that she may continue to suffer that awful experience every moment of her life! And yet they consider vivisectors cruel! We are angels of mercy, for, at least, we would allow this poor wretch the anodyne of death."

Irene's cousin had not arrived, and she was beginning to feel uneasy. She could not bear to abandon the journey. But to cross the Atlantic without a companion! Most girls would have recoiled from the adventure. Irene was attracted by it. Besides, she was bent upon seeing more of that weird and gifted genius, Professor Glogoul, who seemed to her to have more capacity for giving her thrills than any other human being she had yet met. He was so bold, and so original. And then, too, he believed in nothing that other people believed in, and had roundly asserted that there was no such thing as sin. Irene hankered after that doctrine, and was already disposed to add the professor to the long list of men with whom she was pleased to fancy that she had been in love. She had spent the morning telegraphing frantically for her cousin. At three o'clock, just as she was on the point of despair, an express letter was delivered to her. It was from her cousin, enclosing his tickets. He had sprained his ankle, he said, and could not come. If she could get any one to take his place, and if she cared to chance it, well and good. If not, she had better make the best terms she could to exchange bookings for a later steamer.

Poor Irene sat in the hall with her cousin's letter spread out before her, the very picture of grief. Dr. Wynne, as he was gathering up his traps, caught sight of her woebegone face.

He crossed the room, and sat down beside her.

"Miss Vernon, you are in trouble. Have you had bad news?"

For answer she pushed her cousin's letter across for him to read.

"Well," said he, looking up, "and what have you decided to do?"

"I am sure I don't know. I don't want to lose this trip, and yet I don't know what to do about the ticket, and—"

"If that is all," said the doctor, briskly, "it is soon settled. Your difficulty pairs off against mine, and all is for the best. That is to say if you assent?'

"To what?"

"To let me take your cousin's ticket, and, so far as is possible to a stranger, to undertake your cousin's duties. I have only the remotest off-chance of getting a ticket otherwise. So, if you don't object, I will be Walter Vernon for the voyage, and now, if it pleases you, I will take my cousin down to the tender?"

Irene hesitated for a moment. Her cousin was a bit of a bear. She did not care for him in the least. The substitute cousin was much more handsome, and, to tell the truth, a much more eligible travelling companion than the absentee with the sprained ankle. But—but—was it not a rather risky thing accepting his offer? He was a complete stranger.

At this moment a telegraph boy came up. "Dr. Wynne, sir."

The doctor, hardly thinking what he was doing, opened the envelope mechanically. The moment he saw the first word he forgot everything about his prospective ticket and Irene. For the telegram was from the friend to whom he had written in London, and it ran thus :—

"Have seen artist. He remembers model perfectly. Name Rose, very poor, and lonely, but respectable. Twelve months since saw her. Present address unknown. Am following up clue."

For a moment the room swam round before Wynne's eyes. He moved instinctively to a couch near by and sat down.

Irene, not much pleased at his sudden loss of interest in her affairs, had gone off to consider as to what she should do.

The doctor, meanwhile, slowly read the telegram again.

"Thank God!" he said. "Oh, thank God! At last. Thank God, at last!" At first he thought of returning at once to London. But something restrained him. He must go to Chicago. After his return he might take up the pursuit. Meantime, his friend would do all that could be done.

"Dr. Wynne," said Irene, coming up with the ticket in her hand, "I suppose I oughtn't properly to accept your kind offer. But that is just the reason why I want to. So I'll go. And I will regard you as my cousin?'

"Certainly, Miss Vernon," replied the doctor. "You have extricated me from a great dilemma. I will telegraph to your cousin, and then we will go on board the tender.'

They were soon at the landing-stage, that wonder and pride of Liverpool, the like of which is not anywhere in the United Kingdom, or indeed in the world. The tide was high, the river was full of life and bustle. The great ship which was to be their home for the next week

EMBARKING AT THE GANGWAY, LIVERPOOL.

lay in midstream. The tender was blowing off her steam impatiently, waiting for the passengers from Euston. Porters laden with luggage threaded their way to the tender. Everywhere there was the lively animation which immediately precedes departure.

"This way, ladies," said the doctor, as he succeeded at last in getting Irene and Mrs. Julia pi'oted safely through the crowd on the gangway, and established them with all their little impedimenta comfortably at the stern of the tender. The London train was in, and the last of the passengers was on board. The tender gave a farewell shriek with its whistle, the gangway rope was cast off, and the gangway was cleared in another minute. They wer rapidly making their way to the *Majestic*, which, wit. steam up all ready to start, was lying at anchor a little distance down the Mersey.

Mrs. Julia's heart was full as she looked back upon the receding city. Irene, gay with the buoyancy of youth, saw before her that infinite vista of a paradise perpetually renewed—the mirage which youth, that cunning magician, casts upon the desert of life. The widow had buried hope in her husbands grave, and looked forward to nothing but the grey unknown darkening down to the grave. And her lip quivered just a little as she thought it might be the last'time she would ever look upon the

THE TENDER ON ITS WAY TO THE "MAJESTIC."

land where she had lived her young life, and loved her love, and buried her dead.

As for Dr. Wynne, he was still under the influence of the telegram that told of the finding of Rose. It seemed to give a benediction to his western tour. Even on its threshold he had picked up a clue which brought him news of the lost one, only twelve months old. Who could say but that his vision at Orchardcroft might yet be fulfilled, since the journey had begun so auspiciously?

Old Nick's Church spire was fading in the background, with the remains of the city house of the Earls of Derby, who used to reside on the Mersey in the days when their lordship of the Isle of Man was 'a living reality, and not a mere theme for the romancer, even though that romancer was Sir Walter Scott. Little thought of "Peveril of the Peak" crossed their mind. They were nearing the *Majestic*. A moment more they were by her side.

Jack Compton was waiting for his friend, with a downcast look.

"Don't know how it is, Wynne, but can't explain it anyhow. This morning I could have wagered my life you would have sailed with us, and, at this moment, I feel you

must somehow. But I have just seen the clerk, and he tells me they have only three 'disappoints,' and as you were sixth on the rota, it is no go.'

"You don't know me, I see," replied Wynne, smiling. "Allow me to present myself to you as 'Walter Vernon,' whose cousin Miss Irene you already know. After I have seen these ladies to their berths, I will look after my own. It is Letter W. Everything is *en régle*; only don't forget my name, Jack.'

In the hurry-scurry of the final scene, there was not much time for talk. The doctor conducted the ladies to their berths, found out his own, placed his portmanteau, rug, and topcoat in his cabin, and came out to see that saddest of sights, when farewells are whispered, and friends look their last, long look into the faces of those from whom they are parting, it may be for ever.

Along the gang-plank, the double stream flows constant, the latest arrivals entering on the right, the friends leaving on the left. Alike on steamer and on tender, an interested and sympathetic bank of spectators watched the busy scene. There is always an absorbing interest in any deep emotion. And the grief which finds utterance on either end of the gang-plank is as real and terrible as that on the side of the grave. For the dead are dead, they have passed away into the invisible world. But the emigrants were never more alive. They are living, but away from us. It is that which seems so hard. The Irish alone of races have given inarticulate but intensely keen expression to the anguish that gnaws in the heart of the living on being torn for ever from their living love.

There was no shrill, weird keening on the side of the *Majestic*. But the wan faces the tear-stained cheeks, the swollen eyes of those who slowly crossed the gang-plank to the tender testified less loudly, but not less vividly to the severity of the wrench that takes place every time one of the great Atlantic ferry boats puts out to sea.

At Amsterdam there is a familiar spot on the quay known as the "Wailing Place,' for there the mothers and wives of the Dutch mariners used to gather, to catch the last glimpse of the departing ships. The tender is the wailing place of Liverpool, and it sees more of it in a week than Amsterdam saw in a year. For Liverpool is the Great Gate of the Modern Exodus, and through its portals have passed in the last forty years over two millions of emigrants, most of whom return no more.

Dr. Wynne was profoundly moved at the silent misery of these farewells. To divert his attention from the weeping women below, he tried to read the printed list of passengers, freely distributed to all who were leaving. He read his own name, Walter Vernon, and smiled.

A hand was laid on his arm. He looked round. It was his friend Compton. The tender had blown her last warning whistle, the gang-plank was drawn aboard, handkerchiefs were waving briskly when they were not being used to stop the tears; the engines began to move, and in a few minutes the tender was churning its way back to the shore. The side of the steamer was still crowded with those who were straining eyes for the last sight of their friends.

"'Tis a sad sight," said the doctor, moodily.

Compton did not reply. He, too, was gazing after the tender, but it was as if seeing he saw not. The strange, glittering, dark eyes seemed to be fixed upon what was never seen on sea or shore. His nostrils dilated; he drew a long breath, and then, turning to Wynne, he said,—

"Is it not written that a t me will come when parting will be no more?"

"Oh, yes," replied the doctor: "when time itself is lost in eternity. Then, perhaps."

"No," said Compton; "before then. Here, in time, it will come. Perhaps in our time. Who knows?"

CHAPTER IV.—ON BOARD THE "MAJESTIC."

"Now, cousin," said the doctor to Irene, "I have seen the deck steward about the chairs. He has got yours and mine, and if I had only known I was to be your cousin, I would have put you up to a device that Compton explained to me. Compton, the professor, and I have our chairs enamelled bright blue. There is no mistaking them. They are the only blue chairs on board the ship. I have arranged to have your chair added to the blue brigade, so that we can find each other without difficulty."

"Are there so many of us, then?" asked Irene.

"About fifteen hundred altogether, not reckoning three hundred officers and crew," said he. "A tolerably good-sized village full, is it not? But only 290 of these are saloon passengers. I have seen the bath steward also, and fixed up our time for the bath, but as we came on board so late, we had to take less convenient hours than earlier passengers had secured. There can be only so many bath-rooms on the ship, and we have to take our turns. I am on the early squad, and shall have to turn in after I have had my tub. But, come, let us go to the dining-room, and settle where we have to sit."

in barbarous Moscow, no restaurant is without its organ."

"Now," said Compton, "let us make a tour of the ship. When we get out into the channel it may be some time before some of us are capable of such a journey. Professor, you take Miss Vernon; and Wynne, I beg pardon, Vernon, come with me. It is a wonderful world, a kind of separate planet, with its own laws, usages and civilization."

They went the round as everyone makes the round, peeping into the galley, where the cooks prepare the daily bread for nearly two thousand hungry mouths, visiting the smoking-room, the temple set apart for the soothing weed and the exciting "pool," looking in at the library, into which no new newspaper was to come for a week, strolling through the drawing-room, and then venturing into the steerage, where nearly a thousand men, women and children, more or less miserable, were crowded together.

"My laboratory," the professor remarked, half to himself, "is at least well furnished with specimens. It is always interesting to sample and analyse the kind of material with which Europe rectifies the extreme nervous temperament of Americans. Nerves, nerves, nerves—our people are running to nerves. But for this phlegmatic lump of Teutonism, I don't know what would become of

THE WHITE STAR LINER "MAJESTIC."

As they went down into the magnificently furnished dining-room they met Compton and the professor.

"We have fixed your seats for you," said Compton, "subject to your approval. We have got a table for six close to the doctor. The captain, when he is able to be present, sits in the place of honour. But he is as often as not absent, and it is better to be near either the doctor or the purser. We have got a very comfortable table. We secured your places, and added Mrs. Irwin and Mrs. Julia to make up the party. Let us show you where it is, so that you will be able to know your places."

So saying, the party made their way through the throng that was still gathered around the purser, that autocrat of the dining-room, who was busily engaged allotting places to passengers. Irene was full of admiration for the beauty and magnificence of the fittings.

"It is more like a palace than a steamer," she remarked. "If only we had a band of stringed instruments to discourse sweet music, it would be complete."

"You are right," replied the professor. "Always eat and make love to music. It promotes the digestion, and facilitates the making of those whispered compliments which are the circulating medium of lovers. On the Hamburg boats and on the German Lloyd they have bands which play all dinner-time. The English are not civilized enough to appreciate this. Yet, even

us. They are like the spiegeleisen added to the charge in the Bessemer converter. Without them, our steel would not be tough enough to stand the strain."

"But, professor," said Irene, "don't you think you are overdoing your spiegeleisen, or whatever you call it? Just look at these creatures!"

She pointed to a shock-headed family of Russian Jews, crouching together "on their hunkers," and jabbering Yiddish entirely oblivious of the passer-by.

"Good stock, that," said the professor, "good, tough, malleable metal; wish we had more of them. Sober, industrious men, virtuous women, children beautiful as the offspring of the gods. Give them a little soap, and they will ruin our Republic. After being pounded in the Tzar's mortar for a thousand years they are as tough as the harpoons which are made out of cast horse-shoe nails."

"A pleasant prospect for your Republic," said Irene. "Before fifty years are gone, Pharaoh will be canonised as Washington."

"Then it will be the Pharaoh who made Joseph his Grand Vizier, not the Pharaoh of the Exodus. But, see, we are nearly on the bar; let us regain the saloon. Dinner will soon be served."

There was a goodly company at dinner that day. They were still in the river, and the motion of the great ship was hardly perceptible.

"What luxury," said the doctor, as he glanced over the menu, with its soups, and fish, and entrees, and joints, and poultry, and sweets, and pastry, finishing up with ample dessert and *café noire*.

"Not unnecessary," said the professor, "when there is nothing to do for a week, but eat and drink and be sick. These steamers are the Halls of Idleness of our time."

"And Satan finds some mischief still for idle hands to do, I guess," said the merry voice of Mrs. Irwin, who was seated on the doctor's right hand. "For hatred, malice, and all uncharitableness—for drinking, flirting, gambling, and all manner of minor vices, commend me to the saloon of a first-class Atlantic liner."

MRS. IRWIN.

The speaker was a hearty Irish lady, who was no stranger to the ocean ferry, whose general geniality and good humour had caused Compton to add her at once with general consent to the Blue Brigade, as the party was now dubbed.

Conversation turned upon the larders of the *Majestic*. A week's provisions for two thousand persons is no small item in the ship's account.

"We have a ton and a half of mutton on board, and about five tons of beef," said Mrs. Irwin, cheerfully, "a ton of corned beef, and another ton of salt pork, but that, of course, is for the steerage. As for the wine and spirits, I should say, we shall drink enough to make the fortune of the best hotel at Liverpool. Here we can cut and come again all day long," she continued; "breakfast between eight and ten; lunch at one, dinner at seven, and as many snacks in between, and nothing to pay for anything except liquor. It's a capital place for a hungry man."

"If he is not sick, madam," said a somewhat lugu-brious-looking cleric on the opposite side of the table.

"Sir," said Compton, sharply, "that word should never be mentioned at dinner-time. Talk of the devil, and he's sure to appear. *Mal-de-mer* is an affair of the imagina-tion. I knew a lady who, when she was going to France, was always sick when she left the Central Station at Newcastle."

"Excellent, excellent," said the professor, mentally adding the case to his list of illustrations.

"How long do you expect we shall be on the trip?" asked Irene.

"Seven or eight days," replied Compton. "The talk about five days' trip is very delusive. The ship in which we are broke the record in 1891, by covering the waterway from Roche's Point to Sandyhook lightship in five days, eighteen hours, and eighteen minutes; but then you have to add on to that the twelve hours' run to Queenstown, and, at least, two hours from Sandyhook to the wharf at New York. If we are out of the ship in a clear week from the time we got on board we shall do very well."

"I suppose there is practically no danger," said Mrs. Julia, "of anything happening?"

"Danger," said the professor, "of course there is dan-ger. Danger is the inspiration of life. We are encom-passed by danger. There is, first and worst, the danger from fog, against which science has hitherto utterly failed to provide any remedy. Then there is the danger from icebergs, into which many a good steamer has crashed, and never been heard of more. Then there is the danger from fire, with its pleasant alternative of cremation or drown-ing. Finally, there is the danger of collision. These four dangers give spice to our journey."

"You have not referred to the danger from storms," said Mrs. Julia.

"Storms!" said the professor, disdainfully; "storms are no danger. There never was a storm brewed in heaven or earth that could wreck the *Majestic*, if she had sea room enough and no fog. No, madam, the wind and the wave have been vanquished."

"And now for all your other perils," said Compton. "Measure them by this fact that, in 1890, two thousand voyages were made between New York and the other side of the Atlantic, 300,000 cabin passengers were ferried to and fro; 370,000 emigrants were landed at Castle Garden, without a single accident."

"But surely," said these, "even Atlantic liners do get lost sometimes."

"Often," said the professor, who afterwards explained that he was trying an interesting experiment as to the effect of fear upon the appetite. "In the first forty years of the steam ferry, 144 steamers were lost between the American and European seaboard; twenty-four of these, like the *City of Glasgow*, vanished utterly, no one knows where, in 1854, leaving no trace behind to tell what had become of her 480 passengers. Others were burnt in mid-ocean, like the *Austria* in 1858, which cost 471 lives. Others, again, went down in a collision, like the *Arctic* in 1854, when 562 human beings perished. Why, the ocean bed beneath the run of the liners is strewn with the whitening bones of thousands who have taken their passages as we have done, but who never saw their destination."

"Yet," said the doctor, "you are safer on mid-Atlantic than in the Strand. Not an Insurance Company raises its premium by a quarter per cent. because you are going to the States. You could not have a better proof than that of the safety of the trip."

"But the immense speed at which we go—is not that a great increase of danger?" asked the clergyman. "Imagine this enormous leviathan of nearly 10,000 tons driven by its double screws and 18,000 horse-power at the rate of twenty-three miles an hour through these crowded seas, in a dense fog."

"Sir," said Compton, "no ship is ever driven at full speed during a fog. And when the sky is clear there is not a captain on the service who will not tell you that the quicker your ship the safer your voyage. When at high speed, she manoeuvres more easily, so as to avoid a danger, and if, by ill-luck, she should run into anything, she will run through it with such momentum that it will do her as little harm as Stephenson's cow did to the locomotive."

"How many steamers are plying on the ocean ferry?" asked Irene.

"There are twenty-nine regular lines of steamships," replied Compton, "plying between New York and Europe. Six of these, however, do not carry passengers, and only eight run express passenger boats. The Americans say that the value of the steamers cleared annually from New York is about £100,000,000. It easily mounts up when you consider that this ship alone costs £400,000."

"I wonder what Columbus would have thought," said Mrs. Julia, meditatively, "if after he had pleaded in vain for a few thousands from Henry the Seventh, to fit out his little expedition, he could have foreseen that we should have been crossing the Atlantic to celebrate his triumph in a vessel which cost ten times as much as he wanted to equip his entire fleet."

"I regard Columbus," said the professor, "as the supreme criminal——'

"Professor!" said Compton, rising, "we will postpone your views about Columbus till another day. The ladies would probably like to go on deck, and take their last look at the English, or, rather, the Welsh coast"——

They went on deck. It was a lovely evening. The sea was as placid as a lake. The sun was still far above the horizon. On either side of the great ship, the sea was flecked with vessels of every size and rig. Coaling steamers were trading along, and, at some distance off, an Atlantic liner was tearing northward towards the Mersey.

Holyhead Lighthouse was left far behind. The majestic summit of Snowdon, radiant with the light of the western sun, rose before them, and then that too was left far away astern.

The ladies sought their berths. The professor betook himself to the smoking room to hunt for a specimen. Compton and the doctor remained at last alone, pacing the deck, as the sun went down and the evening star shone out in a cloudless sky.

"What a strange exhilaration I always feel," said the doctor, "when I am at sea. It is only then I think one really feels what it is to belong to the nation that is Sovereign of the seas. In my own small way I feel what I suppose every Englishman with any imagination must feel, that he is a kind of miniature edition of the Lord High Admiral, and that even if he is too sick to come down to dinner, he helps to wield the trident of Britannia."

"Yes," rejoined Compton, "it is a glorious heritage. But half our people know nothing about it, and the other half think it is not worth while to teach them. For a nation whose daily bread depends upon their supremacy on the sea, we display the most astonishing indifference to the very foundations of our greatness. It is only within the last eight years that a proposal to cut down the Navy was the favourite nostrum of the Liberal party, and even to-day what was perhaps the most sanely imperial Ministry of recent times sent Nelson's flagship to the German shipknacker to be sold for firewood and old iron. What a race it is! Was there ever a people who did so much upon so small a stock of imagination?"

"I think you do our people wrong," said the doctor. "Our imagination is latent. We are an inarticulate race. But we think more than we speak, and, who knows? I am daring enough to imagine that even Mr. Gladstone, deep down in his heart of hearts, sometimes thinks of the Navy with honest pride. He dissembles it, no doubt. But no one who travels can fail to feel something of a lift of heart when he sails across the seas, and everywhere and always finds the British flag to the fore."

"But the majority of our people don't travel," replied Compton, "and you need to go some hundred miles distance from London to begin to understand how vast England looms before the imagination of mankind. I often wish the moment Parliament rises in the autumn we could pack all our M.P.s on board a trooper, and send them on a cruise around the world. It would broaden their views, and we should perhaps have fewer pedlars posing as statesmen when Parliament re-assembled in the spring."

Night was now falling, and as they wished to see the mails taken on board at Queenstown, the friends turned in and slept.

Early next morning they were roused by the cessation of the rhythmic movement of the engines. They were off Queenstown. The tender was steaming out from the harbour with the mail-bags, and those who wished were allowed to go on shore.

It was a lovely June morning, with one of those sunrises which make us envy the policemen "on night duty," who almost alone of modern citizens see the sun rise in summer time. The Irish coast stood revealed in all its wealth of varied beauty. The green hills in the distance, the spacious harbour, the emerald fields, the indented shore,

THE TENDER WAS STEAMING OUT WITH THE MAIL BAGS.

made a picture of such loveliness as almost to suggest that, to hold the balance even, Nature was compelled to compensate the land for its loveliness by the squalid horror of its intestine feuds.

The professor was the first to land, and was eagerly assailed by the innumerable hucksters who, week-day and Sunday, do a thriving business with the passengers on the Atlantic ferry. He bought what he was assured was a typical Irish shillalegh, a hideous abortion of a pipe stalk, with a knob at the end, big enough to be utterly useless at Donnybrook Fair. Compton and the doctor purchased a few trifling souvenirs for the ladies, and Compton carefully secured copies of the Irish papers of the previous day. They heard the Irish brogue, visited the traditional applewoman, and then, as the bell was sounding, they rejoined the *Majestic*.

The tender pushed off from the side of the great liner, the twin screws began to revolve, and once more the Queen of the Atlantic entered for her race against time to the New World. When they passed the Fastnet Rock, and saw the hills of Erin fade away in the distance, they felt as if they had cut the painter which bound them to the Old World.

When the party re-assembled at breakfast Mrs. Irwin was in high spirits, chiefly, it would seem, because she had just seen the last outline of her "native land fade o'er the waters blue.'

"Ireland," said she, "is the loveliest country in the whole world · to get away from. It is really pretty enough to live in, but it is a mighty deal prettier to be out of. When you remember Erin in the watches of the night, she is even

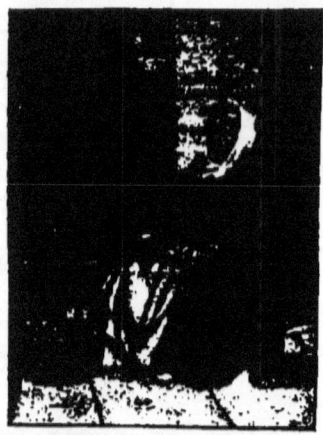

A FAMILIAR FIGURE AT QUEENSTOWN.

lovelier, and much less melancholy, than to live in her day by day. There is something in the air, I think, but I know I'm never in such high spirits as when I've left the dear distracted land so far behind me that it seems like a poetic dream.'

"Madame Blavatsky," remarked Compton, " in her 'Secret Doctrine' tells us that Ireland is a forlorn fragment of an earlier continent, not exactly the Last Rose of Summer left blooming alone, but, literally and truly, a forgotten remnant of what we should call an earlier creation. And you would relegate it to its proper epoch, Mrs. Irwin.'

"That would I," returned Mrs. Irwin, heartily. "It would be tolerable on the astral plane. On the earth plane, somehow, Irishmen in Ireland are like earthbound spirits, imprisoned in uncongenial conditions. Hence the perpetual murmur of Irish discontent. We are all of us spirits from a higher sphere prisoned in a clay compounded chiefly of praties. Imagine a seraph coffined in a potato!" and she laughed heartily at her own conception. "That is the Irishman at his best and worst."

"Well, doctor," said the professor, "and what kind of cabin companions have you chanced on?"

"Fairly good, with one exception. Immediately below me, for I had the good luck to get a top berth, there sleeps a venerable ancient who has a monstrous nose with a snore to match."

"What an infliction!" said Irene.

"I suppose I shall get used to it," said the doctor, resignedly. "But when first I heard that sonorous trumpet blast, I dreamed of earthquakes; when it sounded the second time, it suggested a dream of a fog settling down, and the syren blowing hard; the third time it was like the trumpet of the Angel Israfil, and I jumped up for judgment, hitting my head badly against the top of the berth."

"Snoring," said the professor, "is one of the last afflictions of humanity to be abated by science. But it can be done, although we have not got our data complete. I want a good specimen. I am interested on this account. Would you change berths with me? I have got a cunning little instrument which registers sound. It is an adaptation of the phonograph, and, with a little improvement, I guess it would stop the snoring of the seven sleepers."

"With pleasure," replied the doctor, "if your companion does not object.'

"My dear professor," said Compton, "sacrifice me to the interest of science any time. Besides, the man who abolishes the snore will be canonised, not by the Vatican, but by universal humanity."

"I see you take 'Georgia Water' at all your meals," said Irene. "The sea seems as calm as a lake, and the stewards have nothing to do."

"Just now," said Compton, "I looked at the glass. It is falling, and I should not be surprised if we have a bit of ugly weather before night."

"Glasses round, then," said the doctor. "And if 'Georgia Water' carries us through the storm without a steward, you must get your social organism, my dear professor, to make its use compulsory on all liners."

"Dear me," said Mrs. Julia suddenly, as a lady with her two boys rose from the middle table, and went out, "what an angel face ! It quite startled me as the child passed."

"Yes," said Irene ; "but I liked the elder boy best. There is more snap in his head The other is just too angelic for this work-a-day world. Angels are all very well in heaven, but here they would be insipid."

"For you," remarked the professor, "there should be a cross between angel and devil. You like your qualities so antithetically mixed. Always the extremes. What a salad you would make.'

"But who was she?" persisted Mrs. Julia. "I should like to know them."

"It is never difficult to make acquaintances where there are children," said the doctor. "Before lunch you shall know them all."

He was as good as his word. The Blue Brigade had

FASTNET ROCK : THE LAST GLIMPSE OF THE OLD WORLD.

got their chairs comfortably established on deck under the awning that shielded them from the rays of the sun. When the two children came past, something tickled the younger one in the appearance of the blue chairs. He spoke to his brother, and laughed. Before they could pass, the doctor said,—

"Where is your mother, little man?"

"She is in the drawing-room," he replied, the younger looking at his questioner straight in the face with his black-fringed blue eyes. "Do you want her?"

"Oh, dear, no," said the doctor, "I only wondered how you came to be wandering about all alone."

"Mother's head's bad, and she wanted to rest. So she said we might trot around and see things, and come back to her when we were tired."

"But," said the doctor, "it is

FRED.

pleasanter here than in the drawing-room. Why does not your mother bring her chair, and see the sunlight on the water?"

"Mother has not a chair," said the elder boy. "Has everyone to get a chair? She thought they supplied them on board ship."

"No, each passenger must bring his own. But if your mother likes, she may have the use of ours. We have usually at least one empty in our little colony of the blue chairs."

The boys looked at him, not knowing how their mother would take it. Presently the younger said, —

"Where are you going to?"

"We are going to Chicago, my little man, and where are you bound for?"

"We are going to San Francisco to meet father. He is coming from China. We have not seen him for nearly three years."

"And what is your father?"

"He is a missionary," replied the child.

"And so you are going round the ship," said the doctor. "Perhaps you might let me go with you. I could tell you about things."

They took his offered hands and they set off on an exploring expedition. They peeped down the engine-room, where they could not enter, and saw the great greasy steel slave clanking as he turned the screw, labouring with hot and steaming breath as he drove the mighty ship through the Atlantic. He showed them how there were double sets of engines and boilers, each with its own screw, so that, if one broke or went wrong, the ship could still forge ahead through the sea.

"How fast are we going now?" asked the younger, whose name was Fred.

"About twenty-three miles an hour, a mile and a bit in every three minutes. You know twenty sea miles equal twenty-three land miles. They are strong fellows, these steam slaves of the engine-room. They are like the genii in the 'Arabian Nights,' cooped up by a magician in a hot and grimy cell, and compelled to ferry us all over the sea.

They never rest all the voyage, night and day, day and night, they keep on, never resting, storm or calm. There is the might of 18,000 horses stowed up in their mighty limbs."

"But where does all the power come from?" asked Tom, the elder boy.

"Can you see down there, far, far away down below the engines, right at the bottom of the ship, there is just a little glare of light? They will not let us go down, nor would you care to, even if they allowed you. It is hot, and dark, and dirty. But the power they get there comes from the sun. Ages and ages ago great forests grew in the sunlight, and in their leaves the sun manufactured wood, just as he is manufacturing it now. Then great changes came, and the wood was turned into coal. Deep down in the stoke-hole there are men always busy throwing coal—which is only bottled-up sunshine—into the furnaces, where it burns, and giving off the stored-up sun-heat, it boils the water in the boiler, making it into steam, the steam makes the piston move, the piston-rod turns the screw-shaft, and the screw-shaft drives the ship through the water. It is just like the old nursery story about the woman whose pig would not go over the stile. The moment one thing worked everything followed. Here it was the sun who began at the beginning of all, but in the ship it is the stoker who begins. If he did not constantly shovel coal into the furnaces we should never get to America. We have more than one hundred stokers on board constantly at work."

"Does it take much coal?" asked Tom.

"In order to get the power of one horse for a couple of hours we have to burn three lbs. of coal. It used to be much more. At first it took just six times as much coal. But they improve the engines and the boilers year after year. There is an arithmetic lesson for you. We are now using 18,000 horse-power. It takes 36 lbs. every 2¼ hours to get the power of one horse. How much coal do we burn every day?"

"I don't like sums," said Tom. "Tell us how much it is.'

"Every day," said the doctor, "there is shovelled into the furnaces 290 tons of coal. In six days' voyage we shall burn 1,740 tons. We always take 2,400 to be safe."

"Then the ship is getting lighter every day," said Fred.

"Certainly, 290 tons lighter. But it is not only for driving the ship we use the coal. We steer the ship, and pump the ship, and light the ship, all with the coal we carry in the hold, and which has all to be dug out of

TOM.

the mine deep down in the earth. With plenty of bottled sunlight in the bunkers, we don't mind about the wind."

"If we had to row the ship across the sea, how many oars would be needed?" asked Fred.

"To get the same speed," said the doctor, "we should need 100,000 galley slaves rowing all day and 100,000 rowing all night. The men would weigh just about as much as the coal, but then they would need to be fed and lodged, and there would be no room for them or for their oars. You could not get more than 400 oars on each side a ship like this."

"I want to ask you something," said Fred.

"Well, my boy, what is it?"

"Is this ship—the one we are in now—as big as Noah's Ark?"

"Well, now," said the doctor, trying to gain time, "I wasn't there, you know."

"No," said Fred, "you are not Noah, nor Shem, nor Ham, nor Japheth, and there were no other men on board. But you know the Bible says it was 300 cubits long by 50 broad, and 30 cubits high. How long is the steamer?"

"It is 582 feet long, 57½ feet broad, and 59 feet high, from the keel to the deck. It is much narrower and taller in proportion than the Ark, which was only meant to float, not to drive headlong through the sea."

"How much is a cubit?" asked Tom.

"No one knows. Some say one and a half feet. If so the Ark was nearly 100 feet shorter than the *Majestic*, eighteen feet broader, and fourteen feet lower."

"If the ship caught fire, should we all be burnt alive?" asked the younger boy.

"No," said the doctor. "If the ship caught fire, the fire would be put out. If the captain were only to ring that bell hard for three minutes, every man of the crew would be at work deluging the fire with water pumped in by all manner of engines, and directed upon the flames by great lengths of hose. Before you came on board they had a fire-drill on deck, and all were ready for action in three minutes."

"If a storm came, and the wind was very high, should we not be drowned?"

"Not a bit. You would not have to come on deck, that is all. But you would be as safe as a clock."

"But," persisted the little questioner, "if a great huge wave were to dash right on to the deck, we should go to the bottom, shouldn't we?"

"Nothing of the kind, the wave would simply dash over the deck, taking some things away with it as keepsakes, but the wave never rose that could sink the *Majestic*, and now as the lunch-bell is sounding, let me take you to your mother."

Mrs. Wills was on the deck looking for the boys when they ran up to tell her of the doctor's offer. He now came forward, and repeated it, saying how delighted he should be if he could be of any service.

"I have found your boys most entertaining companions," he said; "and it will be a trivial acknowledgment of your kindness in letting me have your lads to ask you to occupy my chair."

Mrs. Wills, with a sweet and winsome smile, accepted the offer, and she also, with her boys, was formally enrolled in the Blue Brigade.

CHAPTER V. A GALE AT SEA.

"I CALCULATE," said the professor, "that the psychological moment is near at hand." He had just finished lunch, and looked somewhat ruefully upon the remains of the feast. "We're going to have it rather rough. At dinner we shall need the fiddles on the table, but, alas! few will be there to see either table or fiddle."

"Cheer up, professor," said Compton. "Never meet trouble half-way. It may blow over."

"That's just what it will do, my friend. It will blow over, and no mistake. Some of you trust in 'Georgia Water,' and some in Mattei's anti-mal-de-mer, but as for me, I reckon that as regards two-thirds of this company there will be at least two full days before we meet again."

So saying, he solemnly stalked off to his berth. Before turning in, he cast a searching look round the horizon. The sky was clear save where some heavy clouds were banked far in the south-east. There was no wind, but the glass was falling fast, and his experienced eye a v several significant indications that captain and crew, an l especially the steward, were preparing for a bout of rough weather.

On the deck ladies and gentlemen, fresh from the lunch

ON DECK IN THE SUNSHINE.

table, were chatting or smoking, enjoying the bright sunshine, and congratulating themselves upon the halcyon calm of the sea. Some of the young ladies had donned their smart dresses, and were preening themselves in the sunshine.

The professor could not repress a sardonic smile. "In two hours," he thought; "but now, unmindful of their coming doom, the little victims play." Then a certain sinking sensation in the lower portions of the diaphragm, and a curious familiar movement of some of the muscles of the throat, warned him that he had no leisure for philosophizing. He crawled wretchedly to his new berth; summoned the steward, and was soon too much absorbed in his own wretchedness to spare a thought even for the most abnormal of criminal types.

The doctor bestirred himself to prepare his friends for the approaching change. Mrs. Wills was his first care. "She was never sick," she said. "She sometimes wished she was. A certain heavy headachy feeling weighed her down all the time she was on the sea. As for the boys, they were never ill, and she hoped that Baby would not mind."

"Baby!" said the doctor; "I did not know you had a baby with you."

"Oh, yes," she said. "We call her Baby, but she is three years old. It is her first sea voyage, and I did not bring her into the drawing-room. She is so young. But if you will come into my cabin, you will see her for yourself."

Dr. Wynne was, of course, delighted to come. A baby on board ship is something like a primrose on an iceberg. Any ordinarily well-behaved baby is safe to have a better chance of being spoiled on board ship than any it would ever encounter on land. In the steerage babies are somewhat at a discount. In the saloon they are at a premium.

"Where is my little girl?" said Mrs. Wills, as she opened the cabin door.

"Mamma's got no little girl," replied a childish but resolute voice "I's a big girl now, and not mother's 'little' girl any more."

"Well, big girl, won't you shake hands with me?" said the doctor.

The child hid her face in her mother's dress, and did not speak. She was a sturdy little monkey, prettily but plainly dressed, and in her blue eyes lurked a roguish smile.

She was clutching a doll.

"Come, Pearl, won't you speak to the gentleman?"

"No," said the child. "I can't. Kitty's asleep, and we mustn't wake her."

PEARL.

"Well," said the doctor, "it is no use trying to force myself upon the young lady; perhaps, she may be more willing to see me next time. You had better prepare for being a close prisoner with your little one for the next day or two. There is a storm brewing in the south-east, and, before dinner, you will be glad to be safe and snug in your berth."

"Do you think there is any danger?" she asked, anxiously.

"Danger! Not the least in the world. Discomfort? yes, especially for a lady with three children who are making their first voyage I will see the boys, and tell them what to do. Meanwhile, let me help you to make tight all the loose packages you have got in the cabin. When the ship rolls, they are apt to pitch about in a fashion as annoying to you as it is destructive to themselves."

"Thank you very much, doctor," said Mrs. Wills, when he had finished stowing portmanteaus and toys safely under the berths; and even little Pearl held up her chubby mouth to "kiss the nice gentleman Good-bye."

As Dr. Wynne left the cabin, a curious new instinct seemed suddenly to unfold itself in him. He had felt it

before in a dim sort of way, but, now, he was fully conscious of it. He felt a hungry craving longing, not so much for the love of a woman as for the love, the clinging, confiding love of little children. How he envied Mrs. Wills her baby!

But there were the two boys to hunt for, and to prepare for the compulsory confinement that awaited them. They were leaning over the railings, looking down at a sedate old goat which was walking about in the steerage.

"Here, boys," said the doctor. "Do you see those clouds? In half an hour the rain will be upon us, and you had better not stray too far from your berth, or you will have some difficulty in getting back."

The approach of the storm was now beginning to be too manifest to be mistaken. The deck steward was piling up the chairs, all movables were cleared away from the deck, and passengers were scurrying off to their berths.

A puff of wind came sighing past, the surface of the sea became fretful, the sky was almost entirely overcast, and the wind, no longer in fitful gusts, freshened steadily into a gale. The boys were escorted to their cabin; most of the ladies were in their berths. In the drawing-room a few old sailors composed themselves for a tranquil afternoon. There was room enough.

The wind roared and shrieked through the rigging, the waves ran higher and higher, now and again flinging a handful of spray in watery *mitraille* along the deck. In the steerage and in the cabins the stewards were busy. At dinner, a mere handful sat down to table. After dinner, only half-a-dozen seasoned salts were found in the smoking room, and soon after nine, every passenger was in his berth, seeking sleep, but, for the most part, finding none.

It was a rough night, but not exceptionally bad. To those who were making their first Atlantic voyage, the waves seemed mountainous, and each time the *Majestic* plunged down the slope of the billows, it seemed as if she was steaming straight down—down to the abyss. But the next moment, she was climbing up the side of another wave, only to plunge down again, until it seemed as if the unequal contest of the whole roused ocean, in its fight against the cockle-shell of a ship must end in the inevitable catastrophe. But to the captain and his men there was nothing in it. A fresh night, with plenty of sea on, but nothing that gave them even a moment's anxiety.

The engines never for a moment slackened their toil. Come storm or calm, the gaping mouths of the furnaces must be fed, the engines must be oiled, and every minute detail of duty scrupulously performed.

In their cabin Compton and the doctor were talking quietly.

"Is it not glorious," said the doctor, "this wrestle, as of the gods of Asgard with the giants of Jotunheim. Outside, a boiling waste of waters, a whole ocean, scourged by the winds into the wildest fury, all around the darkness of the night, wave after wave surging up as if to overwhelm us, and yet, and yet . . . Listen to the rattle and roar of those engines, as with heart of fire and muscles of steel they steadily tear their tranquil way to their destined port."

"It is a great triumph of the combination of forces," said Compton, "of the might of the scientific brain in command of the ready obedience of a disciplined crew. Yet it is not an ideal system, that which prevails on these liners. From an extreme democratic point of view, it is the quintessence of tyranny. From a humanitarian or philanthropic standpoint, it is in many respects deplorable. On board these boats we have the cash nexus between man and man in its coarse form. Fraternity, comradeship, has hardly recognition. The crew are engaged for the trip only; and although many of them are always re-engaged at the end of the voyage, they are often not a company so much as a crowd. It is a hard, hard life, as Lieutenant Kelly says, 'and as for kindness, or any other raving grace, in the grim pessimism of this iron trade they are never expected.' But grace or no grace, the liners keep their time."

"The kindly graces have not time to flower in a week's engagement," said the doctor, "but the manlier virtues—courage, endurance, discipline, the power to command, the grace to obey, in other words, duty in every shape and form—where will you find it in higher development, or tested under severer strain? From the captain on the bridge down to the grimy stoker who slaves like a naked gnome at the furnace fires, is there one who ever flinches? How the ship labours on these seas! I am glad duty does not call me to tumble out of my berth, don tarpaulin, and face the blinding rain and the bitter blast. All the more do I respect and honour the brave fellows on the night watch."

"No doubt," said Compton. "But take them singly, they are not the elect of mankind. Pool the whole of their brains, and if they were alone in the world they could no more perform their task than they could fly to the moon. They are the heirs of successive generations of builders and mariners; they have the whole science of the world to draw upon, and so the thing is done. Some day, perhaps, we shall see in politics the same concentration and consecration that we see in navigation. But the common sense and science that are recognised as indispensable to drive a liner across the ocean are considered as, quite unnecessary when the ship of State is to be steered across the vast, unsurveyed expanse of the future."

There was a pause. They listened to the reverberations of the screw, which seemed to vary with every pitch of the vessel, and sometimes, as the waves heaved the stern clear of the water, and the screw revolved in the air, its racing was unpleasant to hear.

"How she plunges," said the doctor, as the good ship pitched and strained and forged her way ahead. "What a comment this is upon the croaking of the pessimists upon the bad work, the scamped work of the modern artificer. Whenever in ancient or modern times did the handicrafts-men confront nature in her wildest moods, and challenge the giants of Jotunheim to discover a flaw in their handi-work? Were but a rivet loose, or a plate honeycombed, or any dishonest trick played from stem to stern, such a gale as this would find it out. But after a hundred storms the work of the workman stands the test."

There was another pause. From the next cabin came the familiar, but unmistakable, sound that tells that the world and all things that are therein have faded into insig-nificance, and the only tangible reality is the steward and his basin.

"I wonder, sometimes," said the doctor, "whether, as a mere torture chamber, the Inquisition could be compared at its worst with an Atlantic liner at its best. Think for a moment what is going on around us. Here in this great vessel there are packed about as tightly as the larvæ of wasps in their nests some 1,500 human beings, of whom 1,000 at this moment would probably be grateful beyond words if you could rid them of existence. Life is sweet to all men, they say, but to those who are sea-sick. It is the one malady which overcomes the instinctive longing to persist in living." Not even in toothache do sufferers wish to die. But ask the stewards how many of the sea-sick beg to be thrown overboard. And what good is it all? To what purpose this needless agony?"

"Humph!" said Compton. "It is odd for an Englishman to talk like that. Why, sea-sickness is one of the best gifts

the gods ever gave us. When I heard someone declaring that Georgia Water was an infallible preventive for sea-sickness, I mentally resolved that it would be cheap at a million sterling to poison that Georgian Well. What is sea-sickness but the invisible warder of the English seas, the potent enchanter who tortures by his magic arts all who would approach our sea-girt isle? Why this sea-sickness which you so ignorantly abuse is worth, as a mere shield of defence, a whole armada of ironclads. Even the Spanish Armada itself was cowed by mal-de-mer before it ever came within cannon-shot of the puny pinnaces and fireships of the Elizabethan worthies. Tom Hood's question 'Why, if Britannia ruled the seas, she did not rule them straight?' is easily answered. If she did—if these stormy seas were as smooth as a mill-pond, the trident would more easily be wrested from her grasp, and England might have been the mere appendage of some Continental power. Who can say how much of our national independence and our empire we owe to the inevitable horror which sea-sickness excites in the Continental mind?"

"It may be so," said the doctor, "but I think it gene-rates more misery to the square inch than any other agency in all the diabolical enginery of nature."

"And yet," retorted Compton, "it produces this un-equalled effect upon the imagination by a minimum of injury to human life. Since the Maid of Norway, in Edward the VI.'s time, how many have died of sea-sickness? But, come, let us take a turn on deck before we turn in."

When they went on deck they were saluted by a heavy plash of water from a wave which, striking the ship as it passed, flung disdainfully a giant's handful of brine across the deck. Soaked and chilled, as by a sudden plunge bath, they struggled forward, keeping their feet with diffi-culty as the vessel pitched and lurched. The sky was dark with driving clouds, through gaps in which gleamed, here and there, a lonely star. All around, the waves were running mountains high. One moment, on the crest of a wave, they caught a glimpse far away in the sky-line of the lights of a steamer; then down, down they went, till the wave behind and the wave before shut out everything from their gaze. Up again, they saw the signal rockets that told the captain what steamer they were passing, to which they responded, the hissing rockets with their fiery tails shining bright against the murky darkness. They stood watching the turmoil.

"It is always agreeable," said Compton, "to contemplate chaos from a firm foothold on ever so small a fragment of cosmos. It gives one a pleasant sense of superiority."

"Everything goes like a clock," remarked the doctor, as a fresh watch came on. "It is cosmos; no doubt, the heart beats steady and the pulse is regular, but the stomach of cosmos is very much out of order, I fear."

As the gale seemed increasing rather than abating in its fury, the two friends groped their way down below, and were soon asleep.

There were not many who slept, except from sheer exhaustion, in a kind of deadly lethargy. But among those who slept soundly and awoke fresh as a lark was little Pearl. She was in high glee with the motion of the ship. At first she had been a little frightened, but finding that no one seemed to think anything of it, she had concluded that it was a great swing-swang invented for her own amusement, and enjoyed it immensely.

"A swing, mamma, Pearl's swing; it will put all the dollies to sleep."

Once, when she had her first experience of a thunder-storm, she had come to a similar conclusion. To her they seemed a gorgeous exhibition of celestial fireworks, displayed for her benefit. After some more than usually brilliant flash and thunder peal, she clapped her hands with delight and cried,—

" Do it again! Do it again! ' And it did it again.

The great ship swing-swang did not need being told to do it again. It did it so ofte that, after a time, the little eyes closed, and Pearl slept with her soft out-stretched hand upon her mother's cheek.

Her brothers were less fortunate. They had gone to sleep, each in his own berth, when a sudden lurch of the ship, followed by a heavy roll, landed them both in a confused heap upon the cabin floor. Fred, who was in the top berth, hurt his head rather badly, and set up a doleful howl. The mother rang the bell for the stewardess, who soon bundled the youngsters into the lower berth.

' Better sleep together,' she said ; " there is less danger of your rolling out."

In the morning the doctor came round to see how they were. The boys hailed him as an old friend, and even little Pearl consented to be kissed, " if the doctor would promise to cure Kitty," a doll who was supposed to have suffered severely from being thrown out of the berth in the night

The sea was still running high, although there were signs that the wind was falling. Not more than twenty or thirty passengers had presented themselves at breakfast. The rest breakfasted in their cabins, or, for the most part, did not breakfast at all The professor, when they visited him, was very prostrate

" Compton" said he, in a hoarse whisper, " I think I have thrown up my immortal soul "

" Glad to hear that you ever had one," said Compton, lightly. " You always doubted it."

The professor did not reply. Irene Vernon was all right. She was going to get up before lunch. " She was as hungry as a hawk," she said, " and she would be at table if her cousin had to carry her in a chair."

During the morning the two boys peeped out of their cabin, and seeing the doctor in the distance, summoned him to their help.

" We want to have a look at the waves," said Fred. "Don't you think we could get on deck if you took one hand ? "

" Try," said the doctor. With many a tumble they succeeded in gaining the deck. The waves were not splashing over the bulwarks, and the rain had ceased. The sun was faintly shining through the clouds, and its rays were already beginning to give light and colour to the heaving water.

" Do you know," said the doctor, after he had ensconced his young charges safely in a sheltered spot, ' what a poet once said caused the waves to roar ? "

" Tell us ! " said the boys, eagerly.

" He said that when the north wind blew the old gods of Asgard — "

" Where is Asgard ? " asked Fred.

" Where Thor lived with his thunder hammer, and Odin with his ravens, and Baldur the Beautiful. Well, the poet said that the old gods came forth with the north wind, and chanted the Runic songs of old ; chanted them louder and louder as the wind roared over the waters, until the waves slumbering deep in the ocean, were awakened by the song, and, rousing themselves, lifted their heads to hear it

" KEEPING THEIR FEET WITH DIFFICULTY."

more plainly. And when they heard that mystic chant, they grew mad with excitement, and tossed their great heads on high, and clapped their hands, and danced in frenzied glee. For they, too, belong to the family of gods, and the old song recalled the time before the old gods were dethroned, and the Cross of Jesus smote down the thunder hammer of Thor."

Fred's great eyes dilated as he listened to Heine's pretty conceit, and then they wandered away to the great sea of waters.

Then he said, " Is this a north wind, doctor ? "

" No," said he, " it is a south-easter, but all the winds

have their songs, which the waves hear and understand."

"Where do the waves go to when the wind stops singing?" said Tom.

"They go down deep into the still water at the bottom of the sea, where no ripple ever disturbs their sleep, excepting when, now and then, a dead man settles slowly down.

"What is the bottom of the sea like, doctor?" asked Fred.

"The bottom of this sea is like a smooth, slightly sloping plain. If it were all dried up, you could drive a coach from Ireland to Newfoundland without ever needing to put the brake on. But it is very deep, deeper than even fishes can live in except a few, which you never see. The pressure is too great."

"Could a diver go down to the bottom?"

"No, if he tried the blood would burst from his eyes, and he would die. No one lives down there. Not even mermaids. But do you know what there is down below? All the Atlantic cables are there, which are the telegraph wires of the deep sea. They need no telegraph posts. They lie on the bottom in the ooze, covered all up with gutta percha, and down there at this minute they are pulsing news and messages as quick as thought, from the Old World to the New."

"Doctor," said Fred, after a long pause, "it is not true that story about the wind's song and the wave's dance?"

"No," replied the doctor. "It is only a poet's fancy. But there are far stranger things than that which are quite, quite true."

"Tell us some," said Tom.

"I told you one to-day about this ship being driven through the waves by the bottled-up sunshine. Now, what would you think if I told you that below the keel of our ship, far, far down in the dreamless deep, where no storms ever come, there is going on the making of chalk, out of which is made limestone and the marble on your washstand?"

"Who is making it, doctor?" asked Fred.

"God," said he, laconically. Then, after a pause, during which no one spoke, he said: "Do you know how He does it? By death. There are millions and millions of tiny little creatures in this upper sea. which live for a time, and make their little shells out of the carbonate of lime in the salt water. Then they die; and when they cease to live, their little shells—such wee, wee shells, you can only see they are shells by looking at them through a microscope—fall down, down, down to the bottom of the sea. Day and night, summer and winter, year in and year out, there is a ceaseless, constant downpour of these tiny shells to the ocean floor. It is the great cemetery of the sea. The piled-up corpses of the dead make the oozy mud that is brought up by the deep-sea soundings. In time, that becomes chalk, and chalk, when cooked by the great ovens that are heated down below, becomes marble. To make your marble washstands, who can say how many millions of little shell-fish had to give up their lives?"

"See," said Tom, "there is another ship."

It was a heavily-laden cargo-steamer, floundering along on the waves at a distance of about two miles.

"Come," said the doctor, "I want to show you something."

The children, taking each a hand, staggered and rolled as best they could to where they could see the captain. He was taking observations for the meridian.

"What is he looking through that funny thing for?" asked Fred.

"To see exactly where the sun crosses the meridian," replied the doctor.

"But what good does that do?"

"That is the way in which the captain can find out exactly where the ship is, and how many miles she has run since yesterday."

"Can you get to know exactly where you are?"

"To within about five miles."

"There," exclaimed the captain, "that makes eight bells. It is now exactly twelve o'clock."

"But all the clocks are wrong, and all the watches. Every night at twelve o'clock they alter the ship's clocks, but every hour they go wrong again, because we are racing along and get ahead of time. If I never altered my watch it would show twelve o'clock at New York when New York time would only be about seven o'clock in the morning. New York is just about five hours behind Greenwich."

With such talk the morning wore away. At lunch many more convalescents appeared. Nearly all the Blue Brigade were in their places. But the professor was still laid up, and many anxious inquiries were made on his behalf.

In the evening the wind had almost died away, and after dinner Compton was startled by hearing the voice of the professor.

"Resurrected," said Professor Glogoul, with a forced smile. "Come along to the smoking-room. I want to see the earlier pools. It is the beginning of things that interest me. Their later development follows well-ascertained laws."

They sauntered to the smoking-room.

"Five shilling pool to-night," said a gentleman near the door.

"How many miles did she make to-day?" they asked.

"We are waiting to know," said their informant. "I have bought the minimum, but I fear the wind helped her through the sea. My luck is small."

Presently the exact number of miles she declared to be 486, and the lucky holder of that figure pocketed the stakes. The new pool was opened.

"Are you not going in?" said Compton.

"Certainly not," replied the professor. "Let us sit down, and watch the gamblers make their play. It is quite a Monte Carlo, both as to excitement and morality."

The pool was small—so many passengers were sick; but twenty deposited their crown-pieces, and drew lots for the twenty numbers between 480 and 500. Then the numbers having been distributed, they were all put to auction. The chief competition, of course, is for the lowest and highest numbers, carrying, as they do, all numbers below and above the minimum and maximum. Each player has a right to buy in his own number at half price, but otherwise there is no reserve. The proceeds of the auction are pooled, and the holder of the winning number carries off the stake. At present playing was low, and the stakes small.

"Gambling," said the professor, "is the resource of mankind against ennui. It is mental dram-drinking. The mind gets sluggish and dull. It needs a 'pick-me-up.' That, in many cases, is the pathology of gambling, and as the mind gets jaded it requires a severer spur. So the stakes increase. As people get terribly bored on the Atlantic, gambling and betting tend constantly to increase."

"That is not the worst of it." said Compton. "The fool who has no resource for exhilarating his brains but by emptying his pockets exists everywhere, but the ugly thing is the kind of vultures he attracts wherever he goes. The professional gambler is as well-known on the ocean ferry as in the casinos of Nice. There are not a few sharpers here, even now, and there will be more before another day is over."

"Pool is not so bad," said the professor. "It is most respectably conducted—as honestly as the gaming at Monte Carlo—but it opens the door to gaming which is to pool what the hells of Nice are to the highly respectable establishment of M. Blanc."

Card-playing was going on in many directions, and money was beginning to change hands. The professor watched the players curiously for a time, but after an hour he said, with a sigh,—

"There is not a rook or a pigeon here that is worth a cent for the purposes of scientific investigation."

As they went back to their berth, Compton asked,—

"How have your observations on the Snoring Ancient gone on?"

"Don't ask me," said the professor, lugubriously. "I know no more of what has passed than a Kodak of the pictures it has taken. You know the old joke when *mal-de-mer* has you by the midriff? 'You press the button, the steward will do the rest.' He did."

CHAPTER VI.—IN MID-OCEAN.

SATURDAY was fine. Three-fourths of the passengers came out of their berths, and roosted, more or less comfortably, on their deck chairs. Mrs. Wills, with little Pearl and her dolls, was established in the centre of the Blue Brigade, now doubly distinguished by possessing the only baby on board. The doctor initiated the boys into the mysteries of horse, billiards, deck quoits, and shuffleboard, and wandered with them all over the ship. With the aid of the deck steward he rigged up a swing chair from a cross beam in an out-of-the-way corner, and there little Pearl and her brothers were swinging in turns half the morning. At eleven o'clock they all watched, with intense interest, the starting of the captain upon his daily rounds of inspection. In the afternoon boat drill was held, and the children were delighted at the rapidity with which the boats were manned and made ready for lowering.

The professor and Irene had established themselves close together in the shadow of one of the boats, and seemed to find endless material for conversation. Irene was a wayward, handsome girl, somewhat spoiled, and although she had been twice or thrice engaged to be married, she had always broken it off. She rhapsodised about love, but love she had not known. It was dull to be without a lover, and she could no more have lived without a lover than she would have dressed without a corset. Men went into raptures about her. Three or four had offered her their hand, but the depths of her nature had never been really stirred. She liked the delightful dissipation of love-making, and took a suitor as men take champagne. She disliked to be off with the old love before she was on with the new, for she always felt it was safer to have the new suitor alongside before she sent the old one adrift. Besides, she was an artist, and cultivated her ideals. The favourite for the time being might please her so long as she saw him through a shimmer of novelty, and she could flatter her vanity by imagining him a prince and hero. But when she came to see him closely, she found her prince had freckles, and her hero, instead of being Apollo Belvidere, was manifestly a somewhat round-shouldered mediocrity. Then she got tired of her choice, and looked round for the next one who should come along.

In the professor she found an altogether different man from any whom she had ever met. He piqued her by treating her not in the least as a fine lady, or even as a pretty girl, but simply as a specimen sample of the human female at the age of twenty-two. He had no more feeling about her than if she had been a chunk of old red sandstone, or an obscure chemical compound. She interested him because she was frank, cynically candid, and self-conscious to a degree unusual even in an age in which prime ministers and moralists work themselves up into ecstacies of praise of the journal of a girl which carefully chronicles how admirable she found her hips when she posed herself before her mirror preliminary to going to bed.

Irene was fascinated with him from the first. She was ambitious, and capable of spasms of intellectual aspiration. This man, nearly twice her age, who knew all the eminent *savans* of Europe, who had been everywhere, and who had made friends with the worst criminals in the prisons of two continents, had about him something delightfully, dangerously attractive. So she listened to him by the hour at the time, heard his theories of human nature, shuddered at his stories of his experiences, and looked forward with a fearful joy to seeing some of his wonderful experiments. She was quite willing to have allowed him to experiment upon her, to any extent short of vivisection, but her temporary cousin interposed his veto, and she had to wait until a suitable subject presented itself.

"Permit me, doctor," said the professor one day, "to affix my latest patent to your cousin's little finger. It is a wonderfully simple little instrument which records and registers the degree of excitement or expenditure of nerve force which is going on in the system."

"You can do that if you please," replied the doctor, "but no hypnotism."

"Why does the doctor object to hypnotism?" asked Irene.

"Because he objects to your placing yourself as absolutely in my power as if you were a threepenny bit in my pocket."

"But can you acquire that power over me? It seems too horrible."

"Of course I can," said he. "The power of a hypnotist over the hypnotised is absolute. I can make you insensible to feeling in your own body, and yet keenly susceptible to every pain which I suffer. I can transfer all your sensitiveness to a glass of water, so that if I stir it up you suffer; if I prick it you writhe, if I swallow it you swoon. Nay, I can outdo all that the old witches did, and, by transferring your sensitiveness to your photograph, can cause you to suffer, possibly to die, if I pierce the portrait with a pin."

"Oh," said Irene, "do you think you could teach me to hypnotise?"

"Yes," replied the professor; "but you are not to be trusted. Permit me to affix this to your finger. It will register on this scale the exact expenditure of emotional force caused by every thought that passes through your mind. Every emotion influences every particle of your body. The time is coming when you will be able to write a man's biography from a section of his elbow, and a glance at his shin-bone will enable us to know whether he was what you call good or bad."

"But why won't you teach me how to hypnotise?"

"Because," replied the professor, very deliberately, looking intently as he did so at the registry of his favourite instrument, "because I do not think it safe to give you access to such a facile substitute for the poison with which you will some day try to kill your husband."

"Professor!" she exclaimed, indignantly, "Do you take me for a murderess?"

"The register shows a pressure of 75 out of a maximum of 100," said he, triumphantly. "What an admirable sensitive you are. But why take offence? Facts are facts. You are very easily bored. Any husband will bore you in time. It is a law of nature. You will endure it for a year or two, but after a time you will feel that anything would be better than this awful *ennui*. You will shrink for a long time, perhaps for ever, from poison. But if you could use hypnotism, as the witches did, to kill your husband by piercing his portrait or image with a needle, you would not hesitate a moment."

He went on. "You see, you are emancipated from all restraints. You have lived through your religions. You do not believe in God any more. But you have not yet learnt that the law of the Social Organism is as inexorable as the laws of God, and you——"

"Well," said she, saucily, but half afraid, "what will the laws of the Social Organism do to me?"

"They will sentence you to be hanged by the neck until you are dead! Dear me, how interesting," he said. "The

"THE CLERGYMAN WHO SAT NEXT HER AT TABLE."

register only shows 65 instead of 75 recorded when I spoke of murdering your husband. There must really be some latent altruism in you after all. But, now, allow me to disengage my instrument. I must begin my inspection of the steerage."

Irene was very angry. But what was the use of showing temper when its only result would have been to give her adversary another observation as to the relation between emotion and the nerves and blood vessels of the finger, so she pursed up her lips, and devoted herself for the next hour to an industrious effort to get up a flirtation with her pseudo-cousin. The doctor was not much disposed to respond to her advances. He was somewhat sore with his disappointment at not meeting Rose on the ship. He had roamed the deck at all weathers and at all hours, but he had seen no one who remotely resembled the object of his quest. There was no Thorne in the list of passengers, and so far as he could see his dream of meeting her on the Atlantic was—well, as baseless as a dream.

Sunday came, and with Sunday the regular service by the captain in the morning, and in the afternoon, a discourse

by the clergyman who sat next the Blue Brigade at the dinner-table. In the evening at dinner, the professor, who had listened to the afternoon sermon, remarked:

"Why, he has not even got to Hegel!"

"Who is he, and what is Hegel?" asked Irene.

"Why the parson is he," said Dr. Glogoul, "and Hegelianism is the last refuge of the orthodox. The German pulpit evacuated it fifty years ago. The American pulpit is occupying it now, but that good man—well, after hearing him, I am now prepared to listen to a discourse upon the significance of the flight of the birds, or the comparative efficacy of prayers offered at the shrine of the Ephesian Diana, or the Capitoline Jove."

"You should not be too hard on him," said Compton. "Some men are of their time; some are before it; others, of whom our preacher is one, are far behind it. These old controversies to which he referred, with their battle-cries which he invoked——"

"Are as dead as the feuds of the Guelphs and Ghibellines, or as the Wars of the Roses," said the doctor. "In an age when our friend the professor is prepared to demonstrate that there is no such thing as moral responsibility, and that man is as material as a haggis, it is rather a twiddling of the thumbs to hear grave futilities about the sin of schism, and the pre-eminent importance of the apostolical succession."

"You should have heard him the other night," said Mrs. Irwin, "at our table. He said that the Bishop of Worcester had betrayed his trust by giving the Nonconformists the Sacrament at Grindelwald, that the Church of England was honeycombed with infidelity, and yet that it was the only Church of God with the true credentials left on earth."

"It is such men as these," said Compton, "whose pretensions are as colossal as their ignorance, and whose bigotry is as rank as their pride, who make the very name of Christianity to stink in the nostrils of mankind. At one time I thought the Church might be saved if only as a mere Society for Doing Good. But it will be damned by its own clergy. It will be disestablished and disendowed, not because the English cease to demand a national religion, but because they refuse to tolerate any longer its travesty by a sect whose clerics make up in 'side' what they lack in charity."

"Come, come," said the doctor, "let us go on deck and enjoy the beautiful evening sunlight. I will go and call the boys."

The little company soon was seated in the accustomed cosy corner, little Pearl, as usual, in her mother's lap; Fred stood by her side, and the rest of the Blue Brigade grouped round them like courtiers round their queen.

Tom, who had been reading diligently in the Library, asked if St. Christopher Columbus had sailed this way when he discovered America.

The professor interposed,—

"My boy, Columbus did not discover America. He was not a saint, but a criminal; and we may be thankful that no keel of his ever passed over this track."

"I always thought Columbus was a hero and a saint," said Irene. "And now you speak of him more bitterly than if he were a criminal in a convict prison."

"I would suggest," said Compton, "that as we are a little congregation in ourselves, the professor should address the Blue Brigade upon the subject upon which alone I have ever seen him manifest—what shall I call it?—a sense of moral responsibility other than the obligation of the individual to the Social Organism."

"I accept the invitation," returned the professor, "from a sense of my obligation to the Social Organism. Christopher Columbus was one of the greatest frauds of history.

It was not for nothing, or by accident, that the geographer of St. Die named the new-found continent after Amerigo Vespucci, who *described* it, rather than Columbus, who claimed to have *discovered* it."

"But who did discover America?" asked Mrs. Irwin, "or was it ever discovered at all?"

"America was first discovered," replied the professor, "by the Scandinavians, who visited and described what they called Vinland, but which was part of the coast of the North American Continent, six hundred years before Columbus crossed the seas. Columbus began life as a pirate, achieved renown as a filibuster, tried to recoup his fortunes by slave-dealing, and died in well-merited disgrace. Alike in private and in public life, his character was infamous, his mendacity was stupendous, and it would be well for the world if he had never existed."

"But surely he brought Christianity to the New World?" said Irene, "and added America to the civilised world?"

"Christopher — Christ-Bearer — that was his name, but Diabolus would have been a better designation." The professor was now fairly roused, and declaimed with a fervour very rare in him. "Ransack history for those men who have been named by a shuddering world as the scourges of God, and you will find few worthy to rank with the man whom Europe and America are now delighting to honour in the last decade of this philanthropic and humanitarian century. No! Neither Attila with his Huns; nor Hyder Ali, the scourge of God, rank before this Genoese filibuster, who sacrificed a whole race in order to boom his own fortunes and redeem his lying promises to a deluded Spain."

"What race?" asked Tom, "the Red Indians?"

"Columbus never set foot upon the continent. The scene of his exploits were those islands of Paradise known as the West Indies. Since the days of Joshua, history has recorded many a bloody conquest, and Africa to this hour bears terrible testimony to the crimes of civilisation. But the dealings of Columbus with the Carib stand out in bold relief as the supreme example of perfidy, ingratitude, and ruthless cruelty. When he landed he found the West Indian Islands densely peopled by an inoffensive race, who hardly knew the difference between mine and thine, who had all their land in common, but who dealt truly one with another without books, without law, without judges. Upon these helpless people Columbus descended as a thunderbolt of hell. In twelve years he, and the bloodsuckers whom he let loose in their midst, had extirpated the entire race. The sword of the soldier and the lash of the slave-driver completed a work of extermination which, for rapidity and thoroughness, has few parallels in history. Four hundred years have passed since then, but these lands still lie scarred with the desolation of his rule. When we reach Chicago we shall find his monument set on high for all men to honour, but we shall find no exhibit that would equal in real interest that which we shall not see— a specimen of a single village, or a single family of the manly, simple race which welcomed him with generous hospitality, and were rewarded by annihilation."

After delivering himself of this exordium, the professor departed. He would refresh his mind, he said, and wipe out the hateful memory of a Columbus by cultivating the acquaintance of a Calabrian bandit whom he had unearthed in the steerage.

The boys stared after him in blank amazement. At last Tom said,—

"Mother, I always thought Columbus was such a great man?"

"So he was, but great men are not always good, my boy," replied Mrs. Wills. "And it is not right to judge the people of the fifteenth century by the standpoint of the nineteenth. He was much better than Cortez and Pizarro."

"And for sure," said Mrs. Irwin, "if we have to rake up all the sins of centuries ago, there are some races nearer home than the Caribs who have almost as much to

MRS. WILLS, WITH PEARL AND FRED.

complain of, although their oppressors were never able to clear them off as completely as the Caribs."

"It is odd," said Compton, "how entirely the professor loses control of himself—becomes, in fact, not himself— when Columbus is mentioned. At other times he is cool, scientific, and absolutely ruthless. But name Columbus, and he holds forth like a ranter preacher."

"In the long history of the martyrdom of man," said the doctor, "few chapters are so awful as those which relate to subject races. I don't know that we are much more humane to-day for all our progress. Instead of enslaving the aborigines in the mines, we slowly poison them at a profit per head with opium and alcohol I sometimes think it would be more merciful to do it quick with strychnine and prussic acid. But such mercy would earn no dividends. Therefore, I suppose, the slow process will continue to the inevitable end. It has come in Tasmania. It is not far off in the United States. Australia is not much behind."

There was a pause. Then Fred said,—

"But, doctor, do tell us where Columbus did cross over to America."

"If you look at the map," said the doctor, " you will see he crossed much further south than our road. His little ships sailed down to the Canary Islands before they ventured to leave the Old World behind them. Then they crossed over to the Bahamas."

"Were they very little ships, doctor ?"

"You will see a facsimile model of his caravel when you get to the World's Fair. It is a little ship of sixty tons. It had as its consorts two smaller ships of forty tons. These were manned by crews numbering about a hundred men. Here is a picture of it from a recent photograph. You see it is a mere cockle-shell compared with this great steamer."

"It is not so great a thing to cross the Atlantic in a small ship," said Irene. "Don't you remember that man in the Crystal Palace who crossed it some years since in an open sail boat, navigated solely by himself ? He crossed it again last year, and he is going to show his little 14-

THE CARAVEL "SANTA MARIA," IN WHICH COLUMBUS FIRST SAILED ACROSS THE ATLANTIC.

feet canvas boat at the World's Fair. If it were not for the distance, I should not be surprised to hear that some future Captain Webb would swim across it."

"It is not that things are difficult in themselves," said Mrs. Wills. "It is the thinking them so that is the great obstacle. The Unknown is always terrible. Columbus had no chart. He imagined he was sailing to India. His sailors imagined he was going to destruction. It is not conscience but imagination that makes the coward of us all."

"So," said Compton, "our lack of imagination may be one great secret of England's power. The somnambulist walks safely in serene composure the dizziest heights, from which he would fall headlong if he once opened his eyes."

"Doctor," said Tom, with all a boy's appetite for facts, "how many miles is it to America ?"

"About 3,000," said the doctor. "It is about the same from Southampton and from Liverpool. Columbus sailed from Palos to the Azores ; and from his last Old World port to the Bahamas, it is about 2,500 miles."

"How long did it take to do it in ?" asked Fred.

"About five weeks. So his voyage lasted thirty-five days, an average of seventy miles a day. Nowadays, we should consider that very slow. Yesterday, for instance, we ran 400 miles, and to-day the run will be just as good."

"Columbus did not make such very bad time," said Compton, ' when you consider that down to the beginning of the century, three weeks was regarded as a quick passage between Liverpool and New York. Steam brought it down to a fortnight fifty years ago, and now we make the run in a week."

' Boys," said the doctor, "never forget all through your life that the best authorities are usually the most mistaken, and that the worst person to rely upon is the scientific man who is quite sure that 'it is impossible.' It was so in Columbus's time ; and just before the steam ferry across the Atlantic was established, Dr. Lardner, one of the most eminent men of science of his time, publicly declared that he 'had no hesitation in saying the idea of steaming over from Liverpool to New York was perfectly chimerical. They might as well talk of making a voyage from New York or Liverpool to the moon !'"

" How lovely the sky looks now the sun is going down ! " said Irene. " If the weather would only keep like this, I can conceive nothing more enjoyable than life on the Atlantic. But what is the matter ? ' she asked for the professor had just returned in a state of unwonted excitement.

" Icebergs ! " he said ; " the captain has just learnt from the last steamer that passed us that some icebergs are drifting across our path. We shall be upon them in thirty-six hours."

" Well," said Mrs. Wills, who did not understand the significance of the news, " icebergs or no icebergs, it is time little Pearl went to bed," and with the departure of Pearl, the Blue Brigade broke up in a somewhat sombre mood.

Fred only seemed cheerful. " Tom," said he, as he went down with his brother to his berth. " isn't it jolly about these icebergs ? I wanted to see one, oh, so much. Do you think there will be any bears on them ? "

Tom could not say ; he hoped so, but he feared not.

The professor went aft with Irene, who seemed quite under his spell, the better to see the last of the sunset, he said, but, in reality, to pour into her willing ear, a full and particular account of the bandit in the steerage. The professor, at last, had found a type of the Abnormal which satisfied his utmost aspiration. His new-found type was

THE PROFESSOR WENT AFT WITH IRENE.

a bandit, and a son, of a long line of bandits. When the brigands were hunted into retreat, he became a professional assassin. He had explained to the professor, with the utmost *sang froid*, that the tariff was simple. For a plain murder he only charged £5, but he never did the kill and damn for less than £10.

" Kill and damn ? " said Irene, slightly shuddering.

" Oh, it is a refinement of Italian malevolence only possible when men have not yet emerged from their superstitions. My bandit is most religious ; wears a scapular, and carries a rosary, and his orthodoxy is unimpeachable. It is the creed of the Church that any one dying in mortal sin goes straight to perdition. A ' kill and damn ' order, therefore, necessitated the inveigling the victim to commit a mortal sin at the precise moment the assassin struck the blow. The usual method is by drink. He does not quite remember how many he has despatched, but he prides himself upon the punctuality with which he executed all his engagements."

" What a dreadful man ! " said Irene. " But why is he in the ship ? Is it safe for you to be so familiar with him ? I — I should not like anything to happen to you," she said, impulsively.

If the professor's cunning little instrument had been in position on his own finger the tell-tale register would have shown a not inconsiderable rise of temperature when Irene made that remark. But his instrument was in his portmanteau, and he did not betray the least emotion as he answered her question.

" On the contrary, I assure you, he has already intimated that he is open to despatch any orders I may care to entrust to him, for he evidently thinks the New World is as promising a sphere for his operations as the Old."

" And what did you reply to him ? " asked Irene.

" Oh, I told him that we did not do things in that way in America, and I advised him, if he wanted to make the best use of his talents, to go on the Stock Exchange, or become the proprietor of a newspaper."

" It seems something awful," said Irene, " to think that we are sending over the choicest specimen of European rascality to inoculate American civilisation. But, I suppose, we began it with Columbus, and we do but as our fathers did."

" Oh," said the professor, much touched by this allusion to his favourite aversion, " my poor bandit will never do in all his life a thousandth part of the abominations that Columbus practised in the single island of San Domingo."

" Odd, isn't it ? " said Compton, as he watched Irene and the professor sauntering in the gloaming to the most secluded part of the deck. " I should not be surprised if the girl, in search of a thrill, and the professor in search of a type, have not found themselves mutually suited. But, doctor, come to our cabin. I want to have a few words on a rather important subject."

Wynne, who was sincerely attached to Compton, complied at once, wondering just a little what Jack Compton was driving at. He knew him to be a man of boundless ambition, of immense wealth, and of indomitable force of character, but, hitherto, he had kept his plans very much to himself.

When they were seated in the cabin, Compton began,—

" I don't know what you think of it, Wynne, but it has long seemed to me that the world is ripe for a new movement, based on modern ideas."

" Perhaps," returned the doctor ; " but what kind of movement ? and what do you consider distinctively modern ideas ? "

" To answer your last question first. I regard as distinctively modern the ideas of Democracy, of Home Rule, of Federation, of Socialism, of the Emancipation of Woman, and the restitution of the Lost Ideal of the Church. Equally modern are the ideas of Heredity and of Evolution by the laws of Natural Selection, the Struggle for Existence, and the Elimination of the Unfit. And the kind of movement to which I allude is the world-wide combination of an elect few in every land in an association pledged to dedicate their lives and their substance to the promotion of these ideals."

The doctor shook his head. " It is too vague and it is too vast. What you are thinking of is a modernised Society of Jesus—lay, not clerical—directed towards ends social and political rather than ecclesiastical or theological. But can you generate the self-devotion of the Jesuit for social or political ideas ? "

Compton replied with some warmth . " My ideals are as distinctively religious as Loyola's or Dominic's. I admit the basis of any such Society must be religious, but it need not be ecclesiastical, and religion can be shown as effectively by the Service of Man as by the elaboration of ritual or the definition of creeds."

"Tell me, then, what you are driving at, and remember always that the world is very wide, that the only institution that even partially covers the world has taken nearly two thousand years to grow to its present dimensions, and that the very extent of territory covered by your scheme makes it too cumbrous to work."

"No,' replied Compton. "Herein I must say you are wrong. You reason from the misleading analogies of the past, when things went slow, and when it took a year to get round the world. You forget that we live in the age of the newspaper and the telegraph, and that we are just about to enter upon the Telepathic Era, which will practically annihilate space and make us literally within hearing of each other all over the world."

"With telepathy universalised and systematised you can do many things at present impossible, but after all it is only a means to an end."

"I grant it; but I am as clear as to my end as I am about the means by which to attain it. You object to my scheme as I roughly stated it as vague. It is, as you will see, quite clear and definite, and this Chicago Exhibition has brought them to a head."

"In what way?" asked the doctor. "The Chicago Exhibition and your Society seem far as the poles asunder."

"Then things are not as they seem, For, in reality, this World's Fair may give impetus to a movement which will dominate and transform the whole scheme of the universe so far as this planet is concerned."

"You speak in riddles, Compton," sighed the doctor. "I wish you would be more precise."

"Well, then, what do you think is the real significance of the World's Fair? Is it merely one great International Show the more? Is it merely a glorification of the professor's bête noir Columbus? or merely a great advertisement of the material wealth of the United States? Assuredly not. If that were all, I should certainly not be making my way to Chicago. The World's Fair is a far more serious business than even its promoters have yet conceived. For it puts the issue fairly and squarely before mankind whether or not the time has come for the United States of America to displace Great Britain from the hegemony of the English-speaking race."

The doctor sighed. "Has it come to that already? And this from you, Compton?"

Compton took no notice of the reproach, but continued with the positive air of a man who is laying down a set of mathematical propositions. "What is at stake at Chicago is the headship of the English-speaking world. The great problem of the immediate future in the sphere of high politics is this: Round which centre will the English-speaking communities group themselves? Will the great race alliance, which is the hope of the future, have its centre in Washington or in London? or will our race, permanently rent in two, continue to have two centres? It is because that question seems likely to be decided for good or for ill at Chicago that I am on my way there."

"And which way will it be settled?" asked the doctor, anxiously.

"That depends upon many things, but, so far as Britain is concerned, I fear she will allow judgment to go against her by default. And yet not even a remote glimmering of the momentous crisis upon which we are entering has dawned upon the minds of any British statesmen. They are absorbed in tinkering on with the affairs of Ireland, unwitting that before Home Rule gets well established the United States may have swept into their fiscal system the best part of our Colonial Empire, and that Home Rule may come to Ireland from Washington rather than from London —may, and will, if American statesmen have eyes that see

and ears that hear. But, who knows? They may be as purblind on the other side. That is why I am bound for Chicago."

"You may be right," said the doctor, "but I don't quite see it. But how does this fit in with your Society?"

"The primary object of my Society in the political sphere is the cementing of that race alliance between all English-speaking peoples which is the chief hope of the future peace and civilisation of the world. The great crime of last century was the action of George III. in rending the English-speaking race in twain. It was as the crime of Jeroboam, the son of Nebat, who made Israel to sin. To undo the consequence of that crime, by re-uniting the Empire and the Republic is, of necessity, the supreme task of any such society of which I speak. To promote the re-union by every means in their power would be the duty of all its members. And as it is indispensable to know where lies the real centre of gravity in such a union, you can see how vital is the connection between the World's Fair and the world's future, from the standpoint of our Society."

"Yes," said the doctor, "I understand that. But how are you to bring it about?"

"By using any and every means to the uttermost of the individual and associated capacity of all our members, but chiefly by this: By restoring the Lost Ideal of the Church, that is to say, that we have to re-teach mankind that the primary work of the Church of God is the Service of Man, of man individually and of man collectively, either in state, nation, empire, or municipality. We have, in fact, to use the national ideals of the Old Testament to revivify and energise the Church which was constituted to carry out the ideal of the New: 'Thy kingdom come. Thy will be done on earth as it is in heaven.'

"And do you hope to succeed in the face of such unfaith as there is in the Churches in everything but the mint, and tithe, and anise, and cummin of theological milk-poblets and sectarian watchwords? Why, the very lever which you wish to control is a rope of sand."

"No doubt, and that is why it is necessary to found a Society, including men and women, both within and without the Churches, which will not be a rope of sand, but a twisted strand of tempered steel. Its members would not parade themselves before the world. They would work as often in secrecy as in public. While not a secret society in any sense of the word, it would be a great freemasonry without its aprons, and its mysteries, and, at the same time, a great Society of Jesus without its despotism and its identification with any particular sect."

"But how communicate without a hierarchy? how secure co-operation and concerted action without the outer forms of organisation? The wider your range the more indispensable is machinery, and, at the same time, the more cumbrous and unwieldy."

"Doctor," said Compton, thoughtfully, "you know I have been studying modern psychology for some time past. I cannot explain things to you fully at present. I have not the time and you have not the rudiments necessary to enable you to understand. But I know as a scientific fact that it is possible to communicate instantaneously from a common centre, orders, counsel, judgment, and suggestion, to trained telepathists all over the world, without the use of any other agency than thought."

The doctor looked somewhat sadly at Compton, and said,—

"Where is that common centre to be found, and where are the trained telepathists to be discovered?"

Compton said simply, but impressively,—

"That common centre exists, and at this very moment telepathists in every capital in the English-speaking world are made aware that you have been told of the existence of the Society, in which I hope you will be enrolled as a Helper.

The doctor was startled, and before he recovered from his surprise Compton opened the door and went upon deck.

CHAPTER VII.—COINCIDENCE AND CLAIRVOYANCE.

"GLAD to see you again, Mrs. Julia," said the doctor, the next morning, as the sweet young widow, Mrs. Julia, put in her appearance at the table. "I was afraid you had been quite bowled over by the *mal-de-mer.*"

"I might have been dead, doctor, for all the trouble you took to see how I was," she said, somewhat tartly. "But in truth, I have not been ill at all. While you have been amusing yourself, I have been performing tasks of charity and mercy."

"Not in the steerage, I hope?" said Mrs. Irwin, hastily. "I crossed on the steerage once, but never again; never again, no, not ever, if it was the only way of leaving old Ireland, which the saints forefend!"

"No," said Mrs. Julia, "not quite so bad as that. But I have been in the Intermediates. I found a poor young lady there, quite ill and exhausted, without, apparently, a friend on board. She is not strong to start with, but she is so good-hearted that she persisted in trying to help a poor miserable Jew girl who was ill in the steerage, with the result that the second day she was on board she was regularly laid up. As she cannot leave her berth, and as she has to lie there day after day all day and all night, I thought it only charity to go and take my meals with her."

"Where is she bound for?" asked the professor.

"To Chicago, like the rest of us," replied the widow. "It is a sad errand for her, I fear. Her father has been employed in putting up some special building—I forget the name just now; he has caught the grippe, and she is hurrying over, whether to nurse him or to bury him she hardly knows. I have taken to her greatly. This morning she was a trifle better, and so I slipped round to my old place to hear how the Blue Brigade is getting on."

"The professor," said the doctor, "is in the seventh heaven. He has discovered a professional assassin who has obligingly undertaken to dispose of any of his enemies for a consideration. He has also three confirmed drunkards under observation in the saloon,

" THAT SWEET YOUNG WIDOW, MRS JULIA.

where they drink without intermission from morning to night; and half a dozen professional gamblers who are engaged in emptying the pockets of all the simpletons on board."

"Do not forget," said the professor, "the means with which my little instrument has cured the snorer—it is one of the triumphs of my life."

"And the rest of you?" asked Mrs. Julia.

"Oh," said Irene, "we are developing a passion for deck quoits. We also play cricket every afternoon before dinner, but it is ruinous in balls. At present we are engrossed in arrangements for a concert. You play the guitar. Do you think you could give us a song to your own accompaniment, or would you mind accompanying the professor?"

"Thanks, no," replied the widow; "I think he would play best to your accompaniment," she added slyly. "But does he sing at all?"

"Alas! no, madam. Miss Vernon is only joking," protested the professor.

"Why, I heard him singing 'Oft in the Stilly Night,'" exclaimed Mrs. Irwin, "only last night, when nearly everyone had gone to bed. He was singing it all to himself alone, but there was a feel in the tone of his voice as if he had somebody on his mind or in his heart."

"What, professor!" said Compton, with a laugh, "are you turning a sentimentalist?" And as he spoke he glanced at Irene.

"Really," said that vivacious lady. "I shall be getting quite jealous of Mrs. Irwin. You never sang that song to me, sir," she said to the professor; "you never even told me that you could sing."

As the company left the breakfast-table, and were going on deck, he said, awkwardly, "Miss Vernon, I have too great a regard for you to venture upon making any rash attempt. It was the words, not the music, that I was humming."

Irene flushed just a little with pleasure, and then left the professor to seek Mrs. Wills, who, with little Pearl and the boys, was still in the cabin.

As for Mrs. Julia, she no sooner saw the company disperse than she departed to seek out her new friend in the Intermediates. She found her somewhat better, well enough to be out of her berth, but too weak to venture upon deck.

"Well, well," said Mrs. Julia, "but this is an improvement, indeed. I am glad to see you. But I had come to good to leave you to yourself a little. If I had come to breakfast you would have been still in bed."

"Don't say so," said the Intermediate, feebly. "You

(DECK QUOITS.)

have been so good. How can I ever thank you enough?" and, as she spoke, she laid her delicate, soft hand upon the widow's arm.

"Thank me! Well, I declare," said Mrs. Julia, as she put her arm round her and gave her a tender and affectionate kiss. "It has been a great pleasure to come here and feel I was doing some little good in the world, for, after all, dear, I have helped you a little, have I not?"

"Helped me?" was the reply. "Oh, Mrs. Julia, I never should have pulled through but for you." And she laid her head upon her friend's shoulder and sighed, clinging to her as a child clings to its mother when in fear.

"Come, come," said the little widow; "you are going to be better soon. The voyage is half over, and, dear me, you might as well tell me your name."

"My name is Rose."

"A pretty name," remarked Mrs Julia. "I fear this little Rose has had many a thorn!"

"Oh, don't ask me," sobbed Rose, burying her face in Mrs. Julia's bosom. "Some day, when I am stronger, I may tell you, but not now."

"Poor child, poor child," thought the widow, as she silently stroked the long and lustrous brown tresses which streamed down over Rose's shoulders. "The old, old story, I suppose. It never needs much guessing to know the cause of a woman's grief."

"You don't mind, Mrs. Julia?" said Rose. "I'm ashamed of myself giving way like this, but oh, Mrs Julia, it is barely seven years since I ever met a human creature to whom I could be as close as I am to you. It is so new, so strange, so sweet, to find some one who cares for you enough to let you cry with them."

The widow's eyes, despite her efforts, were blurred with rising tears. The freemasonry of sorrow bound her to this girl not much younger than herself. Was she not also almost alone in the world, and where could she now look for those loving arms to which for two brief years she had flown as a bird to its nest with every sorrow and every joy.

"Cheer up, my dear Rose," she said at last, with a somewhat choking voice. "Cheer up, and remember you are not the only woman who is left alone and desolate."

Rose looked up hastily, and, seeing the widow's face wet with tears, exclaimed, "Oh, how selfish of me, how selfish; forgive me, my dear friend, for forgetting——"

"Nonsense," said Mrs. Julia, with a smile like a sunbeam gleaming through a rain cloud. "Come now, let us sit down like sensible women and talk quietly. And, as a beginning, let me do up your hair."

And then for an hour or more these two lonely ones exchanged confidences, and told each other their hopes and fears until, when the lunch bell rung, they felt as if they had known each other for years.

"Oh, Adelaide," said Rose, for the widow had insisted upon being addressed by her Christian name, "I shall never forget the awful loneliness of that first year in London. Until the day when I left home I had never slept outside my mother's house. I had never known a day when I was not called by my Christian name, and on which I was not constantly addressed as Rose. And to come to a great city, with millions and millions of human beings meeting you every day, not one of whom is anything to you, or you to them—oh, it is awful! My little world in the cottage was a world full of love, and in the village was a world full of interest, perhaps, sometimes not the most kindly, but always interesting. But the great world of London was a world where nobody cared enough for me even to invent spiteful gossip. I was alone, utterly, awfully alone. Oh, Adelaide, Adelaide, it nearly drove me mad," and she shuddered at the memory of that dismal time.

"And had you no one to love you, or care for you at all in the whole place?" asked the widow, lovingly caressing the girl's brow, and occasionally passing her fingers through the girl's hair.

"Not a living soul, not even a dog or a cat!" said Rose, bitterly. "I was no longer Rose; I was only Miss Thistle —for I changed my name so that he might not find me— and even that only to about two or three people—my landlady, my employer, and the little drudge who washed up and waited on the lodgers. I was poor, very poor, so poor that for weeks together I lived upon bread and water, or oatmeal and milk, but the hunger that pinched my body was nothing, nothing to the hunger that consumed my soul."

"How did you manage to get along at all? It is difficult enough to those who know their way about. But for you, poor innocent, with such a face, it is miraculous you escaped."

"I think the good God took care of me," said Rose, simply. "If it had not been for Him I should have gone mad, or thrown myself into the river. Many a time I used to pray to Him, oh, so earnestly, to keep me, and although He sometimes seemed a long, long way off, He never let me go quite under. But, oh, He was so slow sometimes I nearly lost heart altogether."

"Poor lamb, poor little lamb," said the widow, soothingly. "And did you ever hear of him all these years?"

"Yes, often. I watched his career with pride, only feeling now and then as he went upwards step by step that I should never be worthy to stand by his side. Oh, who, even if I had made myself to be his wife, as he was at Stratford, he has risen so much since then; the gulf will be almost impassable. That thought used to harass me for a long time. But I was saved from that by a beautiful dream. I dreamed I was standing in the moonlight close to Ann Hathaway's Cottage. When all the scene seemed strange and new, I was very sad and lonely, and felt as if all was over, and that nothing was left but just to die, when suddenly, in the strangest and most unexpected fashion, Walter stood before me, and said, 'Rose, my own long-lost Rose.' And I fell into his arms, and it seemed in my dream as if we were never to be parted again any more." And although you may think it superstitious, and although I admit there is no reason for such expectation, yet, from that moment, I have never doubted that, some time or other, I shall meet him where I met him at first, close to the dear old cottage, and the long-deferred dream of my life will be fulfilled. Oh, Adelaide, Adelaide, do you think I could otherwise ever have lived through all the horrors of all these years, that constant black desolation of loneliness, night after night, year in year out, with never a soul to speak to, never a heart to confide in, and all round you the constant pressure of tempting fiends?"

Mrs. Julia was a woman of the world, and she appreciated only too well the trials through which her companion had passed.

"It was hard," said Rose, wistfully, "for a young, enthusiastic girl such as I was to come to London, and find men as they were. People said that I had a pleasant face, and I made my living for two or three years as an artist's model. I have been painted many times as various heroines in history or romance. Most of the artists were gentlemen. Here and there, however, were some who were very different; and outside the artistic world, there are only too many who will do everything to spoil a poor girl's life. I remember once living for six months at a time on ten shillings a week, out of which I had to pay five shillings a week for rent and a shilling a week for the reading ticket at South Kensington Library. All that winter, when the struggle seemed almost hopeless, and the blackness of utter despair had settled down on me, I might have had everything the heart could wish except honour if I would but have given in. But I thought of my dream, and I never gave in. Never, never. And when he finds me again at Shottery he will find I am as true to him as that beautiful day of the White Rose, when we first spoke of love."

"What a brave little girl you have been, Rose," said Mrs. Julia. "But you are not a model now?"

"Oh, no. I gave that up nearly four years ago. I always

which I had to live into a new and ideal region. What is more practical, nothing ever brought me more money than fairy stories. So, by degrees, I gave up being a model, and devoted myself altogether to fairy tales. You see, I lived over and over again, in every story, my own life. My Prince Charming was Walter, no matter how disguised, and I was the maiden all forlorn. I wrote my stories with my heart's blood, fairy stories though they were. I sent some of them on chance to a magazine editor. He printed them, and asked for more. And so I am authoress now," she said, with a wan little smile. "And

JACK COMPTON AND MRS. IRWIN IN THE LIBRARY (*page* 43).

had a craving to write. I had it even when I had parents, relatives, lover, on whom to pour out the fulness of my heart. But when I was all alone, with not a living creature whom I knew by their Christian names, and to whom I could ever express any sentiment more profound than a remark about the weather, writing became a necessity. I wrote verse, I wrote prose, I wrote novels, I wrote anything and everything that could serve as an escape from the pressure on my heart. But these effusions were never printed. Most of them were burnt. Then, at last, almost by sheer accident I discovered that I had most satisfaction in writing fairy stories. Don't laugh. Nothing ever gave me such relief. I got out of the sombre, everyday world in

although not rich, I can supply my own wants, and have enough to spare to go to Chicago to my father."

"I hope your father will be well when you arrive," said Mrs. Julia. "But there is the lunch-bell, and now I must leave you. Poor, dear Rose, I am so glad to have been some little help to you." So saying, the pleasant little woman tripped away to lunch with the rest of the Blue Brigade.

The doctor—Dr. Vernon as he was called—was absent from lunch, as he and the professor had arranged to lunch in the steerage with the Calabrian brigand.

At table Mrs. Julia, full of her subject, discoursed with vehemence upon the virtues and the beauty of her friend

In the Intermediate. Miss Thistle, she declared, was one of the most charming, lovable women whom she had ever seen in her life—such grace, such beauty, such pluck ; in short, she exhausted her vocabulary of eulogy in describing the lonely woman in the second-class cabin.

Irene listened with languid interest, feeling rather bored, and resenting the absence of the professor.

Compton was absorbed in his own thoughts, and even Mrs. Irwin, usually very sympathetic, seemed weighed down by an unwonted gloom.

So, as soon as possible, Mrs. Julia finished lunch, and departed to pour out her tale into the sympathetic ears of Mrs. Wills who, before night, was marched off to visit the lovely "Intermediate."

Mr. Compton was abruptly aroused from his reverie by a direct appeal from Mrs. Irwin.

"If you have ten minutes to spare, Mr. Compton, I will be glad to have a word with you by yourself."

"Certainly, madam, will you come to the Library ? It is sure to be empty just now, and we can speak at leisure."

They soon found themselves ensconced in a corner of the Library. There were only one or two ladies present, and shortly afterwards these left Compton and Mrs. Irwin alone.

"I would not have ventured to trouble you," said Mrs. Irwin, "but I know that you are no stranger to occult things. If I had not seen that in the face of you I should not have ventured to speak."

"Yes, yes," said Compton, somewhat impatiently, "but what has that to do with it ?"

"It has everything to do with it, sir," said she ; "because, if you did not understand, it would be no use trying to explain. I must tell you that I come of one of the oldest families in Ireland. We have the Banshee, of course, but, what is more to the purpose, I have occasionally the gift of second sight. Now, last night——"

Compton, who at first had listened with hardly concealed impatience, suddenly manifested eager interest.

"My dear Mrs. Irwin,' he exclaimed, "why did you not tell me this before ? Nothing interests me so much as to come upon those rare but peculiarly gifted persons who have inherited, or acquired by some strange gift of the gods, the privilege—often a sombre and terrible privilege—of seeing into futurity."

"Sombre and terrible you may well say it is," said Mrs. Irwin, "and fain would I be without it. It is a gruesome thing to see, as I have done, the funeral in the midst of the wedding-feast, and to mark the shroud high on the breast of the heir when he comes of age. But the gift comes when it comes, and goes when it goes ; it seems as fitful as the shooting-stars which come no one knows from whence, and disappear no one knows whither."

"Well," said Compton, "you were saying that last night——?"

"I was saying," said Mrs. Irwin, "that last night, as I was lying asleep in my berth, I was awakened by a sudden cry, as of men in mortal peril, and I roused myself to listen, and there before my eyes, as plain as you are sitting there, I saw a sailing ship among the icebergs. She had been stove in by the ice, and was fast sinking. The crew were crying piteously for help: it was their voices that roused me. Some of them had climbed upon the ice ; others were on the sinking ship, which was drifting away as she sank. Even as I looked she settled rapidly by the bow, and went down with a plunge. The waters bubbled and foamed. I could see the heads of a few swimmers in the eddy. One after another they sank, and I saw them no more. I saw that there were six men and a boy on the iceberg. Then, in a moment, the whole scene vanished, and I was alone in my berth, with

the wailing cry of the drowning sailors still ringing in my ears."

"Did you notice the appearance of any of the survivors?" said he, anxiously.

"As plainly as I am looking at you," she replied, "I noticed especially one man, very tall—over six feet, I should say—who wore a curious Scotch plaid around his shoulders and a Scotch cap on his head. He had a rough red beard, and one eye was either blind or closed up."

"And did you see the name of the ship before it foundered?"

"Certainly I did ; it was plain to see as it went down headforemost. I read the name on the stern. It was the *Ann and Jane* of Montrose."

Compton rose from his chair, and took a turn or two in deep thought. Then he stopped, and said,—

"Mrs. Irwin, you have trusted me, I will trust you. What you said has decided me, or rather has given me hope that we may be able to induce the captain of the *Majestic* to rescue these unfortunates, one of whom is a friend of my own."

"But did you know about it before I spoke?" asked Mrs. Irwin.

"I need not explain to you," said Compton, not heeding the interruption, "for you understand that there is no impossibility in the instantaneous communication of intelligence, from any distance, to others who have what some have described as the sixth sense. To some it comes in the form of clairvoyance, to others as clairaudience, while to a third class, among whom I count myself, it comes in the shape of what is called automatic writing. I have many friends in all parts of the world who also have this gift, and we use it constantly to the almost entire disuse of the telegraph. At least once every day, each of us is under a pledge to place his hand at the disposal of any of the associated friends who may wish secretly to communicate with him. This morning, at nine o'clock, I placed my hand with the peculiarly dispatch safe, it wrote off, with feverish rapidity, a message which I will now read to you :

"'To John Thomas. Tuesday morning, four o'clock. The *Ann and Jane*, Montrose, struck on an iceberg in the fog in North Atlantic, and almost immediately foundered. Six men and a boy succeeded in reaching the ice alive. All others were drowned. For God's sake, rescue us speedily ; otherwise death is certain from cold and hunger. We are close to the line of outward steamers.—John Thomas.'

"The signature, you see," said Compton, "is the same as that appended to the last letter I received from him, which I hunted up after I had received this message. I have, therefore, no doubt that 'John Thomas' with five other men and a boy are exposed to a lingering death on the iceberg some hundred miles ahead."

"But," said Mrs. Irwin, "what can we do ?"

"That," replied Compton, "is my difficulty. To have gone to the captain with this message, without any confirmation but my word, would probably have exposed me to certain ridicule, and might have led the captain to steer still further to the south. Now, however, that you also have had the message, I will hesitate no longer."

Without more ado, he wrote a short note to the captain, begging to be allowed to communicate with him on a matter of urgent and immediate importance, involving questions of life and death.

Hardly had the messenger departed with the note when the professor and the doctor entered the library.

"Halloo, Compton," said the professor, "are you not coming on deck to see the fog ? But, in the name of fortune, what is the matter ? Doctor, I think you had better look to Compton."

"It's nothing," said Compton faintly, "only a passing qualm. Is the fog very dense?"

"You can see it in the distance like a dim grey wall lying right across the bows of the steamer. We shall be into it in half-an-hour. But," persisted the professor, "something is up. Can I not help?"

"Professor," said Compton, a sudden thought striking him, "if I send for you from the captain's cabin, please hold yourself in readiness to come."

"Certainly," said the professor. "But what, in the name of common-sense, are you troubling the captain for just as the ship is entering an ice fog?"

"Mr. Compton, the captain will see you at once in the cabin," said the returned messenger.

"Now, Mrs. Irwin; not one word to any one! Professor, I may send for you shortly."

So saying, he followed the messenger to the captain's cabin. It is but seldom that any passenger ventures to intrude into that sanctum. But Mr. Compton was not an ordinary passenger. He had often crossed the Atlantic in vessels under the command of the present captain. He was known to be a man of power, of influence, and of wealth. More than that, he had, on more than one occasion, given invaluable information, procured no one knew how or where, which had enabled the captain to avoid imminent dangers into which he was steaming at full speed. He was, therefore, assured of a respectful hearing, even from the autocrat of the *Majestic* on the verge of an ice fog.

"Now, Mr. Compton," said the captain, "what is it you wish to say to me? I have only a few minutes to spare. We shall have to steer southward to avoid the ice floe which is drifting across our usual course."

"I want you," said Mr. Compton, imperturbably, "to continue your usual course in order to pick up six men and a boy, who are stranded on an iceberg from the ship *Ann and Jane*, of Montrose, which foundered at four o'clock this morning, after collision with the ice."

The captain stared. "Really, Mr. Compton, how do you know that? It is impossible for any one to know it."

Mr. Compton replied. "There is the despatch from one of my friends, John Thomas, who was on the ship, and is now on the iceberg, received by me in his own handwriting at noon this day."

The captain took the paper with an uneasy expression of countenance.

"Entering the fog, sir," said an officer, putting his head into the cabin.

"Slacken speed," said the captain. "I shall be out in a moment."

He carefully read and re-read the paper, and then said —

"Well, really, if you were not Mr. Compton I should consider you a lunatic. What possible reliance can be placed upon such a statement?"

"I received this," replied Compton, significantly, "in the same way that I received the message of 1889, which enabled you to ——"

"I remember," said the captain; "otherwise, I should not be listening to you now."

"But this story has not come without confirmation;" and then Compton repeated Mrs. Irwin's clairvoyant vision.

"What do I care for these old women's stories," said the captain. "But even if they were true, what then? I have nearly 2,000 passengers and crew, all told, on board the *Majestic*. I dare not risk them and the ship, hunting for half-a-dozen castaways on an iceberg on the North Atlantic."

*I need not say that the whole of this story is purely imaginary. Although I illustrate the account of the voyage with a portrait of the real captain of the *Majestic*, he must not be in any way identified with the captain of this story.

"But," said Compton, "if you are convinced that the men are there, dare you leave them to their fate?"

"But I am not convinced. They may have died ere now, even if they ever were there at all."

"Might I ask you to give me pencil and paper," said Compton.

The captain handed him what he wanted. Compton at

THE CAPTAIN OF THE "MAJESTIC."

once grasped the pencil, and placed it on the paper. Almost immediately it wrote :—

"John Thomas. Iceberg. Three o'clock. At one o'clock the iceberg parted under our feet, three men and a boy were carried away. Three still remain, frost bitten, without food or fire. We shall not be able to survive the night. When the *Ann and Jane* foundered, we were on the outward liners' route, 45 by 45, on the extreme southern edge of the ice-floe. Since then, it has rather receded. For God's sake, do not desert us —John Thomas."

The captain stared at the curious writing, which was not Compton's, and then stared at Compton.

The latter merely said, "How far are we off the position mentioned?"

The captain looked at the chart.

"We are steering by our present altered course directly upon the spot where he says the berg is floating. If I believed your message, I would steer still more to the southward, to give the ice a clear berth. It is no joke shaving round an iceberg in such a fog as this. But I do not believe your message, and I will not alter the course of the *Majestic* by one point, for all the witches and wizards that ever lived."

"Captain," said Compton, "your niece is on board, I believe?"

"Yes," said the captain. "But what in the world has she to do with it?"

"If you will allow her to come here, and permit me to send for my friend, the professor, I think we shall be able to convince you that these sailors are waiting deliverance."

The captain rang the bell. "Bring my niece here instantly," he said, "and Professor Glogoul. Thank heaven," he added, "the fog is so dense, no one will be able to see them come, or else they would think—and think rightly—that I had taken leave of my wits."

In a minute or two, the niece and the professor had both arrived.

"Captain," said Compton, "will you let your niece sit down? The professor hypnotized her on a previous voyage, and cured her of sea-sickness. He can cast her into hypnotic sleep with her consent, by merely making a pass over her face with his hand."

The captain growled, "Do what you like, only make haste. If it were any one but Mr. Compton," he muttered under his breath, "if it were any one but Mr. Compton, I should very soon have cleared the cabin."

The captain's niece had hardly taken her seat when the professor's pass threw her into a hypnotic sleep. A few more passes and the professor said she was in the clairvoyant state.

"What is it that you want?" he asked.

"Tell her," said Compton, "to go ahead of the ship in the exact course she is now steering, and tell us what she sees."

The professor repeated the request. Almost immediately the captain's niece began to shiver and shudder, then she spoke—

"I go on for half-an-hour, then for an hour; it gets colder and colder. I see ice, not icebergs, but floating ice. I go through this floating ice for an hour, for two hours, then the fog gets thinner and thinner, it almost disappears. I see icebergs, they shine beautifully in the sunlight. There are many of them stretching for miles and miles, as far as I can see. What a noise there is when they break and capsize."

"Do you see any ship or any thing?" asked the professor.

"No, I see nothing, only icebergs. I go on and on for another hour. Then I see on an iceberg, near the foot, some one making signals. I come nearer, I see him plainly. It is a tall man with one eye and red hair. He is walking up and down. Beside him there is one man sitting, and another man who seems to be dead. It seems to be the edge of the iceberg. There is clear water beyond."

"That will do," said Compton.

The professor blew lightly on the girl's face. She opened her eyes, and, stood up looking round with a dazed expression.

"Well," said Compton to the captain, "are you convinced?"

"Convinced!" said the captain. "It's all confounded nonsense. Out with you! If you ever had to steer the *Majestic* through an ice fog in the mid-Atlantic you would know better than to fool away the captain's time by such a pack of tomfoolery."

The niece and the professor left the cabin.

As Compton turned to go he said, "Captain, that tall, one-eyed man on the iceberg is one of my friends. You will keep on your course, as you say:—I desire nothing better. Will you promise me, if only for the sake of the past, that if you strike drift-ice in an hour and a half, and if you emerge from the fog two hours later on the edge of the floe of icebergs, you will keep a look-out and save John Thomas if you can?"

"If, if, if," said the captain, contemptuously. "Oh, yes, if all these things happen, I will promise; never fear, I can safely promise that!"

As Compton left the cabin the captain remarked—

"They say it is always the cleverest men who have got the biggest bee in their bonnet, and upon my word I begin to believe it."

CHAPTER VIII.—THE CASTAWAYS.

WHEN Compton left the captain's cabin he felt a spring of exhilaration. The very incredulity, the natural and proper incredulity of the captain, would lead directly to the result which he desired. He would save his friend. The chances against it seemed a million to one—to pick up a castaway on an iceberg, the exact location of which was uncertain, and which might be anywhere within fifty or five hundred miles. What seemed more utterly hopeless! But Compton had seen too much of the marvellous perceptions of clairvoyant subjects under hypnotism to doubt that, if the captain only kept on the southward course, which he had marked out in order to avoid the floe, the rescue would certainly take place.

Mentally transmitting a telepathic message to his friend on the iceberg, to let him know that his friend would be able to receive it owing to the difficulty, or not impossibility, of practising automatic hand-writing on the shifting ice, Compton made his way through the fog to his cabin, where he found the professor waiting him.

"Well," said that worthy, "what is it all about? It is rather unusual to summon one to an experiment when the experiment is kept so totally in the dark."

Compton soon satisfied the curiosity of the professor, and sent him to tell the doctor and Mrs. Irwin and the captain's niece what had happened. He then sat down in his berth with his despatch book open before him and pencil in hand awaiting the arrival of further messages from the iceberg.

Meanwhile, the steamer was forging her way onward through the fog. The passengers were either in their berths or in the saloon, or the smoking-room. None were on deck. Mrs. Wills and Mrs. Julia were with Rose in her cabin. The doctor had undertaken to look after the boys and Pearl. Irene was looking out for the professor, whom she soon discovered, not at all to her satisfaction, in close conversation with Mrs. Irwin. Somehow or other, she did not like that Irishwoman, and every minute Dr. Glogoul remained with her the more she felt that Mrs. Irwin was the most objectionable of her sex.

The dense, cold fog filled the air. You breathed it and swallowed it, and saw dimly through it across the saloon. On deck all was strained attention. The captain on the bridge kept constant look out, bearing upon his shoulders the responsibility for 2,000 lives, and a ship with cargo worth at least nearly £400,000. The quartermaster outside the pilot house passed in the commands given by the captain to the first officer and to his messmate at the wheel. Every half-minute the fog whistle boomed its great voice into the fog. Sometimes, as from a far away distance, they heard the boom of another fog horn, but they could see nothing. At the bows, the deck look-out peered into the impenetrable mist; and the quartermaster posted to the leeward, and lowered the thermometer in a little canvass bag to test the temperature of the sea in hopes of timely warning of the coming ice.

The boys cowered close to the doctor, and asked him endless questions about the fog.

"Where does it come from? Who made it? What was the good of it? How could they sail through it without being able to see the end of the ship?"

"This fog," replied the doctor, "came from icebergs."

But that opened up another range of questions.

"What were icebergs? Where did they come from? Would there be bears upon them?" And so forth. A sharp child will ask more questions in ten minutes than a clever man can answer in an hour.

"Icebergs," said the doctor, "are mountains of ice floating about in the sea. Ice, you know, does not sink in water. The bergs float just a little above the surface. All the rest is below. These icebergs are born in Greenland. The snow falls on the high land, and as it does not melt, and ever more and more snow falls, the great mass presses the lowest snow downwards and ever downwards to the sea. Thus glaciers are formed, slowly-moving solid rivers of frozen and solidified snow. When the glacier pushes its way into the sea, its end breaks off, tumbles over into the water with a noise like thunder, and becomes an iceberg. The glaciers are constantly making icebergs. These icebergs drift slowly away into the sea. Sometimes they get caught by the frost, and are winterbound. When summer comes, they drift off again into the current which carries them southward. A whole archipelago of icebergs will sometimes sail southward right across the ocean route to America."

"Isn't it very dangerous?" asked Tom.

"It is the greatest danger of the voyage. For the icebergs bring fogs with them, and the fogs hide the icebergs until the steamer is close upon them. Imagine a country as big as Ireland without lighthouses, foghorns, or any beacons, suddenly towed across the path of the steamer, and then enveloped in this dense frost-fog, and you can imagine. Hark, what is that?"

There was a sound as if the steamer were crashing through ice, and the screws were churning away amid the ice blocks. The doctor ran out to see what was the matter.

When he was gone, Tom said to Fred, "It is very terrible and cold. Are you not afraid?"

"Rather," said Fred. "I wish mother were here. Are you frightened, Pearl?"

"No, I am not," said the little lady, with emphasis, "and Kitty is not frightened either."

"But, Pearl," said Fred. "The fog——"

Pearl interrupted him disdainfully. "Can't God see in the fog, Fed?"

The conversation was interrupted by the doctor's return. "It is not icebergs, boys. It is only the floe ice which the

great ship goes through as Tom here goes through sugar candy."

"What is floe ice, doctor?" asked Fred.

"Loose drift ice, formed in winter off Labrador and Newfoundland. It is not dangerous. It is only icebergs that are dangerous."

"Do ships ever run against icebergs, doctor," said Tom.

"Oh, yes, about four are lost every year in that way. But even if we did strike an iceberg, we probably should not sink. The *Arizona* once went full speed into an iceberg, and crumpled up thirty feet of her nose. She did not sink, but got safely to Newfoundland. I hope, however, we shall not try a similar experiment."

"Doctor," said little Pearl, "could you go to find mamma?"

"Certainly, Pearl," said the doctor, "and where must I look for her?"

"HUSH, THE POOR GIRL IS ASLEEP.

Tom replied, "She went with Mrs. Julia to see the sick lady in the second class. I think I can take you there if you will take my hand."

"All right, Tom," said the doctor, cheerily, "I can leave Pearl with you, Fred, till we come back. Ta-ta."

They felt their way cautiously to the deck. It was wet and clammy and bitterly cold. Every half minute the fog whistle blew; the clashing of the floe ice against the sides of the ship, and the champing of the ice under the screws made it difficult to speak so as to be heard. Tom, however, felt his way along to the second class cabin where he had left his mother an hour before with Mrs. Julia. The doctor knocked at the door.

"Hush," said Mrs. Wills, as she came out, "the poor girl is asleep." She pointed to the upper berth. His eyes dazzled by the sudden glare of the electric light, saw nothing clearly beyond a prostrate form under the rug.

"Good-evening, Mrs. Julia," said he, "I have come for Mrs. Wills. Pearl has sent me to bring her along."

There was a slight movement in the upper berth. "I'd better go at once," said Mrs. Wills, "she is stirring," so saying, she closed the door, and the three made the best of their way back to the saloon.

Half-an hour later, Rose awoke. "Adelaide," she murmured. Mrs. Julia reached up, and kissed her. As she did so, she saw a strange light in her face, a kind of radiance that was heightened rather than diminished by the tears that filled her eyes.

"Adelaide," she said, "I have seen him! He has been here."

"Nonsense, child," said Mrs. Julia. "You have been dreaming. I never left you since you fell asleep."

"You may not have seen him," said Rose, calmly. "I did. I cannot be mistaken. I heard his voice, that voice which I have never heard from his lips for seven long years, but which I have never ceased to hear in my dreams. I heard his voice quite distinctly. I looked up, and there he was standing, older than when I knew him, with a sadder, more wistful look than he had in the old days. But it was he."

"My de.r child," said Mrs. Julia, authoritatively, "you must have been dreaming. Your illness has made you a little light in your head. I assure you, I have been here the whole time, and except Mr. Vernon, who came to bring Mrs. Wills to her children, not a living soul has entered the cabin."

"Adelaide," she replied, "I am not weak to argue. You may not have seen him. I did. He is on the ship. I know it. You cannot deceive me."

Mrs. Julia saw it was indeed no use arguing So, bidding her lie quite still and take a good dinner, she departed

All this while Mr Compton was in the cabin, watching the movements of his hand, as a telegraphist watches the movements of the needle. It wrote a good deal Messages were written out, and signed by telepathic friends in Melbourne, London, and Chicago. Then came the writing as before.

"John Thomas. Iceberg. 4.0. Are you coming? We cannot hold out much longer. One of the men is too frost-bitten to move. The fog is clearing.—JohnThomas"

Then came more messages from Edinburgh, the Cape, and Singapore. It was singular to note the confidence with which correspondents in such distant regions communicated with their chief in mid-Atlantic But he had only eyes for one correspondent. At half-past four, it wrote again.—

"John Thomas. Iceberg. 4.30. The fog has gone The sun is shining. We are on the outer edge of the iceberg field. If you skirt it, you cannot fail to see us—unless the iceberg falls over again. The frost-bitten man is dead. We can hold out till sunset—no later.—John Thomas."

Again more messages from other correspondents, which his hand wrote out without his eye following the lines. At half-past five came the writing.—

"John Thomas. Iceberg. 5.30. I cannot now see the time. My companion can no longer keep his feet. My strength is failing.—John Thomas."

Compton could stand it no longer Closing his despatch-book, he hurried upon deck. He saw and heard the floe ice, and it seemed to him that the fog was not so dense He saw the captain on the bridge. He went forward where the look-out was keeping a sharp look-out on deck. Suddenly he heard the cry,—

"Icebergs on the starboard."

The captain shouted something inaudible in the crash of the ice, the engine bell rang the engines slowed down their speed, the steamer steered a trifle more to the southward, but still kept pounding her way onward. He could only see ghastly shadows looming darkly to the northward. If his friend was there? Sick at heart he sought out Mrs. Irwin.

"Should you know the iceberg which you saw in your vision if you saw it again?"

"Certainly, I would," she replied. "It was very irregular, with huge overhanging pinnacles. I could swear to it among a thousand."

"Stand here, then, near the deck look-out, and keep your eye fixed on the north. It may be that the mist will rise."

He went back to his cabin. The professor was awaiting him.

"Well?" said he.

"It is not well," groaned Compton. As he opened his despatch-book to see if any fresh message was waiting to be taken down, his hand wandered a little over the paper Then it began;—

"John Thomas. Iceberg. My companion is dead. I am alone on the iceberg. I can no longer stand or walk. In another hour all will be over.—John Thomas."

"Halloo!" said the professor. "The fog has lifted!" Compton rushed from the cabin, and tore madly to the bridge, where the captain was standing.

"Captain," he cried. "remember your promise!"

And as he spoke, he pointed to a great flotilla of icebergs. Behind the steamer the fog was as thick as a blanket. Before her was open water. On the north stretched the dazzling array of icebergs, ever shifting and moving. Now and again a great berg would capsize with reverberant roar. The captain was cowed. There was something uncanny and awesome about the incident. He had seen icebergs before, but he had seldom had such good luck as to pass clear by the dangerous edge of floes, and he to have clear sky.

"Agent for Mr. Compton to the bridge Captain," said Compton, before the other had time to speak, "remember your promise. Here we are in open water outside the fog, just off the southern edge of the iceberg. Will you save John Thomas?"

The captain shrugged his shoulders. "How do I know where he is? Am I to use the Majestic, with 2,000 souls on board, to go hunting for John Thomas among that wilderness of icebergs? Ask yourself, Is it reasonable?"

Compton replied. "If I am able to point out the exact iceberg where John Thomas lies, will you stop and send a boat to bring him aboard?"

"Yes," said the captain, "I could not well refuse that." The Majestic was now driving ahead at full speed. All the passengers were on deck enjoying the novel and magnificent spectacle. Suddenly a cry was heard from the bows. It was a woman's voice, shrill and piercing.

"There it is! That is it! That is the iceberg!"

A rush was made forward. Mrs. Irwin was carried to the captain. Then she said: "We are abreast of it, and will be past it in a minute. Oh, stop her, for the Lord's mercy! You are not going to leave three men to die?"

The captain took no notice, but keenly scrutinised through his glasses the peculiar-shaped iceberg which she indicated. "Tis curious," he muttered. "I seem to see a speck of something on the base of that berg."

The bell in the engine-room sounded, the engines stopped, and the great steamer, for the first time since leaving Queenstown, came to a standstill.

The ship was full of buzzing comments and eager inquiry. Why had the engines been stopped? What was the matter? Never was such a thing heard of—to bring to off an ice floe. There was now very little floating ice. The sea was tranquil. But who could say how soon the fog might fall again, or the northern bergs drift across the ship's route? The captain must be mad? Was there an accident in the engine-room? No, nothing was wrong there. What then? In that hubbub the voices of those who held the highest numbers in the pool were loudest in angry denunciation of the captain.

And in all this hubbub where was Compton? In his cabin, eagerly deciphering the words which his hand wrote, hardly being able to do so for the tears which blinded him. It wrote:

"John Thomas. Iceberg. I am dying. I have lost all use of my limbs. I can see a steamer in the distance, but it will not stop. I cannot make any signal. Good-bye, chief; good-bye.—John Thomas."

While he was deciphering this in his cabin, the crew, by the captain's orders, were busily engaged in lowering one of the ship's boats. A whisper ran through the ship that there was a castaway on one of the icebergs, and in a moment everyone on board, excepting the holders of the larger numbers, was intensely interested, and even enthusiastic.

Compton came up to the captain. "Captain," he said, "I am afraid it is too late, but grant me one favour?"

"Well?"

"Let the professor and me go in the boat. My friend cannot help himself. He is motionless and frost-bitten. Someone must climb the iceberg. It is not a task his friends should throw upon others. The professor and I are ready."

The captain said "Go."

The boat was now launched, the men were at the oars, when the professor and Mr. Compton, carrying ice axes, a rope ladder, a coil of rope, and a bag with brandy and other restoratives, climbed down the side of the ship and took their seats.

How the passengers cheered as they rowed away; cheered, too, in spite of the angry order to desist lest the sound should disturb the very slender equilibrium of some floating mountain.

They were about a mile from the iceberg. The officer in command of the boat conferred with Mr. Compton, who briefly explained what was to be done.

As the boat approached the iceberg, they could distinctly see three bodies, but they could make out no signs of life.

Nearer and nearer they rowed, cautiously but boldly, although every now and then huge blocks of ice detached themselves from the berg, and fell with ominous crash into the water.

Nearer still and nearer the boat rowed, until it was almost within a stone's-throw of the iceberg. Then Compton, standing up, hailed his friend. There was a dull echo from the perpendicular ice-cliff, but the silent, motionless figures made no sign.

"Too late, I fear," muttered Compton through his clenched teeth. "Never mind, let us bring him to the ship, dead or alive."

The three bodies were lying on a ledge about twenty feet above the level of the water. When the berg had split, the portion that broke off was that which had afforded the crew a tolerably easy landing-stage. Now there seemed nothing for it but for the boat to lay up alongside : 12 steep

ice-wall, and for the rescue party to climb aloft as best they could.

Then another difficulty revealed itself. The sloping ice stretched under water for some twenty or thirty yards, so that the boat could not draw up to the face of the ledge.

"There is nothing for it," said Compton, "but for you to pull on until you feel the ice beneath your keel; then the professor and I will wade to the face of the cliff, and climb up."

The boat soon bumped on the ice. Compton got out into the water first, followed by the professor. The latter insisted upon carrying some strange machine round his

waist. Each had an axe, and they carried with them a rope-ladder, a small coil of rope, and a flask of brandy. They got out cautiously, fearing lest a sudden spring might possibly bring the whole mountain down upon their heads. In that case, not only were the boat's crew doomed, but even the *Majestic*, a mile away, might be in danger.

They imagined they felt the ice give a little under the water, but they ignored it, and were soon at the foot of the ledge on which lay three motionless figures.

Compton and the professor were experienced mountaineers. They had little difficulty in cutting steps, on which they could climb, but the ice was rotten, and often gave way beneath their tread. On one occasion Compton, who was leading, came down with a heavy crash on the professor, laming his left shoulder. They began again at a place where the ice seemed more solid. This time Compton went up alone.

The momer t he gained the ledge, an enthusiastic cheer went up from the *Majestic*, where his every movement was followed with breathless interest. Compton went directly to the longest of the prostrate forms.

"John Thomas," he said.

There was no answer. He laid his hand upon his face; it was all frost-bitten, and as if it were dead.

"Too late!" he muttered; "too late!"

The professor's head was just appearing above the ledge, when a heavy boulder, so to speak, of ice fell with a sullen crash out to the sea, dangerously jeopardising the safety of the boat.

"I am afraid it is too late," said Compton, sullenly.

The professor stepped blithely to the side of the apparent corpse.

"No," said he; "you will see the use of my patent galvano-vitalizer."

He undid the machine he carried round his waist, and uncoiled some wires, to which plates of copper were attached. One he placed at the back of the neck, the other on the abdomen. Then he proceeded to turn a handle.

"Sit by his head, Compton," he said, "and if he shows any signs of reviving, give him a small mouthful of brandy."

For a time it seemed as if the handle might be turned for ever without producing more effect upon the body than upon the ice on which it lay. But after a while the apparent corpse began to twitch, the eyelids began to move, and then the mouth opened, and a heavy sigh told that vitality had been restored.

Compton tried, at first in vain, to pour some brandy down his throat. It only choked him, and it almost seemed as if John Thomas had survived the cold only to be killed by restoratives. At last, however, they got him sufficiently revived to get him to swallow some spirit, and to take a spoonful of strong beef-tea.

The professor then took off the galvano-vitalizer, and proceeded to fasten the rope-ladder down the side of the cliff. He fixed the two ice-axes securely in the ice, and slung the ladder over the edge. He then fastened the small cord round John Thomas's waist. Compton and he carried the half-senseless, frost-bitten man to the top of the ladder. The professor then descended until he was in a position to take John Thomas's legs on his shoulders. He then began slowly to descend, Compton relieving him of as much of the weight as possible by means of the cord. By this means they got safely down to the water, and from thence it was comparatively easy to carry him to the boat. The professor was just returning for the ice-axes, the rope-ladder, and, above all, for his admirable galvano-vitalizer, when a cry was raised in the boat which made his blood run cold—

"The fog! the fog!"

Looking round, he saw that the fog was sweeping over the sea, and the outline of the *Majestic* could hardly be distinguished. Another ten minutes they might not be able to find their way back. The professor forgot even his machine and leapt into the boat. The men bent to their oars as for life, and sent the boat flying over the water like a bird.

Denser and denser grew the fog, but they could see the *Majestic* right before them, and in another moment they were alongside. Just as they reached the ship they heard a long roar like the reverberation of a park of artillery, and then the water heaved violently and dashed the boat heavily against the side of the *Majestic*.

There was a moment of agonising suspense. No one knew whether the displacement in the iceberg might not

lead to a sudden upheaval of an iceberg under the keel of the *Majestic*. There was a deathly silence. Then the water began to subside, and the boat's crew, with Compton and the professor, and the frozen, half-dead survivor were brought safely to deck.

There was too much alarm about the fog for much demonstration of enthusiasm. But, when the engines were once more started, and the *Majestic* felt her way slowly through the fog to the clear waters beyond, there was not one passenger on board who did not feel glad that the liner had laid to for two whole hours to save that one miserable castaway.

But there were some on board who were filled with deeper feelings than those of mere admiration and sympathy. During the whole of the two hours they had been absent from the ship Irene had watched their progress with a strained interest of emotion which left her no room even for the thought that she was experiencing the most terrible thrill of her life. She had hurriedly thrown an old waterproof over her dinner dress, and leant against the bulwarks following through the glass every movement of the professor, for it was he and he alone for whom she cared. She feared he did not care much for her. Why should he? She was but a silly girl with a pretty face. He was one of the greatest scientists of the world. She would rather be trampled on by him than be made love to by all the other men in the ship. She had always been piqued by his impersonal method of regarding her as alkali capable of yielding certain results when tested with acids, and she was honestly dazzled by his learning and genius, but this excursion of his to the iceberg suddenly transformed him into the prince and hero of her dreams. None of the other men in the boat, not even Compton, seemed to be worth a thought. The professor, and he alone, was the hero-leader of the expedition. How noble he seemed! His very eye seemed to glow with divine light as the boat left the ship. That he seemed supremely indifferent to her only added to his charm.

From all which meditations it may be inferred that Irene was experiencing for the first time an entirely new sensation of utter humility and of self-effacement. As the boat lessened in the distance, she had kept her glass fixed upon the professor, following him with an emotion too deep for utterance until he landed below the ice ledge.

An indefinable feeling of horror came over her as she saw he was in the water. She watched them cutting steps in the ice, but her indignation knew no bounds when she saw Compton go up first. What effrontery to thrust himself before her hero! But when, just as Compton was nearing the top, his foothold gave way and he fell heavily upon the professor below, both falling into the water, it seemed to her as if she were witnessing a murder. In that one terrible moment the flame of her love and her life seemed to flare up with one fierce spasm and then go out for ever in horrible darkness of nothingness and despair. She gave a piteous scream. Her glass dropped from her hands over the bulwarks into the water, and she fell swooning on the deck. So great was the excitement at the moment that she lay for some minutes unnoticed. Then the doctor and one of the stewards carried her to the saloon, where they applied restoratives. She lay quite insensible, but as she was breathing heavily and evenly, they left her, and returned to watch the attempt at rescue.

There was another spectator who was only one degree less interested than Irene. That was Mrs. Irwin. She had been deeply impressed by the straightforward manliness of Mr. Compton, and attracted to him by his occult gifts. The incident of the wreck off the iceberg established a sympathy between them, and she felt naturally intensely interested in the rescue of the tall, red-haired, one-eyed man whom she had seen more than twelve hours before when they must have been distant nearly 200 miles. She would have gladly gone in the boat, but it was idle proposing it. So she had perforce prepared to choose the more arduous task of watching while Compton risked his life to save the castaway.

Mrs. Irwin was of a practical nature amid all her dreams and mystic imaginings. She did not merely watch, she prayed, prayed with all the intensity of a passionate nature for the safety of the man for whom alone she felt reviving in her breast the stormy emotions that she believed had been hushed for ever in her husband's grave. "Something had gone snap inside," she used to say, "when she heard the clods fall on the coffin lid." She could never feel again as she felt in the glad old days when she wandered with her lover under the olive trees of the Riviera, or sat on the promontory rock of Monaco, and saw in the cool of the night the great moon shine double in sky and sea. All was dust and ashes within, and yet she felt, almost with a sense of profanation, the quickening throb of the old emotion as she watched Mr. Compton climb up the ice cliff. When he fell she cried, "O God, let it be the other one!" for her quick nature never hesitated a moment to sacrificing the professor or a hecatomb of professors to save Compton. She felt as if her prayer was granted when Compton struggled to his feet and the professor .se rubbing his shoulder. Every step up the cliff was accompanied by passionate prayer, the outpourings of a woman's will, so potent often for ill as to justify the witch's tar-barrel, but this time employed to bless, not to curse.

The moment she saw them reach the boat in safety, and pull off through the mist, her practical common-sense asserted itself. She bustled to the steward and made him prepare the most commodious berth in the ship for the reception of John Thomas, supply warm blankets, and provide all manner of creature comforts. She brought out the steward of Mr. Compton's cabin, and induced him to provide plenty of warmed wraps, and the doctor got ready every kind of medicament and cordial.

When Compton stepped on board the ship, the impulsive Irish woman seized his hand with both of hers, and exclaimed :

"Mr. Compton, Mr. Compton! the Lord reward you for this day."

He looked up at her glowing face and sparkling eyes, from which her whole soul was beaming in admiration and worship, and then moved slowly towards his berth without saying a word. She accompanied him with the doctor. When he reached the door, he said :

"It was a very near thing, Mrs. Irwin, nearer than I ever care to be in again. I am faint. The doctor will look after me. Good-night."

She seized his proffered hand, wrung it passionately, and rushed away.

"Doctor," said Compton, slowly, "undress me, and let me sleep."

The doctor undressed him, but did not let him sleep. He chafed his frozen hands, he plied him with strong and heated cordials, and made him drink a cup of the best clear soup the cook could provide, and then, when at last after an hour spent in this way he was allowed to sleep, all danger was passed.

As for John Thomas, he was cared for by the ship's doctor. With skilful treatment and constant care life began to return, and by the morning he could speak.

As for the professor, he slipped away in the confusion, and was making his way through the saloon to his berth when he was startled by seeing Irene, her long black hair streaming behind, her face pallid as death, her eyes swollen, her whole appearance that of one almost distraught. She did not seem to see him, but moved as if

"THEN YOU ARE NOT DEAD!"

she were in a dream. They were in a narrow corridor where two could pass with difficulty. He was obliged to speak; all wet as he was he could not allow her to spoil her dress. "Miss Vernon," he said, "do you not see me?"

She gave a frightened cry, turned to run, with horror on her countenance.

The professor sighed for his cunning little instrument which measured emotion, and then, before Irene had time to run two steps, he caught her hand.

"Miss Vernon, this is a poor welcome," he said.

Irene stopped instantly, turned, and regarded him intently.

"Then —you—are—not dead?"

"No," he said, somewhat snappishly; "but I soon shall be if I cannot get off these wet clothes."

Then, to his immense dismay, with a hysterical laugh, poor Irene flung herself upon him, all dripping wet with ice water, kissed him over and over again before he could get breath:

"O professor, professor, I thought I saw you die!"

The poor professor felt he would have given the whole world to have had his instrument in position. "It would have been the highest reading on record," he said to himself. "The complexity of conflicting emotions would have put the instrument to a higher test than will ever recur again."

"Brain fever, I fear," said he, as, grasping Irene firmly with both hands, he led her, talking incoherently about her hero, to her berth, where he delivered her over to the stewardess, telling her to summon the doctor, and keep note of her temperature.

Then he turned to his own berth, and, before he took off his dripping garments, he fixed his instrument on his finger and tried to read the register. But it was too fitful, or his arm was too numb with the bruise on his shoulder, for its record to be valuable. So, calling the steward, he undressed, ate a hearty dinner, and was soon in a sound sleep. But, before he dozed off into unconsciousness, a new and unwonted sensation of mingled regret and desire stole over him.

"Steward," he said, "give me my instrument. I want to measure—" but before he finished the sentence, he had dropped off to sleep.

CHAPTER IX.—THE THRESHOLD OF THE NEW WORLD.

AFTER the rescue from the iceberg no incident of any importance diversified the usual routine of the voyage. The captain recovered his good humour when he found the fog lifted again before sunset, and he saw a straight course of open water before him. That night the gamblers, after making up the pool on the next day's run, found that it was necessary to keep up the excitement of the day by novelties in betting. When once a craze is started, it runs apace. It began in one man offering to bet that the rescued castaway would die after all. This was taken several times over at even money. When the doctor appeared and gave a favourable report the odds went up two to one on his recovery, with few takers. Then they varied the bets. This time it was how old he was. Then when he would first sit down with the captain at dinner in the saloon; in short, as is usual towards the end of a voyage when novelties are few, there was nothing about the unfortunate John Thomas that did not form the subject of a wager.

When morning came, John Thomas was pronounced out of danger, though with great probability of losing one foot from frost-bite. Mr. Compton was almost well. The professor's left shoulder was sore and stiff from the blow caused by Compton's fall. Irene was too weak to leave her berth. Her mind had wandered during the night. When she awoke she, too, took her breakfast in her cabin. She was quite collected, but with very little recollection of what had passed, but with an eager longing, an unquiet, passionate craving to see the professor. As for Mrs. Irwin, she was in the highest spirits. It was a wonderful thing to her that she had the evidence at last that her heart was not all dust and ashes. Whatever had snapped, it was not the string that vibrates in response to the touch of love. She loved Compton, that she was sure of; and if unfortunately he did not return her affection, that, of course, was a misfortune. But compared with the re-

covery of the power of loving it was a mere bagatelle. As a man who, after believing he had for ever lost his sight, rejoices when he once more sees the light of the blessed sun, even although he may never again see the particular landscape on which he feasts his gaze, so Mrs. Irwin rejoiced that day.

She flitted about here and there like a busy bee. She had long talks with Mr. Compton as they walked to and fro on the deck, the observed of all observers.

"Well," said a deck lounger, "if that's the wizard and that's the witch, they are a very well-matched couple, and very different from the warlocks and broomstick-riders of old."

Gamblers sought her secretly to ask if she could foresee the winning number in next day's pool. "Thank you," she said, "my gifts are not for the likes of you. Faith, you can cheat quite well enough as it is, without my coming to your assistance."

And Rose—where was Rose all this time? She was still weak, too weak to be more than an hour a day on the deck in the sunshine, and very piteous it was to see her wistfully gazing along the deck in search of one dear familiar form, for which she looked and always looked in vain. Mrs. Julia would not listen for a moment to the suggestion that he might be on board. She brought her the list of the cabin passengers, and showed her that there was no "Walter Wynne" mentioned. But when she was asking the purser one day if he had ever heard the name, she was not a little startled to hear him say, "Walter Wynne, yes, I remember now. He was down sixth on the list for the places of 'disappoints.' We only had three places left vacant at the last hour, so we had to leave him behind."

"Strange," said the good woman, "that he actually tried to come on this very ship. I had better not tell her, or she will break her poor little heart to think how near he actually was to coming on board."

Still, notwithstanding her disappointment a new life and fresh hope seemed to have entered into her. She talked a good deal with Mrs. Julia about her father in Chicago. A telegram, she said, would be waiting her at New York, and she hoped it would tell of his recovery. She could hope for any good news now, she said, since her Walter had come back. Being an intermediate, she could not be allowed in the part sacred to cabin passengers, or she would no doubt have found the doctor. As it was, Rose could only lie in her berth.

And so it was that Rose lay and wondered day after day, night after night, how it was he came not again. She heard a good deal about Dr. Vernon, and how busy he was with the invalids and the children, but she took the most languid interest in any but the one for whom she looked who never came again.

As the *Majestic* passed the banks of Newfoundland a long trail of fog clung about the sea, through which they steamed at full speed, sounding the fog-whistle almost continuously. Irene was quite well now, and spent every hour she could, if not with the professor, then within range of his voice. He was at first somewhat bored by this dog-like devotion, but after a time he grew accustomed to it. It was a new sensation for him to have a beautiful and sympathetic listener, who was never offended at anything, and who only asked to be allowed the privilege of being subjected to the endless series of moral and mental shocks which he administered impartially to all with whom he conversed. As for her, when Mrs. Wills said to her one day she wondered how she stood the disgusting and horrible things which the professor was in the habit of saying, Irene replied—

"I love colour, bright colour, with vivid contrasts, for

any one bright colour would become monotonous. I long for variety, for sauce, for spice, for anything and everything, that gives salt to existence. Your have ten commandments I believe—or is it eleven? I should only have one. 'Thou shalt not be bored.' But as it would have even less respect paid to it than the old decalogue, I suppose it would be no use. I hate drab and grey, and all these horrid mashed-up neutral tints. Why should I live in this eternal grey fog, when outside there is the bright sun and the blue sky, and the myriad-coloured rainbow? You scold me for longing for thrills, or for any fresh sensations. But what good is it to live unless you make life yield up the heights and the depths, and all the intensity of thought and feeling? Life to me is not worth living unless I have new experiences, and lots of them. Quantity is essential even if the quality is somewhat crude."

" My dear Miss Vernon, said Compton, who was listening, " you remind me of the Aissowa Arabs, who eat scorpions for a thrill, and swallow red hot coals just by way of a sensation."

" Dr. Glogoul is not a scorpion," said the pretty girl, drawing herself up indignantly. " He is the kindesthearted man I ever met. His zeal for human vivisection is the purest philanthropy I ever heard of, and he literally spends his life in studying how to do good to mankind."

" No doubt," said Mrs. Wills drily. " I suppose you have heard of his scheme for settling the Irish difficulty by transfusing sheep's blood into the veins of the turbulent and excitable Celts. He was quite full of that the other morning."

" Oh," said Irene, " that is one of the least of his schemes. He was telling me the other day of a new trepanning machine by which he thinks it will be possible to root out all the abnormality which is the root of vice, crime, and misery."

" What is his particular scheme ?" asked Compton.

" Oh," said Irene, enthusiastically, " every baby within six weeks of birth is to be sent to a State phrenologist. If he condemns its skull as hopelessly abnormal, the baby is fed from a lovely feeding bottle containing mother's milk sweetened with a sedative so powerful and painless the child never wakes again. If however, there is only sufficient abnormality to admit of correction, the child is subjected to a series of surgical operations under anæsthetics by which the great law of the general average is made the rule for each individual. Excess of brain in the lobes of criminalism is suddenly raising the skull over the faculties of spirituality and conscientiousness, benevolence, etc., and vice versâ. Trepanning used to be constantly practised in the Neolithic age. Why not now? I asked, Why not graft brain at once? But he said it would probably be fatal. So he contents himself with remodelling the skull to give the brain room to grow into normality.

" Well," said Mrs. Wills, " of all living beings you and the professor are the last whom I should have suspected of heading a crusade against the abnormal."

" Oh, but the professor is the most self-sacrificing of men," exclaimed Irene. " He frequently says, ' My mission in life is to destroy the abnormal which is my exclusive study. When my work is done, I shall have no more object for which to live.' But there he is. I must leave you, for we have to hypnotise the Calabrian assassin."

As she hurried away Compton muttered sotto voce, " If these two really marry, there is no fear of the immediate extinction of the types of the abnormal."

" Mr. Compton," said Mrs. Wills, " do you think Miss Vernon would allow her babies to be treated like that—supposing that she ever had any ?"

" If she would, madam, said Compton, " I sincerely hope she never may have any. But she would not. Girls are as different from matrons as chalk from cheese. The schoolgirl, who in our grandmother's days ate slate pencils and drank vinegar, now poses à la Bashkirtzeff, and takes up the wildest immoral nonsense that is labelled ' Advanced.' But the cradle deals with all that flatulent balderdash as the strong east wind dealt with the frogs of Egypt. Maternity is at once the salvation and the education of your sex. I could wish that couple no better corrective of their fantasy than for them to become Mr. and Mrs. Glogoul, with a colony of little Glogouls rising up to correct their abnormality by a little common-sense."

The fog was left behind, and soon the betting on board centred not upon the length of the day's run, but upon the pilot boat which was already expected with feverish anxiety as the first tangible proof of their approach to the New World. They had not been six days out from Queenstown, but they had already the feeling that they had somehow lost touch with the universe. There was not a newspaper on board ship that was not six days' old. In England the Ministry might have fallen, or France might have declared war, or the Pope might have died, or the German Emperor have started for Chicago—they knew nothing of anything. Hence the sight of the pilot boat on the far horizon was an event of immense importance. All the New York pilot boats have great numbers on their sails, and for days before they are sighted books are made, and bets laid as to what number the pilot boat would bear that awaited the Majestic. The number, which was 15, was no sooner settled, and the stakes handed over to the winner, than betting began anew as to the person of the pilot. He was as yet too far off to be seen, and bets were freely exchanged as to his height, age, the colour of his hair, etc., etc., which kept up the excitement until he was on board.

After that, the near approach of disembarkation did away with the need for any further gambling. Bags and boxes were overhauled, preparation made to receive the customs officers, competing routes were critically canvassed, and there was everywhere that charming atmosphere of bustle that must have been nowhere more pleasurably appreciated than in the Ark the day after the dove returned with the olive leaf.

The ship swept past Fire Island, and soon the passengers began to catch their first glimpse of their destination.

Mrs. Julia stood with Rose on the deck and endeavoured to cheer her with many assurances of good fortune. Rose was grave and sedate, although as white and as frail as a lily.

" Adelaide," she said, " I have seen him on this ship. If I leave this ship without meeting him I shall never meet him again. To be so near and yet so far; to cross the sea in the same steamer, and yet never to come together, would prove that between us there is an unfathomable abyss. The sands are running fast in the hour-glass. If I do not see him before we land I——!"

" My dear Rose," said the matter-of-fact little widow, " do not torture yourself by idle imagination. I have proved to you a dozen times over that he is not on board the Majestic, but you shall see every saloon passenger leave the ship. If you don't see him then, dearie, you will believe that it was all a hallucination, won't you ?"

" You have been very kind to me, Adelaide," said Rose simply. " For seven years no one but you has ever called me Rose, and now, just when I have learnt to love you, and to prize your love, we separate."

" We shall meet in Chicago at the World's Fair, where I hope you will find your father quite better," said

·Mrs. Julia, brightly, and then moved off to make ready for
the dreaded customs inspection.

"You need not be alarmed.' said the professor, who
was standing by Irene. " The officers will not trouble
you much. They will ask if you have dutiable goods in
excess of the personal luggage allowed to each passenger.
You answer no, sign declaration to that effect, and then
wait till the landing to let them have the run of your
boxes. If the officer suffers from indigestion he will turn
them inside out ; if he has breakfasted comfortably, and
feels at ease with the world and with himself, he will
merely rumple a few frocks, smile graciously, and then
pass your trunks. Whether you get a good digestion or a
bad one inside your particular customs officer no one can
say. It is an even chance."

"Are you joking, professor ? " asked Mrs. Wills, who
was busily engaged in doing up Pearl's dolls into a manageable package, much to the distress of the little lady,
who was sure " Kitty would be smuddered, she would.
She was crying so. She could not breathe."

" Madam," said he, " I never joke. In a well-regulated
state, no one but dyspeptics passed as incurable should be
allowed to act as customs officers. Sometimes, it must be
admitted, the New York officers display such a high average of incivility as to suggest that the dyspeptic test has
been rigidly enforced."

" What are the dutiable articles?" asked Irene.

" Pretty nearly everything," said the professor, " that
you are not able conscientiously to swear you require for
your own personal use during your visit. If you have anything as a present for a friend it is an import, and must
contribute to the exchequer of Uncle Sam on the spot.
which, being interpreted, means that you pay the officers
here from thirty to seventy-five per cent. on the value of
the article in order that the manufacturers of similar
goods within the States may continue to charge
high enough prices to make their fortunes. The chief items
upon which passengers have to pay duty are the following :
Tobacco, photographic cameras, cutlery, new clothes, etc.,
etc., etc."

Few sights are more welcome to the traveller than the
distant view of New York. The approach is not particularly beautiful, but the charm of contrast between the
crowded narrows, with the shore on either side, and craft
of every description passing, or being passed, and the wide
expanse of the lonely Atlantic, is sufficient to impress it
pleasurably on the mind. The sun was setting as the
Majestic finished her run, and its fading rays lit up the
distant spires of the Empire City. Then night fell, and the
stars came out, and from the Statue of Liberty a great
ribbon of electric light streamed forth over the water. It
was a vestibule worthy the entrance hall of the Republic.

The customs officers had almost completed taking their
declarations. A whole horde of interviewers had boarded
the ship on the first whisper of the romantic story of the
rescue from the iceberg, and before the ship was moored
at the wharf, half-a-dozen special editions of the evening
papers were selling in the streets, with the story of the
rescue of John Thomas from the iceberg in mid-Atlantic.

Mrs. Irwin was unanimously deputed to give the story
to the press, and the way in which she discharged her
difficult duty, when confronting the pencils of a score or
more of the sharpest interviewers in New York gave Mr.
Compton quite a new conception of her capacity. Mrs.
Irwin, who was self-possessed, told her story perfectly, and
when one luckless reporter ventured to question the accuracy of her story, she simply extinguished him, to the immense entertainment of all present, for she was sarcastic as
well as kind-hearted, and when it came to close quarters
there were few who were a match for her in repartee, or

the franchise brutale which tells most where it is least
expected. It was agreed beforehand that nothing was to
be said about the occult side of it, and as this was only
known to half-a-dozen persons, it was not difficult. All
the credit for the rescue was given to the captain, and this
not because he deserved it so much as to encourage the
others. Mrs. Irwin had protested against this at first, on
the ground that historic truth required the facts to be set
out as they actually occurred, and that it was unjust to
give the credit properly belonging to Mr. Compton to "that
apalpeen of a captain, who had done nothing at all." Mr.
Compton overruled her objection, saying, " If the credit is
due to me, then it is mine to bestow where I please. I give
it to the captain ; it will make it easier for those of our
helpers who may come after."

So Mrs. Irwin told the story minus its telepathic acces-
sories, and encircled the captain of the Majestic with such
a halo of glory that the Messrs. Ismav increased his
salary, the Directors of the other lines grew green with
envy and ordered their captains at all risks to rescue
some castaways from icebergs, even if they had to
plant them there themselves. Mrs. Irwin's conscience
smote her sore, but she went through with her task
to universal satisfaction—universal, minus one. For
Irene was heard to observe, as she read the papers the
next day at the Fifth Avenue Hotel, that "the story was
entirely wanting in perspective ; for no one on reading it
would imagine what she who saw everything with her own
eyes could declare to be the fact—that the real hero of the
whole adventure was not the captain, nor yet Mr. Compton,
whose name was quite absurdly pushed to the front, but
the illustrious Professor Glogoul. to whose heroic exer-
tions and supreme scientific skill the rescue was really
due."

It was about eight o'clock in the Friday evening when
they sighted the land. It was a little after twelve when
the great ship was brought up alongside the wharf, the
final adjustment being effected by the bull-headed steamboats, which, aiding the alternate working of her double
screws, soon brought her into position.

As it was past midnight, the landing and the examination of the luggage was postponed till the morning. A
few passengers, in light marching order, in deadly haste to
make connection with trains across the Continent, were
allowed to land, but, with these exceptions, the company
remained on board all night.

There were many wakeful occupants of the berths that
night. The sudden cessation of the throbbing of the
engines, the substitution of perfect motionless stillness for
the heave and roll of the Atlantic, were in themselves sufficient to keep many awake. But, in addition to this, there
was all the restlessness of highly strung expectation.
There were few Americans on board. Most of the passengers were in the New World for the first time. The
majority hoped to begin life anew, and were naturally full
of anxiety about the conditions of their new existence.
They were now close upon the threshold of the promised
land. By every berth sat Hope and Fear, and Imagination,
borrowing a wing from each, fluttered tremulously around.

Compton and Wynne were long in retiring to rest.
The professor was sleeping soundly enough, undisturbed
by the unwonted silence In coming up the harbour he
had been engrossed by Irene, who seldom looked
more radiant. In a lovely white dress which adapted itself
to every movement of her graceful form, with a creamy lace
mantilla lightly thrown over her head, where one red rosebud glowed in her raven hair, she seemed, even to the un-
sentimental professor, a vision of almost ideal beauty. He
was conscious of an unusual stir of obscure feeling, and
he noted with complacency the admiring and partly-envious

looks with which he was regarded by the men who saw them standing in the evening sunlight. He felt he ought to say something complimentary, but his tongue, long unused to any but scientific terms, did not lend itself easily to the softer phrases of the drawing-room. He made an effort, and failed. Irene was not unconscious of the effect which she was producing, especially on him. She encouraged his lame and stammering effort by a smile. It gave him courage, as of new wine.

"Miss Irene," he said, recklessly; "I guess, if we

saying something that would ruffle the plumage of this beautiful bird of paradise, with its caressing ways. He looked at her again, with a glance that was pathetic with the speechless misery of the dumb. Then, making a great effort, he said. -

"Miss Vernon, the bell rings at six in the morning. It is about time to turn in."

Irene flushed, and moved towards the saloon. The professor followed, feeling miserable, but about as able to say what he felt as if she understood nothing but Chinese.

IRENE AND THE PROFESSOR IN THE SALOON.

had the universal self-registering thermometer of the emotions. It would bid fair to break the record to-night for admiration and envy, and," he went on awkwardly, "so far as I am concerned, I admit that I cannot conceive of any instrument which would register the height it would have to record in my particular case."

Irene appreciated the effort, but she could not resist the temptation to say, somewhat archly,—

"Really, professor, and which of the emotions you specify is it that would be so immeasurable?"

The poor professor looked at her as he had never looked at man or woman. It was a good opening, but he had exhausted his resources of compliment. A dim sense of the absurdity of silence struggled with as vague a dread of

She was put out, he saw plainly; and yet, as she turned to bid him "Good-night," the glow of resentment still lingering in her face, he felt he had never seen anything more beautiful in his life. As he took her little hand, he held it awkwardly between both of his, and said.—

"Good night, Miss Vernon. I think," he hesitated, and she withdrew her hand as he opened the saloon, "I think, Miss Vernon, that I begin to understand something more of the religion of the Greeks than I ever learned at college."

As the professor climbed into his berth that night he said nothing to himself, but he thought the more. Dim, confused dreams of stately temples reared to the Goddess of Love and Beauty flitted before his eyes, and, somehow, the statue of Aphrodite in all the changes of his vision bore the strongest resemblance to Irene.

As for that young lady, she was even better satisfied with herself than usual. "I have had many declarations," she said, "but none that charmed me as much as this. To order me to bed like a dog one minute, and the next to pay me that lovely compliment about the Greeks! what a man it is! He is an inexhaustible galvanic battery of surprises. With him I am always on the switchback, and one never knows just when the jolt is going to happen."

Far different were the thoughts which absorbed the attention of Compton and the doctor, as they pa the deck of the steamer long after all the other passengers had gone below.

Dr. Wynne, now that the voyage was ending, was very sad. He had not seen Rose. For him that was the forlorn hope that had lured him across the Atlantic. Now that the port was gained, he felt that it was but another case of "Love's labour lost." But for the apparent absurdity of the thing, he was more than half-minded to take the next boat back to Liverpool, without going to Chicago at all. An inexpressible sadness weighed down his spirits. The glimpses of domestic life he had gained when romping with Pearl and explaining things to the boys intensified his feelings of disappointment and unrest. Was it to be ever thus? Why should he shut out from Paradise, the door of which had been so long locked in his face? But the key seemed to be lost, lost more hopelessly than ever. What was the use of keeping up the vain quest for that which never could be found? And yet what was there in life worth living for if he found it not? Better the endless search which kept at least some glimmering of hope alive in his soul than the abandonment to the outer darkness of endless night.

While the doctor was chewing the cud of such bitter fancies, his companion, equally silent, was full of very different broodings.

The lights of New York, dimly visible through the soft twilight of June, seemed a mystic hieroglyph, in which he read a prophecy of things to come. The city lay a dark, shapeless, indistinguishable mass, its very extent but imperfectly outlined by the twinkling lights that could be faintly discerned far up the island. Across the water glided the great ferry-boats, plying ceaselessly between the densely crowded banks. Their whistles, from time to time, could be heard in the distance like the lowing of cattle on the prairie. Here and there, an electric light shed a brilliant riband of white light across the gloom.

After a time he spoke.

"Doctor," he said, "do you think the English race will ever awaken to a consciousness of its destinies?"

"Who knows?" said the doctor, with a laugh. "Is there much hope that the race will realize what such component parts as that city yonder so utterly ignores?"

"New York," said Compton, "is hardly an English-speaking city. It is the cosmio-politico-polyglot antechamber of the New World. You could carve a German city out of it more populous than Hamburg, and an Irish town twice the size of Cork, and still there would remain a more heterogeneous composite amalgam of peoples, and multitudes, and nations, and tongues than is to be found in any city in the whole world."

"London has a fairly large foreign contingent," objected the doctor.

"London is English," replied Compton, "through and through. Numerically strong as are its foreign elements, they are hardly more in the immense current of English life than the pollution which a stream gathers in its course through the moorland and farm. New York rather resembles the Thames below Barking, heavily laden with the sewage of the capital. It is the Cloaca Maxima of Europe at the very portals of the New World."

"Are other American cities so much better?" asked the doctor. "We hear more about New York, because it is the window through which the Western Republic looks out upon the Old World. But although some what worse than the average, it is not much worse."

"You exaggerate," said his companion, "although there is reason enough for pessimism. But it is just because things are in this evil pass that I feel within me the stirrings of a new hope. On the surface you may say truly enough that this people is wholly given up to materialism and to covetousness, which is idolatry. But there is a spirit moving upon the face of the waters, and again, as in old time, it will result in the genesis of a new world."

"I confess I don't see much promise of its coming," said Dr. Wynne, who, however, was beginning to be roused by the fervour and passion of his friend.

"Perhaps it is because you do not take the trouble to look for it," said Compton. "But if you will look below the surface, you will find everywhere in America a deep although vague unrest, a blind groping after a new ideal, a consciousness, stronger than you dream of, that even an infinity of dollars cannot feed a hungry soul."

"Unrest," said the doctor, "undoubtedly. Labour brutalised confronts Capital, striking with the cruelty of fear. Here and there a few dreamers, like Bellamy, but for the vast expanse of the continent, are there even as many light points as we see in the city that stretches darkly before us?"

"What is that city?" said Compton. "It is the city of millionaires—nay, of billionaires. And what is this enormous wealth to the individual who inherits it? A burden too great to be borne. Increase of wealth up to a certain point means increase of comfort, increase of power. Beyond that point it means for its possessor increase of burden without compensation. A man may spend £100 or £1,000 a week in luxurious living or in lavish expenditure, but beyond the latter sum few millionaires ever go. But the revenues of many far exceed that sum, and every penny of that excess, although it may bring them the miser's sordid exultation, brings with it the miser's fears, the miser's foreboding."

"That is all very well," said the doctor, "but even if it be granted that the millionaire is of all men most miserable, I do not see how the misery of the millionaire, which after all most millionaires seem to support well enough, is to minister to the making of the Millennium."

"Wait a little," replied Compton. "The billionaire is a new portent of civilisation. The race of millionaires by inheritance is but newly established. Can you imagine a more tragic contrast between the boundless potentialities of power and beneficence that lie glittering as a mirage before the eyes of a young millionaire of generous enthusiasm and philanthropic instincts, and the treadmill round of mere hoarding to which they are all doomed? I could point out to you millionaire after millionaire who left the University longing to do something, or at least to be somebody, who are now nothing more or less than safe-keys in breeches, the whole of their life consumed in the constant worry of seeing that their enormous investments do not deteriorate, and the not less arduous task of investing to the best advantage, their surplus revenue. What a life for an immortal soul! They are like the men-at-arms in the old wars, so laden with their own armour, their strength was used up in merely conveying themselves about, that they had none left with which to fight. Their imagination is crushed by their millions. A political career is barricaded against them by their own money bags. A crowd of parasites and beggars swarm round them like mosquitoes round a weary wanderer in a Southern swamp. They can do nothing, dare nothing, risk nothing. They sit in the Republic like golden Buddhas, cross-legged in an eastern temple, eternally contemplating their gilded paunch."

"That may be said," the doctor replied, "but it is easier to see the evil than to foresee the remedy."

"My friend, said Compton, "there is a beginning of a great revival of civic religion in this New World. A Church which has forgotten man stands in the midst of a

"No," said Compton. "I do not think that will be needed. For the revived Church, in the fervour of its new love, will startle the world by the success of its Mission to Millionaires."

They were silent for a time.

"It's a sublime dream," said the doctor.

"It is none the worse for that," said Compton. "Most of the best things we have begun by being dreams."

The next morning at six, the passengers were summoned to the last breakfast before landing. The taking of declarations from the customs was almost complete. After

JERSEY CITY.   NEW YORK: BIRD'S-EYE VIEW.   BROOKLYN.

world which has forgotten God. Through the apparently dry and sapless branches into which they have endlessly sub-divided Christendom, there is an upward pulsing of a new life. For, lo! the winter is past, the rain is over and gone, the flowers appear on the earth, the time of the singing of birds is come, the voice of summer is heard in the land. The new impulse which the worship of God is receiving towards the Service of Man will create endless demands upon those who have to supply the necessities of those who have not, and when that day comes, we shall discover that each of these billionaires is but a money-bag, which will be open for the necessities of God's poor."

"Which the poor will open with dynamite, if need be," said the doctor.

breakfast they would stream across the gangway into the wide, wide world.

Rose, with heart obstinately sanguine, although sometimes feeling as if her last hope was flickering in the socket, took her stand close to where she could see every cabin passenger as he crossed the gangway to the wharf. She was alone, and she leant wearily against a projecting rail. All were busy about their own affairs, their own packages, their own settlements with the bedroom steward, the bathroom attendant, the deck steward, and all those for whom tips from half-a-crown to ten shillings are expected at the close of a voyage. There was a rush to obtain American money in exchange for English at the purser's office, but the wise and prudent r.ho had supplied themselves before the steamer had sighted the Sandyhook lightship now began to leave the ship.

Mrs. Julia was still struggling in the throes of packing a portmanteau too full to close. The professor, carrying his bag, passed out alone, not caring to face Irene so soon after the scene of last night. Compton followed shortly after.

Dr. Wynne had promised Mrs. Wills to carry little Pearl across the gang-plank, and to take charge of the youngest boy during the process of luggage inspection. Irene had attired herself in one of the smartest of walking dresses, and produced for the occasion the prettiest hat she had in all her store. At breakfast she said to the doctor, "Now, sir, pray remember that I have not been exacting during the voyage. I shall require your cousinly services on landing."

"I shall not fail you," he replied, gravely, "but you will have to take my arm, as I have promised to carry Pearl, and also to take charge of Fred. And I shall need you more than you need me, you see. for I have unfortunately broken my glasses, and since my illness at Hamburg I am almost as short-sighted as a bat. You must, therefore, personally conduct your cousin across the gangway."

"Really!" said she, laughing. "we shall be quite a family party."

As it was arranged, so it came about. The passengers were now streaming across the gangway in an unending stream. Little Pearl was hoisted upon the doctor's shoulders. Fred, his round eyes full of wonder, firmly grasped the doctor's left hand. Irene rested her hand upon his right arm. Mrs. Wills with Tom came behind. In the crowd the party got separated, and did not meet again until they were on the wharf.

On and on and on poured the stream of life. Rose, supporting herself as best she could upon the rail against which she was leaning, gazed with eyes intent upon every one who stepped upon the plank. Some hundreds had passed, and she was dazed and weary with watching for one who came not, when suddenly she heard a laughing voice she remembered only too well. Her heart nearly stopped, but raising herself to her full height, she gazed with feverish anxiety in the direction whence she heard the voice. Again she heard it. There was no mistake. It had deepened somewhat since that June day by the Avon, but she would have known it among the multitudinous voices of the whole earth. As it drew nearer a strange, indefinable terror seized her, almost choking her breath. Presently she heard it again, almost close at hand, and although from her position she could not see the speaker, she could distinguish the words, and every syllable sank like molten lead into her brain. She clung convulsively to the rail, and listened as one might to the words of her death-warrant. For the voice was saying :—

"Sit tight, little Pearl! Hold on, I will not let you fall. That's a brave little pet! Now Fred, keep tight hold of my hand.'

Almost as she heard the last word, Walter, her Walter, stepped on to the gang-plank. There was no mistake ; it was he, just as she had seen him that night. But a chubby little girl was seated on his shoulders, with her hands clasping a big doll. A lovely little boy, with beautiful curls, held his hand, and hanging on his arm, a stylishly-dressed, beautiful lady ' They were so close to her she could almost have touched them. As he turned to step on the plank she looked straight into his eyes. But there was no answering look of recognition. He turned his back, and walked down the gangway.

"Now, Pearl," he said, "be a brave big girlie, and show mamma how well you can ride !"

Rose heard no more. Everything swam before her eyes. A great dizzying darkness seemed to swallow her up, and she fell forward upon the rail with the pitiful, wailing cry :—

"Oh, my God ! my God !"

CHAPTER X.—THE RE-BIRTH OF HOPE.

WHEN the passengers found themselves upon the wharf, their luggage was piled up in sections, alphabetically numbered. This secured the immediate sub-division of the luggage into twenty lots, and, being so sub-divided it was comparatively easy to identify your own property. The owners who had painted their boxes some glaring colour, such as red and yellow, were the luckiest, but in any case there was li.tle delay. Whether or not the dyspeptics were off duty, or whether the influx of visitors to the World's Fair made the officers more than usually gracious, there was very little ruthless rummaging in the passengers' luggage, and even Miss Irene's lavish provision of dinner and ball dresses passed without notice. There was, however, an hour or more spent on the wharf, but the delay was pleasant enough. The early morning air was delightfully fresh, the scene was new, and whether regarded from a scientific or merely from a human point of view, the debouching of another regiment of the invading European was full of interest. The professor, who had rejoined Irene, was chiefly concerned in noticing the steerage passengers. As they came ashore, he was careful to point out one and another who, in any well regulated state, would not be allowed to land.

"Mark his head," he would say. "There is the type of a born criminal. That man has his head full of the germs of all manner of dishonesty and fraud. You could only cure him by decapitation. Before Uncle Sam has done with him and his progeny, he will cost us more than would have provided for him in frugal comfort to the end of his life, in his native land. What a farce it is !" he continued, bitterly. "We turn back the penniless pauper, be he never so industrious and honest ; we turn back the sufferers from any epidemic disease that affects the body, and yet we allow the greatest continent in the world to be overrun by the moral refuse and human sweepings of Europe, with full and sovereign right to give their decayed and criminal organism a new lease of life, by crossing with the stronger and less debilitated stocks of our spacious homestead."

The professor was never so eloquent as when on his favourite hobby, and he was quite willing to stand on the wharf all day like the cattle sorter at the Union Stockyard in Chicago, and classify the immigrant "for slaughter," "for fattening," or "for export to the west." "There is not enough phlegm," he said regretfully. "Too much nerves, too little beef. Oh, for a few broad-bottomed Dutchmen ! We shall have to contract for all Dutch criminals and practise transfusion of blood on the largest scale if our people are to last. They are pining down to the Red Indian type, and, like the red man, they will perish before a tougher, beefier race that has mastered the secret of repose."

Irene at last got tired of waiting. "How much longer are you going to stand there," she asked, "when the officer is worrying for your declarations ? You will have to sign three separate papers before they let your instruments through, and even then I am afraid you will have some trouble."

Compton had already despatched his business. But he lingered watching the steam ferry-boats plying in the river, the great overhead beam rising and falling conspicuously before the eyes of all men.

"Look," said Compton to Mrs. Irwin, who had ap-

HE TURNED HIS BACK, AND WALKED DOWN THE GANGWAY. "NOW, PEARL," HE SAID, "BE A BRAVE BIG GIRLIE, AND SHOW MAMMA HOW WELL YOU CAN RIDE."

ROSE HEARD NO MORE. SHE FELL FORWARD . . . (page 56).

proached him to say good-bye, "in this country even the steam engines relish asserting themselves. Everything in America must be *en évidence*—even the piston-rod of a ferry-boat."

"I came to say good-bye, Mr. Compton," said Mrs. Irwin, "and to thank you for all you have done and said on the voyage. It is rare indeed to meet a man who lives like you on two worlds at once. Most, with your gift on the astral plane, turn silly in their own affairs. But with you it is different. Good-bye, and thank you."

"Good-bye, Mrs. Irwin," said Mr. Compton, "but remember the Secret of the Telepath. If at any time you wish anything you wish to say to me; it matters not where you are, nor what hour of day or night, my hand will write your message the following noon. By-the-bye, where are you going?"

"To Chicago direct by the New York Central; and you?"

"To Chicago to-morrow by the Pennsylvannia route. We shall perhaps meet at the Fair. *Bon voyage.*"

By this time most of the luggage had been attended to, and handed over to the Express officer who undertook its delivery to the respective destinations.

THE ELEVATED RAILWAY.

Compton took the Elevated Railway, carrying only a light hand-bag. He intended to engage a room and medical attendant for John Thomas, who, although capable of being moved, was still quite helpless, and then he would return to the wharf with a carriage to transport him to his hotel.

Outside the wharf stood several hackmen waiting for fares.

"Don't you think," said Mrs. Wills to the doctor, who had handed over his cousinly duties to the professor, "that we had better take a cab, and drive straight to the Victoria Hotel. It would be simpler, and it cannot cost much, as the distance, according to the map, is only two miles."

The doctor hailed a cabman.

"Take this lady and children to the Victoria Hotel."

"The Victoria *H*otel," said the man, laying great stress on the aspirate.

"Yes," said the doctor; "I will follow immediately, as it will rather crowd the cab if I come too. Ta-ta, Pearl," said he to the baby, who was beginning to fret about her doll, which, she was sure, was being "scumfitted" in the bundle.

The professor drove off to deposit Miss Vernon at the Fifth Avenue Hotel, intending to rejoin Compton in the

quieter quarters selected for the recovery of Mr. Thomas. The doctor took a train that passed near his hotel, and very soon the wharf was almost cleared of cabin-passengers.

But Mrs. Julia had not yet left the steamer. As good fortune would have it, she was following very close behind the doctor when Rose uttered her piteous cry, and fell forward on the deck. She heard it, looked round, and, seeing Rose, at once left the procession going ashore, and hurried to the prostrate form. Rose at first did not speak. She was not weeping; she lay as if stunned by a pole-axe.

"Rose dear," said Mrs. Julia, "let me help you to a cabin. You will be better there."

Finding that she did not move, the kindly widow summoned a steward who was standing near, on the look-out for parting tips, and between them they helped, or rather carried Rose to a state-room. She was deathly pale, and quite conscious, but she seemed to have lost all volition or power to move or speak. The steward brought her some brandy; Mrs. Julia plied her smelling-salts. Rose feebly put them away.

"No," she whispered, "it is not that."

"What is it, then, poor dear?" said she, soothingly. "You need not wait," she added to the steward, who needed no second bidding.

Nothing could exceed the kindness with which the widow devoted herself to Rose. She made her lie down on the sofa. She insisted upon her drinking some nourishing soup, and a glass of old champagne. She smoothed her forehead, and in half-an-hour the poor stricken woman seemed to regain possession of her faculties. All this time she had never wept. Her eyes were hard and fixed, her lips bloodless, her face pinched and shrunk. She raised herself from the couch, and stood up with a great effort.

"Rose dear," said her friend, "you are better now."

"Yes, thank you," she said, with a voice so strained and hollow, Mrs. Julia could not repress a little start of surprise.

Rose continued with forced calm—"Adelaide, you have been very good to me. You are my only friend. But I cannot tell even you what has happened. It is worse than death."

Her voice trembled, and she bit her under lip. Then, recovering herself, she said,—

"Come, it is time we were going ashore."

They crossed the gang plank, and stood on the wharf waiting for their luggage to be examined.

"Now sit there," said Mrs. Julia, "and I will go to the office and see if there is a telegram for you."

Presently she returned saying, "There is no telegram for you at all, nor any letter."

Rose looked at her for a moment, and said, "No telegram! What name did you ask for?"

"Why, Thistle, of course," replied the widow. "Rose Thistle."

Rose said, "That is the name I took when I left home. My real name is Thorne. I will go for the telegram."

Presently she came back with a telegram in her hand. "My father is better," she said.

"Where are you going?" asked the widow.

"To Chicago," answered Rose, as if Chicago had been across the street.

"Yes, yes, I know," said Mrs. Julia. "But where are you going now?"

"I thought of taking the train right through," she said, wearily.

"Really, Rose," said the good-hearted widow, "you must be out of your senses. You are hardly strong enough

OUTSIDE THE ELEVATED RAILWAY STATION.

to cross the street, and you talk of starting right off an express railway journey of nearly 1,000 miles "

"But," said Rose, "there is nowhere else to go." She spoke with a deadness of feeling, as if the question in no way concerned her.

Mrs. Julia hesitated for a moment, then, crossing to the Express office, she booked her luggage and Rose's box to the same address.

Then she returned, and taking Rose's arm said to her, "Come."

Rose did not ask a question. She followed her silently to the Elevated Railway, leaning on Mrs. Julia's arm; she mounted the platform, and soon they were on their way to a station at the other end of the island.

Rose sat perfectly still. The strange spectacle of the railway running, as it were, on the first floor level over the heads of the roaring traffic of one of the busiest cities in the world, the tall buildings, the hideous telegraph posts, the staring advertisements—everything, in short, that provokes the attention and excites inquiry on the part of a stranger, left her perfectly unmoved. If she had been a corpse in a hearse going to her own burial, she could not have shown less interest. Mrs. Julia also was silent. She was revolving in her own mind some schemes which she had not quite thought out. Presently a contented little smile came over her beautiful countenance. She had arrived at some satisfactory solution, but she said nothing.

At last they reached their station. "Now, Rose dear," she said, "we alight here." Rose obeyed mechanically, descended the steps and followed Mrs. Julia to a pleasant little house looking out over the park. "We will stay here for a day or two," she said, "and then we will go on to Chicago."

Rose made no answer. She did not even seem to understand. They entered the house. A comely Quaker lady cordially greeted the widow.

"Welcome," she said, "dear Adelaide, and thy friend whom thou hast brought with thee. Wilt thou come to thy bed-chamber, for thou seemest to have sore need of rest?"

They went upstairs into a beautifully neat and simply-furnished room. "Here thou wilt rest," said the lady of the house.

Mrs. Julia assisted her to undress. "Now, dearie, you had better lie down for a little, and take a sleeping draught and forget all about it for a time."

Rose submitted as if she were a doll. Soon the doctor arrived. He shook his head. "A shock so violent as almost to paralyse the nervous system," he said. "Sleep at once, and for as long as possible, is her only chance."

She submitted to drug and morphia injection unresistingly, and was soon happily unconscious.

"Adelaide," said Aunt Deborah, "thy friend suffers much. When did the Lord send her to thee?"

"Auntie," said Mrs. Julia, "I have heard you say 'The Lord setteth the desolate in families,' and He seems to have sorted out one even more forlorn than myself to keep me company for a time."

Aunt Deborah folded the young widow in her arms, and both were silent for a little space.

Long before Rose had even left the ship a fierce altercation had begun at the doors of the Victoria Hotel. When the driver had deposited Mrs. Wills and her family and handbags at the door of the hotel, she asked the fare.

"Ten dollars," said the hackman.

Not believing she heard aright, she repeated her question. "I asked you how much I was to pay you."

"A COMELY QUAKER LADY GREETED THEM."

"And I say y'ere to pay me ten dollars," said he.

Mrs. Wills went into the hotel, and inquired at the office what the fare was. "That's as you fix it up," was the reply. "You pay what you agree to pay."

"But," said the bewildered lady, "I did not engage the cab. The doctor engaged it. He is following us, and will be here directly."

"Better tell him to wait till the doctor comes," said the clerk.

"And you had better go to your room, No. 236," said the porter.

"The gentleman who engaged the cab will be here directly," she said; "tell the driver to wait."

And then, entering the elevator, she and her children were whisked up to the fifth floor, where, for the first time for a week, they felt themselves almost at home. Little Pearl, who was rather bewildered at the lift, soon

"TEN DOLLARS," SAID THE HACKMAN.

recovered her equanimity when the wraps were unpacked and her beloved Kitty was discovered not to have perished of asphyxia.

"Pearl," said Tom, "cares more for that doll than for all America."

"I does," said Pearl. "I loves Kitty. I does not love Melica. Does you?" she asked.

"Well, no, not exactly, not yet," said Tom.

"Does Melica love you?" she persisted.

"No," said Tom.

"But Kitty loves me," said Pearl, triumphantly, and Tom didn't care to pursue the conversation.

Downstairs, in the spacious vestibule, a pretty storm was raging. Dr. Wynne had arrived, and was at once tackled by the hackman, who declared that the lady had promised him ten dollars. The doctor ridiculed the idea, and offered him two, which the driver scornfully refused. An American, who was an amused spectator of the altercation, at last interposed. "Better leave it to the clerk to settle. He'll see fair."

Dr. Wynne accepted the reference. The driver grumbled a good deal, but ultimately accepted three dollars—twelve shillings for two miles' drive—and departed after considerable expenditure of bad language.

The American, whose name it appeared was James Young, who had himself returned from Europe the previous day, said to the irate doctor,—

"It's a peculiar institution of ours, the hack-driver, sir; an institution specially established and maintained to teach the Britisher, at the moment of entry, that our ways are not your ways, nor our thoughts your thoughts. He is a pretty considerable nuisance, the hackman, but he saves his cost by teaching the stranger it's unsafe in a new country to assume anything. After such an experience as yours, I guess," he continued, "you'll be more careful about hiring things without knowing what's to pay. The poor fellow you will see is, after all, a blessing in disguise."

"The disguise is a trifle thick, isn't it?" said the doctor. "And it is rather rough on the stranger to give him so stiff a lesson before he has had time to look round."

"Well, sir," replied Mr. Young, "perhaps you are right. But it's well not to lose time. Uncle Sam begins with the tariff, and then rubs it in with hackmen; and after two such lessons, he hopes you'll need no more to make you look spry."

The doctor laughed, and went up the staircase to see how Mrs. Wills was "located," and to take the boys out for a run. The marble steps were magnificent, but they were better for looking at than walking on. On the first-floor he was glad to take the elevator and be deposited without more trouble at the door of No. 236. He found Mrs. Wills had made up her mind to start at once for Chicago by the New York Central, stopping on the way at Niagara. The doctor said he was going to stay in New York till Tuesday, and then go round by Washington. He offered to take the boys and the luggage, so that their mother could be free to devote herself to Pearl. The boys were delighted, and so it was arranged.

The next day Rose was somewhat better. But her eyes lacked their old lustre. She looked wan and haggard. She assented to everything that was proposed with the utter absence of interest that made one feel that the mirror of her mind had suddenly been transformed into lead. No image of outer things was reflected thereon. The soul had withdrawn itself. The eye saw not the bustle of the streets, the vivid green of the trees, the loving faces of her friends. She moved almost as in a trance. But, behind that outer calm, bitter thoughts were trampling down all the flowers of her youthful love.

Whenever Mrs. Julia left her she crouched up in a chair or laid her head upon the table, and would sit motionless and mute for hours. She shed no tears, she made no moan. She suffered in outward silence, out within all was tumult and desolation and despair. Her outward life was the vainest of vain shows, and its events and surroundings were as indifferent to her as the colour of the curtains of his bed to a dreamer in the grasp of a nightmare.

Nor was it to be wondered at that she should be thus overwhelmed and crushed into dumb agony. For seven years her whole life had centred in the service of the temple of her love. No vestal virgin had ever trimmed the sacred flame with more reverent hand. She had kept her heart as a sacred grove surrounding the garden-shrine in which all the sweet flowers were tended with loving care to weave garlands for the altar. That altar reared in the inmost holy of holies of her nature was dedicated to this worship of the Supreme Love. Even the remote precincts of this sacred grove had been jealously guarded from all intrusion. In the garden of the shrine no foot but hers had ever trod. Even the winds of heaven were forbidden to blow upon the shrine itself, so shaded was it and so secluded, nor had any knee but that of its vestal priestess ever knelt before the altar in the inmost sanctuary. To guard that grove, to tend that garden, to pray in that consecrated shrine, for seven years had been her life. If, for some hours every day, necessity had driven her to do other work in the outside world, it was only in order that she might keep herself alive and well, to minister at the altar, and to be ready for the coming of the Beloved.

And now, she sees, or thinks she sees, that the rude and brutish hoofs of actual fact trample into remediless ruin all the fair fancies of her maiden meditation, that the axe of the spoiler is laid to the trees of the sacred grove, that maddening thoughts like demented Furies rage round the shrine, and that all this was done by order of him for whom she trimmed the deathless flame by night and day, and day and night, for seven long years. Was it wonderful then that reason should reel on its throne, and despair should mould her prayer unto one vague longing for death?

If he had died she could have borne it. She could cherish her love for his memory when he was near her in the spirit quite as well as when he was absent from her in the flesh. But to forget her, and to marry another who had borne him children, and surrounded him with the new ties of a new love that made it seem wicked for her to love him any more, this was more than she could bear. For, no matter how wicked it was, she could not help loving him. He was another woman's husband, no doubt, and never should the shadow of her presence darken the happiness of his home. But, though he were a hundred times the other woman's husband, that could not and would not prevent her loving him still. Here he could no longer be in life. But in that strange shadowy world in which Rose had passed so much of her actual life, no power in heaven or earth could thrust him from her. That consolation, at least, fate could not deny. There they could live in love, and cherish for each other all the old affection.

But even this melancholy consolation of despair became a new source of torture, for Rose was tormented by doubts whether the solemn and awful words of the Sermon on the Mount, which declare that the thoughts and intents of the heart are even as deeds and acts before the eye of God, did not cover more than the grosser crimes of murder and adultery. If she imagined herself wandering once more by Avonside with her lover's arm around her waist in the dreamy glory of the setting sun, was that not a sin? What right had she to caress the husband of another, to assure him of her love, and might she not possibly, in some mysterious way, involve him in the doom which would overwhelm their lawless love—even though that love were of the imagination only?

So the gloom grew deeper upon her, and the lines on her face became more rigid and her haggard look was pitiful to see. In vain the kindly doctor told her to make an effort to rouse herself and shake off the depression. He might as well have exhorted a watch to resume its movement when the mainspring was broken. He gave her drugs, but they did nothing for her. All that he could do was to administer opiates, which gave her temporary insensibility.

But even sleep became dreadful to her, although she longed for it with a fearful longing, not for oblivion, but because when she slept she dreamed. And she always dreamed the same dream that she dreamed so long ago. And she was there, and he was there, and once more they were locked in each other's arms—to part no more for ever. And always as she awoke, fresh from the glowing rapture of that great love to be confronted by the hard

stern reality of things, her conscience used the sacred words as scourges to lacerate her bleeding flesh.

The day after landing it was evident that she was going to sink into melancholia unless something could be done to rouse her from her misery. The good Aunt Deborah prayed long and fervently for this wandering lamb. Mrs. Julia racked her wits to devise means for exorcising the fiend that possessed the lonely girl. All efforts to make her speak of the cause of her melancholy were quietly but stolidly repelled.

But in a way which they thought not the relief came. Rose was sitting in the drawing-room in the afternoon, as usual taking no notice of what was going on around her. The widow was showing to Aunt Deborah the spoils of the voyage. Among other things she had accumulated a store of portraits of her acquaintances among the passengers. She had Mr. Compton's portrait, and Irene's, and Mrs. Irwin's, and the doctor's, and Professor Glogoul's. But she said, "I prize more than all these the portraits of Mrs. Wills and her dear children. She had the only baby in the saloon, such a duck of a little girl, whom everybody spoiled. But I like the portrait of Fred best, with his long curly hair. He was just like a little angel in a Scotch cap."

"A dear boy," said Aunt Deborah, "with a sweet expression. Wilt thou not let me have his portrait to put upon the mantel? Thou wilt give much pleasure to many who will look upon it."

"Certainly, dear aunt," said the widow. "I am unwilling to lose it, but you will keep it for me, and if I cannot get another, you will let me have it back."

"If thee wishes it," said Aunt Deborah. "But I hope thou wilt let it remain there," she said, as she fixed it in a frame and placed it conspicuously on the mantel-piece.

"Rose, poor dear lamb," she added, "come and say if thou dost not think it a beautiful child?"

Rose, thus appealed to, rose mechanically from her chair and approached the picture.

The moment her eyes fell upon it they dilated and flashed with fire. Turning round upon the astonished widow, she cried—

"I think you at least might have spared me this."

She started for the door. A savage, sombre look of anger and pain had suddenly replaced the listless expression.

Hardly knowing why, Mrs. Julia sprang to the door just in time to prevent Rose leaving the room.

"Let me go," said Rose, imperiously. "I will not stay another moment in this house."

"Why, Rose, what on earth is the matter?" said her friend. "What has happened?"

"Let me go," she cried. "I will go! you shall not stop me! Why do you wish to keep me here to torture me? I cannot bear it," and then she tried with the utmost of her frail strength to force the door open.

"Rose," said Mrs. Julia, gravely, for she saw that a crisis had come, "I will let you out. But you must tell me why you have taken so sudden a desire to go."

"Let me out," she said, impatiently, "let me out! You have no right to keep me here. And that too," she added, "in order to taunt me by thrusting in my face the portrait of his child."

Mrs. Julia was so utterly astounded she let go the door. Rose instantly opened it and ran upstairs. But before she reached her room she slipped and fell heavily at the foot of the marble statue that stood at the top of the stairs.

Mrs. Julia and her aunt ran to her help. Rose was only partially stunned, and still full of resentment. She said, "Go away, I do not need you!" She could not

BEFORE SHE REACHED HER ROOM SHE SLIPPED AND FELL HEAVILY AT THE FOOT OF A MARBLE STATUE AT THE TOP OF THE STAIRS *(page 61)*.

walk, however, and they carried her to her room, where she lay sullenly on her bed, while they busied themselves in bathing the bruise on her brow.

She closed her eyes, and lay quite still as if asleep. Then she heard the two good women talking in whispers at the foot of the bed.

"What dost thou think now?" said the good Quaker. "Thy friend hath revived, but her anger, poor frail lamb, has brought her a snare."

"I cannot imagine what she means," said the widow, "about taunting her. You merely showed her the portrait of Mrs. Wills' boy!"

"Yea," said Aunt Deborah. "Is it possible that poor Rose knew Mr. Wills aforetime? She said something of 'h s' child."

Rose lay silent, but her heart was throbbing as if it would burst. A vague, impossible hope began to struggle into her mind, as the first glimpse of the sunrise struggles almost in vain through the black storm clouds on the eastern sky. She waited for the answer as a convict on the scaffold for the reprieve. She had not long to wait, for almost immediately, the widow replied—

"No, that is impossible, he was not on the ship. Mrs. Wills was bringing the children to meet him at San Francisco, where he returns from the Chinese Mission field. The doctor was very good to her on the voyage, and took charge of the children just as if he had been their father. In fact, I believe he is with them now,—But, what is that?"

A low, sobbing, choking cry brought them at once to the bedside. Rose had swooned, but her eyes were filled with tears, and there was a strange look of ecstasy about her face which had in it something unearthly, so wonderful was the change it had wrought in her haggard features.

"She has been weeping," said Aunt Deborah. "She will be better now. When she comes out of her swoon, I will leave thee alone with her for a time."

As Rose lay unconscious, Mrs. Julia bathed her temples with aromatic vinegar. The swoon gave place to a natural sleep.

She slept quietly as a child for six hours. When Mrs. Julia came from time to time to see if she had awakened, she found the pillow wet with tears, but on the face the same beautiful smile.

It was nearly nine o'clock. The light was beginning to fail, although the sunset splendour still flamed on the western sky, when Rose stirred, opened her eyes, and seeing Mrs. Julia standing by her side, she stretched out her arms. The widow bent down and kissed her. Rose kept her close to her for a long, silent minute. Then she said:

"Oh, Adelaide, it is not true, then; it is not true?"

Then she wept. The widow let her weep for a time, and then, gently disengaging herself from Rose's clinging grasp, she persuaded her to drink, as she would not, some egg and milk. Rose drank it, and then made Mrs. Julia sit close by her on the bed.

"I have had such a beautiful dream. I was in a strange and lovely place by the seaside. I was all alone, seeking my love. I wandered among myriads and myriads of men, and there was none like unto him, none to be compared to him. And I saw Mrs Wills again, and her angel-faced boy, and the little girl. And then things changed in the strangest way as dreams do. I dreamed my old dream again, and I was at Shottery once more, although the surroundings were strange. And then I saw him coming to me. And as I ran to throw myself upon his breast, he put me back, and said, 'Oh, Rose, why did you doubt?' I wept and said, 'If you knew how I have suffered you would be very sorry for me, and forgive.' Then he smiled, and said, 'Fred and Pearl are Mrs. Wills' children. Ours are

still to come.' And he embraced me as he used to do, and then I woke up, and you were there, and though it was only a dream it will some day be real. Won't it, Adelaide?"

"Certainly," said the practical Mrs. Julia. "But if you had only told me at the first, I could have told you all about it. Now I understand many things. But why did the doctor not call himself by his right name?"

"His name was 'Walter Wynne,'" said Rose.

"But they called him, 'Walter Vernon.' Ah! now I think of it, I have his portrait downstairs."

And before she could notice the startled joy on Rose's face, she tripped down to the drawing-room, and, a moment later, burst into the room.

"Well, I declare," she said, "if the portrait has not got 'Walter Wynne' written on the back."

Rose took that photograph, and hid it in her breast.

CHAPTER XI.—ROUND NEW YORK.

"Now," said the doctor to the youngsters, after seeing Mrs. Wills off to Niagara within two hours of landing, "we have got two days and a Sunday in which to see New York, so I propose that we go back to the beginning. Before doing anything else let us take a steamer and go off to the Statue of Liberty. You remember seeing it when you came up in the *Majestic?*"

STATUE OF LIBERTY.

"Whose statue is it?" asked Fred.

"It is the Statue of Liberty enlightening the world, and was put up by Frenchmen, who loved the Americans, seven years ago. The Goddess of Liberty stands on a gigantic pedestal holding a torch in her hand, from which streams a bright electric light at night time. It is the biggest statue in the world."

They soon reached the base of the statue and then began to climb up the staircase which led to the top. They were somewhat tired before they got up, and rested a good while at the top of the pedestal, which is itself 155 feet high.

"Sir," said a companion whom they picked up on the way, "there is nothing like this in the Old World, I guess? The pedestal cost 250,000 dollars, and the statue another 300,000. Half a million dollars you may take it at. Half a million dollars for the Statue of Liberty enlightening the world, and cheap at the price. One half a free gift, and the other half subscribed by Americans."

After resting at the summit of the pedestal they began the ascent of the interior of the figure which is made of copper plates rivetted together. They were very tired when they found themselves in the head of the goddess, in which there was room for forty people to stand.

"What a long nose it has got!" said Tom.

"Three feet long," said the doctor. "But now, let us go up the arm."

After a short climb they reached the torch-chamber, and looked down upon New York, which lay at their feet. The great water-way, along which countless vessels were steaming to the great ocean-gate of America, made a picture which it was worth while climbing twice as far to see.

After admiring the view for some time they descended, finding it much easier to come down than to go up. They had some lunch, and then sailed back to the Battery.

"Now," said Dr. Wynne, "as we have seen the biggest statue in the world, let us go and see the largest suspension bridge that has ever been built."

They took the tram to the City Hall, passing on the way many interesting points, among which were Wall Street, Trinity Church, and the Post Office. They climbed up the tower of the *World* office, which is nearly seventy feet higher than the Statue of Liberty. From the top of this tower they were informed they could see

FROM BROOKLYN BRIDGE: A SNAP-SHOT.

BROOKLYN SUSPENSION BRIDGE.

forty-five miles of country. No other newspaper office in the world has such an outlook. The doctor did not trouble to inspect the office, but made his way straight to the Brooklyn Bridge.

Standing on the bridge, Tom tried to bring his Kodak to bear, but the result, as will be seen by the accompanying plate, was rather peculiar.

"Is it really the biggest suspension bridge?" asked Fred.

"Yes," answered the doctor. "It took thirteen years to build it, and it cost three million pounds sterling. You see, it is 135 feet above the high-water mark. The middle span is nearly a mile long, and the bridge itself spans a distance of over a mile. 150,000 people on an average pass over it every day."

"How is the bridge suspended?" asked Tom.

"By wires," said the doctor. "You see those four large cables, which are attached to the high towers; each of them contains over five thousand galvanised steel wires."

After walking across the bridge and back again, they took the elevated railway.

"Now," said Dr. Wynne, "you have seen the largest

statue and the greatest suspension bridge in the world; I am going to take you to see one of the finest parks that you will see in your lives. It is Saturday afternoon. The Central Park will be full of people. Come and see the turn out."

At Fifth Avenue they took their seats in one of the open carry-alls for a drive round the park. For a dollar a head they made the round trip, greatly enjoying the drive round the great park. It was crowded with vehicles. They were frequently blocked, and admired much the patience of the crowd. What they did not admire was the surliness of the policemen.

"See, Tom," said the doctor, "the Americans only have one class in their railways, but they have three classes in their park, and they never let them mix. They have what they call drive-ways, bridle-paths, and footpaths, and carriage-riders and foot-passengers are all kept rigidly distinct. You are never allowed even to make a short cut across a drive-way or a bridle-path. If you try it, up comes a policeman and turns you back."

"Do they let carts into the park?" asked Tom.

"Never," said the doctor, "except the park-carts. They have a clever plan for keeping the heavy traffic out of

POLICEMAN IN CENTRAL PARK.

sight. Four transverse roads—sunken streets, in fact—cross the park, so that all the street-traffic can be kept out of sight, and the people can feel, in the midst of the crowded city, that they are in the heart of the country."

After they left the carry-all they re-entered the park, to stroll among the people, to visit the pretty lakes, to look through the Menagerie —they had not time to see the Museum and to have late dinner at the capital restaurant, the Casino. When they were dining, an affable New Yorker, sitting at the same table, gossiped with them about the park.

"If it were sold up for building sites," he said, " it would nearly pay off the National Debt."

He named the dollars, but after a while a Britisher's head gets addled with the incessantly recurring million dollars. They remembered that he said the park was over a mile in length, but so cunningly was it laid out that they had nine miles of drives, six miles of bridle-paths, and thirty miles of footpaths within its 840 acres, forty-three of which are under water. The Central Park, he said, was but one of the best of their parks ; they had any number more. In fact, you could hardly fire a musket in any part of the city without scaring birds in one of the parks or open spaces with which it is studded.

Dinner over, they took a car, after a little bargaining in which their American friend assisted them, for an hour's drive just before sunset. A dollar and a half was to be paid, and their new acquaintance kindly offered to accompany them, and point out some of the sights they saw on their way. They drove first through Fifth Avenue, the street of the millionaires. As marble palaces and brown stone fronts were passed, one of the boys asked if the people who lived there were nobles.

"Guess not," said the New Yorker, grimly, " they are only their uncles and fathers-in-law. There is enough real estate in that row, I reckon, to buy up—stock, lock, and barrel—the whole titled aristocracy of more than one European country. But we have no titles in this country, except those of office—honorary or otherwise. Every other man is president or secretary of something, just as in the South pretty nearly every white man is a colonel, unless he is a general. If we started a peerage there would be more dukes than dudes. No, sir, give us the power of the purse ; you can keep the gilded gingerbread in Europe. Our girls marry titles, but the boys mustn't wear them."

"What are these huge houses?" said the doctor, as they drove into Fifty-ninth Street.

"They are the flats which ascend into the heights. Land is dear, servants are scarce, so New York imitates Paris, and crowds many families under one roof."

"Then these tenement houses——"

"Sir," said the New Yorker; " these tenement houses ? You might as well call them slums. Tenement houses are only for poor folks. These flats or apartment houses, for we have both sorts, are almost the crowning achievement which associated effort brings to luxury. But -stop for a moment," he said to the car-man. " I want to show you the scene of one of our little battles. This is Eighth Avenue—fine business street, is it not ? Well, it is here, of all places in the world, in which a pitched battle took place only twenty-two years ago, between the Orangemen and the Catholic Irish. The Catholics swore they would stop the Orange procession celebrating the Battle of the Boyne. We swore they should parade if we had to call out our whole army. We did call out the militia, and the parade took place. When they were passing Twenty-fifth and Twenty-sixth Streets, the Catholics opened fire from the windows. The militia replied. When the fight was over we reckoned up. It cost forty dead men and

two hundred wounded to teach the Catholics to respect liberty of procession in a free country. Unfortunately, the Butchers Bill had to be met by both sides."

"Forty killed and two hundred wounded ! why, that is nearly as many as we lose in one of our little wars,' said Tom.

"Yes, sir," said the American, "but life is cheap here, especially Irish life. If the Irish would only kill each other we should not mind. It is when they take to killing us we begin to wake up. Do you see that building there?" he asked, pointing to the Grand Opera House at the corner of Eight Avenue, "that was where Fisk and Gould were once besieged, and where Fisk used the Erie Railway funds to run opera bouffe and maintain his seraglio. Yes, sir, we have no doubt to put up with many imported ruffians, but it is only the indigenous American who carries rascality to a scale of sublimity."

"What came of Fisk ? " asked the doctor.

"Got shot, thank God ! " was the reply.

DINNER OVER, THEY TOOK A CAR.

"Here is Madison Square, the very heart of the city. It is quiet now, but when elections are on, here is the place to note the throbbing pulse of our great democracy. Down Madison Avenue there is Dr. Parkhurst's Church - you had better go and hear him to-morrow. He doesn't live with Melchisedek and archæologize in Babylon while New York is left to the rum-seller and the Evil One. Near by is another live man of a different type, Dr. Marcus Rainsford, who is rector of St. George's Episcopal Church. He believes in running a church saloon. He has got as far as a club and a gymnasium. If you go to-morrow you will see his women choristers in white array."

"I want to go to Plymouth Church," said the doctor. "After Plymouth Rock, it is to me the most sacred place in America."

"So," said their friend, " that is over in Brooklyn, close to the bridge ; but here we are in Sixth Avenue. Do you see that store ? "

"With R. H. Macy and Co. on it ? " said Fred.

"That is what I mean. That is about the biggest store in the entire world. Paris has got one or two big magazines, and in London you have Whiteley's. But that store

MADISON SQUARE, NEW YORK.

there takes the cake. The figures " (suppressed groan from Fred)—"Never you mind, sir, the figures are a romance. Why, sir, it takes an engine of twenty-five horse-power merely to operate the blowers of the pneumatic tubes through which all change is paid."

"Really," said the doctor, "how is that done?"

"Why, the whole of that building before you, with its floor space of 200,000 square feet, is threaded through and through with pneumatic tubes, all centring in a change-room, where sits one change-girl at the mouth of every three tubes. All the money is whisked to her by the pneumatic blower, with the account. She takes the bill, checks the additions, and sends back the change and the receipt. There is no delay, no robbery. There are 4,000 persons employed in that store in busy times, 2,500 are constantly on duty in the slackest time. You will find all the cunningest notions under that roof. One hundred thousand people pass in and out of its seven doors every day, more than half as many as cross Brooklyn Bridge, and all is done for cash—ready money down, as you say. There are two hints that may be useful to your shop people. One is the Mail Order department. This is a staff of buyers, shopmen who receive orders from customers at a distance, whose whole duty it is to go and buy from the various departments just as if the customer was there herself. The other is the dark Hall of Mirrors where all purchasers of coloured silks can see how the material looks in the glare of the electric light."

"Are there any other firms as big as Macy's," asked Tom.

"Ridley's is as big, or even bigger. They have eighty-five departments as against fifty in Macy's. Their stables alone cost them a quarter of a million dollars."

From Madison Square they drove to Washington Square where they saw the Judson Memorial Church, a branch of the Church militant which is devoted to social work. There is a club house, apartment house, and a nursery all centring round this church. They looked at the Astor Library, and then drove down the Bowery.

"Here," said their guide, " we come to the slummy region, which is low class European rather than American. You meet here Chinese, Italians, Jews, and any number of Germans and Irish. I showed you a little further up where we had our last pitched battle; we are now passing the place where there was a still more determined fight just before our Civil War broke out. It was in 1857 when two factions, the ' Dead Rabbits ' and the ' Bowery Boys,' had a stand-up fight with barricades, rifles, and even cannon. The police – of whom we have only 3,200 in New York now, whereas by the London standard we ought to have double as many—were quite powerless. The fight went on until the militia were called out, and it was not stopped until six men had been killed and 100 injured."

"But what was it all about?" asked Tom.

"One target company refused to give precedence to another, and so they killed each other—'Irish fashion.' But we do not think much of these things. Eight years before a theatrical row about Macready ended in a riot which was only quelled by calling out the soldiers—100 of whom were wounded and several killed before the riot was suppressed. You are too squeamish about killing people in England. Instead of letting them fight it out as we do, you coddle them up, and make far too much ado when, now and again, your authorities do not hesitate to shoot. I suppose," said he, meditatively, "it is because you kill at such a wholesale rate in your wars, you cannot afford to have it done retail as we do. Now," said he, " we will see the outside of the institution which keeps the Bowery Boys in order."

They then drove to the Tombs, the city prison of New York. It was getting late, and they drove down past the City Hall and the Post Office, at which point they dismissed their carman, and betook themselves to the hotel.

Next day being Sunday, they spent it quietly. In the morning they went to Old Trinity, the oldest Episcopalian church in New York, which stands just opposite the end of Wall Street, and then went to hear Dr. Parkhurst In the afternoon they looked in at St. Patrick's Cathedral in the Fifth Avenue, admiring the building, which is said to be the finest church edifice in the New World. They then crossed over to Brooklyn, and looked in at Dr. Talmage's Sunday-school in Clifton Avenue, and in the evening visited Plymouth Church.

"I want to go there," said the doctor to the boys, " because it was one of the cradles of the religious and civil liberty of the United States."

"Who is the preacher?" asked Tom.

"Dr. Lyman Abbott is now in the pulpit, but although he is a good man and eloquent, it is not because of the man who is in it, but because of the man who used to be in it that we are going to Plymouth Church this evening. None of you young people will quite understand how useful Henry Ward Beecher was in his day and generation. For twenty years and more he was the foremost preacher in the English-speaking world, and his influence was always on the right side. He was for every good cause everywhere, and while advocating broad views, he never left the foundation on which he had been reared. In the great struggle for the emancipation of the negro, and the still greater struggle for the maintenance of the union upon which depended the industrial as opposed to the military aspect of the New World, Beecher fought ever in the van. These issues have, however, gone by.' What was of more permanent value was the service which he rendered in broadening the theological horizon and ex-

THE VESTIBULE TRAIN.

panding even the narrowest and straitest of the sects till they could see their doctrine from the point of view of a genial humanitarianism.'

Fred was very tired when he came back to the hotel, and the doctor was silent, thinking of many things, and recalling from the recesses of his memory the watchwords of the great pulpit orator, whose voice still reverberates in the memories of hundreds of thousands of men who are carrying out to-day the work which Beecher began.

Next day Dr. Wynne took the boys down to Wall Street to see the crush and bustle of business. After visiting some of the historic places in the neighbourhood of Battery Point, he took the Albany Day Line steamer up the Hudson. It was a fine day. The splendid three-decker was not uncomfortably crowded. After tearing about the city, it was a great relief to be able to sit on deck and watch the beauties of the American Rhine as they unfolded themselves before their eyes.

"The Americans beat us hollow," said the doctor, "in the organisation of locomotive comfort. If they only made their pavements and roads as good as they make their three decked steamers or vestibule cars, they might have some claim to lead the world in that civilisation which is interpreted by making smooth the paths of the travelling man."

Two and a half dollars each carried them the round trip from New York to Albany and back again. The foliage on the banks of the river was in its freshest green, and both young and old heartily enjoyed the excursion.

The next day they were up betimes. After settling their bill and getting their boots polished like mirrors by the omnipresent boot-blacks, they took their tickets through to Chicago *via* Philadelphia, Washington, and Pittsburg. They had no anxiety about luggage, as they checked it through. They bought their tickets at the ticket agency office close to the hotel, and booked their luggage through at the same time. The Express Office official tied a small metal check, with the place of destination on it, to each of the portmanteaus, and gave the counterpart of the numbered metal check to the doctor, who was thus relieved from all further responsibility for his impedimenta. Then crossing the river to the New Jersey

side by the biggest ferry in the world, they went to the station of the Pennsylvania Railroad and took their seats in a vestibule train.

The vestibule train is locomotive luxury, where everything is done to make you comfortable except motionless stillness, and that is attained as far as possible by the excellence of the metalled way, the solidity of the rolling-stock, and the perfection of the fittings. The boys, who had never been aboard a Pullman car in their own country, but had occasionally seen them at the London stations, were delighted to find a train made up of Pullman cars, and superior Pullman cars, so arranged that you can walk from one end of the train to the other while it is going at full speed.

In England, where the distances are so short that people think the journey between Edinburgh and London covers quite a considerable stretch of country, one can hardly realise the necessity for railway comfort in a country where cities are separated from each other by thousands of miles. The vestibule train is, therefore, a hotel on wheels. It is fitted with library, bath-room, barber's shop, writing-desk and type-writing staff, dining saloon, smoking-room, and sleeping accommodation.

Soon after they had taken their seats, the bell rang and the train started. At first it went slowly, but as soon as it got out of the city it quickened speed and rattled along as rapidly as any of the Scotch expresses.

In three hours they were in Philadelphia. Here they got out, intending only to look round and go on to Washington by a later train.

"Whatever you do," said one of their travelling com-

THE OBSERVATION CAR.

panions, "don't forget to see three things in Philadelphia. There is the City Hall, which is one of the largest buildings in the world that is used for public business; Wanamaker's Stores, and Independence Hall."

On getting out of the station Dr. Wynne found the City Hall immediately confronting him. Wanamaker's Stores were not far off. But the element of size had already begun to pall upon him, so without more ado he started for Independence Hall. This is the building in which the Declaration of Independence was first read. It is interesting as the birthplace of the Republic, and they were glad to see with what care the place had been preserved. Every chair is said to stand exactly where it did on the eventful day on which the independence of the American colonies was declared. The walls are crusted over with relics of the men who founded the American Republic.

"Did they do right, doctor," said Tom, "these men who declared their independence?"

"Yes," said the doctor, "it was not they who were wrong, but England."

THE CAPITOL, WASHINGTON.

"But would it not have been better," said Tom, "if they had never broken loose from the old country?"

The doctor sighed. "It may seem so to us, my boy, but Providence thought otherwise. If our ancestors had been wise, things would never have come to this pass, but the folly of our king was punished by the rending in twain of the English-speaking race. The blame of that great schism lies at our door, not that of the men who drew up the Declaration of Independence. Some day perhaps that schism may be healed, but of the day and the hour knoweth no man."

They hurried back to the station and were soon speeding southward to the National capital. There they remained the night, rising early in the morning to drive round one of the most beautiful cities in the world, and pay a visit to the Capitol, which America has a right to claim as being one of the finest buildings in either hemisphere.

From Washington they took the cars and were soon ascending the Alleghanies.

"Fifty years ago," said the doctor, "America was believed to consist of the States east of these mountains. Now they are little more than the skin of the apple; the

real core of the Republic lies far within. Even Chicago is now almost an Eastern city."

The weather was fine and the railroad well made. Nothing could be more beautiful than the mountain scenery through which they passed. The train then began to descend into the heart of the Black Country in a region famous for its iron, its coal, and its oil, and still more for its great store of natural gas, which, however, they were told, was beginning to give out.

They had no wish to stay at Pittsburg. The doctor looked with a melancholy interest upon the iron district which had been the scene the previous year of the fatal and sanguinary collision between Labour and Capital at Homestead.

"I wonder," he mused. "I wonder if this century will pass before mankind has found the solution to the riddle of the Sphinx."

CHAPTER XII.—THE QUEEN CITY.

"THERE are in all 147 ways of spelling Chicago," said Mike Dooley, the interviewer, who, having exhausted the resources of copy manufacture in the car, was graciously disposed to be communicative in his turn.

"And how do you pronounce it?" said little Fred.

"Shee-gaw-ger, or Chick-ar-go, accent on the second syllable," said Mike. "Queer name, is it not? It is the oldest thing about the place. They say there is a map in the Expo' 200 years old with Fort Checagow printed on it. There is nothing else in the city so old, no, not by a hundred years."

"It is an old Indian name, I think," said the doctor. "What does it mean?"

"Skunk's Hole, they say," answered Mike. "But others say it is Indian for strong and mighty, and a mighty strong city it is for sure, and there are skunks in it to this day," he added seriously, as he recalled how Ned Flannigan had "done a beat" on him just seven days gone by.

The train was now coming within sight of the outskirts of the city. The line was crossing a great plain, intersected by an endless series of railways radiating like an immense fan to the horizon, but all centring in Chicago.

"The railways make the State look like a gridiron," said Mike, "an almighty big gridiron, too, with Chicago as a rasher of bacon grilling on the lake shore."

"Sir," said a stranger, who had been sitting silent for some time, "you're from the old country, I presume."

"Yes," said the doctor. "And we've come like everyone else to see the Show."

"You have done well, sir," said the stranger, whose name was Hiram Jones, "but there is no show in the Expo' that is anything like so wonderful as Chicago. No, sir, Chicago is the great exhibit, the greatest exhibit of all."

"Well," said the doctor, "I suppose it is a pretty fair size—Chicago is rather less than half as big as London, I hear."

Hiram Jones surveyed the doctor with a look of supreme disdain, not unmixed with compassion.

Before he could put his look into words, Mike broke in with an exclamation of surprise.

"London!" he said. "Well, I reckon London is nowhere compared with Chicago. She's had 1,800 years to grow, and Chicago less than 80. Four millions in 1,800 years is not in it beside 1,500,000 in 80 years. Why, we kill more pork in a month than London can eat in a year."

The doctor laughed. Hiram Jones looked serious. "Stranger," he said, "you've got to expand your mind before you even begin to take in the size of Chicago. It's cramping to the faculties living on a small island. Why, all your railroads put together in all your three kingdoms are less than one quarter the roads operated from Chicago. Eighty thousand miles of rail centre here. You have barely twenty thousand all put together."

The train was now slowing up as they approached the city. Before them hung, like the pillar of cloud that guided Israel through the wilderness, a dense pall of smoke.

"Look, doctor," said Tom, "how smoky it seems.'

"Smoky," said Mike. "Chicago can b at even London follow at smoke. We have 2,000 factory chimneys always at it, and as we burn four million tons of bituminous coal every year; we're tied to have some smoke."

"Where no oxen are the crib is clean, but much increase is by the strength of the ox," said Hiram Jones. "Did not your Mr. Gladstone lament there was not smoke enough in Paris? He would not make that complaint here."

Dimly through the smoke the lofty buildings began to be more clearly seen against the sky line.

"Now," said Mike to the boys, "if you've got no crick in your necks you will have one before to-morrow dinner-time. For it takes a man to walk with his head at right angles to his spine to see the top of our buildings. They used to say that it took two men and a boy to see to the roof of our sky-scrapers, each one beginning where the other left off—but that is an old chestnut now.'

GRAND CENTRAL DEPOT.

The bell was ringing its warning notes, and the train was going very slowly. They were nearing the depôt.

"There are seven central terminal depôts in Chicago," said Mike, "and over 100 other stations, but I suppose we will all run on to the Terminal."

The boys were looking out of the window, full of eager curiosity at the strange city. The doctor was busy putting his odds and ends together. Mike was pouring into his ear, with Hibernian volubility, the statistical information with which the citizens are crammed.

"1,360 trains," he said, "arrive and depart every 24 hours, 260 of which are through expresses; 35 different railway companies bring 175,000 people to and from Chicago every day."

In the midst of his figures the train came to a stand-still, and they landed at one of the largest and finest rail-way stations in the world.

Summoning a cab, they were soon driving through the busy streets to the Auditorium Hotel.

"What a blessing," said the doctor, "Chicago is civilized enough to have its cab fares fixed by city ordinance. Pretty stiff," he added, as he looked at the regulations, "six shillings for taking the three of us less than a mile; nothing less than a dollar if we just cross the street. But

anything is better than the hideous jargoning at New York. We might have taken the hotel omnibus, but at two shillings a head we should have saved nothing."

THE AUDITORIUM HOTEL.

The boys were full of eager interest at the bustle and rush of the street. Cable-cars, carriages, cabs, drays were intermixed in apparently inextricable confusion. They had never seen streets at once so broad, and yet so crowded. But more than anything else, they marvelled at the height of the buildings.

"Do people really live up there in the sky?" said Fred. "How do they ever get upstairs?"

"They never go upstairs at all," said the doctor, "they are shot up in elevators so quick it makes hardly any difference which floor they occupy. Indeed, I am told the rent of the topmost rooms is heavier than those lower down. It is quieter up aloft."

The cab traversed the heart of the business block, the most crowded half of a mile on the earth's surface. On either side towered the "sky-scrapers," with sixteen and twenty stories.

"That man was quite right," said Tom, "that man in the car, when he said we should get a crick in the neck if we tried to see the top of these houses. I wonder if the Tower of Babel ever got so high."

The car stopped. They were at the Auditorium Hotel. In a few minutes they were whisked up to their rooms in the elevator, and they found themselves ten stories high. It was not so very far up for Chicago, although it was twenty feet higher than the top of the Duke of York's Column in London.

After they had washed, and made themselves comfortable, they went in search of Mrs. Wills. She had arrived the previous day. Little Pearl was delighted to see her brothers again, and "the kind gentleman"—as she called the doctor.

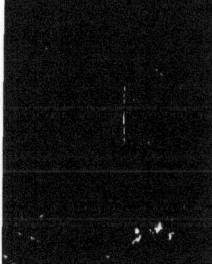

CHAMBER OF COMMERCE, CHICAGO.

At dinner, in the midst of a bewildering variety of dishes, the doctor heard all the news about the rest of the party. The professor and Compton were at the Palmer, where Irene had also established herself. Mrs. Julia had been lost sight of at New York. Mrs. Irwin was staying at the Leland.

"This hotel is very splendid," said Mrs. Wills, "but it is too big for me. I don't like a palace where 1,000 beds are made every day, and the figures they give you about the hotel are simply bewildering. I feel as I used to do at school when they made us learn the distances of the stars."

RAND MC NALLY BUILDING.

"The Americans," said the doctor, "certainly do beat all creation in their familiarity with detail. In describing this hotel, for instance, they tell you its exact weight, 110,000 tons, and they even tell you that 17,000,000 bricks were used in building it. Who can conceive 17,000,000 bricks? It is easier to realise the 10,000 electric lights, the twenty-five miles of gas and water pipes, the 230 miles of electric wire, but even that is somewhat of a strain."

"Doctor," said Tom, "what a lot of machinery they have in this hotel. It is almost like a factory. They have eleven dynamos, thirteen electric motors, four hydraulic motors, twenty-one pumping engines, and thirteen elevators. It is just like the *Majestic*, which you used to say was nothing but a great box of machinery."

After dinner Dr. Wynne started for the Palmer Hotel to look up his friends Compton and the professor. He found them enjoying a cigar in the smoke room.

"Wonderful place! ' said Compton ; "the marble staircase is a wonder, while as for the marble panels, and all other kinds of architectural luxury, the place is like a dream suddenly solidified by the word of some magician."

"Yes," said the professor, "it is a wonderful people ; if they could only learn to eat as cleverly as they have learned to build who knows what they might not do? But although I have only been two days in Chicago I have already seen that here, least of any place in the world, have they learned that leisure is life. It is a great people. It has rebuilt Chicago, it has put up the World's Fair, and it is perishing from indigestion.'

"Well," said the doctor, "I came here to ask you to stroll round the business quarter now that the throng is off the streets, and we can look about without being hustled off the sidewalk."

The professor, however, pleaded an engagement. He said he had promised to take Miss Vernon to McVicker's Theatre, one of the thirty-two theatres in which Chicago endeavours to forget for a moment the price of grain and pork. He said apologetically, "I will meet you here after the play."

Compton and the doctor then started on a little tour of inspection. On their way they picked up an old travelling acquaintance who had crossed on the *Majestic*, and who, as good luck would have it, happened to be engaged on the engineering staff of the municipality. Seeing they were doing a little sight seeing he

offered his services, which were gratefully accepted, and the three set off to see the heart of the busiest city in the world.

"The heart of Chicago," said John Adiram, for such was the name of their companion :-"the heart of Chicago in proportion to the whole city is not much larger than that of the heart to the human body. Within the city limits we have a hundred and eighty square miles, but the whole of the business is practically concentrated within an area of half a mile square, in which we are now standing. It is this extreme concentration which forces the growth of these gigantic buildings you see on every side. Outside this half mile square we live and manufacture, but the actual business is centred in this small section. As the ground is limited, these buildings tend every year to climb higher and higher into the sky."

"My first impression,' said Compton, "when I saw the sky-scrapers was that one of our great chimneys had been suddenly unfolded, like a Chinese puzzle, so that its walls were stretched round a great quadrangle which was then pierced with windows and used for offices. Architecturally these huge piles offend our European eye."

"I suppose it is only the elevator that makes them possible ?" said the doctor.

"Yes, sir, but for the elevator there would be such a getting up and down stairs that business would be impossible. One of these big buildings," said Adiram, as they stopped opposite one in Dearborn and Jackson Street, "one of these big buildings will have as many as fifteen or sixteen elevators constantly going with such rapidity that there is no loss of time between the first storey and the sixteenth. Some of them have restaurants close to the roof with a kind of summer garden at a height usually supposed only to be attained by monuments."

"I noticed," said the doctor, "as I was coming here that your business premises are about as high as our tallest monuments in London. The Monument at London Bridge, which was built to celebrate our great fire, is only 202 feet high, and I see that some of your buildings are well up to that height. Most of your ' sky-scrapers,' as

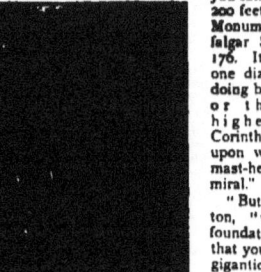

A TYPICAL SKY-SCRAPER.

you call them, are up to 200 feet, and Nelson's Monument in Trafalgar Square is only 176. It almost makes one dizzy to think of doing business twenty or thirty feet higher than the Corinthian column upon which we have mast-headed our Admiral."

"But," said Compton, "what kind of foundations have you that you can rear such gigantic piles ?"

"The foundations are one of our greatest difficulties. Even if we dig down thirty or forty feet we still fail to find a sufficiently solid base on which to rear buildings such as these, which weigh from 100,000 to 200,000 tons. Therefore it is necessary to make a foundation consisting of a solid mass of steel girders and cement grouting, upon which the buildings can safely be reared. The soil is about the worst that could have been chosen on which to rear such monstrous edifices

They are all built upon the sand, or rather through the seven or fourteen feet of sand which forms the surface of the soil, and are floated, as it were, upon a soft jelly-like clay, which yields like dough to the pressure from above. Hence, when one of these buildings is begun the first thing done is to cover the site with flat pads, eighteen inches thick and eighteen feet square, made of alternating courses of steel beams laid crosswise, filled in, and solidified with cement. By this means every pillar on which the structure has to rest has under it such a pad, and all the pads together cover the whole of the basement. Experience has proved that these enormous buildings so supported do not sink, while much lighter buildings built in the ordinary way settle ruinously. The outside shell of a building has nothing whatever to do with the structure itself, and could come down without endangering the solidity of the main building, which is made of steel girders bolted together. The outside is filled in with terra cotta or whatever material is deemed advantageous for the sake of ornament. But the interior is quite distinct."

"Apart from the economy of ground space, what advantage do these huge buildings offer?" asked Compton.

"Oh," said Adiram, "they immensely facilitate business; you have everything under one roof. Take, for instance, the Monadnock block, which we are just passing. It is the largest business building in the world, although it is only sixteen stories high. It has nearly 1,000 feet frontage on this street, and accommodates no fewer than 6,000 persons, or more than the population of Chicago when first the city was incorporated. To run a building like that properly will require the services of twenty elevators. This block, by the way," added Adiram, "is the first building in which the aluminium elevator was first used. Before long they will be the only elevators in use."

"The disadvantages of these monsters," said the doctor, "are, however, by no means inconsiderable. They darken the street, and depreciate the value of surrounding property, and are practically out of the reach of all fire-extinguishing apparatus or ordinary fire escapes. And then all your buildings are so hideously rectangular. Everything is at right angles in Chicago. All your streets are laid out with mathematical accuracy like a well-constructed gridiron, and your model of architecture seems to be the packing-box. This Monadnock block, for instance, is simply a gigantic conglomeration of packing-boxes."

"You can hardly say that of the building we are now approaching," said Adiram; "it is the Board of Trade, whose tower rises 300 feet above the pavement. It is one of the landmarks of Chicago. It may not be one of the most beautiful buildings in the world, but at any rate it is not a packing-case. Even if it were a packing-case it would deserve attention, for we fix the price here for the bread-stuffs of the world. Christendom prays, 'Give us this day our daily bread,' but in this building Chicago fixes its price."

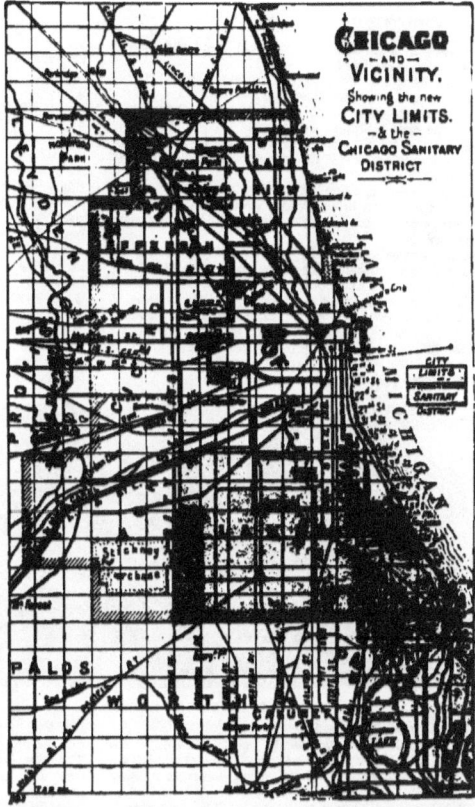

" By the bye," said the doctor, "is this what was called the burned district?"

"Certainly," said Adiram, "the fire swept over the whole of this. It is only twenty-one years ago since the whole of this region was one mass of smoking ruins, but a disaster which would have crippled most cities was to Chicago no more than the singeing of your hair at a barber's shop, which only makes it grow the more, yet the net loss of property amounted to nearly 200,000,000 dollars. It was about the biggest burnt-sacrifice on record. At nine o'clock on the 9th of October, 1871, Mrs. O'Leary's cow kicked over a paraffin lamp in a shanty in De Koven Street. There was a high wind, the weather was dry, and the flames simply ate up everything covering a tract of territory three and three-quarter miles along the lake-front and a mile back into the city."

"I was only a lad when it happened," said the doctor. "Were many lives lost?"

"Considering that it burned out 100,000 people, it is very surprising that not more than 300 perished in the fire; 11,000 buildings went down, including eight bridges and half of the best buildings in the city. It was a terrible disaster, and yet it did more to make Chicago what Chicago is than the greatest benefit that could have been desired by her citizens.'

As they were strolling along, admiring the immense width of the streets, in which four street cars ran side by side, with ample room for the rest of the traffic, they came to the City Hall.

"Something better than the packing-case style of architecture here," said Adiram. "We started to build this six years after the fire, and it has cost us nearly two million dollars."

"Is Chicago as bad as New York?" said Dr. Wynne.

"As bad as New York, sir!" said Adiram, as if he could not trust his ears. "Did you say as bad as New York? Sir, the Chicago Municipality is not perfect, but there is not a town in your country which would not be glad to change places with Chicago in this respect."

RAILWAYS RADIATING FROM CHICAGO.

"In what respect?" said the doctor.

"First of all in the death-rate," said Adiram. "We have built a city upon a bog, and one of the tasks which we had to undertake, about the time when you were fighting your Crimean War, was the hoisting up of the best part of the town about eight feet higher than the level on which it was originally built. We had to put screw-jacks under the foundations and hoist the buildings up to such a level as corresponded to the new grading of the streets. It was an unparalleled enterprise. To build the city was remarkable, but to take out its foundations and hoist its buildings eight feet in the air was a still more remarkable feat. Well, we had hardly accomplished it, when the fire came and burned us up. Since then we have rebuilt the city as you see it. But, notwithstanding the marshes on which we stand, and all the difficulties we have to meet, our death-rate is only twenty-two per thousand, which is lower than almost any city in the world, excepting London. Even London is only a unit or two below Chicago. From a sanitary point of view, therefore, Chicago may be said to stand at the top of the tree."

"But how about crime?" asked Compton.

"Sir," said Adiram, "if we are a little behind London in the matter of sanitation, we are much ahead of her in the matter of police."

As he was speaking they were startled by the clanging of a gong some distance down the street, on hearing which the drivers drew to one side to leave a clear space for what at first Compton and Wynne took to be a fire-engine. On its nearer approach, however, they saw only a blue-painted wagon, drawn by a team of spirited horses which were galloping down the street as hard as any fire-engine. In the wagon were some policemen.

"What is that?" said Compton.

"Oh, that is a patrol wagon," said Adiram, "bringing up officers to where they are wanted. We have got some thirty-five of these in Chicago. They are kept constantly ready. The telephone-call system is so perfect that nothing can happen in any part of the town without its being immediately telephoned to the police head-quarters. This enables us to do with much fewer police than would otherwise be necessary. Every constable knows that if he has a job which is too much for him, he has only to make a call to head-quarters and in a couple of minutes a patrol wagon will be galloping to his relief.' The consequence is that in Chicago, with a population of 1½ millions and an area of 180 square miles, we manage with 2,000 policemen, although we have as motley a population of the scum of Europe as any city in the world. If London were policed at the rate at which Chicago manages, you would have to disband half the Metropolitan constabulary."

"Yes," said Compton, "that is true; we police 5,000,000 of people with 15,000 constables, whereas you police 1½ million with 2,000. At this rate we ought only to have 6,000."

"Yes," said Dr. Wynne. "But what I was meaning was not so much sanitation or police as municipal government. Is Chicago governed by the best of her citizens or the worst? Do the rum-sellers rule the roost, as they do in New York, or is the work of governing the city undertaken by the most public-spirited citizens?"

"Well," replied Adiram, "the proof of the pudding is in the eating of it. There are no doubt things which need mending in Chicago. The clearing of rubbish from the streets and of garbage from the houses leaves much to be desired, and there are here and there blots upon which you can put your finger. But Chicago has a right to be judged by three things. First, that we have the most beautiful system of parks and boulevards of any city on the continent; secondly, that no emergency has ever come upon Chicago with which the municipality has not been able to cope; and thirdly, the unparalleled difficulties which have beset the city have been overcome so economically that the finance of Chicago is a marvel of all those who know the figures."

"And what are these figures?" said the doctor.

"The revenue of the city is about twenty-five million dollars and the expenditure about the same. The debt, however, is the smallest in proportion to the population of any city in the world. Including five million dollar bonds issued in connection with the World's Fair, the city debt is not twenty million dollars, or less than one year's revenue. The real estate property of the city many times exceeds the whole of her debt. The twenty-five million dollars include the whole cost of police, fire department, education, and water."

"Your boulevards are all very well," said Compton, "but they must interrupt traffic terribly."

"It is easier," said Adiram, "to keep business traffic off a boulevard, even if it stretched like your imaginary Rotten Row from the Marble Arch to the Bank, than it is to keep them off the railroads which cross Chicago in all directions. People get used to anything, but they take longer to get used to our railroads than to get used to the perils and the far more fatiguing delays that come from the way in which trains are run at level-crossings right into the heart of the town."

"The railroads made Chicago, they say," remarked the doctor, "and is the clay to grumble against the potter?"

"But," said Mr. Adiram, "they might diminish their blood tax. Six hundred lives offered up per annum constitute the heaviest sacrifice of human beings which Moloch ever exacted from a single city."

"What is that stately building?" said Compton, as a turn of the street brought them in view of an immense and newly erected pile surmounted with graceful pinnacles.

"Oh," said Adiram, "that is one of the handsomest buildings in Chicago. Nothing of the packing-case about that," said he, rather savagely. "That is the Women's Temple which has been put up by the Women's Christian Temperance Union, of which you, of course, have heard. It is the greatest women's association in the world. It is a much more handsome edifice than any other of the same kind, and it is a standing monument of the energy, zeal, and business capacity of the women who built it."

THE WOMEN'S TEMPERANCE TEMPLE, CHICAGO.

THE MASONIC TEMPLE.

"Is there much need for temperance work in Chicago?" asked the doctor.

"Temperance work, sir," said Adiram, "is needed everywhere, especially in Chicago, where the pace is so fast that stimulants are often resorted to as a whip or a whet. You can take a drink more speedily than you can eat your lunch even at Chicago, where the meal only lasts fifteen minutes."

"Have you many public-houses in Chicago?" said Compton.

"Well, sir," said their friend, "we reckon we have about six thousand of them in Chicago. They pay for their licenses about three million dollars a year. Of course our Germans drink endless quantities of beer, and we have forty-three breweries turning out twenty-one million barrels every year."

"How does the price of beer run?" asked Compton.

"Five cents a glass."

"I never saw such a twopenny-halfpenny country as this," said Dr. Wynne; "2½d. in the elevated railway, 2½d. in the tram, 2½d. for a glass of beer; even for blacking your boots, it is always 2½d."

"But as the sun is setting," said Adiram, "you had better be making your way back to the hotel. You are staying at the Auditorium," said he to Dr. Wynne, "are you not? In that case we had better go there by the Masonic Temple and the Tacoma, which is one of our largest sky-scrapers. We will also pass the new public library, and return by the Lake Park."

"The Masonic Temple is large enough in all conscience," said Compton, "but I can't say that architecturally I think it an addition to the beauties of Chicago."

"Stands 260 feet high. and has 20 storeys," said Adiram. "Has an elevator capacity for 40,000 passengers, and a drill-room on the eighteenth story large enough to hold 1,500 people. There is a garden on the roof in which an orchestra plays while refreshments are served. It could not be built much under three million dollars. What more could you desire?"

Compton was silent. To such an argument he could make no reply.

After passing the splendid new library, the party came to the lake front, and sauntered slowly home through a small park, which was little better than a large boulevard by the sea.

The sun had set, and the stars were faintly visible in the sky. There was a slight breeze from the lake not so refreshing as that which is laden with the salt sea foam, but all the same very pleasant. It was with a feeling of complete satisfaction that Dr. Wynne found himself back in the palatial hall of the Auditorium.

"Well," said Mrs. Wills, as he called at her room to bid her good-night; "what do you think of Chicago?"

"I shall sleep without a pillow to-night," said he, "or rather I will put my pillow under my shoulders in order that I may train the vertebræ of my neck to an angle of forty-five degrees, otherwise I shall never be able to see the tops of the buildings."

CHAPTER XIII.—ON THE SHORES OF THE INLAND SEA.

"WHAT a bewildering impression the Great Show leaves upon your mind," said Compton to Mrs. Irwin, with whom he was sitting at dinner in the Palmer. The rest of the company had dined earlier, and the two were alone together, in an arrangement which, if not devised, was at least in no way opposed to the inclinations of either.

THE SEA-GATE OF THE SHOW.

"Then you have been there?" said she "And all by yourself?"

"Yes," he replied. "I wished to see the Fair alone, and receive the impact of its impression without any disturbing influence; so early this morning—early that is for me, although the day seemed well advanced for the multitude of people, who make the streets of Chicago as busy as an ant hill—I walked down to the harbour and took the lake steamboat for the Exhibition. The lake, for anything

that the eye can tell you, might be as boundless as the Pacific. This it is which, to my thinking, differentiates the World's Fair from all the other Exhibitions I have ever seen.

"You have been in most of them then?" said his companion.

"Yes, I may say all of them, including the Moscow Exhibition twenty years ago, which is not usually included amongst the World's Fairs. And none of them could for a moment compare with the Chicago show, for none of them had the inestimable advantage of combining the attractions of land and water. Paris did her best with her miserable little mill stream of a Seine, and the few duck ponds in the grounds. But her best was nothing at all to this splendid expanse of ocean with the great lagoons running inland. There is an illimitable expanse about Lake Michigan."

"I had enough of it," said Mrs. Irwin, "in crossing the Atlantic. I shall go to the Fair by rail. It will save time at least. It is seven miles off, and we can get there in half-an-hour by rail, as against three-quarters of an hour by boat or cable car. The fare, a shilling the round trip, is the same by rail or water, and it is only 2½d. each way by tram. So I save time by avoiding the uneasy deep with its horrible suggestions of sea-sickness."

"You need not fear sea-sickness on the lake," said Compton. "This morning it was like a mirror, and there was hardly any perceptible motion on the magnificently equipped steamer. There is no doubt about one thing, and that is that in the art and mystery of combining luxury with safety on passenger steamers, the Americans beat the Old World folk out of sight. And although you lose fifteen minutes, you gain in that fifteen minutes what you might well cross the Atlantic to see. The approach to every Exhibition is one of its greatest charms. Who can forget the stimulating, eerie attractiveness of the first sight of the cupolas, the pillars and the quaint oriental domes, all flag-begirt and colour-bright, which caught the eye as you crossed the Place de la Concorde in Paris, in 1889? Multiply that effect a hundred times and you have some idea of the fascination that you lose if you go by rail or train to the World's Fair. If you want to see London, see it from the top of an omnibus; if you want to see Chicago, look at it from the deck of a lake steamer. For it is not only the Exhibition that looks well from the sea—I cannot call it a lake, to me a lake is a sheet of water you can see the other side of, and there is no other side visible in Michigan; you start for the outer harbour, the mouth, of which the dirty Chicago river is the narrow gullet. You see the whalebacks steaming into the port, tug boats are plying busily about, in the offing the white sail of a pleasure yacht flaps against the mast. All is animation, movement, life. You think New York is a great shipping port? Chicago last year had fifty per cent. more arrivals and clearances than New York. It is the greatest shipping place in America."

"Are the ships lying in the docks?" enquired Mrs. Irwin.

"Docks!" said Compton. "No, there are no docks in Chicago. Chicago receives its ships as a man receives his meals. You see them go in at his mouth, but he tucks them away out of sight. So it is with Chicago. A dirty river enters the city from the lake, crosses its business quarter at right angles, and then dividing to right and left gives the city a river frontage of a kind of twenty-two navigable miles. All along the banks of the river and its branches you see the huge elevators, or great timber yards where the ships discharge and load their cargo."

"A river in the heart of the city!" said Mrs. Irwin. "Does it not play the mischief with the street traffic?"

"They say there are fifty bridges in Chicago," said Compton, "most of which swing open to allow ships to pass. The delay is, of course, considerable, but the convenience of water transit to your warehouses is so great, Chicago prefers to put up with the loss of time, and is even

"I got aboard the steamer at the dock between Monroe and Van Buren Street. We steamed past the American gun-boat which patrols the lake, and then passing the

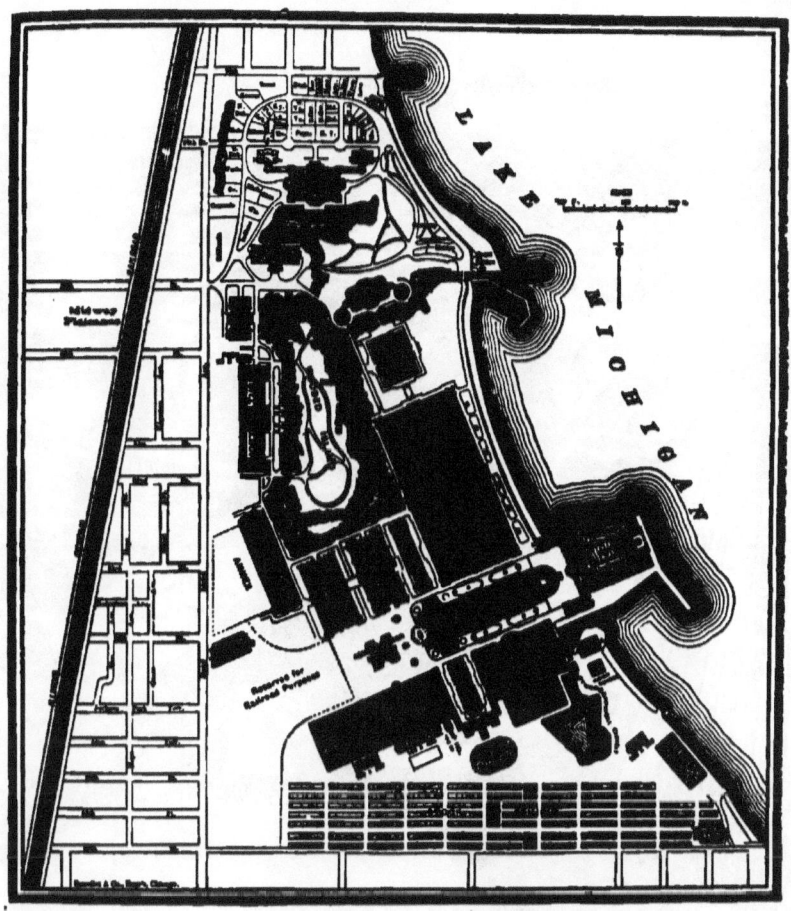

GROUND PLAN OF THE WORLD'S FAIR.

developing a bridge-sense by which the citizen is able to divine beforehand when a bridge is about to open."

"I am glad I don't live in Chicago," said Mrs Irwin, "but tell me about the Exhibition?"

southern breakwater, we steamed along the shore. You see the city, 'the best built and the busiest in the world' they say, stretching mile after mile under its cloud of smoke. The worst of the smoke-pall, however, is left

BIRD'S-EYE VIEW OF THE FAIR.

KEY PLAN.

1. Manufacturers and Liberal Art Building.
2. Agriculture Building.
3. The Great Peristyle and Music Hall Cafe.
4. Casino and Pier
5. La Rabida Convent (Where Columbus Retired).
6. Forestry Building.
7. Dairy.
8. Live Stock Exhibit.
9. Stock Pavilion
10. Machinery Hall.
11. Administration Building.

12. Railroad Buildings.
13. Electricity Building.
14. Mines Building.
15. Transportation Building.
16. Horticulture Building.
17. Midway Plaisance.
18. Washington Park.
19. Woman's Building.
20. Moving Sidewalk.
21. Reserved for States Buildings.
22. Building of the State of Indiana.
23. Building of the State of Illinois.
24. Fisheries Building.

25. U. S. Government Building.
26. U. S. Navy Exhibit.
27. buildings of France, Mexico, Germany, etc.
28. England's Building.
29. Art Galleries and Annex.
30. Building of the State of Washington.
31. Building of the State of Pennsylvania.
32. Building of the State of New York.
33. Building of the State of Massachusetts.
34. Pavilion.
35. Wooded Island.

behind you. Out at sea all is bright and cloudless blue. As you get a mile or two southward the smoke thins, and by the time you catch the first sight of the Exhibition buildings you might almost be in Paris, the air is so clear."

"And were you disappointed? You expected a great deal, and 'blessed are they that expect nothing.'"

"Disappointed!" said Compton. "I was prepared for disappointment, for ever since I landed every second person we had met had performed a special fantasia of his own in praise of the World's Fair. But I was agreeably disappointed in not being disappointed. The first view of the distant domes gleaming like gold in the morning sunlight reminded me of the great cathedral of St. Isaac's, St. Petersburg. When we came nearer and saw the immense white palaces looming large over the trees, I thought of Constantinople with its mosques and its minarets, and when we steamed alongside the Jackson Park, near enough to see the architecture, and the statuary, and the fountains, and the electric launches glancing like dragon flies over the surface of the lagoon, I thought only of Venice. 'She seems a new Cybele fresh from ocean,' but even Venice itself, that fair bride of the Adriatic, must fall back upon the traditions of her history in order to compare with the splendour and the glory of the World's Fair. The white city of gorgeous palaces which they have reared by the shore of the tideless sea is indeed a lordly pleasure-house not unworthy of the dreams of the uncrowned monarchs of this vast and fair dominion."

"Dear, dear!" said Mrs. Irwin, "you are getting quite romantic about the show. Did it look as well when you landed?"

"Nothing could exceed the first impression," he re-

ROUND THE EXHIBITION IN A GONDOLA.

plied. "That vision of radiant loveliness will dwell for ever upon the mind. But it is no small praise to say that a nearer view did not disenchant, although it could not heighten the general effect. Too often, as in Rome for instance, you are charmed with the beauty of a building or a ruin at a distance which, on nearer approach, is as fœtid and filthy as a dunghill. At the World's Fair there is no hideous contrast of that kind. Of course, every Exhibition is more or less like every other Exhibition, and the contrast between this World's Fair and other World's Fairs is greatest when the sea comes in. Machinery in motion in Paris or Chicago is still machinery in motion, and the exhibitions of manufactures, wherever you find them, are more or less like a great dry goods store. But the lagoon and the wooded island in the lake, and the stately buildings, and, above all, the great grey, limitless expanse of the sea stretching far away to the horizon— these have never been seen before in any Exhibition."

"Do you find much difficulty in finding your way about? Most exhibitions are a mighty maze without a plan!"

"Oh, dear no. I had no plan with me. My invariable custom is to lose myself on a first visit. You never get to know where places are so well as when you lose yourself. But in Jackson Park you can never lose yourself for long. For the lake is always there, the smooth sea walk is a landmark that cannot be mistaken. Whenever you doubt, make for the lake; then you can discover where you are. You are always close to water, and whenever you are at a loss, take a gondola."

THE GONDOLIER ROWED ME INTO THE SHADE.

"I like that idea," said Mrs. Irwin. "In most exhibitions you have to walk till you are footsore, or resort to the humiliation of a bath-chair. But to do the World's Fair in a gondola—that sounds lovely. How do you take them?"

"Hire them as you do in Venice. But there are steam and electric launches constantly plying round the exhibition waters. Some, which carry quite a cargo of from thirty to forty passengers, make the round trip, stopping at every landing; others, the express, make the round trip without calling by the way. But the third is the cab of the lagoon, which you engage by the hour or by the trip. I went in a gondola, rowed by a gondolier who, by his make-up, might have been born in Venice, were it not for his delicious Irish brogue. I told the man to take me round slowly, and he obeyed my instructions. I went to sleep in the sun as we neared the convent of La Robida, and the gondolier rowed me round into the shade, and had a comfortable smoke until I woke up, when he took me down the great central lagoon, past the statue of the Republic to the Administration Building; then we turned northward, and circumnavigated the Wooded Island. I then left the boat, and took a stroll down the Midway Pleasance, where all the side-shows are. It will be the most popular part of the Fair. After that I retraced my steps, took an omnibus-steamer at the nearest landing-stage, caught the return steamer at the harbour, and here I am."

"You don't seem very tired," observed Mrs. Irwin.

"No, I am not," he said. "I usually get exhibition headache, but to-day, whether it was because of the air, or the water, or the nap which I had in the gondola, I cannot say; the fact, however, is indisputable, I am as fresh as if I had not spent eight hours in the World's Fair. But where shall we go now we've finished dinner?"

"I want to go to the Libby Prison," said Mrs. Irwin. "Don't be dismayed! It is not a prison really. It is the famous fortress in which the Union prisoners of war were confined. It was brought to Chicago two or three years ago, and set up as a National War Museum."

"Well, said Compton, "as I have spent the day in the great World's Temple of Peace, let us spend the evening in the midst of the memorials of the great Civil War."

Compton and Mrs. Irwin got into a Wabash Avenue cable car, and were soon landed at the castellated gate of Libby Prison.

"How things have changed!" said Compton. "I am not an old man, but I remember when Libby Prison was a name which filled the North with wrath, sometimes too deep for words. It was then the dungeon of the captive in the capital of the Slave State. To-day it is the trophy of the conqueror in the capital of the Free North."

When they were producing the small charge for admission—for Libby Prison, like the World's Fair, and like everything else in Chicago, is a financial speculation—who should come up to the doorway but Mrs. Wills.

She greeted them eagerly. "Oh, Mrs. Irwin," she said, "how glad I am to see you; and you, Mr. Compton, and where is the professor? and where is the good kind doctor?"

At the moment they were passing the entrance. Mrs. Irwin turned deadly pale, and did not answer.

"Dear, dear!" said Mrs. Wills, "what is the matter with Mrs. Irwin? She seems as if she were going to faint."

"It is nothing," said Mrs. Irwin. "Never mind, it will pass. Could you get me a glass of water? I'll be all right presently."

Compton assisted her to a chair, iced water was procured, and Mrs. Irwin said she was better, but there was a scared look in her eyes Compton thought he had seen once before. He did not exactly remember where or when. But it made him uneasy.

"Take Mrs. Wills through the Museum," said Mrs. Irwin. "I will stay here and rest awhile."

Reluctantly Compton obeyed, and soon Mrs. Wills and he were inspecting the thousand and one relics of the great Civil War.

Mrs. Wills, however, cared little for relics of battle-fields. Torn banners did not appeal to her. She had no imagination of that kind. Pictures interested her more for art than for their subject. As for cannon and rifle and bayonet, and all the memorabilia of the hard-fought field,

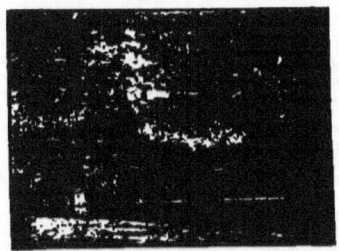

LIBBY PRISON MUSEUM.

she passed by them as if they were wash-tubs by the curb-stone. She was in her cradle when Lee surrendered, and the heroes and glories of the Great Rebellion were almost as shadowy as the heroes and the glories of the Peloponnesian War. She talked more of the doctor than of Grant and Lee. "The doctor," she remarked, "has been about a good deal with my children. He seems very fond of them. Do you know whether he has any of his own?"

Compton laughed. "Not that I know of; never heard of any, although I must say he would be a capital father. But Walter has led such a knock-about life, he has never had time to set up a house for himself."

"You don't mean to say such a charming man has never got married," said Mrs. Wills.

"Ladies," said Compton, "don't seem to interest him—at least, not now. At the University he was the most sentimental young Romeo who ever conjured up a flawless Juliet out of any inanity of girlhood. But when I met him again, he was strangely changed. Why, I don't know. He never opened his heart to me and I never asked him."

"A disappointment, do you think?" said Mrs. Wills.

"I do not pry into the silence of my friends," said Compton; "they are like the tomb, an unbidder foot may raise a troubled ghost, which no enchantment can lay."

"Do not talk of tombs," said Mrs. Wills, shuddering, "the atmosphere of death seems to hang about this place."

"Nonsense," said Compton; "I never saw you looking more radiant since I met you at Liverpool. But the associations of the Museum are depressing. Come, let us go back to Mrs. Irwin."

They turned back, making their way through corridors of relics and trophies, each of which had cost at least one brave man's life, and soon found themselves once more at the entrance. But Mrs. Irwin was gone. They inquired. She had not remained five minutes after they had left her. Wondering at this hasty flight, they took the first car back to the Leland. Mrs. Wills went off to the Auditorium. Compton, ill at ease, and disquieted more than he could say, hurried up to inquire about Mrs. Irwin.

He found her in the drawing-room, pale and weary.

"For Heaven's sake," he said, "what is the matter?"

"I'm sorry," she said; "pray forgive me! It is the curse of my temperament."

"What on earth do you mean?" said he, impatiently.

"I took you at your own request to the Libby Museum, and the moment you cross the threshold you turn faint, and the moment my back is turned you fly off to the hotel. It surely cannot be"—he was going to say "that you are jealous of Mrs. Wills," but he arrested himself in time.

"Don't be vexed with me, Mr. Compton," said she, "I cannot help myself. You have heard about the sixth sense of the psychometrist, by which one can hear and see the sounds and sights which are inaudible and invisible to all other mortals. It is hereditary in our family. Give me the knife with which a murder is committed and I see the face of the murderer, the form of his victim, and hear the fatal blow, and hear the dying groan."

"I understand," said Compton. "I have read Professor Denton's 'Nature's Secrets,' where it is all explained, and where a psychometrist who is given a burnt bean from Herculaneum is able to see the whole course of the eruption which overwhelmed the doomed cities. According to this, every object becomes a photographic negative, which only those who have this sense can develop."

"Yes," said Mrs. Irwin, "it is not only that, but also a phonograph, for you hear the sounds of the vanished voices of the dead. I ought never to have wanted to go to Libby. I remember when I went to the Naval Exhibition at Kensington, and went over the model of the *Victory*, I nearly died. There were so many relics of Trafalgar fight all around that it seemed as if I were actually in the midst of the battle. My ears were deafened with the roar of the cannon. The air was hot and sulphurous with the smoke of powder, and it seemed wherever I went the deck was slippery with blood and littered with the dying and the dead. If I had only remembered that experience I should never have dreamed of going to the Libby Museum."

"But what really happened there?" said Compton.

"I had no sooner crossed the threshold of the Museum," she said, "than I became conscious of being, as it were, in the vestibule of hell. A sense of unutterable despair, of physical exhaustion, and of hot, fevered pain and gnawing hunger, rose up, as it were, like exhalations from a marsh at sunset, and I lost all sight of everybody and everything. In a moment or two the mist cleared before my eyes, and I found myself alone. You were gone, and so was Mrs. Wills. But I was not alone. For defiling before me in dread procession entering into the Libby Fort, I saw an endless throng of war-worn soldiers, haggard, weary, broken-spirited captives, driven within the gates by armed men as cattle are driven into the slaughter-pen by the drover. On and on and on they came in an unending stream. And it seemed to me as if the interior of the fort must have been one horrible reservoir of coagulated horror, of pain, of pestilence, of famine, and of torture, ending only with death. From within I heard despairing prayers, wild blasphemy, bitter curses, and sometimes I thought I heard the death-rattle in the throat of the poor fellows who were still marching, marching, marching in unceasingly to their doom. I bore it as long as I could, but I felt I should go mad if I watched it much longer. So I staggered out into the open, and took the car back to the hotel."

She looked very beautiful as she lay on the couch, her lustrous blue-black eyes seeming all the more magical from their contrast with the pallor of her face.

"Forgive me leaving you, won't you?" she said, with a beseeching smile. "If you knew how much it cost me," she added, with some confusion.

Compton bent over her, fascinated by the glamour of eyes to which the past as well as the future seemed to be unveiled. "My dear Mrs. Irwin," he said, "I think you really must allow me to take you for a drive, it will do you good. Get a warm wrap, for the air from the lake is apt to be chilly after sunset, and an hour in the park will soon set you up again."

"I will try," said she, and taking Compton's arm, she walked slowly to the elevator that whisked her up to her room. Compton remained below, pondering many things.

He was in love with this charming Irish widow. The he now admitted to himself for the first time, not without much misgiving. His heart was gone, but his head was not convinced. He was the heart and head and centre of a world-wide organisation. Was Mrs. Irwin capable of standing by his side? He had considered the question in the abstract long before, and had come to the practical conclusion that no woman of his acquaintance would be other than a hindrance. For with him his work was first, and would always be first. He might love a woman, but he was possessed by his work. If the woman crossed the work, it was not the latter which would give way, so hitherto he had been celibate, and had lived solely for his work. He had conceived a vast scheme compared with which the work of all existing agencies was but sectional and fragmentary, with the exception of the Catholic Church. Even the Catholic Church was less catholic and more sectarian than the dream to which he had consecrated his wealth and his energies from earliest manhood. He was an Englishman; Mrs. Irwin was Irish. He was single; she was a widow. He was wealthy, powerful, the centre of an association as world-wide as the Freemasons, as powerful as the Jesuits. Was she fit to be his partner? Was any woman competent to share his life? Must not the founders of great societies be as celibate as the Popes? The familiar verse of Longfellow hummed in his brain:—

> "'Oh, stay,' the maiden said, 'and rest
> Thy weary head upon this breast,'
> A tear stood in his clear blue eye,
> But still he answered with a sigh,
> 'Excelsior.'"

"Excelsior," he muttered. "Yes, but if he had accepted that maiden's invitation he might have scaled the mountain height safely the following day instead of perishing in the snow before he even reached the hospice in the pass." From which it may be inferred that Compton was badly hit. He resented it.

"Wa, Wa!" cried Clothaire, when the mists of death were dimming his eyes. "Who is this strong one who pulls down the strongest kings?" And in like fashion, Compton could have cried out against this strong one who made mince-meat of his logic, laughed at his resolutions, and compelled him to think much more about the owner of one pair of saucy blue-black eyes than of the myriad multitude of all sorts and conditions of men whom his association was to save.

"I hope I have not kept you too long," said the object of his meditations, as she stepped out of the elevator. She was still pale, but she seemed stronger, and she hardly needed to lean upon his proffered arm, as he conducted her to the hansom in which they were to take their drive.

"By the hour," said Compton to the driver. "To Lincoln Park."

Compton at first was silent. Mrs. Irwin was not in a

humour to talk. The hansom made way across the business block, now almost deserted, to the river. Had they been going to almost any other park they could have driven by boulevard all the way.

Chicago is a city of boulevards. It is villadom democratised. The boulevard is the western substitute for the London square, whose gates and bars are falling before ruthless Demos. If a certain proportion of property holders along any residential street wish to exclude business traffic, they can do so by a simple formality provided it does not lie next to any other such street. Then the Park Commissioners take it in hand, improve its road bed and put up notices, " For Pleasure Driving. No Traffic Teams Allowed," and its inhabitants sleep in peace and dream in comfort. One such pleasure-driving boulevard runs right into the heart of the business quarter from Garfield Park. Imagine Rotten Row rolled out and extended straight to Threadneedle Street !

These boulevards are laid out specially for pleasure drives. There are 100 miles of them already, and more to follow. They are planted with trees and edged with cool green lawns.

Compton began to find the silence irksome. They were crossing the Chicago river. He must say something if only to break the silence.

" Do you see that huge building by the waterside ? " he said.

" Yes," she said, " I see it ; is it a warehouse ? "

" Yes, and no," he replied. " It is one of the wonders of Chicago. I was over it the other day. It is a grain elevator. You know how grain is carried in England, in sacks. They could not do that here. They have not the time. Grain in sacks is a solid ; in bulk it is, so to speak, fluid. These elevators are gigantic grain pumps, built like dredgers."

" How do they work ? " said Mrs. Irwin.

" A great 'm arine leg,' like a gigantic elephant's trunk, filled inside v ith an endless belt carrying buckets, each holding 1⁸ ...s of grain, is thrust down into the ship's hold where the grain is lying loose. The belt revolves. The buckets fill themselves, and are whisked up to the top of the building at the rate of 10,000 bushels an hour. After that it works itself down by gravitation, weighing itself and delivering itself just as it is wanted."

" These Americans are very ingenious," she remarked, " what I cannot understand is why other people are so slow in copying their inventions. But where are we going now ? "

" To Lincoln Park by the Lake Shore drive," said Compton. " It is a lovely view at sunset."

" Why Lincoln Park ? " she asked.

" Chicago calls its parks after presidents. They have Lincoln, Garfield, Jackson, Jefferson, and Washington. I suppose they will now have a Cleveland Park seeing that the president was nominated at a Chicago Convention."

When he was talking of elevators Mrs. Irwin was thinking of far different subjects. She was too astute not to have divined by her own unaided woman's instinct that Compton loved her, but she was not dependent upon her instinct. Mrs. Irwin had developed the faculty of thought-reading to an extraordinary extent, and she was often able, without being in contact with her subject, to read all that was passing in his mind as clearly as if it were written in an open book. When, as in the present case, she was in close contact with her subject, she simply read him through and through. She saw, as in a crystal mirror, the whole confused and confusing discussion that was raging within. He had relapsed into silence again, merely remarking, as they came out upon the Lake Shore Drive, that this was the

most magnificent boulevard in the world, stretching for miles along the very lip of the great lake, and that the mansions of many millionaires studded the wooded country inland. It was a lovely evening, reminding Compton of the delightful drive he had had many years before to the islands at St. Petersburg. But the islands had none of the illimitable swe e,: of ocean expanse which they were enjoying on the Lake Shore Drive.

" I am afraid that you find me a v, r, dull companion," said Compton, after they had driven for half an hour without exchanging monosyllables.

" Not in the least," said Mrs. Irwin ; " nothing entertains me more than your thoughts."

" But," said he, hastily, " I have not said a word for the last half hour."

" I did not say you had," said she. " But you thought the more if you talked the less ; your thoughts were more interesting than your words."

" You speak in enigmas,' he rejoined. " But we are now at the entrance of the park, and there is the great statue of the greatest of modern Americans —President Lincoln."

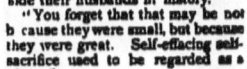

THE LINCOLN
MONUMENT.

" Yes," said Mrs. Irwin, " a striking likeness, they say, and certainly a notable monument. But," she added, quietly, " you are not thinking of the man, but of his wife."

Compton started as if he had been s ung. As a matter of fact, he had been wondering whether it would not have been better if Lincoln had never been married. " I was thinking, it is true," he said, " how small a figure most men's wives cut beside their husbands in history."

" You forget that that may be not b cause they were small, but because they were great. Self-effacing self-sacrifice used to be regarded as a virtue."

" You would hardly say that of Mrs. Lincoln," said Compton, " or of Mrs. Wesley."

" No, perhaps not. Dear me ! " she suddenly exclaimed, what a beautiful spectacle ! "

They were driving past the electric fountain which plays not far from the entrance of the park. There was a great crowd of sightseers, and the sight stopped a conversation which was becoming embarrassing.

Compton, anxious to force some kind of a conversation, talked of the La Salle Monument. " How little," said he, " the original pioneers, French and Catholic, thought of the huge Protestant English Babylon that would rise at the mouth of the Chicago river ! "

" Not much more than Columbus imagined the New World which he brought within sight of Europe," said Mrs. Irwin. " But what a cosmopolitan collection of monuments we have : the Swede Linnæus, the Frenchman La Salle, an Indian group, the German Schiller, while America is represented by Lincoln and Grant."

They drove up to the base of the Grant monument—a colossal man on a colossal horse. Here they got out and walked round the statue. Compton proposed to go in the corridor beneath the arch. " No," said Mrs. Irwin, " the dead are there ! " Compton remembered that three persons had been killed beneath the statue by a thunderstorm in the previous year, when the statue had been struck by lightning.

" How do you know ? " he said.

" I see them," said Mrs. Irwin, quietly.

They went back to the hansom, and resumed the drive

along the lake. It was very lovely, with the lake on one side, darkening after the summer sunset, and the long winding canal on the other. They were silent. Compton's heart was beating wildly, but his head was cool, and the head and heart held a stormy debate. Many a man has held similar debates; perhaps every man has at various

AT THE GRANT MONUMENT.

times discussed the rival claims of intellect and affection. But Compton's case was almost unique for while he discussed, she listened; he did not speak, but she heard. She saw the whole conflict in her companion's mind as the Empress in the Imperial box saw the gladiatorial combat in the Coliseum. She loved Compton had loved him ever since the famous adventure on the iceberg; she knew he loved her, but she did not care to be married unless her husband felt she was helping and not hindering him.

Some women are so lost in the delirium of love and the selfish pride of conquest that the consciousness of their own utter unfitness for the position to which marriage would bring them but adds zest to the pleasure of receiving a proposal. "He loves me, all unfit as I am! He would marry me, although I shou'd probably mar his career!" These reflections were foreign to the nature and experienced mind of the widow. She was a widow, to begin with. She was clairvoyant, psychometric, and a thought-reader. She knew that Compton's life was in his work; if a woman helped his work, she might be happy as his wife; if not—not. No glow of passion, no intensity of affectionate emotion, could stand the test of the daily-renewed disappointment of having to share his life with a woman who did not understand his work.

Watching the tumult of his emotions, Mrs. Irwin was somewhat piqued by noticing how entirely Compton assumed that she was unequal to the post of wife of the Great Head Centre. His heart pleaded that she was charming, that he was in love with her, that his life was very lonely, and that it was time he had a home. But all these arguments were overborne by the imperious representations of the head that Mrs. Irwin was not up to the position of John Compton's wife.

At last she could stand it no longer. Suddenly breaking the long silence, she said—

"Well, Mr. Compton, I am much obliged for your kind feelings towards myself, but if I cannot be your helpmate I do not want to be your wife."

"Really, Mrs. Irwin," he began, somewhat helplessly, for he had just formulated to himself the dictum that no one could do for a wife who was not fit to be a helpmate, but he was unprepared for so frank an answer from the person most concerned.

"Oh, I know what you will be after saying," said Mrs. Irwin, with a gleam of amusement in her eye. "You'd be remarking that I'd better wait till some one asked me to be either one or the other before I volunteer any opinion on the subject. But I have watched you turning it over and over in your mind this whole hour, and I am tired of watching a man's indecision when a woman's concerned. Now, Mr. Compton, you assume that I am not up to the work of being your partner in your great world-wide enterprise. If I am not, say good-bye to me once for all, for if I can

not help you I would not have you—no, though twenty Mr.
Comptons came begging for my hand. But I offer you a
bargain fair and square. You want to marry me, but you
fear I am not up to the work; well and good. I am willing
to come and serve you as your secretary, for twelve
months. If at the end of that time you have proved
that I can be a real help to you, and you still wish to make
me your wife, I will marry you If not, I will leave you,
and for ever. I will never link my life to a man unless he
thinks he will gain strength from the union; no, though
I love him as much as I—I fear I love you."

Her voice trembled as she spoke the last words.
Compton was profoundly moved.

"Mrs. Irwin," said he, "it is I who am unworthy of you.
I misjudged you. Forgive my conceit. You humble me to
the dust by your magnanimity; at the same time that you
reprove me for my unmanly indecision. I have great interests at stake. Were I alone concerned I should never

"Well, Jack," she said.

He folded her in his arms, kissed her tenderly, and then
went to his own room, to dream of the consequences of
that fateful cast of the die.

CHAPTER XIV.—ROSE AT CHICAGO AND NIAGARA.

ROSE rapidly recovered, so rapidly as to amaze Mrs. Julia
and the good Quakeress. In place of listlessness and indifference, she was consumed by a feverish impatience to
get to Chicago Her whole mind fastened upon the single
thought. The World's Fair, with all its wealth of garnered
store, the tribute of vassal continents, the triumphs of art
and invention, all these were to her as nothing, and less
than nothing. The one consuming thought was that
among the midst of the myriads who were visiting the
Great Show, there was her Walter. The great Columbian
Exhibition was a loadstone to her eager soul, but its

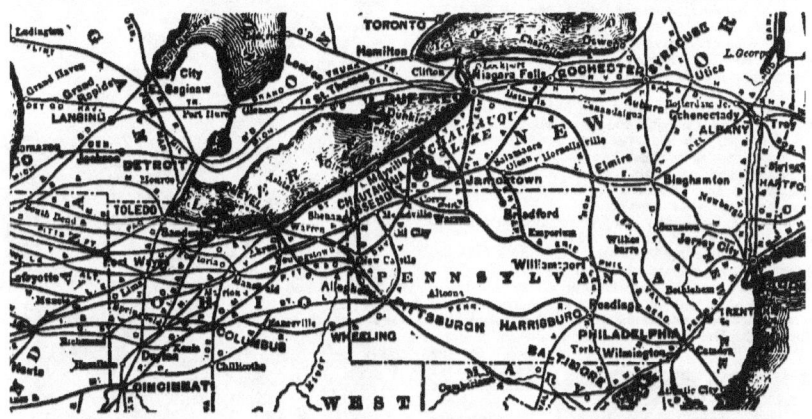

RAILWAY ROUTES TO CHICAGO.

have hesitated, but now I see those other interests would
be safer in your hands than in my own. I do not
make any protestations of my love for you—you read my
thoughts far too clearly to need that; but I will ask you to
be my wife, and not only to be my wife, but to espouse the
cause to which I have devoted my life.'

And Mrs. Irwin, seeing that he was perfectly sincere,
said simply—

"Very well; as you think I can help you, I will try.
When do you think we should marry?'

"The sooner the better," said Compton. "I have no
time for ceremonies. A quiet marriage in Chicago, a fortnight in the Yellowstone Valley, and then back to work.
Will that suit?"

"Perfectly. I am free. I want no bridesmaids and no
trousseau."

"All right," said Compton, and no more was said until
they reached the hotel.

But as they parted at her door, he said to her, somewhat
pleadingly—

"Marion?"

magnetic quality was due simply and solely to the
expected presence there of one person, who, but the other
day, had seemed to be banished as far from her as the
fixed stars, but who had now, in some unaccountably
blessed manner, been brought close to her, almost
within her reach.

Chicago was a thousand miles off, but Chicago was but
a day's journey, or two days' at the most. There were
100,000 persons in the show every day, but if there were
a million she would find him. And when she found him
—ah, then she did not care if she died in the ecstasy of
the longed-for reunion. Such bliss was too exquisite
to be thought of calmly. She would find him—that was
enough.

All day long she thought about it, and lived over again
all the brief and beautiful May day of their lives; all night
long she dreamed it over again, until the seven long terrible
years, during which she had struggled alone against the
awful odds which beset a young friendless and beautiful
girl in London, seemed but as a far-away nightmare,
vanished never to return Sometimes in her dream she

GRAND CENTRAL STATION, NEW YORK.

saw the old vision of Ann Hathaway's cottage standing in strange surroundings; once she thought she saw the wide expanse of a great blue sea, but always, alike on sea or land, the vision never passed until *he* appeared, and after that, she remembered nothing but a joy that passed all understanding, a peace that filled her with a measureless content.

At last the day came when she had made sufficient recovery to make it possible for her to take the cars. The good Mrs. Julia, who had lived over again her own too brief experience of wedded love, had become warmly attached to her lovely *protégé* and when, with many blessings, the good Quakeress bade Rose farewell, Julia accompanied the latter to the car.

"Thou must break the journey at Niagara," said she on leaving. "It is a good half-way house."

"I will not leave her" said Mrs. Julia, "until I see her safe in Chicago, where .er we stop on the road."

They took the New York Central at the splendidly equipped depôt in the city, and were soon hurrying north-wards at a splendid rate on one of the best managed lines in the world. Mrs. Julia in vain tried to attract her attention to the beautiful scenery of the Hudson. Rose looked at it absently from time to time When the train stopped, she was almost angry. "What is it stopping for?" she asked, nor could she be convinced that it was really necessary for the most rapid of express trains to stop once and again in a thousand miles run. When the train moved on, Mrs. Julia, exhilarated with the rapid motion, and delighted with the beautiful scenery of the

THE HIGHLANDS OF THE HUDSON.

Catskills, was in a state of enthusiastic delight. Rose looked at her with pained surprise, but said nothing. After they had been an hour in the car, she said wearily—

"I never knew so slow a train in all my life!"

But the gods, who have not yet annihilated time and space to make two lovers happy, have a gracious anodyne in sleep, and, after two hours' run, Rose lay unconscious as the wheels reverberating beneath. She seemed to hear them echo with monotonous iteration her own thought, "I'm coming, I'm coming, I'm coming."

So far from the train being slow, it was one of the fastest in the world. It was timed to make the run from New York to Niagara, 462 miles, in less than nine hours. To keep up a speed of over fifty miles an hour for a journey of nearly five hundred miles is a record no English

THE DINING CAR.

railway can break and very few American. It was a lovely day. Mrs. Julia, relieved from the care of Rose, who was sleeping tranquilly by her side, abandoned herself to the full enjoyment of the beautifully varied landscape through which they were hurrying. An impression of the size of the new world began to dawn upon her. A run of nine hours, in the fastest train in the world, would not take them out of the State of New York. The English habit of regarding American States as if they were English counties gradually began to dissolve. This State, at least, was as large as a kingdom. From New York to Niagara was farther than from London to Paris or London to Edinburgh. She remembered and began to appreciate the point of the Mormon's remark that the whole of the Land of Canaan would not make more than a cow-lot in the territory of Utah.

The train had left Albany behind and turned westward. Mrs. Julia, looking tenderly at the sleeping Rose, began to wonder whether after all there was any chance of her

NIAGARA FALLS.

attaining her heart's desire. It seemed a forlorn hope. Seven years work strange transformations in a human life. Who could say whether the doctor's heart had remained true to the girl with whom he had fallen in love so long ago? No one could have blamed him if he had wiped her from his memory. She had fled from him no doubt acting under the highest motives, but still, she had left him all these years—what right had she to hope that a man so brilliant and so strong would remain faithful for so long to the memory of what might have been a dead love? Suppose that Rose got to Chicago, and found him indifferent or engaged, or possibly married! Yet the chances were heavy in favour of such a horrible *dénouement*.

To rid herself of these unpleasant fancies, and as Rose began to stir, she awoke her, and, proceeding to the well-appointed dining-car, they passed a pleasant half-hour at the table. The novelty of dinner on the rail, and the care and comfort that surrounded them, had a good effect on Rose, who was better for her sleep. To her companion's surprise, she was not only willing, but resolute to make a stay at Niagara. Mrs. Julia had been very much afraid that she would insist at all hazards upon going through to Chicago. Rose, on the contrary, was full of Niagara, and talked of little else all dinner-time; and after they returned to their own car Rose said to her friend—

"Adelaide, dear, I saw you looked surprised when I spoke so strongly about stopping at Niagara. You don't think it showed indifference to—to—him?"

"Poor dear!" said Mrs. Julia, "I was only too glad to hear you were willing to make the break in the journey."

"But," continued Rose, earnestly, "it is all for his sake I want to see Niagara. In the dear old days, when we used to wander hand in hand by the quiet Avon, he used to tell me about Niagara. He pictured it to me in contrast to the silent flow of the peaceful stream at our feet. Often when I lay awake at night and heard the ceaseless rumble and roar of traffic in the street, I thought of what he told me of the thunder of the great Falls as the cataract plunged over the rocky ledge into the abyss below. It seemed sometimes like a parable of my own life. In my girlhood of poetry and peace, day after day glided smoothly by, unmarked save by the fresh flowers that blossomed in the fields. Afterwards I was but as a foam bubble upon the cataract of life, swept irresistibly along over cruel rocks, around whirlpools, through tortuous gorges, only to be flung headlong into the abyss. From the Avon to Niagara—they are the two poles of my life."

"Nonsense," said Adelaide, caressingly; "you are not going over Niagara. You have had a bad time, no doubt; but you are coming out all safe, never fear."

Rose made no answer, but drawing the doctor's portrait from her breast, she looked at it silently. Then she said, "Niagara will seem lonely without him; but perhaps—" and her face lit up with a glowing light, "perhaps we may come there afterwards."

Mrs. Julia's heart smote her, but she did not speak. Both of them dozed off to dreamland, and when they awoke the engine bell was clanging, and the train slowly running into the station at Niagara.

They were soon in the station, and drove at once to the International Hotel. The murmurous roar of the Falls filled the air. "I know it," said Rose. "It seems like home. I have listened to it so long. And, do you know, I almost seem to hear the tone of his voice in its solemn music."

After tea they rested, looking out from the window of their hotel upon the Falls. They spoke little. The sound of the falling waters filled the air. The sun set in a cloudless sky. After a while the stars came out, and the crescent moon. Then Rose said, "Come!"

"Not now," said Mrs Julia; "it is quite dark and chilly. We cannot go out at this time of night."

"Come!" said Rose, "I want to stand close to the Falls at night. It was always at night I heard their voice in London. I want to see them in the silent moonlight. If you would rather not come, I will go myself."

Mrs. Julia heaped on wraps, and they were soon standing where they got the best view of the Great Fall. For a long time they stood there silently. Then Rose laid her hand on her companion's arm, and they slowly returned to the hotel.

When they reached their room Mrs. Julia was startled by the look of almost ecstatic joy that shone in her companion's face.

"Rose?" she said, inquiringly.

"Oh, Adelaide!" she replied, "we have heard the voice of the glory of God, and—behold!—it is perfect peace."

Next day they took the cars again, and after a long and weary run they reached the great city of the World's Fair. When they reached the Central terminus, Mrs Julia and Rose got out on to the platform. Rose, weak and weary, clung to the kindly widow's arm, not even daring to speak. She was in Chicago at last. Hailing a cab, they drove off to the address of the place where Rose had last heard from her father. Thorne was the name she gave to the cabman. It reminded Mrs. Julia of a point on which she had wished to speak.

"Rose," she said, "your real name and your father's name you say is Thorne. How was it you took the name Thistle?"

"Oh," said Rose, "it was a foolish idea of mine. But I thought the thistle stood for independence. And when I sent him back the little white rose, I tied up with it a tiny little thistle, making a lover's knot with a lock of my own hair. When I got to London I did not want to be traced, so I changed my name, and as I did not know exactly what name to choose, it suddenly occurred to me to call myself Thistle. So I was Miss Thistle for seven years. When I published my "Tales from Fairyland," I took my real name, but the publishers think it a *nom-de-plume*."

"Silly little girl," said Mrs. Julia, soothingly. "Let us hope you have had enough both of thorn and of thistle. You have got to change your name to Wynne next."

Rose flushed and said nothing. Then as the cab wound in and out through the crowded streets, Mrs. Julia saw her companion's eyes glitter with a strange lustre, while her cheeks seemed to become paler and paler. For a whole hour they drove through endless streets that crossed each other at right angles, wondrously uniform. Rose's lip quivered.

"Oh, Adelaide," she sobbed at last, burying her face in her companion's breast, "how shall I ever find him in all this wilderness of a city?"

"Courage, Rose," said Mrs. Julia, "you'll find him, never fear. But first, we've to find your father. We're getting near his district now, and it will never do for his bonny Rose to come to him in this forlorn fashion."

Rose sobbed silently. The long strain had been too great. Expectation, braced up too much, gave way before the stern realisation of unwelcome fact, and her only relief was tears.

At last the cab drew up before a neat two-storey house. Mrs. Julia got out, and inquired if Mr. Thorne lived there. Yes, was the reply, but he was busy at the Expo'. He would not be back till late. Would the ladies come in and wait?

Nothing loth, they paid the cabman, and entered the

house. The house-keeper showed them up to the bed-room, and seeing how weak and exhausted Rose appeared, offered to get them a cup of real English tea, which Mr. Thorne always insisted upon having.

Hardly had they closed the bedroom door, when Rose exclaimed, "Oh, Mrs. Julia, see, there it is ! Just as it was when —" She clasped her friend's hand and pointed to where Mrs. Julia saw prominently on the wall a large photograph of Ann Hathaway's cottage at Shot-tery.

It was some time before Rose was calmed, but she was quite rested and quiet when she heard the familiar steps of her father on the stairs. "Ladies upstairs in my room !" she heard him say. "Who can they be, I wonder ? I don't have any ladies coming to ——" Rose opened the door.

"Oh, father," she said, "don't you know me ?"

would take her to see it next day, but, f r the present, she must rest. She gratefully assented, and, after a few more words, she retired to rest. As she fell asleep, the light of the sunset had not quite died from the western sky, and the last thing she saw was the photograph on the wall.

CHAPTER XV. —THE FIRST PARLIAMENT OF THE ENGLISH-SPEAKING RACE.

"HERE," said Dr. Wynne, as he stepped ashore from the electric launch, which swept him rapidly up the waters of the lagoon to the steps leading to the terrace of the Art Palace, "here, at least, the Princess of Caprera would have found a dome with a figure on it.'

He pointed as he spoke to the colossal figure of Victory.

THE ART PALACE—MEETING-PLACE OF THE WORLD'S CONGRESS AUXILIARY.

Thorne was mystified. He was just from work, with lime-dust on his clothes, and infinite astonishment on his honest face.

"Way, Rose, lass !" he said at last. "My own daughter, where have you sprung from ?"

"Oh, father," she said, as she flung her arms round his neck, and kissed him tenderly, "how glad I am to be at home once more."

For it was seven years since she had been in a house that she could regard as her own. Mrs. Julia pleaded an engagement elsewhere, promised to come back to-morrow, and l ft Rose with her father. Taking the cable car, she returned to the city, and established herself at a modest but comfortable hotel close to the centre of the town.

Rose was too weary to talk much. Her father told her that he was doing well, and had quite recovered from the illness which had led him to cross the sea. He was busy at a special job in the Fair, he said. It was not quite fin shed, although the Fair had been opened a month. He

for which the dome of the Art Building serves as a pedestal.

"Yes, sir," said his American cicerone, "that building is reckoned the most beautiful palace in the Exposition. That is why we crowned it with the winged Victory. It cost 670.000 dols. to build, and covers nearly five acres. It is 500 feet long, and——"

"Have mercy," said Irene, with a gesture of mock dismay. "You Americans are quite too awfully statistical for anything. Ever since I came to this country, I hardly dare open my mouth to ask a question for fear of being drenched with a shower-bath of statistics. I really begin to be afraid, when I remark that the sun is bright, that I shall be told how many miles he is distant, and——"

"How many dollars he cost to put together," said Compton. "Without that item of information, no thoroughbred American ever rests content. It is a splendid illustration of the genius of this wonderful people. They have only one measwa d of value, and they never rest till they have reduced everything to its measurement. The Parthenon is worth so many dollars, the Coliseum so many dollars, the Holy Sepulchre so many dollars, and so forth. What the dollar cannot reckon is not worth reckoning, I guess. But, come along, don't let us begin philosophising. I want to tell you about the World's Congress Auxiliary, which meets here."

"The what?" said Irene. "Why cannot we have a shorter name? All American societies seem to have as many titles as a royal prince or princess has in the Old World. What is the World's Congress, etc.?"

"Madam" said the American, stiffly, "it is what your Tennyson foresaw fifty years ago, when he sang of

"'The Parliament of Man, the Federation of the World.'"

"Yes," said the doctor, good-naturedly, "you are quite right, Jackson, quite right. It is a great idea this of the Auxiliary. Here is the great Senate of Humanity; here we have as exhibits the ideas that shake the world. The great minds which think in every language under heaven will assemble here to exchange their conclusions and to register their convictions, but in whatever language they think, they must express them in English."

"A great parade-ground for all the cranks of creation," said Irene, with a laugh, "with an agenda-paper of 'How to Inaugurate the Millennium.' I don't see exactly how they will ever get through. I am sure it would bore me to death. But here comes my professor. I wonder where he is off to?"

The professor was in high spirits.

"Oh Miss Vernon," he said, reproachfully, "where have you been? I waited exactly five minutes for you before I descended to inspect the sewerage system of the Exhibition. It is delightful. I have been a whole hour watching the functioning of that superb masterpiece of sanitary engineering. If only we could deal as effectively with our human refuse!"

"Why," said the doctor, "what is there remarkable about the sewerage?"

"Sir," said the professor, "it is perfection. I think there is nothing on the surface so wonderful. Six thousand five hundred lavatories empty their contents into a system of drains sufficient to carry off the refuse of a town of 600,000 inhabitants. After passing through precipitation-tanks, everything solid is pressed into cakes, and burned in the boiler-furnaces."

"But," asked Compton, "is there not a great deal of water to be dealt with?"

"No, sir," said the professor. "All the rain-water from the roofs is run directly by pipes into the lake, and all the surface-water is carried off by a second service of pipes. The sewage proper occupies the third set. But now, Miss Vernon, are you not coming with me to the Exhibit devoted to Penology?"

"Well, but first tell me what Penology is?" objected Irene.

"Penology," said the professor, "is the science of dealing with the failures—the refuse of the human race. If you will come with me I will show you the electrocution chair—that triumph of applied science—and you can contrast it with the hangman's rope and the headsman's axe, those effete bungling appliances of the Old World."

"Oh, go by all means, Miss Vernon," said the doctor, laughing. "The professor will show you all manner of horrible things—instruments of torture, model cells, treadmills, cunning little methods of identifying criminals, and, in short, a veritable Chamber of Horrors."

"Well," said Irene, "that is promising; at any rate, it is better than the prosy palaver of your Congress Auxiliary."

As they departed for the Exhibit of the Bureau of Charities and Corrections, the doctor said: "Miss Vernon would go anywhere for a sensation. I should not wonder if she were to end by going to a slaughter-house."

"Oh, dear me, yes," said Compton. "She would go anywhere with him. And the more horrible and improper the place, the greater her craze to go. But, come, let us go into the buildings. I believe I have to take part in the debate."

The three friends entered the spacious place of assembly, which was to be used as a senate house or synod chamber by men of all politics, and nations and creeds. It was, as yet, too early in the year for these World's parliaments to be in session. August and September were to see gathered together in friendly converse representatives of all the creeds by which man has endeavoured to interpret God. Moslem and Christian, Buddhist and Hindoo, with exponents of every other religious and philosophical system, had undertaken to expound in this great meeting-place of nations what they believe to be necessary for the salvation of man. But this great Œcumenical Council of the World's Religions was but one among a series of conferences which were to be held to discuss everything under heaven that is likely "to increase progress, prosperity, and the peace of mankind."

"What's on to-day," said the doctor, lightly, "Industrialism or Spooks, Africa or Catholics, Woman's Rights or the Art of Cooking? I feel my brain bulging at the mere contemplation of their programme."

"To-day," said Compton, gravely, "marks an epoch in the history of our race. For the first time since the great rupture, there are assembled together under one roof representatives from every English-speaking State in either hemisphere."

"What," said the doctor, "a kind of Pan-Anglican Parliament?"

"Sir," said Mr. Jackson, indignantly, "America is too big for your Pan-Anglican. English-speaking is big enough, but Anglican is too scrumpy with pot or with pan."

But now they were within the building, and the conference was about to commence.

It was indeed an imposing assembly. Within the four walls were gathered together the duly accredited representatives of every State in the Union, and of every nation, colony, or dependency of Great Britain. Behind the chair the Union Jack and the Stars and Stripes hung side by side.

The chairman, who seemed to Doctor Wynne to bear a considerable resemblance to Mr. Blaine, was speaking as they entered. He was apparently explaining the difficulties that had to be overcome, before they could secure the attendance of the representatives of all the ocean-severed members of their race.

"With the States in the American Union," he said, "there was no difficulty. Representatives duly accredited were deputed at once to attend this great gathering of the race, and under this lofty dome, surmounted by the winged Victory, there are now gathered together the chosen statesmen of every State and territory from Maine to Mexico. Not one is omitted. Not a single star that gems the diadem of Columbia but adds its lustre to our Assembly. But with the colonies and dependencies that own the sway of Her Gracious Majesty Queen Victoria our task was most difficult. To begin with, how was Ireland to be represented? Was India to be included? Is the Cape Colony an English-speaking state, or the province of Quebec, or the island of the Mauritius? To invite the Imperial Government of Britain was not enough. We wanted to have the representatives of the peoples rather than of the Governments. Endless were the discussions, sometimes not without anger, but ultimately the question was solved by a rough and ready expedient. Every English-speaking community, territory, or dependency was asked to send one representative, and as many more as there were half millions of English speaking inhabitants. Thus India, Ceylon, the Mauritius, the province of Quebec, and the Cape Colony were all represented by two representatives. England, Ireland, Scotland, Wales, Canada, and Australia, one each, plus twice as many delegates as they have millions of population. The choice of representatives was left in all cases to the local governments, in cases where there were local governments, but in the case of Ireland, Scotland, and Wales, the choice was left to the Parliamentary representatives of each nationality. There was a good deal of comment in London over this recognition of nations which had no independent existence under the British State system, but it subsided before long, and we have here gathered together on American soil the first Parliament of the English-speaking world. Our object is simple and eminently practical. We meet to recognise the unity of our race whether under a monarchy or a republic, and we meet to discuss the ways and means by which that unity can be made more manifestly visible and potent for the blessing of the states that are within and of the nations that are without."

"Eloquent old man," said the doctor.

"Hush," said Compton. "Is that Mr. Arthur Balfour who is on his legs?"

The speaker, whoever he was, might easily have been mistaken for the late leader of the House of Commons. He spoke with much earnestness. He said, "Deeply as I deplore the fact that this great assembly should not have met for the first time at Westminster, near the cradle of the Mother of all Parliaments, I rejoice that it has been summoned even although the honour and the glory of the initiative belongs to another land than my own. For of all the duties that lie before us who speak the tongue of Shakespeare and of Milton, the greatest is to heal the schism that has rent our race in twain. Compared with that all other questions are but of the fringe. This is of the essence. But is it possible? Can the memories of the great revolt be effaced? There are some blunders that are irrevocable. It is not enough to deplore a mistake in order to undo its consequences. How often did the prophets of Jehovah deplore the crime of Jeroboam, the son of Nebat, who made Israel to sin! But the fatal rent was never healed. Where shall we find the anodyne that will dull the edge of the memory of ancient injury? How shall we allay the jealousies of a hundred years?"

An irrepressible little man jumped up.

"Carnegie," muttered Compton; "Carnegie of Homestead."

"Mr. Chairman, they did not know everything down in Judee. We need not go back two thousand years for a precedent to paralyse our hopes. Less than thirty years ago this continent was rent in twain by as wide a chasm as ever yawned between nations. Between North and South lay a mountain barrier of a million graves, and the Red Sea of brothers' blood by brothers shed was ten times deeper and wider than that which was filled with the blood shed in Anglo-American wars. But to-day, even the politicians who traded on the bloody shirt are silent. The Union is stronger than it ever was. Americans are prouder than ever of their common flag and their glorious constitution. Why? Because common interest, common sentiment, and, above all, common sense, are stronger than the memory of old feuds or the rancour of ancient prejudice. Has not the time come for a race alliance? Blood is thicker than water, and King Shakespeare more potent for union than poor old George the Third."

"Mr. Chairman," said an Irishman—["Michael Davitt, I think," said Compton *sotto voce* to his American friend]—"the obstacle to the union of the English-speaking race is not George the Third. The salt in the mortar that prevents its binding is the sense of injustice which rankles in the Irish race.

Until you have a hearty union of the Irish and British democracies, there can be no race alliance. Much as I long for peace and fraternity, it must be peace and fraternity based on justice. As long as the Irish are denied the right of self-government enjoyed by every other English-speaking community in the whole world, so long will you find every Irishman everywhere active against that reunion which we meet to promote.

"Permit me," said a silvery voice, which was recognised as that of the wife of the Governor-General of

Canada, "permit me to express my entire accord with the last speaker. Were I Irish I should say the same. But the union of the democracies is at hand, and no one has done more than my friend to promote it. Nor is it only the democracy monarch and peer alike bow to the inevitable—and Britain on the verge of federation gladly proffers the right hand of fellowship to federal America."

"Home Rule," said the next speaker, who the doctor said reminded him of Sir Hercules Robinson, "Home Rule is the key of the situation. As an empire Britain must federate or perish. But without the Irish at Westminster, the House of Commons would never consent to devolve any of its powers on subordinate assemblies."

"No," said an American senator; "it is too late. Never can America and England again enter the same political system. Westward sweeps the star of the empire. Let the effete monarchy decay. The future is to the Republic."

A venerable-looking Australian stood up to speak.

"Why, bless me," said Compton, "if that isn't Sir Henry Parkes."

"Mr. Chairman, I am an Australian. We are from the newest of the new worlds peopled by the English race. You are celebrating your four-hundredth birthday. We have hardly completed a century of growth. We are the land of the Morning Star as well as of the Southern Cross, and denunciations of effete monarchies do not trouble us. We are republican in heart and in head, not-

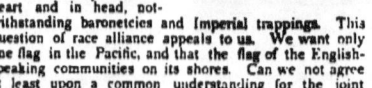

withstanding baronetcies and Imperial trappings. This question of race alliance appeals to us. We want only one flag in the Pacific, and that the flag of the English-speaking communities on its shores. Can we not agree at least upon a common understanding for the joint policing of the Pacific?"

"This is a practical question," said a New Yorker, on the Chairman's right. "We want a regular Court of Appeal; a permanent court to settle the questions constantly cropping up between us. Why should we always be improvising arbitration courts? Why not rig up a court once for all which would sit as regularly as the supreme courts, and to which all disputes about fish, seals, etc., can be relegated? Then there are all the international questions, such as patents, copyright and commercial law. Why not have a joint committee to endeavour to bring about some uniform system? And finally there is the question of policing the seas. Why should we not agree to regard the Stars and Stripes and the Union Jack as one flag against any foreign enemy?"

"Because said a stalwart-looking stranger, immediately before the chair,

"because you Americans have not a big enough Navy to be able to do a fair deal with John Bull. If we are going to have a partnership at sea, let the partners contribute equal numbers of ships to the pool; otherwise, it is not fair. But it is not only on the sea we need the alliance. We need it in China on land, and in Africa. We need it everywhere."

"Who is he?' said the doctor.

"Don't know," said Compton; "but it sounds like Mr. Rhodes."

"You talk of language as if it were the only bond between us. It is a good thing, but it is not the only thing. Not by any means. What does the English-speaking man stand for? A common language? Much more than that. He stands for industrialism as opposed to militarism, for peace as opposed to war, for liberty as opposed to despotism, for order as opposed to anarchy, for local self-government as opposed to centralisation, for civilisation as opposed to barbarism. I do not pose as a religious man, nor is this a church meeting, but the English-speaking race has a creed which it holds, whether it is English or American, in the unity of the faith. Why, then, should we be divided? The work which we have to do is to maintain a Roman peace among the dark-skinned races of the world, to open up Africa to civilisation, to give the best races room to grow by securing them the prior right to the best of the unoccupied lands of the world, to establish in the presence of hostile nations and jealous empires a moral force with sufficient strength at its disposal to boycott the rest of the world into peace. All this lies within our grasp if the crime of George the Third can be undone; all this is impossible if the centrifugal tendency of the colonies and commonwealths is allowed full play. You in this country have solved the difficulty for all dwellers between the Atlantic and the Pacific. The race has now to solve it over a wider area, in many lands, lapped by many oceans. The same Imperial instinct which led the heroes of your Civil War to stake the fortunes of the Republic on the suppression of the Rebellion has now a greater opportunity of asserting over a wider area the same great law of unity and peace as opposed to anarchy and war. We stand at the watershed of our destinies. It is for us to decide whether it be for peace or war, for union or for anarchy, for the arbitrament of the sword or for the supreme authority of law and justice. In the old country, while our statesmen are squabbling about the repair of the village pump, the Empire is slipping from their grasp. Few among them will open their eyes even to the federation of their own half of the English-speaking world. To them the federation of the race is the wildest of dreams. The chance which was ours is now passing from us, and America may seize the sceptre which is slipping from our nerveless grasp."

The next speaker was a smart dapper man of middle age, with somewhat of a metallic ring in his voice, and a jaunty, self-complacent air in the tilt of his nose and the pose of his glass. "I differ from the gentleman who has just sat down,' said he, "in thinking that the old country is played out. If he confines his observations to the men who are now at Downing Street I fully agree with him, but they represent only a minority of the people of England, and hold power only by the support of those whose heart's desire is not

for union, but for dismemberment. If you look beyond Downing Street to the heart of the great English people you will find no shrinking from our destinies. No, gentlemen, the heart of England beats at Birmingham, and Birmingham is ready to-morrow not merely to federate the British Empire, but to lay down the laws upon which the federation of the world will be accomplished. It is as easy as A B C. You have only to expand the principle of the Birmingham Caucus, and the thing is done. English or American, Scotch or Australian, it is all one. The same principles are universally applicable. I wo .ld suggest that a Commit ee be appointed by this Congress which shall be instructed to draw up a scheme, hereafter to be submitted to the representatives of the states and colonies here assembl.d, with orders to report to a Conference to be held in London early next year. I say in London because the movement which has begun upon American soil can only find its natural development in the country from which we all sprang. By that time I believe you will find men in power at Downing Street who will cordially welcome any attempt to realise the world-wide aspirations of the English-speaking race."

"I come from Queensland," said the next speaker,  "and represent nearly a million square miles of territory, upon the edges of which my fellow-subjects are building up a commonwealth not unworthy to rank in line with the best of those represented here to-day. The English race in its old home may have become, as some of the speakers suggest, somewhat effete, but in Australia the British lion is renewing its mighty youth, and its roar will be heard by the American eagle from its eyrie in the Rockies. We may divide Queensland and subdivide it, or we may federate the whole of Australasia into a great dominion ; but whether we seem to step backwards or forwards, our heart is set upon the great scheme which has been so eloquently laid before us to-day, and, whoever hangs back, our motto is ever, 'Advance, Australia.'"

"Permit me to say a word," said the next speaker——
["I think," said Compton, "it is Mr. Bryce, of the 'American Commonwealth,' but how he got over here from his ministerial duties I can  not imagine. But whoever it is, he seems to have the ear of the Congress."]
"It is much to be regretted if this Congress, representing so many states, kingdoms, republics, and commonwealths, should be distracted by any references to domestic disputes by local partisans. Let us take the broadest possible view of things. In England we have been discussing for some time what could be done towards the federation of the British Empire. Many of the principles which have been threshed out in discussion at the Federation League are equally applicable to the Race Alliance which has been discussed to-day. The essentials of a united federated commonwealth may be thus briefly defined : —(a) That the voice of the commonwealth in peace, when dealing with foreign powers, shall be, as far as possible, the united voice of all its autonomous parts. (b) That the defence of the commonwealth in war shall be the common defence of all its interests and of all its

parts by the united forces and resources of all its members. In order that the commonwealth may speak with the greatest authority to foreign nations, there ought to be a body in which all its autonomous parts are represented. The necessity of the maintenance of the sea communications of the commonwealths is most absolute. The primary requirements of defence are therefore sea-going fleets and naval bases. It follows that we can best attain a practical sense of the unity of our race by an understanding by which the naval forces of the Empire and the Republic should not be regarded as two, but as one, under certain contingencies which must be carefully defined beforehand. If, for instance, the example of the Triple Alliance should be followed, the attack by any foreign power upon any of the members of the Alliance would be considered as directed against all its members. It might be further extended so as to deal with certain specific cases. It might be defined as an Anglo-American concert, which would be responsible for the policing of the Pacific, the maintenance of the treaties with China, and the protection of Anglo-American interests in South America. The declaration that ' blood is thicker than water' was first used in relation to our naval co-operation in the trouble with Japan. It is a principle upon which a great superstructure may yet be raised. The comparative weakness of the American navy is a diminishing quantity, and every fresh ship that is launched renders an alliance upon a footing of perfect equality more possible and more desirable. Each power would be free to use its navy in its own interests, but both together would operate as a united force in the defence of our territories from un-provoked invasion, in the policing of the sea, and in the protection of all unoccupied islands against occupation by non-English-speaking Powers. To this could be adde l the suppression of the slave trade and piracy, and the regulation of fisheries, seal and whale-catching, and all other occupations carried on in the high seas. There are many other points to which the attertion of this Congress might be drawn, but I confine myself to the one paramount and most practical step, which would make the Stars and Stripes and the Union Jack practically one flag as against the common enemies of the common peace."

Compton, seeing that no one else rose to continue the discourse, sprang to his feet, and, speaking with much fervour, addressed the chair:
"Despite what has been said by the gentleman from Birmingham and the excellent and practical remarks of the last speaker, I must ask you to look at the facts as they are. We are told that, although the present English Administration may not rise to the height of its great opportunies, its successor will be more in accord with our ideals; but let us look at the facts. Take the English-speaking communities wherever they are to be found, and ask, without prejudice or prepossession, to what type do they most naturally approximate. Is it the type of the Monarchy or the type of the Republic ? I see representatives here from Australasia, from South Africa, and from Canada. Is there one colony on the whole expanse of this planet which has chosen the institutions that differentiate England from the United States? What are these institutions ? First, the Monarchy ; secondly, the peerage ; third, the Established Church. The English-speaking man goes forth into all continents to found new commonwealths, and wherever he goes the polity which he establishes is the polity, not of the United Kingdom, but of the United States. It is unpleasant for an Englishman to have to say this, but it is absurd to refuse to see the facts. The Australian is no more monarchical than the Kentuckian ; the South African would as soon think of establishing a peerage as the New Yorker ; and

everywhere the principle of the Established Church is scouted, even by those who themselves belong to the Establishment in the old country. Nor is it only in these three points that Greater Britain under the Union Jack approximates to the United States rather than to the United Kingdom. The fiscal system of the colonies is like that of the United States. The Protective Tariff may be an incident of growth, but none the less the fact remains that therein colonial Britain approximates to the United States rather than to the United Kingdom. There is more similarity between the colonies and the United States than between the colonies and the Mother Country. Then again, the force of numbers is on your side. You are already sixty millions; in twenty years you will be 100 millions. The attraction of such a homogeneous mass must necessarily be greater than that exercised by a population of half that number struggling for existence on a small island off the continent of Europe. The attraction will be first felt commercially, then politically. Already you are sweeping our West Indian islands into the orbit of your Zollverein. Canada will follow suit; and after Canada, what next? There is nothing to hinder your constitution being extended to include every self-governing colony under the British flag; nay, Great Britain itself could come into the Union if it so chose. Already we have had discussions as to whether or not Ireland might not find Home Rule sooner under the Stars and Stripes than under the Union Jack. On the other hand, the British constitution makes no provision for the entry of other states. If the American Republic were to sue, hat in hand, for admission into the British Empire, there exists no means by which you could be accommodated. It is otherwise with you. Hence it seems inevitable that the hegemony of the English-speaking race will belong to you and not to us. You must increase; we must decrease. The Victorian age marks the culmination of the glory of Old England; the future belongs to the New England beyond the seas. The fact that this Congress should be held in Chicago under your presidency is a significant illustration that the sceptre of the race has dropped from our hands, and that the leadership is ours no more."

The deep emotion under which Compton spoke produced a marked effect upon the assembly. The Chairman, in closing its deliberations, said:

"Whatever might be the ultimate development, no one would dispute that if the Monarchy and the Republic were to join hand in hand in promoting the federation of the race, they would join as equals; nor was there any disposition on this side of the Atlantic to dispute the traditional right of the Mother Country to the first place, *primus inter pares;* but," he added, significantly. "if there is no move on the other side, the ball lies at our feet."

CHAPTER XVI.—THE WHITE CITY OF PALACES.

"You talk about the English-speaking world," said Dr. Hedwig, a keen, sarcastic son of Israel, who had joined the little party. "and you do well; for it is all talk, and if you do not talk there is nothing else left."

"Really, Dr. Hedwig," said Compton, "you can hardly say that in the presence of such a marvellous monument of the world-wide extent and influence of that world as the Exhibition which we are visiting."

"The Exposition," replied Dr. Hedwig, "is the creation chiefly of Chicago, and Chicago is rather German than English. The architecture is an imitation of Rome, with occasional borrowings from mediæval Italy or Germany, but what is there English about the show? Not even its title; for you see, instead of Exhibition, they call it Expo-

DR. HEDWIG.

sition, which is French and not English. But the most distinctive note of the English race is Sabbatarianism. You will find it in London and in Toronto. You will not find it in Chicago. Sunday is the best day for the theatre and the saloon, and the World's Fair would never have been closed on a Sunday if the decision had been left to Chicago.'

"So," said the professor, "the net result of your observations is that Chicago is not to be the capital of the English-speaking race in place of London dethroned?"

"Chicago," said Dr. Hedwig, "may be the new Rome; it will never be the new London. But see, here we are at the Exposition.

Nothing can be more admirable than the way in which the approach to the Exhibition by the railway is contrived. The great Administration Building, which recalls the splendid central dome of the Paris Exhibition of 1889, was built with the express object of being a worthy porch to the World's Fair. This is the Gate Beautiful of the modern Temple which has been reared on the shores of Lake Michigan for the worship of the Time Spirit. It is, according to the plan of the framers of the architectural plan, the ceremonial vestibule of the Exhibition, and it was planned in order that visitors might be appropriately introduced into the old world of art of which the New World of the West at present knows little.

As the little knot of friends passed under the Civic Temple, Dr. Hedwig called their attention to the skill with which the device of Wren had been used in constructing an inner lower dome, 95 feet short of the gigantic dome which rises 275 feet in height, as the monumental gateway of the World's Fair.

"The biggest dome in the whole earth, except that of St. Peter's at Rome," said Hiram Jones, an American acquaintance. "Mr. Hunt, of New York, has beaten every one except Michael Angelo, and if the Pope comes to Chicago he will find a dome near to his new Vatican only 20 feet less wide than that on which he looked this morning. I guess there is not so much gold on Michael Angelo's dome as there is upon Mr. Hunt's."

As they passed the building, they saw before them one of the most brilliant and effective bits of architectural theatricality that has ever been conjured up by the Aladdin's lamp of the modern showman. It was the Grand Court of the World's Fair. It deserved its title.

"Chicago,' said the professor, "has astonished the world. Here she has had the finest opportunity of making a fool of herself that a city ever had, and she has not done it."

"No," said Dr. Hedwig, "but how has she avoided it? By eschewing all originality, and severely following classic models. Chicago, the city of sky-scrapers, is in this court conventionality itself."

"Classic and conventional," said Compton, 'it may be, but it is beautiful. It is imposing. Never had any previous Exhibition so magnificent a chance, and Chicago has made the most of it."

The scene certainly was very lovely. On either side rose great palaces, which, if they had been executed in marble instead of the convenient and economical staff, would have been worthy of the palmy days of Greece and

Rome. As the eye wandered down the court, there was nothing to mar the sense of proportion, nothing to jar upon the sense of colour. Down the centre, flanked by the water's edge, were thronged with hundreds of visitors, who had just disembarked from the electric launches which were skimming the water, or from the

THE VESTIBULE OF THE WORLD'S FAIR.   THE ADMINISTRATION BUILDING.

terraces bright with shrubs and gay with flowers, stretched the great basin, an arm of the lake whose grey waters formed an illimitable background, reaching to the horizon. Spacious flights of stone steps, leading down to gondolas which sleepily sauntered down the canals that pass under the monumental bridges to the right and left. The long arcades of the palaces devoted to Machinery and Agriculture on one side, and to the Liberal Arts and

Electricity on the other, sheltered the passer-by from the glare of the sun. A great fountain made rippling coolness in the air round the bronze galley of Columbia, while an austere and colossal statue of the Republic, with both hands raised on high, towered aloft on a pedestal at the other end of the great basin. Beyond the Republican Colossus was a court enclosed by a peristyle, or double open colonnade, like that of St. Peter's, only that Chicago adheres to the universal rectangle, while Rome prefers the more graceful curve. The majestic towers, the graceful domes, the colonnaded pavilions, the statue-crowned columns, and the groups of emblematic sculpture, all executed as it were in mellowed ivory, with the background of the sky and the lake, combined to make a scene of

tical lesson to American architects on the value of strict subordination to the orthodox conventionalities of the schools. American architects have too often the immense audacity of ignorance and are so apt to design buildings all out of their own heads. It was thought a good thing once in a way, to show these bold experimentalists that beautiful effects can be obtained by adhering to the purely classic models."

"If you want originality,' said Compton, "you will find plenty of it at the other end of the Fair. Go to the various buildings put up by the States beyond the Art Palace; or, better still, go and study the barbaric monstrosities of the South American Republics, and you will come back grateful that in the main buildings there was some higher

THE MACHINERY HALL.

beauty and harmony which had never before met the eye of the Western World.

"It is a symphony in colour, an architectural revelation," said Adiram, who had been reading the *World's Fair Illustrated* all the way down in the train.

"Say, rather," sneered Hedwig, "the apotheosis of stucco. 'No doubt it is a revelation to those who have never seen anything better in the shape of architecture than the bloated packing-cases and overgrown monstrosities of Chicago. But an imitation can hardly be a revelation."

"A truce to your sneers, Dr. Hedwig," said Compton, "these buildings are a glory to Chicago, and an object lesson to the whole world."

"I was talking to one of the architects yesterday," said the professor, "and he told me the reason why they adhered so closely to classic models was to give a prac-

canon of art in the mind of the architect than a whimsical straining after originality."

"Come, now," said Adiram, "let us look at the biggest building in the show—the building of Manufactures and Liberal Arts." Suiting the action to the word, he led the way past the buildings of Machines and of Electricity, and came to the south front of the Manufactures and Liberal Arts Building. Entering, they were under the largest roofed-in section of space to be found on this planet. Adiram was lost in wonder and amazement, and kept on reeling off endless figures which to most of those who heard him conveyed no conception as to the real dimensions of the place.

At last Dr. Hedwig interposed, "Really, my good friend, you are wasting your figures. We are quite willing to admit that they have used 17,000,000 feet of timber, and

12,000,000 pounds of steel in putting up this building, but we are no wiser at the end of it. Let us have a look round. Your millions confuse us."

The hall inside was well worth examination. The Machinery Hall of the Paris Exhibition four years ago was the biggest thing of its kind in its day, and was much admired on account of its size. But when it comes to a question of bigness, no American will permit himself to be beaten. The visitors were told until they were sick of it that they could pile the pyramid of Cheops inside the building without interfering with the galleries, that it was twice as large as the Cathedral of St. Peter's, that it was four times as large as the Coliseum, which seated 8,000 persons. Another curious method of impressing its dimensions upon the mind is to say that eleven *Majestics* could be moored side by side and leave room to spare. The ground covered by this building is about 30½ acres, and to secure the wood for this huge building 1,100 acres of Michigan had to be denuded of its pine trees.

"You are staying at the Auditorium, are you not?" said Adiram.

rated, 18,000 of which are used for electrical purposes. The boilers are fed with oil.

After seeing the Power House, the party took the Electric Elevated Railway which runs through the grounds for about five miles. They passed in rapid succession the Great Transportation Building, the rear of the Horticultural and Woman's Buildings, then, rounding the extreme northern limit of the park, they came back and descended on the Government Piazza between the National Buildings and the Naval Exhibit. Lunch-time had arrived, and they made their way to the Clam Bake. They were fortunate enough to obtain seats before the crowds began to come in.

"The restaurant capacity of the Exhibition is," said Dr. Hedwig, "only 30,000 an hour, and as there is a minimum attendance of 100,000 a day, it takes over three hours for them all to dine if they dine comfortably in an hour, but Chicagoans dine much more rapidly."

"Well, what do you think of the Exhibition?" said Adiram to Compton.

"I am beginning," said he, "to get the Exhibition headache. The show is beautiful, and gigantic, but although

MANUFACTURES AND LIBERAL ARTS.

"Yes," said the doctor, "and a fine building it is."

"Sir, you could put twenty Auditoriums upon this floor."

After a time the doctor and his friends would not admit that anything was big, because whatever the object might be whose size they admired, they were always told how much larger this building was than the edifice of whose dimensions they had spoken with admiration. The building is lit with 10,000 electric lights, and when the building was dedicated last October it was seated for 125,000 persons.

"There are eleven acres of skylight," began Adiram. "Large as the building is, we could have filled a much larger building if we had had room. You might spend a lifetime here studying the various products of the manufacturing ingenuity of mankind."

"As we have not a lifetime to spare," said Dr. Hedwig, "we had better not trouble about the exhibits, but take a rapid survey of the grounds. First of all, let us retrace our steps, and go to the place where the power is generated."

Passing through the Machinery Hall, they came to the Power House, where is established the largest engine in the world. Here 24,000 horse-power was being gene-

colossal it is not monstrous. The park is laid out to great advantage. If you leave out the half-dozen large buildings on either side of you, you still have sufficient diversity to satisfy the most exacting critic. A more beautiful Exhibition I have never seen, and it quite comes up to the descriptions with which we are all familiar."

"An Exhibition like this always oppresses me, and yet it is an enormous stimulus to the imagination," said Dr. Wynne. "Like some magician's wand, it calls into visible and palpable existence before our eyes, oblivious of obstacles of time and space, the immense panorama of the labours of man."

After lunch they walked down to the Naval Exhibit.

"This," said Compton, "interests me more than most things in the Exhibition, for the development of the self-consciousness of the race is measured by the interest it takes in its Navy. I am glad to see that this exhibit is one of the most popular in the show."

The Naval Exhibit consists of the complete reproduction of an American line-of-battle ship, and the odd thing about it is that it is made of cement and bricks. Its larger guns are also quakers. They are, however, sufficiently life-like to deceive any but those who have to fire them. Apart from the manner of its construction, the ship is, both in the interior and exterior, an exact *facsimile* of a man-of-war. She has a regular crew, but the space that would be occupied by the engines in the real ship is devoted to Naval exhibits. While not possessing the attractiveness of the *Victory* at the Naval Exhibition held at Chelsea, it is still more instructive, as enabling the continuous swarm of visitors who stand in queue, an opportunity of seeing the conditions under which modern naval warfare is waged.

Close to the Naval Exhibit is the British Pavilion, Victoria House, the headquarters of the British Commission. It stands nearest to the lake of all the buildings in the show. It is an excellent example of an old English house adapted to modern requirements.

The party then separated, each to see that which most interested him in the show, and promised to compare notes when they returned to the Casino Restaurant for dinner.

Compton spent the afternoon in visiting the build-

THE BRITISH PAVILION, VICTORIA HOUSE.

ings put up by the States for the convenience of their citizens, and occasionally for the display of the special products of the State. Here, indeed, free scope had been allowed to the fancy of the architect. Every kind of building is represented in these palatial clubhouses, and some of them, like California, are miniature exhibitions. For the most part, however, they are no more than pavilions with conveniences for reading, resting, and correspondence. The Illinois exhibit is the largest, as befits the State in which the Exhibition is being held. After Illinois comes California, whose building is in some respects even more interesting. It is the reproduction of the old Church of San Diego, with its towers—an interesting reminder of the time when Spain had something to say in North America. The Californian building has a garden on the roof, and is cooled with fountains. Its exhibition is rich in fruit, which is the speciality and glory of the Pacific Slope. Another curious exhibit is that of Florida. It is a reproduction in miniature of Fort Marian in St. Augustine. It is the oldest structure in North America, as it was built in 1620, and is the only mediæval fort left in the country. For 100 years its 100 guns and garrison of 1,000 men defied every attack. Although the Spaniards have long left this bastion, Fort

Marian deserves the title of La Pucelle, for no besieging force was ever able to storm its walls. Another interesting historical building is that of Massachusetts, which is a reproduction of John Hancock's residence on Beacon Hill, Boston. Still more interesting is the reproduction of Independence Hall, which is the exhibition of the State of Pennsylvania. It is the exact reproduction of the old hall, and the identical Independence bell hangs in the tower. Another notable building, one of the largest in the grounds, is that which Washington has erected in order to show its timber resources. The first tier of logs upon which the building is raised are 121 feet long and four feet in diameter. Idaho has a very pretty châlet. New York has an Italian villa, with a large relief-map of New York on its basement. New Hampshire has a Swiss cottage; while Nebraska indulges in classic architecture of the Corinthian order.

Compton wandered in and out among the state buildings in order to impress his mind with the conception of the fact that the American Republic is a federation of independent states. It is a fact which an Englishman is slow to learn. The very conception of states as separate national entities is foreign to his mind.

After a time Compton, feeling tired, made his way to the Arts Building, which lies north of the lake, and the State Buildings. He rested and watched the endless flow of human beings who always find the art galleries of an exhibition the most popular part of the great show.

Dr. Wynne sauntered through the Fisheries, admiring the enormous variety of fresh-water fish which disported themselves in aquaria containing 140,000 gallons of fresh water. Salt-water fish were less numerous and more familiar. They had 40,000 gallons of water, which was brought from the Atlantic seaboard. To economise carriage the salt water was condensed to one-fifth its bulk; 8,000 gallons of concentrated brine were brought by rail and then filled up to their original volume with fresh water. From the Fisheries he walked down to the Government Exhibits, where he was chiefly interested in studying a raised map of the United States in plaster. Being 400 feet square it enabled him to see the curvature of the earth, the height of the mountains, and all the leading topographical features of the country. It is only by studying such a relief map that we can form any idea of the real appearance of a country.

After a time Dr. Wynne got tired even of the Government Exhibits and crossed over to the wooded garden in the lagoon. Here he loitered in the shrubbery around the Japanese temple which has been reproduced as the gift of the Japanese Government to the city of Chicago. Japan has taken great pride in the Exhibition, its appropriation being £125,000, a larger sum than was voted by any other government except those of France and Germany. Japan not only rears her temple in the World's Fair; she sends 2,000 Japanese students to travel round and study for themselves the actual results achieved by modern civilization, not in the Show but in the daily life of the Republic. At the other extremity of the Wooded Island, the rose garden was laid out—with its 50,000 rose trees. But the whole island was one brilliant scene of floral beauty. Ten of its dif-

THE FISHERIES BUILDING.

teen acres are laid out in flower beds, to furnish which the loveliest treasures of Flora's garden have been despoiled. And there again the unique character of the World's Fair, the combination of land and water, has been made the most of. The waters of the lagoon are only one degree less beautiful than the shores. The island is simply encircled by water-lilies of every description. The air was heavy with fragrance of roses and lilacs. The rhododendrons are just beginning to flame into colour. "This," said the doctor to himself, "is surely the paradise of the World's Fair. It is the Isle of Calypso without the goddess," and he sighed as he thought of Rose.

After crossing the bridge to the smaller island on which was exhibited a Hunter's Camp, the doctor went back the whole length of the Wooded Island to the north end of the lagoon to one of the most interesting exhibits of the Show. This is the Indian Encampment. Here are located the representatives of the red men who, when Columbus set sail from Palos, roamed in undisputed ownership over the whole continent. It is but a remnant of the vanishing race that furnishes the Indian Exhibit. The utmost pains

have been taken to make the exhibit characteristic and complete. At the extreme north end of the lagoon you come upon the tents and houses of the Esquimaux and Canadian Indians, among the stunted pines and firs of the snowy north. Next to them are the Indians of the temperate zone, while at the southern end, among tropical palms, are the Indians of Central and Southern America. Here we have representatives of every existing tribe, living as much as possible as if in their original habitat, braves and squaws with their little papooses carrying on the industries of the wigwam. Among the most interesting of the Indian groups is an encampment of Carib Indians, the sole representatives of the populous nation upon whom the Spaniards fell like a thunderbolt, desolating and destroying to the verge of extirpation. "It is like a Roman triumph," thought the doctor. "Civilization, like the Cæsars, is not without her Tarpeian rock."

It was a welcome relief from the sombre reminiscences called up by the spectacle of these scanty remnants of a race which once held a continent in fee to enter the spacious, bright edifice known as the Woman's Building.

WOMAN'S BUILDING.

This structure, designed by a woman architect, is the first in any World's Show that has been dedicated to the art, the industry, and the invention of woman. The Woman's Building, of which Mrs. Potter Palmer is the presiding genius, is the social headquarters of the fair sex. It is beautiful within and without, with gardens on the roof, where, beneath spacious awnings, you can lounge and gossip and take light refreshment, and look down the ever-changing kaleidoscope of life in the Midway Pleasance and on Calypso's Isle.

It was the proffered pledge of Isabella that enabled Columbus to finance his first Atlantic journey, but four centuries had to pass before members of her sex were considered to deserve a place for themselves in any International Exhibition. Women exhibit freely in all the departments of the Fair, competing on equal terms with men, without fear or favour. But this building is sacred to woman's work. It contains everything for the model kitchen—woman's peculiar domain; the model nursery—where she reigns without a rival near her throne; the model hospital—where both nurses and physicians are women; the model kindergarten, while the interior is full of exhibits shown by invitation of the best workwomen, and especially American women, have done in our time. A portrait of the unfortunate Pocahontas, one of the few Indian heroines whose story has touched the heart and lodged itself in the memory of mankind, is one of the treasures of the Woman's Building. There is a library of books written by women, illustrated by women, set up by women, and bound by women. A vast array of inventions patented by women confound those libellers who say that women never invent anything except excuses. The walls are hung with paintings by female artists. Statuary from the studios of women sculptors adorn the hall. Everywhere the doctor found himself confronted by evidence of the science, the art, the industry—in one word, the capacity of women.

He turned into the library and glanced over the catalogue. As he was carelessly turning over the pages he saw a name that rivetted his attention. There were the simple words, "THORNE, ROSE, 'Tales from Fairyland.'

THE LIBRARIAN: WOMAN'S BUILDING.

London, 1891." For a moment he thought he was dreaming. He rubbed his eyes and read it again. There was no mistake. A mist swam before the page. Then he rose and went to the librarian.

"Could you let me look at 'Tales from Fairyland,' by Rose Thorne?"

"Certainly," said the lady librarian; "but you cannot take it away with you."

"No," said the doctor, "of course not. But may I sit down and look at it just here?"

Something in his manner impressed the girl, and she answered kindly, "By all means," and then tripped off to find the book.

Dr. Wynne tried to persuade himself that it was not his Rose; she had never written anything, that he knew, in her life, except her diary. There might be a thousand Rose Thornes. Why should he jump to the conclusion that this was his Rose? It was in vain he argued, trying to still the beating of his heart. For him there was only one Rose Thorne in the whole world.

"Here is the book, sir," said the librarian.

It was a daintily-bound volume. He took it mechanically and sat down. For a time he did not open the book. His hands trembled. He bit his lip. "This is absurd," he muttered; and, forcing himself, he opened the book. In a moment he knew that it was she, and none other. With difficulty repressing a cry of exultant delight, he devoured page after page. Then he drew a long breath and closed the book.

"Are you ill, sir?" said the librarian, hurrying to his side with a glass of iced water.

He looked at her in some amazement. "No, madam; thank you kindly all the same."

Then he opened the book and re-read the chapter he had just read. It was entitled, "The Little White Rosebud."

It was a simple fairy tale, simple enough to those who did not know—a mere fairy tale. But to him who knew it was as the unfolding of the innermost recesses of a human heart.

The story of "The Little White Rosebud," told how a fairy prince had loved a village maiden, and had given her as a token of his devotion the first little white rosebud that blossomed in his garden. But the witch's spell had cast a glamour over the lovers, and the village maiden had feared and fled. Before she fled, she sent back to the fairy prince the little white rosebud to keep till she returned. And with the rosebud, she sent a tiny little thistle, tying them together in a lover's knot—indissoluble till death. The fairy prince, forlorn and deserted, sought everywhere in vain for his lost one. She was under the witch's spell, and all the letters which she wrote withered into dust as they were written. But one night as she stood at her window in the moonlight, weeping for her fairy prince, and wondering if he still carried near his heart the little white rose, a bright hope flashed into her heart.

And she sang a lovely pathetic little song, telling the fairy prince far away that as she could not send him her letters through the silence, she would send her heart.

And, lo! it was not in vain. For the fairy prince, far in the West, heard the music of her song. He took out the white rose and kissed it, and the witch's spell was broken. The fairy prince wedded the village maiden under the branches of an old oak tree, and they were as happy as the day was long; and ever after in the fairy kingdom the royal arms were the rosebud and the thistle, tied with a lock of brown hair in a true lover's knot.

It was but a simple tale, but as he read it again, eagerly drinking in every word as if it were the elixir of life,

Wynne felt that the story, which was true history, would yet be true prophecy. Was the witch's spell broken? He had heard the music of her song. Where was the little white rose? He took out his pocket-book and reverently extricated it from its wrappings. There it lay, the rosebud tied up with the thistle, with the lover's knot indissoluble till death. He kissed it reverently, but with exultant joy. Was the witch's spell broken now? He looked up almost expecting to see his Rose standing before him. She was not there. He only met the curious glance of the librarian, and he hastily restored the precious keepsake to its abiding place.

Then he settled himself down in the chair and read the "Tales from Fairyland" from cover to cover. The light began to fail. He took no heed. The crowd increased. He had no eyes for anything but the printed page, in every line of which he recognised the delicate, poetic fancy of his idolised girl. The electric lights were turned on. He had finished the book, but as he read the last page he turned at once to the first. And then he noticed what he had not seen before, that the book was dedicated, "To Walter ——." He closed the volume abruptly, handed it to the librarian, and hurriedly left the building.

The rest of the company had long before sat down to dinner in the crowded restaurant at the Casino. Mrs. Irwin had found them, and the professor and Irene.

"I have been at the Dog Show," said Dr. Hedwig, "the greatest canine parliament that ever assembled since the first dog bayed at the moon. It is below the live-stock sheds, behind the Machinery Hall. I should think you could hear them here but for the clatter of the knives. I was particularly delighted with one dog—a huge St. Bernard from Pennsylvania. He stands three feet high, weighs 247 pounds, or, as you English would say, nearly eighteen stone. He is the dog to hunt your mastodons."

"That dog," said Adiram, "cost 3 750 dols. He is the biggest dog in creation. He is quite in his place in the World's Fair."

"And where have you been, Mr. Adiram?" said Compton.

"I have been in the Transportation Building for the most part," said Adiram, "where I was chiefly impressed by the marvellous superiority of the American locomotive over those of other countries. There are eight acres of railway exhibits. You see the whole history of the locomotive from the old grasshopper to the latest leviathan. It is an exhibit worthy an industry in which sixty thousand million dollars are invested."

"When I was in the Transportation Building," said Dr. Hedwig, "I was much more interested in the electric cars than in the locomotives. Steam—pah! it is a thing of yesterday. At the next Exposition the gigantic locomo-

TRANSPORTATION EXHIBITS.

"Where can the doctor have gone?" said Mrs. Irwin. "I wanted particularly to see him."

"He'll turn up," said Compton, "never fear. But meantime, we must either dine, or give up our places to those who will. He may turn up before long."

"And where have you been?" said Compton to the professor.

"Grubbing in old tombs," said Mrs. Irwin, with a laugh. "Poor Miss Vernon! I came upon them both in the Ethnographical section, in the midst of the Ohio skeletons."

"Why poor Miss Vernon!" said Irene, bridling. "It is a great deal more interesting learning everything about these dead men from the professor than merely lounging round among a hot and vulgar crowd, whose chief anxiety is to know how many dollars everything is worth."

"The exhibit of prehistoric Americana,' said the professor, "is one of the most complete and valuable in the World's Fair. The collection embraces all varieties of aborigines, from the Aleuts of Alaska to the stone ruins of Yucatan. The models are most wonderful. It is a resurrection of a vanished world. We have been back among the mastodon, and have been the whole afternoon face to face with the races which perished long before the white man set his foot on the continent."

'Do you think your psychometric gift,' said Compton to Mrs. Irwin, ' would enable you to restore the language of the mound-builders of Ohio?"

"I fear not,' said she. "I am clairvoyant, and am not clairaudient. But I should like to see the mastodon."

tive engines which Mr. Adiram saw will be shown as historical curiosities, beside the professor's mastodons. Electricity is the motor of the future."

"The electrical exhibits," said Mrs. Irwin, "are far the most interesting to me. Have you seen the electrical model house? That is a sight that alone is well worth coming to Chicago to see. Why, it is like the Kodak! You press the button, and we do the rest."

"Really," said Irene, "that is the kind of house I should like to live in. Where is it?"

"In the Electrical Building," said Mrs. Irwin. "Everything is almost ideally complete. You touch an electric bell—the door flies open. You enter the parlour to wait for the hostess. You touch another button, and the loud-speaking phonograph on the table repeats a selection from 'Faust.' The hostess comes down to dinner. She touches a button, and the dishes descend on dumb electric waiters from the kitchen in the attic. When they are placed on the table, they are kept hot by wires laid on under the table from electric warming furnaces. After dinner, the dishes mount upstairs by the electric lift, in five minutes they are washed by the electric automatic dish washer, and dried by an electric dish-drier. On washing day, the dirty clothes and a piece of soap are thrown into a tub, electricity beats the water, rubs and scrubs and cleans the clothes. After being rinsed and blued, they pass into an electric wringer, and are dried in an electric oven, and then are ironed by electric ironing machines. The sewing machine is run by an electric motor, another cunning little

THE ELECTRICITY BUILDING.

electric machine sweeps the carpet, and electric thermo-stats keep the temperature of the house perfectly equable. It is a jewel of a house."

"Now," said Compton, rising. "we must be going. The doctor must have dined elsewhere. We had better get a good place, from which we can see the illumination of the grounds."

The illumination had already begun. The huge Shuckert light, with 25,000 candle-power, was turning great streams of brilliant light upon the harbour and the lake shore. Other great search lights of almost fabulous power were wandering around the great white palaces within which, when the light passed, could be seen the rays of innumerable lamps.

"There are 10,000 arc lights," said Adiram, in awed whisper, "and 100,000 incandescent lamps within this park."

"Oh, how beautiful!" exclaimed Irene, as the great electric fountain began to play and the rainbow coloured rays fell upon the springing water that soared aloft far above the lofty walls of the surrounding palaces.

"See," said Mrs. Irwin, "they have lamps under the water."

The whole basin was gemmed by coloured lamps, burning like glow-worms under the water. Gondolas, gaily festooned with Chinese lanterns, flitted to and fro, and the strains of music from distant bands floated dreamily through the air.

"Now,' said Dr. Hedwig, "the electrical fireworks are about to begin."

A Frenchman seated himself at what looked like a piano, and began to play. Instantly, a pyrotechnic display, un-dreamed of by Messrs. Brock, flamed forth before the eyes of admiring thousands. Set piece succeeded set piece, each more beautiful, more amazing, than the last. The display culminated in a magnificent tableau in which

flame figures representing all the great Powers defiled before the fire Statue of Chicago, laying down their trophies at her feet.

"The New World has beaten the Old," said Adiram. "There has been nothing like that before ; no, not even in the Arabian Nights."

CHAPTER XVII.—ROUND THE FAIR WITH THE CHILDREN.

THE moment Dr. Wynne reached the Auditorium he despatched a cablegram to London, to the publishers of the "Tales from Fairyland," prepaying a reply to the question as to the address of Rose Thorne. Then, without waiting to hear of the others whom he had left at the Exhibition, he retired to his room. Early next morning he was downstairs inquiring for a telegram.

On receiving it, he tore it open and read :—

"Left for World's Fair in May."

Then she was here ! The secret instinct which drove him across the sea was not at fault. But where ? How could he find her in this whirling maelstrom of humanity ?

He went back to his room and considered the situation She had gone to the World's Fair. He would then live at the World's Fair morning, noon, and night She would probably visit the Woman's Building. He would leave his address with the librarian. He would see if they knew anything of her at the British Commission. How he wished there existed a centre where every British visitor could register his name and address. It seemed so hopeless hunting without a clue.

He had got to the end of his resources, and he was rather relieved when there was a knock at his door, and little Pearl came running into his arms. "Mamma says it's bekfast time," said the little lady. The doctor followed the child to Mrs. Wills's room.

"Doctor, doctor," said the boys, "you promised to take us to the Exhibition to-day."

"I suppose we may get breakfast first?" said he, smiling. "Had you a good night, Mrs. Wills?"

"Thanks, pretty fair," she said. "But to-morrow we must start for San Francisco. Do you think you could find out the best way of making our way thither?"

"I am so sorry to lose you," said he. "I shall be quite forlorn without the boys, and as for little Pearl——"

"Pearl will ky," said the child, "and Kitty will ky. We don't want to go away in the rasty puff-puff. Pearl wants to stop here. Dollies all want to stop here."

"Come, come," said the doctor, hoisting his little pet on to her accustomed seat on his shoulder, "we must come down to breakfast."

When breakfast was over they agreed to take the cable-car down to the South Park entrance in Fifty-seventh Street, and to spend the whole day in the Fair, returning late after the fireworks to the hotel.

The boys were in high glee. Mrs. Wills was not in such high spirits. She hated Exhibitions she said. For her own part she would not have visited the 'World's Fair, but for the children's sake she would go.

"I am sure you will enjoy it," said the doctor. "We will take it easy, and I will not take you to see anything that will not interest and amuse you."

When they got into the cable-car Pearl was uneasy. "Where are the nice gee-gees?" she kept asking. Nor could she for some time be made to understand that the car was drawn by an underground cable which made it independent of horses. On the way down the children were wild with excitement, wondering what the Fair would contain. The Red Indians and the Esquimaux, with their real huts and wigwams, fascinated Tom. Fred wanted to see the performing animals, and the fireworks. As for Pearl, she thought of the dollies and the flowers and the sweeties, which the doctor assured her abounded in the Fair.

"Melican sweeties," said Pearl, for the child had already learned that the making of confectionery is one of those arts, like the fitting up of river steamers and vestibule cars, in which the Americans stand first of the human race.

It was a pleasant morning when they paid their half-dollar at the gates and were free of the World's Fair. "Are there many extra charges?" said Mrs. Wills.

"No, not as Exhibitions go," said the doctor. "There are, however, many side shows where you have to pay. If, for instance, you want to go to the theatre, take a ride in the gondolas, go up in a balloon, or see any of the special performances in the Midway Pleasance, you pay extra. But all the regular exhibits are free.'

"What are these funny men?" said Pearl, as they approached the bridge across the north pond, pointing to the Esquimaux village which occupies the extreme northern corner of Jackson Park.

"Would you like to see them, Pearl?" said the doctor. But Pearl did not want to go. "Nasty, ugly 'ittle men,"

SOME OF THE STATUARY IN THE EXHIBITION.

MODEL OF THE CONVENT OF LA ROBINA.

she said. So they crossed the north-west pond and found themselves among the State Buildings.

"I want you just to look at the fruit in the Californian Building," said the doctor, as they made their way into the reproduction of the old monastery of San Diego. They were in the paradise of fruit. Pearl wanted some to eat, but was consoled by some peanuts, the vendor of which had paid £24,000 for the monopoly of sale within the Fair, so that he would have to make a net profit of nearly £200 per day before clearing the price of his concession.

"What is that huge, round thing under the glass dome?" said Tom.

"Oh, that," said the doctor, "is a section of one of the trees they grow in California. It is 23 ft. across and 30 ft. high. You see it is hollowed out, there is an upstairs room and a downstairs, each 14 ft. high. You could cut a tunnel through that tree and drive two omnibuses abreast through. For at the ground it was 33 ft. in diameter, or more than 100 ft. round about. But now, as it is comparatively early, let us go into the Art Palace before the crowd makes it hot and uncomfortable."

There is an unfailing attraction about pictures, especially pictures with stories in them. And here were the pick of the best pictures in the whole world. They wandered slowly round, stopping here and there before the pictures that pleased them best and resting whenever Mrs. Wills felt weary opposite her favourite pictures. Pearl was in high glee. As they went on from gallery to gallery, the morning imperceptibly slipped away.

"Dear me," said the doctor, "if it is not twelve o'clock! Let us take the electric launch that starts from the steps, and run down the ornamental water to the Casino at the pier."

They were soon on board the launch; the pretty awning overhead screened them from the sun, while the rapid motion of the launch made them feel as if a pleasant zephyr were fanning their cheeks.

"What are those big buildings on either side?" said Tom.

"One is the Illinois State Building, the other is the Brazilian Palace. But see, we are now coming into the lagoon."

They dived under the ornamental bridge that connects the wooded island with the Fisheries, passed the Japanese temple, and skirted Calypso's Isle so closely that they almost ran among the water-lilies, and could see the roses, and smell the lilacs that were blossoming on the island.

"How beautiful," said Mrs. Wills "and how pleasant.

There is no steam, no fear of an explosion, no disagreeable smell of engine oil; it is the ideal of luxurious motion."

Gaily decorated gondolas passed them on their way, and occasionally a great omnibus launch with thirty or forty on board swept by.

"Look, look," said Fred, "look, doctor, what a beautiful building we are coming to! '

"It's the Electricity Palace," said the doctor. 'You must see that to night when it is all ablaze with a myriad lamps."

"What is it all made of?' said Mrs. Wills; "it looks like marble with an old ivory tinge.'

"The buildings are constructed of wood and iron and glass, but what you see, the outside mask, as it were, of the real building, is made of staff—the veritable staff of life, so far as the architecture of this Show is concerned. It is a mixture of cement, plaster, and hemp-fibre, which can be moulded like plaster, carved and worked like wood, and which, if it is but painted and cared for, will last for years."

"Oh, how beautiful," said the boys, as the launch, after threading the North Canal came out into the Grand Basin. The imposing Columbian fountain was in full play, its waters gleaming like crystal in the sun's rays, and falling in snowy spray over the figures of the rowers of the barque of Progress. The great gilded dome of the Administration Building glowed in the mid-day sun like a flame of fire. On either side were flower beds and statuary leading up to the great palaces which rose to the right and left. Immediately in front was the Statue of the Republic, and behind the many pillared Peristyle, through which they caught glimpses of the infinite expanse of the lake. A few minutes more and they were landed, and made their way to the doctor's favourite restaurant, which stands at the shore end of the great pier.

They were fortunate enough to secure a seat near the window which commanded a view of the harbour, bright with a thousand sails, and the great lake beyond, stretching far away, as illimitable as the ocean, to where it met the horizon of the cloudless sky.

"Ships," said Pearl, "but what little ships. I don't see our nice big ship anywhere." She was soon consoled, however, by a delightful lunch of fruit and sweets, and a glass of iced milk.

"What is that funny building that we see there just across the water?' said Fred.

"That," said the doctor, "is a famous place which you must take a good look at before you go. More than 400 years ago there was a disappointed, and almost heartbroken man who was wandering about the Old World like a tramp. One day, when he was just ready to perish, he came to the door of that place which you see there, and asked them to take him in and give him shelter. Now the abbot of that convent—for it is a convent—was a wise, good, and kind man. He took the poor fellow in and gave him food and lodged him, and listened to all that he had to say, and then helped him to carry out the idea upon which he had set his heart. Do you know who that poor tramp was?"

"No," said Fred. "Who was he?"

"That tramp was Christopher Columbus, and it was in that Convent of La Robina where he first found the friends without whose aid he would never have got Queen Isabella's support, and would never have discovered America."

"Do you see that curious little ship that is lying beside the convent?" said the doctor. "That is the model of the S-n'a Muria, the ship in which Columbus crossed the Atlantic. Isn't it a queerly-shaped ship, with its high poop and strange build?"

"I suppose," said Mrs. Wills, "that such a ship could not cross the Atlantic now?"

"Oh, dear me," said the doctor, "that very ship at which we are looking has crossed the Atlantic. Although the rig and build of the ship seems strange to us, it is nevertheless perfectly seaworthy. As a matter of fact, that little model was built in Spain last year and crossed the Atlantic without danger or difficulty. Everything is done to make it like the old ship, even the crew, who are in old Spanish costume. Fortunately those who are on board are not the offscouring of the Spanish gaols with which Columbus had to be content 400 years ago."

"How little a ship can you cross the Atlantic in?" said Tom.

"If we have time, I will show you Captain Andrew's ocean cockle-shells, which are on show in the Marine Department. They are little sail-boats; one, the *Dark Secret*, with a twelve-foot keel; the other the *Nautilus*, which is only nineteen feet long, but in these tiny craft he has crossed the Atlantic all alone, at least three times."

"How did he get any sleep, doctor?" asked Mrs. Wills.

"He took it in snatches of a few minutes at a time. When the weather was fine, he adjusted his sails and lay down by the helm. When it was stormy he did without. But there are some sailors and ships which seem to have a charmed life. Do you see that old whaling bark that is lying near the *Santi Maria?* That is the famous old *Progress* from New Bedford. She is fifty years old; she has been seventeen times round Cape Horn, and has always been successful. Forty times she has been in the Arctic Ocean and always came back safe. Twenty-two years ago all the whaling fleet was destroyed but that small ship, which brought back seven captains and 300 sailors whose vessels had perished.'

After lunch they went down to the Krupp Exhibit, in order to see the biggest gun in the whole world. It was made by Krupp and weighs 122 tons

"You can take the boys if you like, doctor," said Mrs. Wills, "but I do not care for such things, neither does Pearl."

"No," said Pearl, "I don't like shooter-guns, they make a noise like froggy signals. It frightens Pearl. I will stay with mamma.'

"All right," said the doctor, and he marched off with the two boys, one in each hand, to see the exhibit from Essen. Afterwards they went a little further along the shore to see the Forestry Exhibit. There are over 400 trees which are native to America, and specimens of these are to be found in this exhibit. Each State in the Union contributes three typical trees to the construction of this building. Another fact which the doctor pointed out was that no iron whatever is used. Wooden pins are used instead of bolts and nails.

They did not stay very long in the Forestry Exhibit, but after a passing glance at the Dairy Hall they came back to the station of the Elevated Electrical Railway, where Mrs. Wills and Pearl were waiting for them. There was a small crowd, and they had to wait their turn

FORESTRY BUILDING.

THE DAIRY BUILDING.

for some time. At last they took their seats, and were running along behind the great palaces and the Administration Buildings; then they skirted the extreme north edge of the park and past the Midway Pleasance, where the doctor said they would get out on the return journey. After making a circuit of the north end of the park with its State buildings, they were ultimately deposited close to the ironclad, which Pearl and Mrs. Wills both refused to inspect. The doctor and the boys therefore did not leave the cars, and taking the return journey went back to the Midway Pleasance. where they alighted.

"This is the place for amusement," said the doctor. "I think the boys will like it better than going through those endless buildings and wandering through the exhibits in the Mining, Manufactures, and Liberal Arts Buildings."

"What are we going to see?" said Tom.

"Now," said the doctor, "we will just run up the Tower of Babel which stands at the entrance. It is a tower 400 feet high, with a diameter of 100 feet at the bottom. The peculiarity of this tower," he said, "is that they take you up in an electric railway. You can also ascend by an elevator or by walking."

Before he had finished his explanation the car was in motion, and as they went spirally round the tower they obtained beautiful views of the Exhibition, the Midway Pleasance, and the city of Chicago as far as the eye could see. When they had reached the top they were higher than any other buildings in the Exhibition.

"Yes," said the doctor, "it is a good view, but it is not half as high as the Eiffel Tower. In that respect the Americans have been beaten. It is the one thing in which they have not outdone everything that has been attempted in former Exhibitions."

Having gone up by the railway they descended by the elevator.

"Now," said Dr. Wynne to Mrs. Wills, "do you feel tired? If so, you had better go into the Woman's Building; there is a Department of Comfort for tired children and for ladies who want to have a rest. Y u can put Pearl to sleep and lie down yourself. We will be back in an hour or two."

Mrs. Wills, who was no great sightseer at the best, gratefully accepted the suggestion, although Pearl somewhat demurred. She was, however, really very sleepy, and,

in a few minutes after going into the Comfort Department, was sound asleep.

"Now," said Dr. Wynne, "we had better take a walk first right through the Pleasance, and coming back we can look at the exhibits which we like best more in detail. First we pass on our left Lady Aberdeen's Irish Village, with Blarney Castle. It is as like an Irish village as it could be minus the pigs running about the street, the roofless, ruined, and desolated houses, and the omnipresent dirt, which would be needed to make it homelike. On the other side of the Pleasance, separated from the Irish Village by the tower up which we have been, is the Bohemian Glass Works, where you can see the process of making the beautiful Bohemian Glass."

They then crossed the great Illinois Central Railroad. Here there were more glass works. "There is a place," said the doctor, "at which we will not fail to call as we come back?"

"What is that?" asked Fred.

"It is the wild beast show. They should not be called wild beasts, because they are tame. It is Hagenbeck's wonderful collection of tame animals. We shall see them perform on our way back. Immediately opposite the wild beast show you have Little Japan. The Japanese bazaar is the first of the foreign settlements which make the Pleasance like a section of Europe or Asia. A little further on, on both sides, you have the Dutch Settlement. Then you come to the panorama of the Bernese Alps. They could not send the Alps, you see, as an exhibit, so they sent a panorama as the next best thing."

Opposite the panorama on the other side of the covered walk they came to the German Village. which is the largest exhibit in the Pleasance. Near it was the Turkish Village. Then they came to a group of buildings which reminded them of the Paris Exhibition of 1889. There were the Moroccan Palace, the street in Cairo, and the Algerian and Tunis exhibits.

"But what is this huge thing right in front of us?" said Tom.

"Oh, that is the Ferris Wheel. We shall go up that when we come back," said the doctor. "On the left of that is another place you will like to go and see—that is, the ice railway. A little further on is the sliding railway, which was on exhibition at Paris. Then we come to another panorama, at which we shall look as we return.

It is a panorama of an eruption in the Sandwich Islands. As you are not likely to see a volcano in eruption you had better see this. On the other side of the covered way you see the Austrian Village and the East Indian Village, and last of all there is the village from Dahomey. Then come the nursery gardens, with which the Pleasance ends. Now, boys,' said Dr. Wynne, as he came to the end of the walk, "which of all the things we have passed do you wish to see most?"

"The wild beasts," said Fred.

"Yes," said Tom, "I agree. Then we want to go on the Ferris Wheel, and see what the ice railway is like."

"Then," said Fred, "I want to ride on one of those Indian elephants which were wandering up and down for hire."

"And," Tom chimed in, "I want to ride an Egyptian donkey in the Cairo street."

"Well," said the doctor, "we shall have our work set before we get back. Let us begin at the beginning, and look at this East Indian Village. It is something like what there was at Paris, it comes from the Dutch East Indies. The natives are living as they do in their own homes, and if we had time to wait we should see them performing juggling feats and charming serpents. But we must hurry on. Close beside this village is a house from Pompeii, which was buried by an eruption of Vesuvius, nearly two thousand years ago. Near it we have the Dahomeyan Village, as a type of the savagery, which the French have been endeavouring to civilise by means of Lebel rifles. There are about fifty to sixty men and women of what was, till last year, the one independent negro kingdom, and the only state where women are regularly trained to war. Fortunately,' said the doctor, "we are just in time to see them give one of their war dances."

It was not a very edifying spectacle, although shorn of the horrors which are the usual accompaniment of Dahomeyan festivals. In great contrast to this is the Austrian Village which is the reproduction of a street in old Vienna, called Der Graben. They walked through this, looking at the quaint old houses on either hand, and then came back to the Chinese Village and sat for some time to see a Chinese play. A Chinese play is like a serial in a magazine. It begins some time or other, and seems to keep on for ever, and a very little of it will go a long way.

"Let us go into the Chinese tea-house and have a cup of tea, made by the Chinese themselves," said the doctor. "But before we cross the way, we will look in at the panorama of the volcano of Kilawi."

When they got inside the circular building, they found that they were supposed to be standing in the centre of the crater, and the fire was spouting out around them on all sides. But, safe on their plat . ," they were able to look out upon the scenery which surrounds what is believed to be the biggest crater in existence.

They went across the way and had a cup of tea, after which all three took their seats on the ice railway. This is like an ordinary toboggan, but the ice is real, and is kept frozen in the hottest weather by machinery.

"Now," said the doctor, after giving a passing glance at a model of St. Peter's, "for the Ferris Wheel."

The Ferris Wheel is a gigantic concern. It is a wheel of 250 feet in diameter, nearly 800 feet in circumference, and is mounted upon towers 135 feet high. The doctor and the boys took their seats in the cars, which were suspended from the perimeter, and waited until the rest were filled. Then the huge wheel, weighing when fully freighted over 2,000 tons, it is said, slowly revolved, carrying them up 250 feet high, and then bringing them down again. The sensation was not unpleasant, the great

curve being sufficient to prevent any feeling of dizziness in turning.

After they had descended, they went straight into the Cairo street. Here below the minaret of Kaid Bey, from which at stated times the muezzin calls to prayer, the water-carrier clinked his glasses and cried his drink. They were in the unchanging East. Mosque, bazaar, donkey boys, the Musharabeeayah, lattice work, the alcoves, the street sellers are a condensed epitome of Oriental life, with its framework complete, conveyed as if by Solomon's carpet from the banks of the Nile to the heart of Chicago. There are scores of donkey boys, youths from eighteen to twenty, who exhibited their asses—which are whitey-grey for the most part, with a curious blue pattern stencilled on the legs. Imagine this section of Cairo suddenly plumped down in the midst of the Exhibition, fill the shops with native merchants, plant turbaned street sellers at each corner with sweetmeats, keep the donkey

STATUARY" IN THE TRANSPORTATION BUILDING.

boys running hither and thither, crowd the whole place with sightseers, and you have the Rue du Caire.

The two boys were soon accommodated with two Egyptian donkeys, and enjoyed the luxury of a brief ride. From Egypt to Turkey was a short transition. The Turkish Village, a reproduction of a square in Constantinople, lay on the other side of the covered walk. It had much the same characteristics as the street in Cairo. They then visited the German Village.

"Here," said the doctor, "if we had time, which we have not, you could study various styles of houses from all parts of the Fatherland of to-day combined with a German town of mediæval times."

More interesting to the boys than the German Village or the Dutch Settlement was Hagenbeck's Wild Animal Show. They watched the performance with intense interest. Mr Hagenbeck is a German who has brought over with him 100 animals, including lions, tigers, elephants and other animals, which form a happy family. "It is a kind of fulfilment of the prophecy that the lion and

seen the authoress of that book ' Tales from Fairyland' which I was reading yesterday?"

Alas! no, the librarian had not seen Rose Thorne save in the catalogue.

"Well, said the doctor, "if she comes and you happen to see her, might I ask you to give her this card?"

"Certainly," said the librarian, whose sympathies were aroused by the open secret of the interest which the doctor showed in Rose Thorne. "But is she in Chicago?"

"I hear so," said Dr. Wynne, and not caring to stand any further cross-examination he returned to the party on the roof.

They had finished their tea, and Pearl was eager to begin again the round of the grounds. The doctor took them to the White Star exhibit. The children recognised the staircase of the *Majestic* with a cry of delight, and Mrs. Wills was pleasantly surprised at coming upon this reminiscence of their journey across the Atlantic. As they lingered in the model of the saloon of the *Tautcon*, Mrs. Wills asked the doctor if he had ever seen Mrs Julia

HORTICULTURAL HALL.

the lamb shall lie down together," said Dr. Wynne; "it is quite wonderful the things he has taught them to do. They are as tame as cats."

"And a great deal more obedient," said Fred, "for our cat will not do what it is told. Mr. Hagenbeck makes his lions stand on their head or hind legs just as he wishes."

More than two hours had passed when they found Mrs. Wills and Pearl anxiously waiting their return at the entrance of the Woman's Building. "We are going to have tea on the roof," said Mrs. Wills; "the sun is not so hot now, and I am sure you must be tired after having seen so much." Nothing loth, notwithstanding their cup of tea at the Chinese Village, they settled themselves comfortably on the roof, and were soon engaged in an animated conversation on the comparative attractiveness of the various exhibitions which they had seen on the Pleasance.

While Mrs Wills and the children were having their tea the doctor slipped down to the librarian. She recognised him at once and asked him if he was better.

"Oh, I am all right, thank you," he replied, "but would you mind telling me whether you have ever heard of or

since they had landed. On hearing that he had heard nothing of her since he left the *Majestic*, Mrs. Wills went on to say that she was very sorry, for Mrs. Julia was a real good soul. Her kindness to poor Rose——"

"Rose," said the doctor quickly, "what Rose?'

"The girl in the Intermediate cabin. Don't you remember," said Mrs. Wills, "you came to bring me back to Pearl the evening before the fog."

"Good heavens!" said the doctor, "can it be possible! Tell me. Do you know Rose's name?"

"I am not quite sure,' said Mrs. Wills, "I think I heard it once but I have forgotten it."

"I remember," said Tom; "it was Thistle or something like that, because when she was a little better we used to tease her and say she was a thorny, prickly Rose."

The doctor turned away in silence. Thistle—Rose Thistle—Rose Thorne. He had no doubt it was she. It was too cruel. She had been on the *Majestic*. He had even been in her berth, and yet they had not met.

The little company walked on for a space, wondering somewhat at the doctor's agitation, until they reached the

Horticultural Exhibition. The boys looked up at him from time to time with wondering eyes; Mrs. Wills did not like to speak; Pearl alone was unconcerned, and made quaint observations upon all that she saw.

When they reached the entrance of the Horticultural Building the doctor pulled himself together with an effort, and giving a hand to each of the boys he led them through the most magnificent collection of flowers that had ever been brought together under one roof. Every continent had been ransacked for the choicest beauties.

The orchids exhibited are alone said to be worth £100,000. There were roses there from every country, and a wonderful collection of beautiful flowers from Australia, South America, and Europe. Each State exhibited its own fruit, and the oranges from the Southern States were something enormous. There were orange trees in full bloom and peach trees in full fruit. On coming out of the hall they noticed three large trees, much larger than those usually to be seen in Jackson Park. They were an elm, an ash, and a sugar maple. On in-

of the enormous collection of models and exhibits of every conceivable method of locomotion. They only looked through the long corridors of vehicles varying from a leviathan locomotive down to a tiny bicycle. They were most interested in the exhibits showing the progress made in flying.

"I had hoped," said Dr. Wynne to Mrs. Wills, "that we should have been able to come here by air, but that triumph is to be reserved, it would seem, for the next century."

"I should never take your aeroplane or flying machine. I prefer the solid ground," said Mrs. Wills.

From the Transport Building they walked through the Mines to the Electrical Building, which was just being lit up. It was not to see the beauty of the effulgence of the electric light of every shape and design with which the interior of the Electrical Building was ablaze, that Dr. Wynne had brought Mrs. Wills and her children, who were now getting somewhat weary of tramping about the grounds. He could not let them leave the Exhibition, he said, until they had seen Mr. Edison's kinetograph

MINES AND MINING BUILDING.

quiry it was found that they were brought there by a nurseryman, and were the first exhibits on the ground. The elm was seventy-five feet high, two feet in diameter, and weighed ten tons. The tree was growing and was an interesting specimen of the way in which full grown forest trees can be transplanted without injury.

From the Horticultural Exhibition the doctor led his little party to the Fisheries in order that they might notice the flowers of the sea which were displayed in the aquarium. The tanks seemed endless. The curator said they were 570 feet long.

Pearl was much impressed with the extraordinary shape and colour of many of the fishes which swam close to the glass as if on purpose to show off their peculiarities. The boys were most interested in the papier-maché models exhibiting the method of catching seals. These models, which were extraordinarily life like, contained hundreds of seals, Aleuts, and walruses, all dramatically arranged.

On leaving the Fisheries they took a gondola and were rowed to the entrance of the Transportation Building, which lies at the other end of the lagoon. They made no pretence of making an exhaustive examination

"What is a kinetograph?"

"You will see," said the doctor. "It is a combination of the phonograph and the photograph."

An exhibition was being given when they entered the hall. There was a picture of a prize-fight being thrown on the canvas by a magic lantern. The scene was continually changing. The combatants were now up, now down, now giving a blow home on the face or chest, then sparring round the ring. All the while the loud-speaking phonograph was reproducing the incessant sounds that were audible when the picture was being photographed.

"I think it is a disgusting exhibition," said Mrs. Wills, "and it is a great pity that Edison could not have found a better subject for his invention than in bringing the oaths and brutality of the prize-ring before the public in that fashion."

Mrs. Wills was not alone in her opinion of the exhibit. It was soon taken off, and a picture substituted of Patti singing. The lantern threw her picture upon the screen with such life-like realism that you could almost have said she was standing before you. Each movement of her figure was reproduced by means of instantaneous photo-

IDEAL: FROM A FRIEZE IN THE AGRICULTURAL BUILDING.

duty at the dedication of the show last October. They were all lit up with electric light, so that the outline of the emblematic groups could easily be made out. Behind them were ten large flat boats, with set pieces of fireworks, which were discharged in the course of the evening. A score of small steamers decorated from stem to stern, covered with lamps and well supplied with bombs and rockets, were kept plying in a sort of aquatic waltz along the whole of the lake front of the Jackson Park. As each of the steamers had bands on board there was plenty of music. Pearl was delighted, and clapped her hands from her position of advantage on the doctor's shoulders. Even the bursting of the maroons did not frighten her, for her eyes were so absorbed by the splendour and glitter of the fireworks that her ears had not much chance of protest. Messrs. Brock, the pyrotechnists whose displays at the Crystal Palace are familiar to Londoners, had the contract for the fireworks at the World's Fair, and it is unnecessary to say that they were worthy of their reputation. Long before the last set piece had been displayed, Dr. Wynne, Mrs. Wills, and the three children were making their way back to Chicago. The crush back at night would have been tremendous. There must have been at least 250,000 people in the Exhibition ground, and the scramble for even the early cars was more exciting than pleasant.

One of the exhibits* which most pleased the doctor and the boys was the Children's Department, where they saw a reproduction in miniature of the Ducal Palace at Venice, and many other buildings, all designed by a clever and original American girl, who hit upon this plan of teaching architecture. *à la* Ruskin, in the nursery. These Stones of Venice were all built up of separate bricks exactly ten times less than the original, but of the same colour and shape. It was like a course of Ruskin-made-easy to build up the Palace, and the word-book which accompanied the bricks, was a sufficient introduction to one of the most fascinating of all sciences. In order to complete this object lesson in architecture, Miss Etta had lived in a houseboat on the waters of the Adriatic, for months at a time, acquiring materials at the same time for a delightful girls book, "How I Lived in Venice on a Shilling a Day."

graphy. The phonograph moved exactly in accordance with the procession of the pictures through the lantern, and thus enabled all those present to hear the music and at the same time see the prima donna as it were in the very act of singing.

"Now," said Mrs. Wills, "I think we should be going home."

"No," said the doctor; "this is a festival night, and there will be a great illumination upon the lake."

When they came out of the Electrical Hall, they found themselves in the midst of a fairy-like splendour. All the trees in the park were decorated with Chinese lanterns. On the lake were anchored innumerable wooden frames, made in the shape of stars, crescents, eagles, and shields, which were lit up with red, white, and blue lamps, that seemed to float on the surface of the water. Around these groups of lamps illuminated gondolas and electric launches gay with Chinese lanterns were flitting to and fro. But it was on the lake shore that the chief glory of the fête was to be witnessed. Along the shore were twenty-four floats representing the procession of the centuries, which did

REAL: A BULLOCK-WAGGON OF TO-DAY.

CHAPTER XVIII.—FROM THE SLAUGHTER HOUSE TO THE ALTAR.

NEXT day Mrs. Irwin went out to purchase such additions to her wardrobe as her marriage seemed to dictate. She went to the Fair, not the World's Fair, but the Bon Marché of Chicago, and soon lost herself in the many-acred store.

* It is proper to say that as none of the exhibits are as yet in the Fair, all the descriptions in this and the preceding chapter, of what was seen there in Midsummer, are necessarily based upon the present arrangements of exhibitors, which may be varied before then. As a rule, however, with here and there an exception, it may safely be taken for granted that what is described in this Christmas story will actually be found in the World's Fair. I am sorry to say that one of the exceptions seems likely to be the facsimile model of Ann Hathaway's Cottage.

" Big shops are all very well," she said afterwards, "but a shop with 2,400 shopmen is rather more than I can stand." After lunch Compton and Mr. Adiram called upon her to take her to see some more of the sights of Chicago. She would have preferred Mr. Adiram's room to his company, but seeing that he had attached himself to Compton as a cicerone she accompanied them with a sigh.

" Talk about gold mines," said Adiram, as they walked along one of the less frequented streets of the business

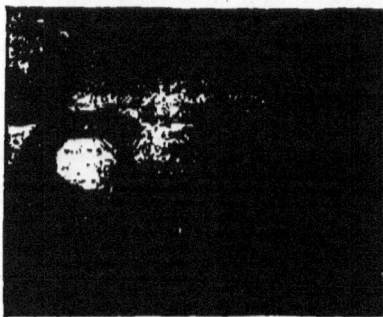

THE SITE OF CHICAGO : PRICE FIVE SHILLINGS !

quarter, " what is a gold mine to a good corner lot in this section of Chicago. The original founder bought the site of the city and 300 miles round about for the handsome sum of five shillings. That was two hundred years ago. But within the memory of men now living the whole ground rent of Chicago could have been bought in open market for a thousand dollars. It would hardly have brought that in 1812, the day after the garrison of Fort Dearborn was massacred by the Redskins. But we don't need to go back so far as eighty years. Corner lots that went for 1,500 dollars in 1845 are worth 200,000 dollars to-day. The Union Block, sold for 2,000 dollars in 1841, is now worth a million. The Custom House Block was bought in 1833 for 500 dollars. It is valued to-day at 750,000. In the Michigan Avenue forty years ago land sold at a dollar a foot, which now would be snapped up at 400 dollars."

" What about the unearned increment ? " said Compton.
" Our increment is not unearned," said Adiram, " it is the produce of honest brain and untiring energy. We don't take much stock in that kind of Socialist talk in Chicago. At least," he added, " not since 1887."
" Why since 1887 ? " asked Mrs. Irwin.
" Do you see that statue ? " said Adiram, pointing to the Police Monument that stands at the corner of the Haymarket. " That monument answers your question."

They approached it and read the inscription. " In the name of the people of Illinois I command peace." On the pedestal stood a policeman in uniform with his hand raised. " Well," said Mrs. Irwin. " It's the first time I ever saw a policeman on a monument. But what happened ? "

" It was just seven years ago," said Adiram, " that the Anarchist element got out of hand. Anarchists with us are imported, and we had some lovely specimens in those days. They were keen for an eight hours' day as pre-

liminary to the general Socialist divide-up, and as it did not come along quick enough they tried dynamite. Seven policemen were killed by a bomb and many injured. How many of the mob were killed is unknown. We hanged four of their leaders twelve months later and one of them blew his head off with dynamite in gaol. Since that time the policeman has been on the monument and in the saddle."

" Then that is why," said Mrs Irwin, maliciously, ' they are so rude A London policeman is a born courtier compared with the boors whom you have in uniform in Chicago."

" Let us hope that the World's Fair will give them better manners and a little gentler method of asserting their authority," said Compton. " There is certainly room for improvement. I suppose your officers have a somewhat rough time ? "

" Rather," said Adiram, " they have pretty well cleared out Little Hell now ; but the foreign element is too strong to render it possible to enforce either strict Sunday or liquor laws. The Lager Beer Riot settled that as long ago as 1855."

" Dear me," said Mrs. Irwin, " that is the sixth ice-cart I have seen. Ice seems an absolute necessity of life to Americans."

" Yes, madam," said Adiram. " that's just so. We consume ten thousand tons of ice per day in Chicago in summer-time. Half of this is used in the stock-yards, the rest is for private consumption. Each big hotel uses ten tons a day. Even the dead need it, for the undertakers consume two tons a day. We reckon we consume more ice and drink milk per head than any other city in the Union. But, my good friends, it is no use going on this way, sauntering about a city like this. If you want to see Chicago you ought to divide it up into sections, and do it systematically."

Mrs. Irwin sighed. " I spent an hour the other day reading Flinn's 'Standard Guide to Chicago.' I find the industrious Flinn plans out excursions for thirty-one days, during which time he says we shall see a great part, but by no means all, of Chicago. Now, we have not thirty-one days to spare, and as we cannot see all of Chicago even in a month, I think we had better stop before we begin."

" Tell us," said Compton, " what you think is best worth seeing in Chicago."

" Everything," said Adiram, " because Chicago is the sum of everything it contains. I cannot discriminate. But if you must begin somewhere, and you have already seen her lofty buildings, her railways, her parks and her avenues, her elevators, and her shipping, you ought now to see her University, so splendidly endowed by Mr. Rockefeller, the Baptist and Standard Oil Trust millionaire ; the *Herald* newspaper office, one of the most magni-

THE POLICE MONUMENT, CHICAGO.

ficent in the world ; then you should see the Union Stock Yard, the slaughter-houses, and the packing factories. On Sunday you should look into Farwell Hall, the headquarters of Moody and Sankey, and see the Armour

Mission. Then you should drive along State Street, one of our long streets, measuring eighteen miles from end to end. But when you have seen all these things you will only be at the beginning. I have lived in Chicago twenty years, and I have not seen half of it yet. Its annual growth is forty thousand citizens per annum, and it builds fifty miles of new buildings every year."

"Now," said Compton, " let us sit down and have a cup of tea. I suppose you have tea here? although coffee and cocoa seem more in demand."

"Sir," said Adiram, "there is one professional expert in this city who draws a salary of 25,000 dollars per annum as a tea taster.'

When they were drinking their tea Compton asked Adiram if he attributed the phenomenal growth of Chicago to the superior energy of the Western breed.

"Western breed, sir," said Adiram, who was from the

sleepy way like an open sewer into the Lake, poisoning the water the citizens had to drink. How did we do it, sir? Why, we simply turned it right round about, and now our river flows south instead of north, and empties our sewage into the Gulf of Mexico instead of Lake Michigan. It cost us twenty million dollars, but we faced the music and paid the bill.'

As the good Adiram seems likely to hold forth till the crack of doom upon the incomparable qualities of this great modern city, it may be well to leave him with Compton, and to follow the fortunes of the professor and Irene. These children of the *fin de siècle* were now almost inseparable. The professor had not proposed marriage, nor had he talked of love, although for the first time in his life he had felt it as a sentiment. As for Irene, she was about as much in love with the professor as she could ever be with anyone. For she had drabbled her soul out in alternating thrills and sensations, until there was not enough womanhood left in her to rise up majestic and irresistible in the might of a great passion. She was pleased with the professor. He was always giving her shocks, sometimes pleasant, sometimes not. But he never bored her, and he never made love to her, and that in itself was a secret of his attraction. For Irene had been spoiled with attention as pastry-cooks' apprentices lose their taste for sweets. She had had too much of it. If a girl has a pretty face, a saucy tongue, good serviceable eyes, and a smart figure, she can simply swim in admiration from the time she is eighteen till she is twenty-six. And after eight years of that kind of thing, even love-making by relays of lovers grows irksome. Hence, Irene and the professor were thoroughly enjoying themselves. They had been "doing Chicago"

GENERAL GRANT'S OLD HOME, SOON TO BE REMOVED TO CHICAGO.

State of Maine, "who is talking of Western breed? Chicago stands on the road to the West, but even the site is in the Eastern half of the Continent, and as for her citizens, they are more Eastern still. Chicago was financed from the East, settled from the East, and manned by Eastern men. Look over the list of her mayors, the men whose executive ability and force has commanded the recognition of their fellow citizens. Eight out of ten were born in New York or the East coast. Illinois has only produced two; two or three came from Kentucky. Chicago is the product of Eastern youth settled on Western soil, in the most central and convenient location in a territory 1,000 miles square."

"Then is the location what has made Chicago?" inquired Mrs. Irwin. -

"No," said Adiram. " What did the location do for the French, who had it first; or for the British, who cleared out afterwards? No, sir. The world hereaway was only half made until Chicago arose to improve it. Why, the very Chicago river itself did not know which way to flow until the city took it in hand. It used to flow in a slow,

ever since they had arrived. "Chicago first," said the professor; "the World's Fair afterwards." So they had been exhausting the sensations. They always lunched in the highest restaurant, tor the sake of the lift. The rapid elevator that whisks you up and down with electric speed delighted Irene. "It is like a switchback with a 200-feet drop," she said. " It would be just perfect if you could be jerked into the ascending lift the moment you touch the bottom."

The professor studied Irene, and humoured her to the top of her bent. He was interested in the girl, and occasionally he felt as if the inherited instinct of courtship might assert itself unawares. But the acquired instinct of the passion for experiment was far stronger than his incipient affection. Irene was to him a good type of the girl of the period, who in sheer loathing of *ennui*, would do anything for a thrill, and he did not hesitate to subject her to experience from which any other man would have recoiled, and which occasionally, to do him justice, touched even his hardened heart. He took her round all the worst streets—slumming, he called it—and then, still trying it on, he took her to an opium den ; of course only for the gratification of curiosity. She was keen to go, but she experienced something even more shocking than she had bargained for, when the police raided the house while they were on the premises and carried them both off to the police-station along with the degraded Celestials and their half-stupefied customers. They were conveyed in a patrol-waggon to the lock-up, where, however, after an altogether too exciting quarter-of-an-hour, they were liberated by the officer in charge with a reprimand. This excursion was kept a profound secret. No one knew of it, and the mystery of the secrecy made it all the more delectable to Irene. If Dr. Wynne had heard of it there would have been a fuss. So he was kept in the dark, and the professor, to do him justice, never repeated that escapade.

For the most part he took Irene to public institutions. He took her through the Bridewell in California Avenue, through which 10,000 prisoners pass annually on the first day of their arrival. But their favourite visiting place was the penitentiary. Here the professor was at home, and as he was one of the first experts in penology in the world, he was allowed to take Irene almost where he pleased. Of the 1,500 convicts in that institution, about 150, he said, were persons who deserved to be "micro-scoped," and he succeeded in introducing her to some fifteen of them before she found that even murderers pall when they come to tread one on the heels of another. He then introduced her to Michael Dunn, the English thief and ex-convict, who, in his old age, has turned philan-thropist, and after spending thirty years in British prisons, is utilising the experience gained in these public institu-tions by scanning Homes of Industry and Refuges for Discharged Prisoners in Honore Street, Chicago, in New York, San Francisco, and Detroit. She liked the gaol-bird, whose conversion, the professor explained, in a fashion she could not understand, was due to certain physiological changes in the cells in the base of the brain.

Irene loved to hear the professor talk, and as he loved to be listened to, it soon came to be a settled thing that they went everywhere together. Irene was delighted to hear from the lips of so eminent an authority, the most delight-fully destructive doctrines as to the absence of all moral responsibility on the part of the human automaton. "But professor," she ventured to observe one day, "what do you make of an uneasy conscience ?"

"Conscience!" he answered, "an uneasy conscience—oh, it is a species of indigestion."

When he took her to the World's Fair, he bade her note that the progress of civilization depended much more upon material inventions than so-called moral ideals. "What has made Chicago? Christianity? philanthropy? God Almighty? Stuff and nonsense. The only lord and maker of Chicago is the Almighty Dollar. His temple is the Stock Exchange, his scriptures the stock list. Why, when we came from New York in the express train, we had the quotations of the Chicago produce market telegraphed thrice a day to the vestibule car."

Irene, who had been brought up in Church and Sunday-school, was somewhat shocked, and at the same time pleased, although she could not altogether rid herself of the lingering remains of that indigestion, conscience.

"They talk," the professor went on, "of Columbus, and the Cross, of the men of the *Mayflower*, and the Bible. What did Cross or Bible do for the wilderness for three hundred years? Less than the steam-engine and the telegraph have done in our lifetime. Less than the man of science—the inventor, the engineer, the chemist—who subdues continents and conquers worlds. And people are beginning to see it. What is the World's Fair but the very apotheosis of Materialism, the triumph of Science."

"There are 200,000 people at the show to-day, said the professor, "and there are probably not two hundred who noticed the two things in the Fair which will most profoundly affect the outward appearance of American civilisation."

"What are these ?" said Irene, feeling quite certain that she was not among the two hundred.

"Medusaline and pergamoid,' said Glogoul, oracularly. "Medusaline is the pavement of civilisation. It is a compound of granite and cement that is as smooth as asphalt, as durable as adamant. It has been laid down throughout the Fair, on all footpaths, and it will be used throughout the world. Pergamoid is a preparation of celluloid, which will be the universal material for all per-manent advertising. As tough as bone, as flexible as cloth, and almost as cheap as paper, it will revolutionise the outward appearance of the United States."

"Really," said Irene. "Is not that rather a large order ?"

"No," said the professor. "What is the outward appearance of the United States—the Rockies, the prairies, the great lakes? Nothing of the kind. They only appear on maps. What appears to the natural eye every day is not mountain ranges but advertising posters, and for one man who sees a lake or a prairie, there are a thousand who see the various artifices by which quacks and other tradesmen disfigure their country in order to puff their goods."

"Dear me," said Irene. "I never thought of that before."

"It is everywhere the same," continued the professor. "What is going to revolutionise the roads of the continent. Preaching about the wickedness of mud and mire? Ex-hortations about the duty of promoting human intercourse? All the sermons since the days of Jonathan Edwards have done less to mend the roads than has been effected by the invention of the bicycle. The electric motor will complete what the bicycle has begun. What is it that will end wars? Brotherly love? Religion? No; it will be found by a chemist who will discover Vril, or by a mechanic who will give us the secret of flight."

"Then if you wanted to change the world?" said Irene.

"I would only ask for one thing," he replied promptly, "and that is ten per cent. Give me ten per cent. and I can work miracles. It was said by them of old time, 'If ye have faith but as a grain of mustard seed, ye shall say to this mountain, be thou removed and be thou cast into the sea, and it shall be done.' But I say if you can but pay ten per cent. you can trundle the Rockies into the Pacific. All things are possible to ten per cent. With ten per cent. you can do all things. Yes, for ten per cent. men will sell their lives—for their souls they can now-a-days find no purchasers."

"Do you really think men will sell their lives for ten per cent. ?" said Irene.

"I know it. Guarantee ten per cent. for draining a miasmatic marsh or laying down a railway through a hostile country, the sacrifice of life is not even thought of as an obstacle. Money can buy all things—even life Pshaw, what is life ?"

Irene was silent. "It is very pleasant to live some-times—at least, I find it so now and then," she said, look-ing up at him somewhat archly.

The professor accepted the compliment with a smile, and by way of showing his gratitude he suggested that next day she should accompany him to the famous Union Stock Yards, where eight million pigs, three million and a half cattle, and one million sheep are handled every year. Of these, about two million cattle and six million pigs are slaughtered in Chicago. Without thinking much about it,

Irene said she would be delighted to go with him anywhere.

"The girl is game," said the professor to himself, "she has never flinched yet." Then he said aloud, "All rignt, I will call for you at nine, and don't dress too gaily, for these places are not exactly like the World's Fair.

That night as he lay awake the professor found himself engaged in calculating whether he had not exhausted the experimental possibilities of celibacy, and whether, even if he had not done so, it would not be wise to begin the experimental study of matrimony.

"If I am to marry I ought to have a wife who would be willing to learn, who would be a good listener, and who would have plenty of pluck. And so far as my observation has gone, Miss Vernon seems to fill the bill better than any. No doubt marriage would not be paradise, but it is the purgatory of the race, and why snould I not go through it like the rest?"

Revolving these things he fell asleep. At nine next morning he called on Irene. To his dismay she was arrayed in a beautiful white dress with a coquettish little hat, and a gauzy jacket fastened in front with a blood red rose.

"But Miss Vernon," he stammered, "we are going to the slaughter-house. Do you think that dress——?"

"And is it not good enough for the butchers?", she asked, laughing. "Why I thought it looked very smart as I looked at myself in the glass!"

"Oh, yes," said the professor, "very beautiful indeed. But, but——"

"But me no buts, professor. I am not going to change my dress for any one. So if you are ready we will start."

ENTRANCE TO THE STOCK YARD.

The professor yielded, and they were soon driving rapidly to the Union Stock Yards. Irene was in high spirits. Never had she seemed more beautiful, not even when her evening toilette, as the *Majestic* neared New York, revealed to the professor the secret of the worship of Aphrodite.

"Here we are," said he, as they drew up opposite the main entrance of the stock-yards. A guide instantly accosted them, and was chartered to take them round. "But the lady's dress?" said the guide

"Never mind my dress," said Irene. "Goodness, what a smell!"

The wind had slightly veered round to the west, and the odour of the packing-house was unmistakable. From the restaurant gallery they looked down upon the swarming acreage of cattle pens where forty thousand head of we stock are handled every week-day in the year. They saw the agent of the Live Stock Commission riding up and down, keeping a keen look-out upon the cattle for evidences of suffering or lameness or disease. "There," said the professor, "is philanthropy on horseback – earning a living. But look at that bunko steer who is trained to act as guide and decoy to the cattle doomed to slaughter.

He is a noted character in the yard is 'Old Bill.' From morning to night, he is employed in luring his kith and kin to walk tranquilly from the stockyard to the killing-rooms. He leads them to the gate, and then steps aside, waits till they pass to their doom, and then quietly goes back to lead another contingent to the slaughter. It is murderous treason on four hoofs—earning its living. Yet no one blames the bunko steer. No one holds him up to moral reprobation. He does but as he is taught, no doubt; and so do we. But when will men recognise 'that they also are creatures of their environment?"

"Come," said he to Irene, "and see what kind of thing is life; how easily it is taken, how simple is the transformation from the living pig to merchantable pork."

Irene held a scented handkerchief to her nose as she followed the professor, who picked his steps through the dirt as of a farm-yard, leading the way to the killing-house. Up an inclined plane towards the chamber of death walked a drove of pigs marked for slaughter. With many a bewildered grunt and squeal the porcine company was driven on and on until they entered a pen on the landing where the killing was going on.

"Life, you ask, what is life?" said the professor. "What is it to these poor creatures? They are using their sharp, inquisitive eyes to the best of their ability and understanding nothing for all their looking. Who knows what beatific visions of limitless swill-tub and juicy and succulent mash gleam before these doomed porkers. Life has not been unpleasant to them I daresay. They gambolled merrily in their days of litterdom, they fed freely, and slept soundly on the breezy prairie. They are full of lusty life, and probably never loved it more than they do to-day. But let us go inside."

They entered the slaughter house. The stench was almost unbearable. The floor was slippery with blood. At the door a stalwart man slipped a running noose round the hind leg of the nearest pig. In an instant the rope was pulled tight, and the pig was jerked head downwards, and swung on a long iron overhead runner dipping downwards towards the other end of the room, where stood the vat over which they bled to death.

Standing ready to receive his prey was the slaughterer with a long, sharp knife in his right hand. Seizing the pig by one ear with his left hand, he plunged the knife into its throat, gave it a murderous twist, and drew it out. The warm blood spurted over his hand, but the pig had already begun to slide towards the vat. Another pig was swinging ready for sticking, and so the procession went on. A dozen or more pigs in progressive stages of inanition were bleeding to death, those further down were almost motionless, the last stuck were struggling horribly. The steam of the hot blood made a mist before their eyes. But still they could see that sharp, bright steel "going always," and they knew that a life went with every thrust. "Smart man that," said their guide, "he kills 5,000 hogs every day." Irene was looking on as if fascinated, when a more lively porker than ordinary, on receiving the knife in his throat, shrieked horribly, as with a human-like voice, and twisting himself round, flung some of his spurting blood upon Irene's dress. She stepped hurriedly back, her foot slipped, and before the professor could catch her, she fell full length into the gory, greasy mire with which the floor was covered.

Irene struggled to her feet. Her face was deadly pale, but her beautiful white dress was bedrabbled from head to foot with blood. The professor looked at her and remorse filled his soul. "My dear Miss Vernon," he said anxiously, "what shall we do?"

Irene felt she was on her mettle. She had not been a fortnight in constant company of an experimental physiologist without knowing the importance of such a test of her self-possession and self-control. "Do!" she said coolly, "why, I thought you were going to take me through the place."

"But, my dear Miss Vernon," he began, "your dress——'

"You seem very difficult to please about my dress to-day,' said Irene, affecting a laugh, although she felt deadly faint and much more inclined to cry. "Why can we not go through the programme here and now?' she said to the guide, who had been scraping the thickest of the dirt off with a bit of hoop-iron. "That will do, I am quite ready to go through with it."

But the professor would not hear of such a thing. She must not dream of it. She must retire at once and send for another dress or borrow a cloak. Irene, delighted at seeing that she was much more self-possessed than the professor, at last gave in, with every appearance of reluctance, although she was so deadly sick it was with the utmost difficulty she kept her feet. "Remember," she said, "it was not I who flinched." And they led her out into an ante-room, where after a time a maid was procured, and she was divested of her soiled and blood-stained dress.

Before retiring she begged the professor to go round the place. She could find her way home alone. But the professor would not hear of it. He hung round the ante-room the picture of misery, waiting until she emerged. She was a good while, and he became more and more wretched. "What a wretch I was," he said

IRENE SLIPPED AND FELL

to himself, "to expose her to this. But what splendid pluck! What iron nerve! That's the woman for me—if only I haven't lost her," he added bitterly "She will never forgive me. And I daresay I deserve it."

But when Irene came out clad in a long cloak that con-cealed all the deficiencies in her toilet, she was quite cordial, although she gently bantered him for not going round the packing-house. But she was obviously faint, and he was very glad to get her into a carriage and drive off with her to the hotel.

As they were on their way, the professor, in an absent-minded kind of way, took one of Irene's hands and pressed it to his lips.

"Really, sir," said Irene, bridling up, "this is too much. After letting me fall in that horrid puddle, to kiss my hand. I should have thought it would have been too blood-stained."

"Irene!" said the professor. Her eyes dilated as she heard him address her for the first time by her Christian name, but she said nothing.

"Irene, forgive me. I beg you to forgive me. But I forgot what I was doing. Or rather, I was thinking of the future. That is——" and he stopped, hopelessly confused.

Irene looked at him calmly, and said, "Is this a physio-logical experiment, professor? or"—and she dropped her eyes: "is it——?"

Dr. Glogoul was grateful for the opening. Grasping both her hands in his, he exclaimed, "It is, it is. Oh, forgive me. I am so sorry. I never admired you more than I did this morning. You were so beautiful. But I never loved you so much as when you got up and wanted to go round. Irene, you have more nerve than I possess. I need such a woman as you. Will you be my wife?"

And he bowed his head to her knee and kissed her hand with more feeling than she deemed possible.

"Well," said Irene, "I think I need such a man as you, and as you ask me I think I will. "But——"

"But what?' said the professor, anxiously.

"I want to be mar-ried in the Mormon Tabernacle in Salt Lake City. That would be so delight-fully amusing."

"Irene," said the professor, "I'll marry you anywhere or no-where. No, I don't mean that," he stam-mered. "But I'll do what you please about it."

And then he leaned forward and kissed her. It is notable, as an instance of the habit of scientific ob-servation and reflec-tion which the professor always cultivated, that when their lips met for the first time he was thinking whether the scent with which she had copiously sprinkled her hair, or the odour of the packing-house, which lingered about them both, would the sooner evaporate.

"Irene," said the professor, thoughtfully, "I am afraid I have behaved very badly to you more than once. But in the future I shall experiment upon you just as if you were myself, I promise you just as if you were part and parcel of myself. Oh, what experiments we shall have, for in vivisection two are better than one."

"He is only marrying me as a subject," thought Irene, as she went upstairs to bathe and purify herself. "Well, perhaps so. And what am I marrying him as, I wonder? As a diversion and as a livelihood? Possibly. It is six of one and half-a-dozen of the other."

With which sage reflection she comforted her soul, and

when she came down to dinner no one could have suspected through what a crisis she had passed earlier in the day.

There was a gathering of the Blue Brigade at the hotel that night, and there was much excitement as first Compton and then the professor announced their respective marriages.

"I congratulate you both," said the doctor, and Mrs. Wills said she thought them all well-matched. After dinner the little company gathered together in the drawing-room of the hotel and began to discuss their next movements.

"Chicago," said Mrs. Irwin, "seems to be one of the easiest places in the world from which to get away. You want to go away east, north, south or west, you pay your money and you take your choice. We have the whole world before us, and where are we going?"

"That depends," said the professor, "upon two things; first, where you want to go and secondly, whether a good number of human beings have had that wish before, in order that you find the necessary apparatus already constructed to carry you there."

"First," said the doctor, "Mrs. Wills has to go to San

was some ten years ago when I was there examining the remains of the cave dwellers who many centuries ago lived on the sides of the Great Canon."

"But what is the Great Canon?" persisted Irene.

"That," said the professor, "you will understand when you get there. No tongue can explain what even the eye inadequately surveys. The ancients would have made it the mouth of hell. Science, however, has stopped the value of these picturesque methods of describing the indescribable. It is a gigantic gorge which the Colorado River has cut through limestone, sandstone and granite. To get to the bottom of this awful chasm you have to scramble down a mule path as steep as Jacob's ladder, for nearly five miles. Long before the bottom is reached the mule path gives out and you have then to descend by means of rope ladders into the abyss along which the waters roar like a cataract, and the mountains rise almost in perpendicular walls 3,000 feet above your head. It is only twenty-six years ago since the first exploring party ventured to survey it, and no one who saw them launch their boats on the terrible river expected to see them emerge alive again."

"Well," said Irene, "I think that sounds promising. But is it big enough? for since I have come to this country I have contracted a taste for dimensions."

"The Grand Canon is just the size of Switzerland, about 15,000 square miles. By the Topeka and Santa Fe Railway you travel within sixty-five miles from Flagstaff, from whence you make the descent into the abyss. From the Grand Canon we shall have several weeks of mountaineering with pack horses, camping out, in order to reach Utah."

"That fixes you up," said Mrs. Irwin. "Now

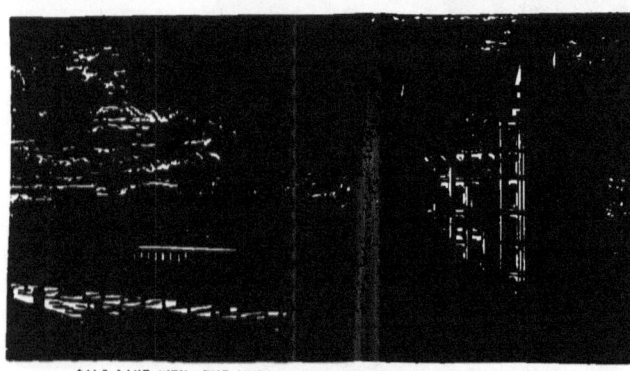

SALT LAKE CITY: THE MORMON TABERNACLE AND THE NEW TEMPLE.

Francisco. I suppose there is no doubt about the way she should go?"

"No," said Compton, who had before him a mass of handbooks, railway-guides, and similar literature, "her course is quite plain. She will go by the Union Pacific through Utah and on to the Golden Gate. It is the oldest Trans-continental railway, and when once you are aboard you need have no further anxiety until you get out at the other end."

"That settles Mrs. Wills," said Irene, "for her it is all plain sailing. But for us——Professor," said she playfully, "where have we to go?"

"I have been thinking," said the professor. "There is only one place on the continent which would give you a strong enough thrill to prepare you for matrimony, and that is the Grand Canon of the Colorado."

"Where on earth is that?" said Irene.

"It is in Arizona. It is the most awe-inspiring, terrible and wonderful place in the whole of the United States."

"I can see that Miss Vernon's mouth is already watering," said the doctor, "but how on earth do you get there?"

"It is not so difficult now," said the professor, "as it

for our turn. Where shall we go?"

"Well," said Compton, "I have been studying the map for some time. I first thought of going to the Yosemite, but it lies just a little too much out of the way; everyone goes to the Yosemite; in midsummer it would be pleasanter to get to a higher region, more to the north. My plan is that we should go through the North West and Minneapolis and strike the North Pacific, and then along the main line to the Yellowstone Park, and spend a quiet fortnight by the side of the Yellowstone Lake. There is no lake so large that lies so high above the level of the sea. From there we will run down to Portland in Oregon and finish our honeymoon on the shores of the Pacific, looking out over the illimitable expanse of sea which divides us from the land of the rising sun."

"The Yellowstone is all very well," said the professor to Irene, "but the whole of the Yellowstone Park, lake and all, could be tucked away in one of the gorges through which we shall have to clamber to get to the bottom of the Great Canon. You have no idea what sort of a place it is. I can assure you that Niagara is but a trout stream when compared with the torrent of the Colorado."

"But doctor," said Compton, "when you leave are you going to travel further afield or going straight home?"

"I shall go home," said the doctor, "by the Lake Shore and Michigan Railway, which will take me to Niagara. I do not wish to leave the country without seeing the Falls. When I was a boy it seemed to be the one attraction which was strong enough to lure a man across the Atlantic."

"And from Niagara——?'"

"And from Niagara I shall strike the beautiful country which is served by the Delaware and Hudson Line, which will bring me back to New York. From there of course it is plain sailing to Liverpool."

"In another week," said Irene, "we shall be scattered to the uttermost ends of the earth. The professor and I shall be at the mouth of hell, Mr. and Mrs. Compton will be at the Yellowstone Park and on their way to the Pacific, and the doctor will be wending his way homewards over the Atlantic. Heigho, who knows whether we shall ever meet again in this world!"

As they left the room, the doctor said to the professor, "It is all very well this honeymooning before marriage, but you must have the civil ceremony over before you leave Chicago, the marriage in Utah can come afterwards."

"All right," said the professor; "but make her believe it is only a preliminary formality. Otherwise it would spoil her thrill!"

GRAND CANON OF THE COLORADO.

CHAPTER XIX.—FROM THE OTHER SIDE.

ROSE was still weak and unable to get about. Mrs Julia made it her duty to call upon her every morning. One day she startled Rose by saying, "Robert woke me last night. I was sound asleep in the hotel, when suddenly I became conscious of a presence in the room. I woke up in a moment, and there by my bedside I saw him as plainly as ever I saw him in life. He looked at me with a yearning look of infinite love in his eyes, and then, as I stretched out my hands, he slowly faded away."

"Were you not dreaming?" said Rose, incredulously.

"I was as wide awake as ever I was in my life," said Mrs. Julia. "Besides, this is not the first time I have seen him. I saw him quite as distinctly shortly after his death. I am almost always conscious of his presence. It seemed to me quite natural that he should appear to me. When we first fell in love we promised that whichever of us died the first would, if possible, come back to the world to comfort the other with news of the other side. But, alas, I am unable to hear what he says, and I grieve to think that he is hovering around trying to communicate with me, and that I am unable to understand his loving messages from beyond the grave."

This made a deep impression upon Rose. She was naturally mystical. Her girlhood had been nurtured on the two books which are of all in English literature the fullest of the supernatural, the Bible and Shakespeare. It did not seem to her unnatural that Robert Julia should have come to see his widow after his decease. She had always counted confidently upon Walter visiting her if he had preceded her to the invisible world. As for herself, she knew that the first and last thought of her liberated spirit would have been to seek him whom she had loved so long.

But she had never imagined that aggravation of misery, the torture of Tantalus, the possibility of the disembodied spirit being able to approach without being able to communicate with the beloved one. She thought over it a good deal. She found in Aunt Deborah's book-shelves some old numbers of the late Colonel Bundy's "Religious Philosophical Journal," and read them eagerly and diligently. There was to be a congress, she saw, of all the psychical researchers of the world at the Chicago Exhibition. Chicago, not content with collecting all the treasures of the Old World and the New, must also cast its plummet into the immeasurable abyss of the infinite, and interrogate the Invisible, demanding its answer to the problems of the world. Rose did not care for congresses, but an article in the paper on automatic handwriting caught her attention. "Take a pen," it said, "hold it in your hand over a sheet of blank paper, keep your mind passive and wait. In many cases your hand will begin to write of its own accord, and after a time you will be able to secure communications from those who are on the other side."

Rose read it, re-read it, and then decided to try it. At first her hand remained as motionless as if it had been made of lead. She was beginning to despair, when it began to show some tendency to move. She watched it with fascinated interest. There was no doubt about it. The pen was moving. She was not consciously moving it, of that she was certain, but it only made quite illegible scrawls. Still, it moved. It might write some day. She tried again. It moved more freely, and its scrawls might possibly be construed as attempts to frame legible words. The third time it wrote quite clearly, "Robert Julia."

"Are you here?" she asked.

Then sl...wly, but distinctly, her hand wrote, in large Roman characters, "I am."

There the pen stopped. Rose's heart was beating hard as she watched her hand, holding her breath, and hardly daring to speak. Then it began to move, forming letter after letter slowly, and with infinite labour, as if some one was trying to use the pen by manipulating her elbow from behind.

"Tell my wife," it wrote—and then paused, then it began again—"not to grieve because she cannot speak to me. I am constantly with her, impressing her mind and reading the thoughts of her mind."

"Yes," said Rose, plucking up courage, "but how am I to know that you are her husband who is writing? Can you give me a test?"

Her pen quivered, and then slowly wrote, "Yes."

"Go on, then," said Rose.

And her hand wrote : "Ask Adelaide to remember what I said to her the last day we went to Minerva."

"Minerva," said Rose, "is that right?"

"Yes," wrote the hand.

"But how could she go to Minerva? Is Minerva a place?"

"No,' wrote the hand.

"Then this is nonsense," said Rose decisively. "How could you go to Minerva, who was an old heathen goddess?"

And her hand wrote, "Never mind. Deliver the message to Adelaide, she will understand."

Rose did not like it. The message was all right; the test was foolishness. She hesitated to say anything about it to her friend, but ultimately decided she had better tell her exactly what had happened.

Mrs. Julia came in next day.

With many apologies, Rose mentioned what had happened, and said she did not like to speak of it, the proffered test was so absurd.

"Well,' said Mrs. Julia, "what was it?"

Rose read it out with some degree of shame: "Ask Adelaide to remember what I said to her the last day we went to Minerva."

"That is quite absurd, is it not?" she asked.

"No," said Mrs. Julia, with deep feeling. "I remember it perfectly."

"But how," asked Rose in amazement, "but how could you go to Minerva?"

"Of course, my dear Rose, you do not understand," said the widow; "but we had a very dear friend whom we always called Minerva, as a pet name, because of a brooch she wore that had on it a cameo of Minerva's head. The last day on which we went to Minerva was the day before he died. Well indeed do I remember the solemn words to which he calls my attention."

Rose was startled. She had never before realised as an actual possibility the establishment of direct communication between the living and the dead.

'Adelaide," she said, "if it is really your husband, let me ask him to give me another test. It is too wonderfully blessed a hope to be admitted on a single test."

The widow did not answer. Her heart was too full of memories of the past. Rose got her pen and paper and, sitting down, said:

"If you are really Adelaide's husband, would you reveal some incident which she will remember but which is entirely unknown to me? Any little trivial thing will do," she added hurriedly, for she feared the possible effect which the revival of more serious events might have upon her friend.

Then she waited. Presently her hand began to move. The two women watched its movements as they might

have watched the rolling away of the stone that sealed the sepulchre. The words slowly formed at first and then more rapidly. When the message was complete Rose read it aloud to the widow. It ran thus :—

"Robert Julia. Yes. Ask her to remember the day we were walking together, when she slipped and sprained her ankle?"

"Well," said Rose, "I certainly know nothing about that. Do you remember it, Adelaide?"

Adelaide, still more or less confused by the first message, said slowly, "Well, no. I do not think I ever sprained my ankle."

"Really?" said Rose in a disappointed tone. Then, addressing the unknown entity which controlled her hand, she said in a mocking tone, "There! what is the use of your test? Adelaide never sprained her ankle, so you are all wrong. Your test is no good."

To her amazement her hand wrote: "No, I am quite right. She has forgotten.'

"It is all very well to say that," said Rose, "but how can you prove it? How long ago was it?"

And her hand wrote: "Seven years."

"And where did it occur?" she continued.

"On the terrace at Windsor; we were walking there shortly after we were engaged, when she slipped her foot and——"

"I remember," interrupted Adelaide; "I remember perfectly! How could I have forgotten it! He had almost to carry me to a cab. I nearly fainted with the pain."

And then she added, awestruck: "O, Robert! Robert! then it is really you? Do tell me what has happened to you since, since——" and her voice broke down.

Rose, very pale and quivering with a sense of the presence of the dead, once more placed her pen on the paper. Adelaide interrupted her, "No, not now; I cannot bear it now. Let me go."

Rose put her arms round her friend's neck and kissed her tenderly. "Yes,' said she, "you had better go. It is too wonderful."

But the moment Mrs. Julia had left, Rose resumed her place at the table, and said: "Mr. Julia, your wife has gone. But had you not better take my hand and write her a letter, just as if you were on earth. I will send it to her."

The pen at once began to move at the top of the sheet of letter paper : "My darling Adelaide." Then after some tender and touching greetings, the invisible writer went on to say that he did not think he could do better than just tell her what had happened to him since he passed over. Then he continued as follows :—

"When I left you, darling, you thought I was gone from you for ever, or at least till you also passed over. But I was never so near to you as after I had, what you called, died.

"I found myself free from my body. It was such a strange new feeling. I was standing close to the bedside on which my body was lying ; I saw everything in the room just as before I closed my eyes. I did not feel any pain 'dying'; I felt only a great calm and peace. Then I awoke, and I was standing outside my old body in the room. There was no one there at first, just myself and my old body. At first I wondered I was so strangely well. Then I saw that I had passed over.

"I waited about a little ; then the door opened and Mrs. Judson came in. She was very sad; she addressed my poor body as if it was myself. I was standing looking at her, but all her thoughts were upon the poor old body I had left behind. I did not try to speak at first, I waited to see what would happen.

"Then I felt as though a great warm flood of light had come into the room, and I saw an angel. She, for she seemed to be a female, came to me and said,—

" ' I am sent to teach you the laws of the new life.'

"And as I looked, she gently touched me and said,—

" ' We must go.'

"Then I left the room and my poor old body, and passed out. It was so strange, the streets were full of spirits. I could see them as we passed, they seemed to be just like ourselves. My angel had wings; they were very beautiful. She was all robed in white.

"We went at first through the streets, then we went through the air, till we came to the place where we met friends who had passed on before.

"There were Mr. Morgan, and Mr. Mitchell, and Ethel Julia, and many others. They told me much about the spirit world. They said I must learn its laws, and endeavour to be as useful as I could. The angel who remained with me all the time helped me to explain.

"The spirit friends had their life much as it was here; they lived and loved, and if they had not to work for their daily bread, they had still plenty to do.

"Then I began to be sad about you, and I wanted to go back; the angel took me swiftly through the air to where I came from. When I entered the death chamber there lay my body. It was no longer of interest to me, but I was so grieved to see how you were all greeting over my worn-out clothes. I wished to speak to you. I saw you, darling, all wet with tears, and I was so sad I could not cheer you. I very much wanted to speak and tell you how near I was to you, but I could not make you hear. I tried, but you took no notice. I said to the angel,—

" ' Will it be always thus ?'

"She said,—' Wait; the time will come when you will speak with her. But at present she cannot hear, neither can she understand.'

"I was then called away. I found myself in a great expanse of landscape where I had never been before. I was alone; that is, I saw no one. But you are never really alone. We are always living in the presence of God. But I saw no one. Then, I heard a voice. I did not see from whence it came, or who spoke. I only heard the words, ' Robert Julia, *He who saved thee would fain speak with thee.*' I listened, but no words other than these were spoken.

"Then I said, 'Who is it that speaks?' And, behold, a flaming fire—really like fire though in human shape. I was afraid. Then He spoke and said, ' Be not afraid. It is I, who am appointed to teach thee the secret things of God.' Then I saw that the brightness as of fire was only the brightness that comes from the radiant love of the Immortals.

"Then a flame-bright One said to me, ' Robert, behold your Saviour !' and when I looked, I saw Him. He was sitting on a seat close to me, and He said, ' Beloved, in my Father's House are many mansions; here am I whom you have loved so long. I have prepared a place for you.'

"And I said, 'Where, oh, my Lord ?' He smiled, and in the brightness of that smile I saw the whole landscape change as the Alps change in the sunset, which I saw so often from the windows of my hotel at Lucerne. Then I saw that I was not alone, but all around and above were fair and loving forms, some of those whom I had known, others of whom I had heard, while some were strange. But all were friends, and the air was full of love. And in the midst of all was He, my Lord and Saviour. He was as a Man among men. He was full of the wonderful sweet mildness which you are acquainted with in some of the pictures that have been painted by the Italian Fra Angelico. He had an admirable look of warm affection, which was as the very breath of life to my soul. He is with us always. This is Heaven —to be with Him. You cannot understand how the consciousness of His presence makes the atmosphere of this world so different from that with you. There are many things I wish I could write to you, but I cannot, nor could you understand them. I can only tell you that He is more than we ever have imagined. He is the Source and Giver of all good gifts. All that we know of what is good, and sweet, and pure, and noble, and lovable are but faint reflections of the immensity of the glory that is His. And He loves us with such tender love ! Oh, Adelaide, Adelaide, you and I used to love each other with what seemed to us sometimes too deep and intense a love, but that at its very best was but the pale reflection of the love with which He loves us, which is marvellously and wonderfully great beyond all power of mind to describe. His name is Love ; it is what He is— Love, Love, Love !"

When the hand had finished writing the letter Rose read it over. She hesitated a moment about sending it. Who was Mrs. Judson? Who were the others who were named? Had they ever existed? Were they dead? It would be ghastly if Mrs. Julia knew none of them ! Rose, however, did not feel justified in keeping the letter back. She posted it and waited anxiously for the morning.

Early next morning Mrs Julia came to see her. There was an exalted look in her eyes—a look as of triumph and of radiant delight. Rose glanced at her hastily, fearing to reveal her anxiety.

"Oh, Rose," said the widow as she kissed her, "it is really Robert. How wonderful !"

"What !" said Rose, "are you quite sure ?"

"Yes," said Mrs. Julia, seating herself, "it is Robert himself. How else could you have written of these people of whom you knew nothing?"

"Then," said Rose, hurriedly, "were the names right ? '

"Mrs. Judsen," said the widow, "was my husband's nurse at the hospital. Mr. Morgan was his brother-in-law who died some years since. Ethel was his little sister who died in childhood. Mr. Mitchell was his most intimate friend. No, I can no longer doubt. It is Robert himself. But oh, I want to know so much more. Do you think he will write again ? "

"We can ask,' said Rose ; and sitting down to the table she once more let her unconscious hand be guided over the paper by the invisible control. It began, " I am here, Robert Julia.'

"Robert," said Adelaide, " where are you, and how do you live now? Tell me everything."

And Rose's hand began writing. "I cannot tell you everything, you could not understand it. But I am in a state of bliss such as we never imagined when on earth. I am with my friends who went before."

"Your father, Robert," said the widow, "is he with you, the dear old man ?"

And the hand went on writing. "He is, but he no longer seems to be old. He is like me, not older than I seem to be. We are both young, with what seems to be immortal youth. We can, when we please, assume the old bodies or their spiritual counterparts as we can assume our old clothes for purposes of identification, but our spiritual bodies here are young and beautiful. There is a semblance between what we are and what we were. We might recognise the new by its likeness to the old, but it is very different. The disembodied soul soon assumes the new raiment of youth, from which all decay has been removed.

"I find it so difficult to explain how we live, and how we spend our time. We never weary, and do not need to sleep as we did on earth; neither do we need to eat or drink; these things were necessary for the material body, here we do not need them. I think we can best teach you what we experience by asking you to remember those moments of exaltation when, in the light of the setting or rising sun, you look out, happy and content, upon the landscape upon which the sun's rays have shed their magical beauty. There is peace; there is life; there is beauty; above all, there is love. Beauty everywhere, joy and love. Love, love is the secret of Heaven. God is love, and when you are lost in love you are found in God.

"You ask me what we feel about the sin and sorrow of the world. We reply that we see it, and seek to remove it. But it does not oppress us as it used to do, for we see the other side. We cannot doubt the love of God. We live in it. It is the greatest, the only real thing. The sins and sorrows of the earth-life are but as shadows that will flee away. But they are not merely on the earth plane; there is sin and there is sorrow on this side. Hell is on this side as well as Heaven. But it is the joy of Heaven to be always emptying Hell.

"We are learning always to save by love; how to redeem by sacrifice. We must make sacrifices, otherwise there is no salvation. What else is the secret of Christ?"

"But, Robert," said Adelaide, "did it not seem all very strange to you, very different from what you had expected?"

And the hand went on writing, "Yes, it was different. I was not prepared for such oneness in the life on both sides.

"When the soul leaves the body it remains exactly the same as when it was in the body; the soul which is the only real self, and which uses the mind and the body as its instruments, no longer has the use or the need of the body. But it retains the mind, the knowledge, the experience, the habits of thought, the inclinations; they remain exactly as they were. Only it often happens that the gradual decay of the fleshly envelope to some extent obscures and impairs the real self which is liberated by death. The most extraordinary thing that came to my knowledge when I passed over was the difference between the apparent man and the real self. It gave quite a new meaning to the warning. 'Judge not,' for the real self is built up even more by the use it makes of the mind than by the use it makes of the body. There are here men who seemed to be vile and filthy to their fellows, who are far, far, far superior, even in purity and holiness, to men who in life kept an outward veneer of apparent goodness while the mind rioted in all wantonness. It is the mind that makes character. It is the mind that is far more active, more potent than the body, which is but a poor instrument at best. Hence the thoughts and intents of the heart, the imaginations of the mind, these are the things by which we are judged; for it is they which make up and create as it were the real character of the inner self, which becomes visible after the leaving of the body. Thought has much greater reality than you imagine. The day-dreamer is not so idle as you imagine. The influence of his idealising speculation may not make him work, but it may be felt imperceptibly by more practical minds. And so, in like manner, the man who in his innermost heart gives himself up to evil and unclean thoughts may be generating forces, the evil influences of which stir the passions and ruin the lives it may be of his own children, who possibly never knew that their father had ever had a thought of sin.

"Hence on this side things seem so topsy-turvy. The first are last, the last first. I see convicts and murderers and adulterers, who worked their wickedness out in the material sphere, standing far higher in the scale of purity and of holiness than some who never committed a crime,

but whose minds, as it were, were the factory and breeding-ground of thoughts which are the seed of crimes in others. I do not mean by this that it is better to do crimes than to think them. Only that the doing is not always to be taken as proof of wicked-heartedness. The sins of impulse, the crimes perpetrated in a gust of passion, these harm the soul less and do less harm than the long-indulged thoughts of evil which come at last to poison the whole soul.

"When the body is cast off the real state of the case is visible. Then it is for the first time that we are seen as we really are or rather have been thinking. The revelation is startling, and even now I am but dimly beginning to be accustomed to it.

"Then there is another thing that surprised me not a little, and that was or is the discovery of the nothingness of things. I mean by that the entire nothingness of most things which seemed to one on earth the most important of things. For instance, money, rank, worth, merit, station, and all the things we most prize when on earth, are simply nothing. They don't exist any more than the mist of yesterday or the weather of last year. They were no doubt influential for a time, but they do not last, they pass as the cloud passes, and are not visible any more."

The two friends remained for some time silent. Then Adelaide said,—

"Good-bye, Robert. I feel you are always with me."

And the hand wrote: "Good-bye; I am, Robert Julia."

Next morning Mrs. Julia was detained at home by a severe cold. Rose, after waiting for her for some time, resumed her seat at the table, and asked Robert if he was present and wished to write.

The hand did not write at once. After a few moments it wrote: "I am here: Robert Julia. My wife is unwell. I have just left her. She cannot come to-day."

Rose said, "Do you wish to write now?"

The hand wrote: "I do; I want to ask you if you can help me at all in a matter in which I am much interested? I have long wanted to establish a place where those who have passed over could communicate with the loved ones behind. At present the world is full of spirits longing to speak to those from whom they have been parted, just as I longed to speak to you, but without finding a hand to enable them to write. It is a strange spectacle. On your side, souls full of anguish for bereavement; on this side, souls full of sadness because they cannot communicate with those whom they love. What can be done to bring these sombre, sorrow-laden persons together? To do so requires something which we cannot supply. You must help. But how? It is not impossible. And when it is done death will have lost its sting and the grave its victory. The apostle thought this was done. But the grave has not been so easily defeated, and death keeps his sting. Who can console us for the loss of our beloved? Only those who can show us they are not lost, but are with us more than ever. Do you not think I have been much more with Adelaide since I put off my flesh than I used to be? Why, I dwelt with her in a way that before was quite impossible. I was never more with her than I have been since I came to this side. But she would not have known it, nor would you have heard from me at all but for the accident of your meeting.

"What is wanted is a bureau of communication between the two sides. Could you not establish some such sort of office with a trustworthy medium or medium? If only it were to enable the sorrowing on the earth to know, if only for once, that their so-called dead live nearer them than ever before, it would help to dry many a tear and soothe many a sorrow. I think you could count upon the eager co-operation of all on this side

"We on this side are full of joy at the hope of this coming to pass. Imagine how grieved we must be to see so many whom we love, sorrowing without hope, when those for whom they sorrow are trying every means in vain to make them conscious of their presence. And many also are racked with agony, imagining that their loved ones are lost in hell, when in reality they have been found in the all-embracing arms of the love of God. Adelaide dear, do talk of this with Minerva, and see what can be done. It is the most important thing there is to do. For it brings with it the trump of the Archangel, when those that were in their graves shall awake and walk forth once more among men.

"I was at first astonished to learn how much importance the spirits attach to the communications which they are allowed to have with those on earth. I can, of course, easily understand, because I feel it myself—the craving there is to speak to those whom you loved and whom you love; but it is much more than this. What they tell me on all sides, and especially my dear guides, is that the time is come when there is to be a great spiritual awakening among the nations, and that the agency which is to bring this about is the sudden and conclusive demonstration, in every individual case which seeks for it of the reality, of the spirit, of the permanence of the soul, and the immanence of the Divine."

Rose said, "But how can I help?"

The hand wrote. "You are a good writing medium. If you would allow your hand to be used by the spirit of any on this side whose relatives or friends wished to hear from them, you could depend almost confidently upon the spirit using your hand. At any rate, I could always explain why they could not use your hand."

That afternoon the Rev. Solomon Stybarrow made a pastoral call upon the household. Rose was intensely interested in the discovery of her automatic gift, and ventured to consult him on the subject. He started as if he had been stung. "Miss Thorne," said he, "have nothing to do with any such spirits. Spiritualism is nine parts fraud and one part the devil. Cursed be he who has dealings with a familiar spirit. If any spirits profess to control your hand they lie. If they are lost souls they would not be allowed out of hell. If they are saved, they are too happy in heaven to come down here to jump tables or to use your hand. What good thing have these spirits ever written since spiritualism began? Avoid it as an imposture based on credulity and cursed by the Bible and the Church."

Rose was startled by his vehemence, but she said, "Are we not told to try the spirits, and how can we try them if we do not listen to them?"

The Rev. Solomon Stybarrow hardly deigned a reply, but departed in high dudgeon.

When he had gone, Rose sat down to her paper, and asked Robert Julia if he wished to write. He began as usual, and then went on:—

"You must not heed that minister. When I was on your side I believed as he does. But I now know that those who have only lived on one side cannot possibly know as much as those who are actually on this side and have already lived on yours."

Then Rose said, "Had you not better take my hand and write and tell Adelaide about your side? What is it, for instance, which makes heaven so much better than earth?"

The hand wrote:

"There are degrees in heaven. And the lowest heaven is higher than the most wonderful vision of its bliss that you ever had. There is nothing to which you can compare our constantly loving state in this world except the supreme beatitude of the lover who is perfectly satisfied with and perfectly enraptured with the one whom he loves. For the whole difference between this side and your side consists in this—without entering now into the question of body and matter—that we live in love, which is God, and you too often live in the misery which is the natural, necessary result of the absence of God, who is love.

"There is much love on earth. Were it not so it would be hell. There is the love of the mother for her children, of brother and sister, of young man and maiden, of husband and wife, of friends, whether men or women, or whether the friendship is between those of the same sex. All these forms of love are the rays of heaven in earth. They are none of them complete. They are the sparkling light from the diamond facets, the totality of which is God. The meanest man or woman who loves is, so far as they love, inspired by the Divine. The whole secret of the saving of the world lies in that—you must have more love —more love—more love.

"You may say that there is love which is selfish and a love which is evil. It is true, but that is because the love is imperfect. It is not love when it leads to selfishness. The love which leads a mother to engross herself with her own children and neglect all her duties to other people is not wrong itself. It is only because she has not enough love for others that her love for her children makes her selfish. The great need wherever love seems to make people selfish is not less love to those whom they do love, but more love for the others who are neglected. You never love anyone too much. It is only that we don't love others enough also. Perfect love all round is the Divine ideal, and when love fails at any point, then evil is in danger of coming in. But even a guilty love, so far as it takes you out of yourself, and makes you toil, and pray, and live, and perhaps die for the man or woman whom you should never have loved, brings you nearer heaven than selfish, loveless marriage. I do not say this as against marriage. I know this is dangerous doctrine. All true doctrine is dangerous. But it is not less true for its danger. There is no doubt that much so-called love is very selfish, and is not love at all. The love, for instance, which leads a man to ruin a woman, and desert her when he has gratified a temporary passion, is not love. It is not easy to distinguish it from the deadliest hate. It is self-indulgence in its worst shape. Now all love is of the nature of self-sacrifice. There are many things also to be borne in mind. We have all not merely to think what is the result to ourselves, but also to other persons, some of whom may not yet be born. To love, therefore, anyone really, truly, means that we are putting ourselves in his place, loving him as ourselves, that we desire for him the best, and give up ourselves and our own pleasure in order to secure it for him. This is true love, and wherever you find it you find a spark of God. That is why mothers are so much nearer God than anyone else. They love more—that is, they are more like God; it is they who keep the earth from becoming a vast hell.

"Now, my darling, hold fast to this central doctrine: Love is God, God is love. The more you love, the more you are like God. It is only when we deeply, truly love, we find our true selves, or that we see the Divine in the person loved. O Addie, Addie! if I could come back and speak in the ears of the children of men, I think I should wish to say nothing but this—love; love is the fulfilling of the law, love is the seeing of the face of God. Love is God, God is love. If you wish to be with God—love. If you wish to be in heaven—love. For heaven differs chiefly from earth and from hell in that in heaven all love up to the full measure of their being, and all growth in grace is growth in love. Love! love! love! That is the first word and the last word. There is none beside that, for God, who is love, is all in all, the Alpha and the Omega, the first and the last, world without end. Oh, my darling Addie, this is indeed a true word. It is the word which the world needs, it is the word which became flesh and dwelt amongst men—Love, love, love ! "

Mrs. Julia arrived in the morning, in radiant spirits.

" Well ? " said Rose.

And Adelaide replied : " O Rose ! I feel as if already there was no more death, and as if the kingdom of Heaven is really about to be established in the earth."*

CHAPTER XX.—ANN HATHAWAY'S COTTAGE, CHICAGO.

THE last days of Dr. Wynne's stay in Chicago were drawing to a close. The party which had crossed the Atlantic in the *Majestic* was scattered far and wide. Mrs. Wills and her three children had met Mr. Wills in San Francisco. Irene and the professor were to be married in the Temple, by special permission from the President of the Latter Day Saints, and they were spending the time before their marriage in the Grand Canon of the Colorado.

" Honeymoons after marriage," said Irene, " were quite too conventional. The professor and she were taking their honeymoon before the ceremony. It sounds awful, but it is quite correct, although the situation is full of exciting incidents. The professor is not a very good hand at love-making anyhow, but, as I tell him, it is a new experience which he should make the most of. We are travelling with some *savans*, and they get so warm about protoplasm and other horrors that the professor sometimes quite forgets that he is engaged."

Compton had married Mrs. Irwin, and they were spending their honeymoon quite in the orthodox fashion in the Yellowstone Valley, that great museum of nature of which the Republic is the vigilant custodian.

Mrs. Julia had gone back to New York, full of a peace and content to which she had been a stranger since her husband's death. Mr. Thorne was putting the last touches to the special job on which he had been engaged, and which was the erection of a correct model of Ann Hathaway's Cottage, and when this was finished he intended to return to England with his daughter.

Rose had almost recovered. She had been several times in the Exhibition, but she was alone, the multitude of strange faces weighed upon her spirits, and after a while she lost heart. It was vain to seek him among so many myriads. Repeatedly she thought she had recognised the well-known figure, only to find, on overtaking it, that the features were not those of him whom she sought. On one occasion she made certain that she saw him. It was his figure, his hat, his moustache, his very walk. Her knees trembled as she leaned against a recess in the wall waiting for him to pass. Another moment and he would be so near she could grasp his hand.

Nearer still, and nearer came the footsteps. Her heart beat hard, she raised her head. He rounded the corner, and lo ! it was not he, but a Spaniard, whose features were as unlike Walter's as his figure was identical with his. After that cruel disappointment, she seldom went into the World's Fair, and never except when her father accompanied her.

As for the doctor, he had literally lived in the World's Fair. He knew every inch of the whole park. He was there the first thing in the morning, he was almost the last to leave at night. He wandered about everywhere alone, with hungry eyes, hawking for any one whose hair, figure, and general appearance might reveal his Rose. A hundred times did he espy some one who seemed to resemble her. A hundred times he was disappointed. But still he renewed the search with unwearied zeal. There were certain favourite spots where he thought she might possibly be attracted One was the Woman's Building, where the librarian, divining the secret cause of his unrest, kept a vigilant and sympathetic eye for every visitor who might chance to be Rose Thorne. And there was Shakespeare's House, the facsimile of which was established in the ground as the Pavilion of the *Illustrated London News*. But no one had ever seen her there. A third place where he loved to linger was at Messrs. Hampton's exhibit in the Manufactures and Liberal Arts. It was a reproduction in facsimile of the famous dining-room of the Cecils at Hatfield, where every night, at dinner hour, the sweet old English ballads were sung by minstrels in the singing gallery. He thought the music of the old songs, which she used to love so well, would attract her, but night after night he watched in vain for a glimpse of the familiar face. He spoke little, and took but small notice of exhibits since the children had left. But the great World's Fair grew upon him day by day, although he noticed its details but little, until it became not so much the World's Fair, but the world itself—a sunless world for him until Rose was found, but still a world.

The mere gazing into the faces of so many hundreds of thousands of human beings, gathered together from all the nations of the earth produced its effect. At first it made his sense of loneliness and isolation almost unbearable. But after a while that feeling gave way to a sense of human brotherhood, of a solidarity real as life felt with men of all kindreds and peoples and tongues. There were none of all the myriad hosts gathered together at Chicago but had some time or other loved, and by some one had been loved. They did not know his secret, nor he theirs in its details. But it was an open secret in the general. They all had loved, and had been loved, and the freemasonry of love seemed a living link which united them all to each other.

Nor was it only the visitors who impressed him. If they were representatives of humanity in its totality as a living, loving, sorrowing, rejoicing entity, the Exhibition itself was a microcosm of the world and all the things

* The narrative in this chapter is not a story, it is a fact. That is to say, the communications professing to be written by the disembodied spirit of Robert Julia, were actually written automatically under similar circumstances to those described in these pages by the hand of a writer, who was unaware of what his pen was writing, and who did not know the persons correctly named, or the circumstances accurately referred to by the intelligence which guided his pen. Names and places of course have been altered, and whereas in the story the communications are represented as having been written by the spirit of a man through the hand of a woman, they were in reality written by the hand of a man under the alleged control of a woman. Whatever explanation may be offered, I am prepared to vouch absolutely for the truth of the following statements—

(1) That the communications were written by the pen of one whose good faith cannot be impugned, and who was quite unaware of what his hand was about to write when he took up his pen.

(2) That the communications began and are continued to this hour, under circumstances practically identical with those in the story.

(3) That the intelligence which controls the hand of the writer, whose own consciousness is never for a moment in abeyance, always alleges that it is the disembodied spirit of a woman with whom the writer had a slight personal acquaintance who "died" about twelve months since.

(4) That the intelligence frequently refers to names, places, and incidents, in the past and present of which the person whose hand holds the pen has no knowledge.

All this is true. In token whereof I am willing to submit all the evidence, and the chief witnesses to the examination of the Psychical Research Society. I know of my own knowledge that the facts are as stated.—ED.

that were therein. Gradually there impressed itself deep in Wynne's heart and memory an imperishable sense of that immense conglomerate of human ingenuity and human skill. Between the rude cave-dwellers, who lurked in holes in the rocks as if they were biped rabbits in stony burrows, and the men who designed and executed that immense sampling case of the world's products, how immense was the distance traversed ! What countless generations of men and women had toiled, and struggled, and fought and died before these remote progenitors of ours could develop the race that built the World's Fair, and bottled up the accents of the human voice in Edison's phonograph ! In contemplating that measureless expanse of unrecorded time, across which these endless myriads of humans plodded their foot-weary way, measuring each day's march as it were by the grave-mounds of a generation, he acquired a sense of the infinite insignificance of the individual, the marvellous potentialities that lie latent in the race. He looked at the Exhibition, teeming with innumerable specimens of human activity, and remembered that there was not a machine, not an exhibit, that was not the slowly elaborated growth of an infinitude of tentative experiments, every one of which by its very imperfection drove mankind by pain and suffering and weariness to discover something better.

The sense of the solidarity of mankind, past, present, and to come, begun by the sight of the visitors, grew upon him as the more striking details of the Great Show merged into one vast whole. How many had laboured before we could enjoy ! With what a new sense of significance did he realise how vast and multifarious are the activities that make up the life of the race to which has been committed the peopling, the cultivation, and the government of the world. On the whole perhaps, that was the thought that most enriched his mind. Here, it is true, there were but samples of the world's labour. But the samples sug-gested something of the immensity of the day's work that goes on without ceasing from the rising to the setting of the sun. If the old monk's saying be a truth, and to labour is to pray, then, what a manifold and unceasing prayer en-circles the world ! That service ceases not, from the cradle to the tomb, filling the whole round earth with the murmur of prayer—prayer not unanswered, as this Exhibi-tion showed.

It was his last day at the World's Fair. His long quest had been in vain. Trace of Rose he found none. He abandoned himself on the last day to the full bitterness of his disappointment. All around, the Fair was full of visitors eager, joyous, intensely interested in all the won-ders they had come to see. The music of the bands throbbed in the air, but no answering chord resounded in his breast. He felt as if he were a broken man, as if henceforth for him stretched an endless vista of chilly November days, dark with fog and chill with frost, but with neither sun in the heavens nor blue in the sky.

    *   *   *   *   *

The work of putting up a reproduction of Ann Hatha-way's Cottage in Jackson Park, in which Mr. Thorne had been engaged since the show opened, was completed. The scaffolding and hoarding which had concealed the ex-hibit from the public eye were removed. Visitors for the first time were allowed to enter the trim old English gar-den and see the house in which the greatest of all Eng-lish-speaking men first dreamed the sweet fond dream of love. Rose had often asked her father to let her see it, but he, like a prudent workman, refused until it was ready for inspection. At last, however, the time had come when she was to come and see with what success the rustic scene of that Warwickshire idyll had been repro-duced on the shores of Lake Michigan.

It was a Festival of Choirs at the Exhibition, and Thorne did not take his daughter down to the Hathaway Cottage till the sun had set and the throng had deserted the rest of the show in order to concentrate on the lake shore, where the aquatic fête was taking place. Rose trembled a little when her father lifted the latchet of the garden gate, and led her with some pardonable degree of triumph into the cottage. The reproduction was very exact. But for the warm sultry air, the great expanse of lake, and the strange and varied scene presented by the Exhibition, all blazing with electric light, she could have imagined herself once more a girl at home in the happy days when she played the May Queen, and the still happier months that followed.

" It is very beautiful, father,' she said, " and very true. I could almost imagine it was the dear old place trans-ported from Shottery by magic."

" I'm glad you like it, my lass ! " said Thorne, looking with honest complacency upon the work of his hands. " It's taken some time putting it up ; and we're rather late. But better late than never ; and no one can say it's a scamped job."

They went into the cottage. Rose examined it closely, room after room. Everything seemed to be as she knew it of old. Each room, almost every article of furniture, seemed to revive some fresh memory, some old associa-tion of the days when she lived in her own life the life of all Shakespeare's heroines in turn.

" Now," said her father, " will you come with me and see the end of the fête near the pier. I'd like a last look at the Show before starting home."

Rose stood on the doorstep and looked out. The distant strains of the band came sighing up the lake. The dull boom of a maroon, followed by a shower of brilliant stars, marked where the fête was in progress. She shook her head. " You go, father, and come back for me when it is all over. It is a beautiful moonlight night. I would much rather stay quietly in the cottage. I don't like fire-works and crowds. Do go, father. I shall be quite happy here till you return."

Mr. Thorne somewhat reluctantly consented.

" I shan't be long." he said, as he hasped the wicket-gate, and strode off towards the pier.

Rose sat down in the front room of the cottage. The moonlight streamed through the latticed window upon the table. She buried her face in her hands and thought. Seven years had passed since she last had seen Ann Hathaway's cottage. How vividly it all came back to her. With what high hopes she had set out for London town ! How bitterly she had been disappointed ! And he, too, whom she had sought to win worthily had been lost, lost for ever.

Meanwhile Walter Wynne, wandering on his last solitary round, came upon the cottage with a feeling of surprise. It lay somewhat out of the regular line of buildings, and as it had been manifestly unfinished, he had not even troubled to inquire as to what it represented. Even now he would not have stepped on one side were it not for an ill-defined association of ideas connected with the thatched roof, which led him to look more closely. When he reached the garden-gate, he recognised the place in a moment.

" Ann Hathaway's cottage here ! " he said to himself. " I wonder why I never heard anything of this before ? There is no one about ; I suppose I may look round."

He unlatched the gate and entered the little garden, Rose heard the gate open, and, rousing herself with an effort, got up and went to the door to meet her father. She was in the shade. The moon shone full upon the path which the visitor must cross, but she saw with some

alarm it was not her father. Half-frightened, she thought of locking herself in the house, when the new-comer stopped, and stooped to pluck a rosebud from a bush. Then the steps came nearer and nearer, and Walter Wynne, with a white rosebud in his hand, stepped out into the moonbeams, and she saw him and knew him, and in a moment she sprang from the door-step, ran down the path, and flung herself upon his neck, crying

"Oh, Walter, Walter, at last! at last!"

"And we shall never, never part again?"

"Never!" he said, "never while life and love endure!" And then he kissed her.

And as they stood together, enfolded one with the other, locked in close embrace, silent with emotion too intense for speech, there came floating over the waters of the lake the voices of one of the choirs singing, as the boat rowed home from the Fair. It was her favourite hymn, that which he had heard at Orchardcroft on Christmas

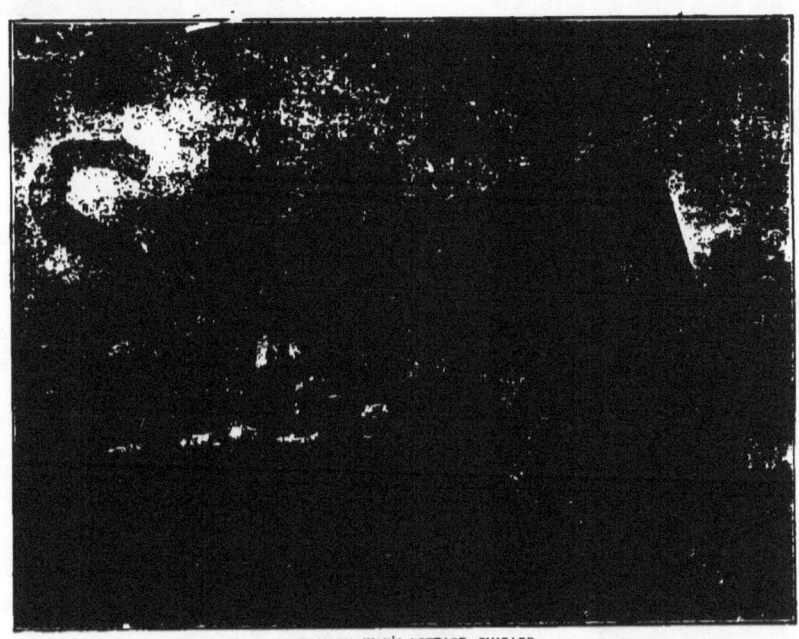

ANN HATHAWAY'S COTTAGE, CHICAGO.

And he, dazed somewhat by the sudden excess of joy, clasped her in his arms, and murmured

"My own Rose!"

For some time they stood there, neither speaking, she throbbing convulsively, and clinging as if she feared he would leave her again. Then he gently raised her face to his.

In the moonlight he could see she had been weeping, that even now her eyes were quivering with tears. Then she said, half to herself, as in a trance of ecstasy

Eve. Nearer the rowers came, and now, clear and sweet, they heard the words of their song, and to Walter and Rose it was as if poetry and music had united to give utterance to their inmost thoughts :—

"So long Thy power hath blest me, sure it still
Will lead me on,
O'er moor and fen, o'er crag and torrent, till
The night be gone,
And with the morn those angel-faces smile
Which I have loved long since and lost awhile."

THE END.

All about HOW TO GET TO

CHICAGO.

Valuable Hints from an

Experienced Traveller.

GRAND CENTRAL STATION, NEW YORK.

 E are in New York, bound for the WORLD'S FAIR. How shall we proceed? It is my province to explain. We will take the New York Central Route, of course—all of us desiring to see the Hudson River and Niagara Falls must necessarily do so—and, indeed, every consideration of expediency tends to confirm our choice.

Owing to its great natural advantages, the New York Central occupies a unique position among American Railways. To begin with, it is the only line entering the City of New York, its trains all leaving and arriving at Grand Central Station, which, by reason of attractive architecture, central location, and the unparalleled facilities it affords to travellers, has become one of the notable features

UP THE HUDSON, ON A NEW YORK CENTRAL "FLYER."

DOBB'S FERRY, ON THE HUDSON

of the city. The remarkably central location of this great metropolitan terminus of the Vanderbilt Lines renders it accessible within from three to twenty minutes from sixty-six of the great hotels of America; it is also the centre from which lines of horse-cars and elevated railroads radiate. It is not only in exactly the ideal spot for a railroad station in New York City, but it is also the only station on Manhattan Island.

Comfortably ensconced in the palatial coach from which we need not emerge until our destination is reached, we have nothing to do but enjoy

A GLIMPSE OF THE MOHAWK.
"The most beautiful sight I ever witnessed was along the Mohawk Valley."—Rev. T. De Witt Talmage.

to the fullest extent our luxurious surroundings —and right here let me say that no trip in the world, of equal length, offers such a variety of beautiful scenery, such indications of wealth and prosperity, such comfort and luxury for the traveller, as the ride between New York and Chicago by the New York Central and its connections. For one hundred and forty-two miles our course skirts the east shore of the historic Hudson, unfolding a wonderful panorama of grand and varied scenery. The threatening battlements of the Palisades rise in bold relief against the sky on the further bank of the noble river, soon giving

THE HUDSON

place to the lofty eminences of the Hudson Highlands and the towering peaks of the Catskill Mountains. [3] Past field and wood, past hill and dale, teeming with memories of Aboriginal, Colonial, and Revolutionary days, the train is swiftly whirled. Crossing the Hudson River at Albany we

NIAGARA FALLS, VIEW FROM PROSPECT POINT.

traverse the charmed region of the Mohawk Valley and the rich agricultural district of Western New York. Approaching Niagara, its roar can be heard under favorable circumstances a distance of fifteen miles, and soon the train pauses upon the very brink of the mighty cataract. We realise in an instant the sentiment under which Anthony Trollope wrote: "Of all the sights on this earth of ours which tourists travel to see, I am inclined to give the palm to Niagara. In the catalogue of such sights I intend to include all buildings, pictures, statues, and wonders of art made by men's hands, and also all beauties of nature prepared by the Creator for the delight of His creatures. This is a long word, but as far as my taste and judgment go, it is justified. I know of no other one thing so beautiful, so glorious, and so powerful."

Arrangements have been perfected permitting passengers holding first class limited tickets, reading *via* the New York Central and Hudson Railroad, during the continuance of the World's Fair, to stop over at Niagara Falls for a period not exceeding ten days, affording travellers ample opportunity to see the World's Greatest Cataract, without incurring additional expense for railroad fare.

A word about train service. It is whispered that next year the New York Central will probably have a train every hour for Chicago. However this may be, of one thing rest assured, its facilities will be ample to meet whatever demands may arise.

We present below an illustration of the Empire State Express, which has so long held the world's record for fast time. This is only one of the five great "Limited" trains of the New York Central, representing in equipment, speed, and attendance the highest development of the modern art of transportation. Though these trains form but a small part of the New York Central Service, they are fair examples of the standard to which all the others conform. A writer in *Herapath's London, England, Railway and Commercial Journal*, of February 6th, 1892, in an article on American Railroads, after commenting at considerable length on the comparative merits of various American Lines, closes with this remarkable sentence: "The New York Central is no doubt the best line in America, and a very excellent line it is—equal, probably, to the best English line." That this will be your verdict there is no possibility of doubt. Its trains are equipped with all the modern safety appliances, its cars are heated by steam from the engine, and lighted by the Pintsch system of compressed gas; a large portion of the passenger equipment having been recently built, it is far superior to that formerly in use on American lines. The New York Central, with its connections, forms the most direct route across the Continent, through Chicago, St. Louis, or Cincinnati to San Francisco on the Pacific Ocean, and is a very important link in the great international highway around the world.

At Buffalo connections are made with the Michigan Central Railroad and the Lake Shore and Michigan Southern Railway, by either of which lines passengers can continue their journey in through cars to Chicago—the city of the World's Fair.

The time consumed in the ride from New York to Chicago is from twenty-four to twenty-seven hours.

"EMPIRE STATE EXPRESS"
OF THE
NEW YORK CENTRAL.
THE FASTEST TRAIN IN THE WORLD.

(From a Photograph by A. P. Yates, Syracuse, N.Y. Taken when the train was running 60 miles an hour.)

™ᴴᴱ MICHIGAN CENTRAL

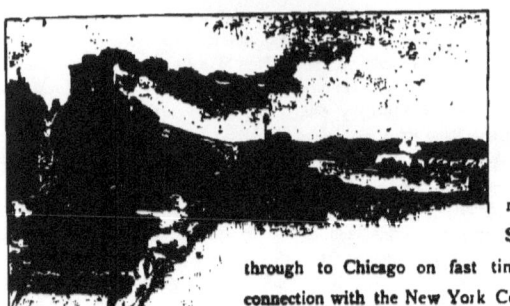

"The Niagara Falls Route"

runs Through-Trains and Palace, Sleeping, Buffet and Dining Cars through to Chicago on fast time, from New York and Boston, in connection with the New York Central and Hudson River and Boston and Albany Railroads.

THE MICHIGAN CENTRAL, which has won its popular title of "THE NIAGARA FALLS ROUTE" from the fact that it is the only railroad running directly by and in full view of the Falls, stops its trains at Falls View Station, directly above the brink of the Horseshoe Fall, from which point all parts of the Falls, the green islands in the river, the raging rapids above and the boiling chasm below, are in full view. No more comprehensive view of the great Cataract is to be had from any one point, yet the traveller who possesses any love for, or appreciation of, the beauties of nature, should be by no means content with the single view.

Niagara offers a thousand scenes of marvellous beauty, of unceasing variety and unequalled picturesqueness, that one should see under the varying conditions of sunlight and shadow, calm and storm, and under the silvery moonlight. Every mile of Niagara River, from Lake Erie to Lake Ontario, especially from the Rapids above the Falls to the Whirlpool and the Escarpment at Lewiston and Queenston, is filled with interesting and charming scenes. The longer the traveller lingers, the oftener he sees the different points of interest, and the more varying the conditions under which they are seen, the greater will be his appreciation of this great natural wonder.

The hotel accommodations at Niagara are ample, excellent in quality, and reasonable in price, while the terrible hackman, so long the butt of innumerable jokes, will be found, upon close acquaintance to be very tame and inoffensive. The banks of the river upon either side of the Falls have been reserved by the Canadian and New York State Governments as public parks, free to all, so that the expense of a visit to Niagara has been shorn of exorbitant charges.

A visit to the Cave of the Winds, with guide and dress, costs a dollar, and the similar trip under the Horseshoe Falls, on the Canada side, fifty cents; the round trip on the inclined railway costs ten cents, and upon the *Maid of the Mist*, fifty cents. The admission fee to the Whirlpool Rapids, and to the Whirlpool from either side, costs fifty cents. The toll over the new Suspension Foot and Carriage Bridge is twenty-five cents, and the same amount extra for each vehicle. The hack fares at Niagara Falls are regulated by law and are very reasonable, while vans make the tour of the entire State Reservation, with the privilege of stopping off at any point of interest, for twenty-five cents.

BIRD'S-EYE VIEW OF NIAGARA RIVER.

Illustrated printed matter, descriptive of Niagara Falls and the route of the famous NORTH SHORE, LIMITED, of the MICHIGAN CENTRAL, will be sent to any address in Great Britain or on the Continent upon application to—

O. W. RUGGLES,

General Passenger and Ticket Agent,
CHICAGO.

The MICHIGAN CENTRAL

"The Niagara Falls Route"

OCCUPIES in Chicago a depot at the foot of Lake Street, soon to be replaced by a new structure, in some degree worthy of the superb location. It is but a few minutes' walk from all the principal Hotels, and easily reached by cable cars. The transfer to the depôts of western lines in the city is easily and speedily made by omnibuses and carriages.

No other eastern line has so eligible a location or route into the city. For miles the smooth steel tracks follow the lake front, with beautiful and varied views of Lake Michigan on the left, and on the right the green turf and bright flowers of extensive parks and the *parterres* of the most elegant residence portion of the city and its southern suburbs. Fronting the Lake Front Park on Michigan Avenue are seen the beautiful Art Institute, the imposing granite pile of the Auditorium, and other magnificent buildings. In this park is now being constructed a stately Art Palace, which will be unsurpassed by any similar structure in this country.

As the Michigan Central approaches the above line, it encloses between it and the lake the splendid group of colossal structures erected for the World's Columbian Exposition. The Woman's Building is nearest to the elevated track of the railroad, with Horticultural Hall and the Transportation Building to the right, while a little farther off rises the stately dome of the Administration Building. No other eastern line runs directly by or to it as does the Michigan Central whose passengers alone enjoy the passing view, as they do also that of Niagara Falls, the great cataract of the world.

All of the Michigan Central's fast through trains are, therefore, "World's Fair Specials" and "Columbian Exposition Expresses," and all run over "The Niagara Falls Route" between Buffalo and Chicago.

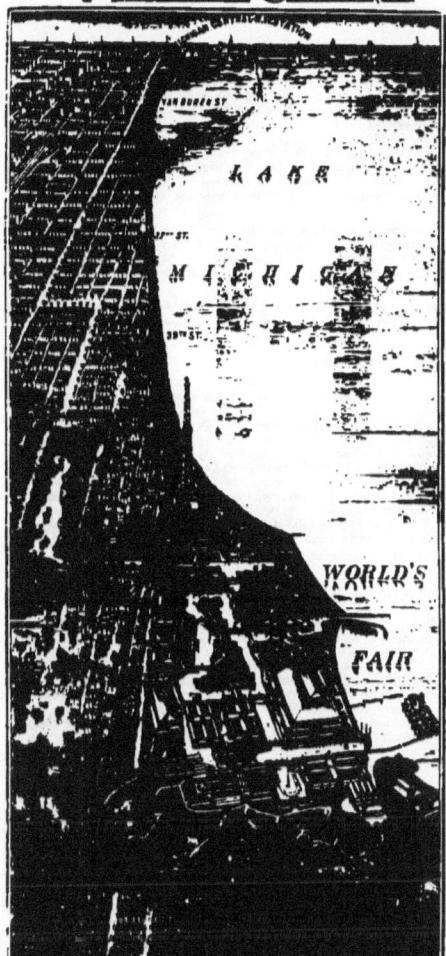

THE MICHIGAN CENTRAL'S ENTRANCE TO CHICAGO.

ROBERT MILLER,
General Superintendent,
DETROIT.

O. W. RUGGLES,
General Passenger and Ticket Agent,
CHICAGO.

"VIA THE UNION PACIFIC."

THIS great national highway is so well known, not only throughout the United States, but all over the world, that a mere reference to it would seem sufficient, yet for the benefit of those who have never had the pleasure of riding over its smooth track, and thus had an opportunity of gazing upon the fine scenery along its route, the following description is given:—

It formed a part of the first transcontinental line of railroad from ocean to ocean, and was conceived, and its construction authorized, as a war measure, the needs of the Government during the war of the Rebellion having clearly shown the necessity for it. Many thought the feat of constructing a line of railroad over the Rocky Mountains an utter impossibility. Many of those who had crossed the plains, deserts, and mountains to California in 1849-50, knew very well a railroad could not be built there, for "how could a locomotive ascend a mountain where six yoke of oxen could scarcely haul a wagon?" In the days of '49-50, when long trains of gold-seekers, after outfitting at Council Bluffs, wended their way over the plains, the country was filled with hostile Indians, herds of buffalo, deer, and antelope. There was scarcely a house west of the Elkhorn River, within twenty miles of Omaha. Now the traveller sits in a luxurious Pullman car, and is whirled over the smooth railroad at forty miles an hour.

This railway is one of the very best on this continent. Its two main stems, the one from KANSAS CITY, the other from COUNCIL BLUFFS, uniting at Cheyenne and diverging again at Granger, one for Portland, and one for San Francisco, are crowded with the commerce of the Orient and the Occident, while people from every nation in the world may be seen on its passenger trains. Every improvement which human ingenuity has invented for the safety or comfort of the traveller is in use on the Union Pacific System.

For nearly 500 miles west of Council Bluffs and 700 miles west of Kansas City there are no heavy grades or curves, crossing the Missouri river from the Transfer Depôt, Council Bluffs, over a magnificent steel bridge, Omaha is reached, and

The Trip Across the Continent

to either Portland or San Francisco commences. This metropolis of the West has now 142,000 inhabitants. Leaving Omaha, the road follows the Platte River through the thickly settled and fertile Platte Valley, and crosses mile after mile of level country, as impressive to those unfamiliar with such scenes as is the unbounded level of the ocean. At Cheyenne (516 miles from Omaha) Kansas main line via Denver connects with the Nebraska main line from Council Bluffs. Leaving Kansas City, via the Kansas main line of the Union Pacific System, one passes through some of the finest farming land of the West. The descent is rapid into Denver, 639 miles from Kansas City, with a population of 126,000. The elevation is 5,170 feet. The dry climate of Colorado is said to be unrivalled for all diseases of the lungs, if the patient goes there in time. The trip from Denver to Cheyenne, Wyoming, along the foothills of the Rocky Mountains, affords a kaleidoscopic panorama of hills, fields, farms, rivers, running brooks, and lofty mountains. Here the eastern traveller for the first time sees fields of alfalfa of a deep green colour, grown by the use of irrigating ditches, the water for which is brought down from the mountains in large canals and thence distributed by means of smaller ditches. After leaving Cheyenne the train climbs a grade 2,000 feet in thirty-three miles to Sherman, 8,247 feet above sea-level, and the highest point of the transcontinental ride.

Across the Continent to Portland, Oregon.

At Green River the trains for Portland, Oregon, are made up, although they do not make their departure from the main line until Granger is reached, thirty miles west of Green River, and the trip across the continent is confined to the great Northwest. The road goes along over moderate curves and grades, through pretty little valleys along the Bear River, until the great Territory of Idaho is entered at Border Station. Then on through Soda Springs and Pocatello—the junction with the Utah and Northern branch for the Yellowstone National Park, Butte, Garrison, and Helena; thence to Shoshone Station, where the junction is made for the great Shoshone Falls via stage, and also for Hailey and Ketchum via rail; from Shoshone Station the road stretches away through Nampa, where the junction is made with the Idaho Central branch for Boise City. From Nampa, Idaho, the Oregon Short Line skirts along the boundary line of Idaho and Oregon, following the Snake River, until Huntington, just within Oregon, is reached, where it starts directly across the State. Huntington is the junction of the Mountain Division with the Pacific Division of the Union Pacific System. Just beyond La Grande, in the Grand Ronde Valley, comes a passage in the Blue Mountains, replete with the dark beauty of the pine and the rippling brook and waterfall.

Absorbing Scenes.

All along, the sights have been absorbing in their varied aspects; but it is only when a pause is made at "The Dalles" Station that the true grandeur of the scenery of the Columbia River is impressed upon the mind. From this point the noble river, surging and whirling to the sea, breaking the image rocks into wave fragments, occupies the mind of the beholder. The Columbia is one of the world's great rivers, affording a waterway that is navigable for traffic for over 200 miles. Upon it, near its mouth, the largest ocean steamers ply with safety. There can be nothing more inspiring than the ride along "The Dalles" of the Columbia, with the shining river on one side and the towering battlements of the shore on the other. The scene is one of continued magnificence. The grottos, in which are moss-garlanded cascades, almost hidden under the dense foliage, are most inviting and beautiful. Multnomah Falls and their surroundings are a bit of fairy land. There are scores of smaller falls—mere ribbons some of them—but all clear and dashing, and banked by a wealth of moss. For miles upon miles this wild scenery continues, and a thousand times the tourist thinks the climax has been reached, only to acknowledge later that something grander has developed, particularly when Cape Horn, 700 feet sheer height; Castle Rock, 1,000 feet; Gibraltar and Hallet's Hades burst into view. Along the Rhine, the Rhone, or the Hudson, there is nothing that will compare with the stately palisades of the Columbia, with their cool recesses, kept sunless by the overhanging rocks, and watered by the melting snows of their own summits. A splendid view can be had of Mt. Hood, Mt. St. Helen's and the Cascades, where the scenery surpasses anything of the kind in the world. From Hood River Station, the traveller can find good stages to convey him over an excellent road to the base of Mt. Hood, twenty-five miles distant. The view from Mt. Hood is simply incomparable, and the trip from Hood River Station to Mt. Hood is made through some of the most extraordinary scenery in the world. Arrived at Portland, the metropolis of Oregon, the tourist can reach other important points in Oregon, and that not far-off country Alaska, an extraordinary and almost unknown domain. To the tourist, Alaska presents many points of interest. Its curious people, wonderful scenery, extinct volcanoes, magnificent glaciers, hot springs, sulphur lakes, and boiling marshes, well repay the tourist for making the trip. A trip to Alaska will be something to think of in after years.

Across the Continent to San Francisco.

From Portland, magnificent ocean steamers depart for the far distant Orient. Fine steamers also ply over the broad bosom of the Pacific Ocean from Portland to Alaska. From Portland to San Francisco, the trip can be made in the iron steamships of the Union Pacific System, or by rail over the Mt. Shasta route. From Green River the trip across the continent to San Francisco is continued. Green River Buttes are objects of interest, and are within sight for miles. At Wahsatch

Station the elevation is 6,812 feet, and at this point the road enters Echo Cañon. Three and a half miles west of Wahsatch, the train runs into a tunnel 500 feet long. One mile east of Castle Rock is a queer formation of rock resembling the ruins of an old castle. "Hanging Rock" is what its name indicates. West of Emory, on top of the Bluff, is a rock called "Jack in the Pulpit," and further on can be seen the heights of Echo Cañon, on the top of which are the old Mormon fortifications. Then comes "Steamboat Rocks." Just before reaching Echo are seen the "Amphitheatre," "Pulpit Rocks," and "Bromley's Cathedral." At Echo Station, Weber Cañon is entered. West of Echo can be seen the "Witch Rocks." Five miles further on is the 1,000 mile tree, and a mile farther on is "Devil's Slide." Echo and Weber Cañons compare favourably with the celebrated Colorado Cañons. About half a mile away, between Petersen and Uintah Station, "Devil's Gate" is to be seen, and shortly after the country widens into the Great Salt Lake Valley, when Ogden is reached. Between Cheyenne and Ogden about ten miles of snow-sheds, altogether, are passed, and these sheds are quite a feature of the ride across the continent. Ogden is 1,034 miles from Council Bluffs, 1,260 miles from Kansas City, and 833 miles from San Francisco; the trip to Salt Lake City and Garfield Beach is made from this point.

The crowning scenes of the trip to San Francisco are not beheld until after leaving Reno, Cape Horn, Emigrant Gap, the Sierra Nevadas, Donner Lake and other objects of more than ordinary interest will be found. The marvellous Carson and Humboldt sinks, in which the waters of all the rivers in the State of Nevada save one are swallowed; the Mud Lakes, the Borax marshes, and countless numbers of thermal springs, have been the wonder of the scientist and the delight of the tourist. From Sacramento, the Central Pacific Railroad branches off via Lathrop to Los Angeles, from which point the prominent cities and noted resorts of California are readily reached. From Sacramento the main line of the Central Pacific road takes the tourist through to Oakland, where a transfer is made across an arm of the bay to San Francisco, and here this part of the trip "Across the Continent" terminates at San Francisco.

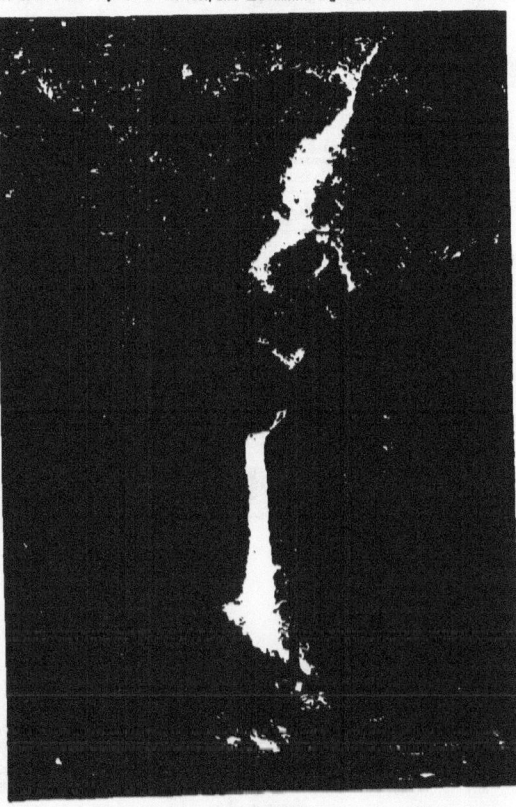

YOSEMITE FALLS, CAL.—HEIGHT 2,600 FEET—reached via the Union Pacific System.

Of all the Railroads leading Westward from Chicago, the site of the
World's Columbian Exposition,

THE NORTHERN PACIFIC RAILROAD,

With its TWO TRAINS A DAY to the PACIFIC COAST, is easily the **TOURIST'S ROUTE,**
without a Change of Cars, in connection with its Leased Line,

THE WISCONSIN CENTRAL RAILROAD.

The Traveller is carried from Chicago, on Lake Michigan, to the young, thrifty, and enterprising
Cities of

Tacoma and Seattle, on Puget Sound,

AND

Portland, Oregon,

The Largest City of the Pacific North-West.

In accomplishing this great distance of more than 2,500 miles, the train traverses in whole
or in part Eight Great States.

➤●◄

LEAVING CHICAGO FROM THE

GRAND CENTRAL STATION,

GRAND TERMINAL STATION, NORTHERN PACIFIC RAILWAY.

Probably the finest railway station in the United States, one enters the vestibuled train of the Wisconsin Central Railroad, and
is whirled over the level prairies of Illinois, and across the timbered lands and among the hills of Wisconsin.

After a ride of a little more than half a day, the cities of **ST. PAUL**, the Capital of Minnesota, with its massive buildings and compact business centre, and **MINNEAPOLIS**, with its world-renowned Flour Mills, are reached. Within easy ride from either of the "Twin Cities," as they are known in Western phraseology, are the noted **MINNEHAHA FALLS**, so well sung by Longfellow.

At St. Paul the **NORTHERN PACIFIC RAILROAD** proper is taken.

The road first winds through the Valley of the Mississippi River, and then enters the Lake Park region. Minnesota contains about 8,000 Lakes, and this particular locality is a charming combination of rolling prairie, with sleeping lakes nestling in the hollows and depressions.

Then comes the Valley of the Red River of the North, where the hard wheat for which Minnesota and North Dakota are famous the world over, is raised.

The train now winds among the wonderfully fashioned and painted "Bad Lands" of North Dakota, a strangely fascinating country, and thence descends into the Valley of the Yellowstone River. Following this for 340 miles, it then clambers over the Rocky Mountains and across the State of Montana, replete with fine mountain views, and some delicious glimpses of valley landscapes, and along Clark's Fork of the Columbia, to Lake Pend R'Oreille in Idaho.

Skirting the northern edge of this most enchanting mountain lake, the course of the railroad is south westward to the Columbia River, crossing which it turns north westward, and heroically fights its way across the Cascade Mountains. Here is found some superb mountain scenery. The western descent of this range through the Green River is a panorama of rare beauty.

Four days after leaving Chicago, and three-and-one-half days after St. Paul has been left behind, the tourist reaches **TACOMA** and **SEATTLE**, the great cities of the State of Washington, and less than eight hours later the train reaches the end of the journey at **PORTLAND, OREGON**.

En route, the two great cities of Montana—**BUTTE**, the greatest Mining Camp of the world, and **HELENA**, the State capital—have been passed, as has also **SPOKANE**, the largest city of Eastern Washington.

The Northern Pacific is popularly known as the

"WONDERLAND ROUTE."

The Gem of Wonderland, the Crowning Glory of the Trip, the Most Wonderful Assemblage of Scenic Splendours on the Known Earth, is the now world-famed

YELLOWSTONE NATIONAL PARK.

LIBERTY CAP, YELLOWSTONE PARK.

The credulity of mankind is tested to its extreme limit in the effort to believe, unseen, that any region of the given area of this Park can contain such a congregation of wonderful and dissimilar features. Such a study and pleasure ground of natural history is it, that the United States Government for ever set it aside for the use and pleasure of the people.

Mammoth hot springs, with its myriad pools flashing the everchanging colours of the rainbow; with its bubbling and pulsating springs; its caves and caverns; its living terraces of dazzling white or glowing colour, and its dead ones with crumbling, disintegrated cliffs; its extinct geyser cones standing like mummies amid the wreck of their former greatness, teach the mutability of life and time.

The Geyser Basins, bellowing and hissing, and belching forth from hundreds of vents, with roar and splutter, thin, fanciful steam clouds, with their wonderful basins of crystal water, contained within rims as wonderfully fretted and decorated, have no counterpart elsewhere.

The mountains sweep to the clouds and hold in their embrace eternal snows and glaciers. Luxuriant forests crown the hills; cataracts plunge in wild abandon over precipices; bear and elk, deer and antelope, haunt the glades and valleys; glorious lakes lie scattered all about.

The *pièce de résistance*, the grandest feature of this region, however, is the renowned

GRAND CAÑON OF THE YELLOWSTONE.

From 1,200 to 1,500 feet deep, its indescribably coloured and carved walls, its wonderful river and thundering falls, its grand and extensive prospective, make it a wonder of wonders.

The cañon walls in their ornate warmth of colour are a noon-day dream. In their buttressed cliffs and fantastically wrought columns and pinnacles, they are an architectural study. The Grand Cañon is a fit culmination of the powers here shown forth by the great God of the Universe, and truly of this part of Wonderland it may be written, "The firmament showeth His handiwork."

To reach this Wonderland, the tourist leaves the main line of railroad at Livingston, Montana, about half-way between St. Paul and Puget Sound, and takes the Yellowstone Park Branch Railroad to Cinnabar; whence comfortable stages make the tour of the Park in seven days, with convenient stops at large hotels supplied with modern conveniences.

The marvellous recent development of the Puget Sound country is known of all men. Growing cities, prosperous towns and villages are scattered along its coast line. Its valleys yield abundant harvests, its hills are clothed with umbrageous forests of cedar, spruce, pine and fir, and its mountains afford rugged scenery.

MINERVA TERRACE, YELLOWSTONE PARK.

To the north Mount Baker lifts its snow-crowned head, while from all the regions round about Seattle, Tacoma, and Olympia, the magnificent pile of Mount Tacoma, monarch of monarchs, its haughty crest hoary with the snows of ages and wreathed in the white fleeces of the air, greets the vision.

Tacoma is the point from which the tourist who, in connection with his trip over the Northern Pacific, adds to it the Alaskan Tour, starts upon this experience of a life-time. For over 1,000 miles the comfortable steamers thread the stormless inland passage; for 1,000 miles a panorama of mountain peaks, inland sea, picturesque islands, glittering snow-fields, cracking glaciers, frozen rivers, glittering bergs, lovely bays, and Indian villages passes before one. The experience is a new, a novel one, unlike anything in the usual routine of travel.

In addition to this wealth of scenic attraction the Northern Pacific Railroad offers a car service of great excellence. Its Pullman Sleeping Cars are the best made; its Dining Car Service is unexcelled, and its Tourist and Free Colonist Sleeping Cars, place sleeping car accommodation within the reach of all.

To epitomise: The Round Trip from Chicago to the Yellowstone Park, and Return, can be made in eleven days, at a cost of about $145. This charge includes Railroad Fares for the Round Trip, one Double Berth in Pullman Sleeping Car, Meals on Dining Cars, Stage Transportation from the end of the Railroad at Cinnabar to all principal points of interest in the Park, and Meals and Lodging at the Park Hotels during a stay there of six-and-one-quarter days.

The Round Trip from Chicago to Tacoma on Puget Sound, and Portland, Oregon, can be made comfortably in two weeks, spending on the North Coast at its several points of interest Five Days. The Expense of this trip for Railroad Transportation, Sleeping Cars, and Meals in Dining Cars, approximates $150.

The Round Trip from Chicago to Tacoma, thence to Sitka, Alaska, and return by Steamer, can be made in twenty-one days, at an expense for Railroad Fares, Sleeping Cars, Meals in Dining Cars, and Berth, and Meals on Steamer for twelve days, approximating $240.

For Tourist Books, Maps, Folders, and detailed Information as to Rates, etc., address—

SUTTON & CO.,
22, GOLDEN LANE,
LONDON, E.C., ENGLAND,
Or Branch Offices;

HENRY GAZE & SONS,
142, STRAND, W C.,
LONDON, ENGLAND,
Or Branch Offices;

THOMAS COOK & SON,
LUDGATE CIRCUS, LONDON, ENGLAND,
Or Branch Offices;

OR,

J. M. HANNAFORD,
General Traffic Manager,
ST. PAUL, MINNESOTA, U.S.A.

CHARLES S. FEE,
General Passenger Agent,
ST. PAUL, MINNESOTA, U.S.A.

Chicago to the Rockies,

Denver, Colorado Springs, etc.

EITHER ONE DAY OR ONE NIGHT OUT, BY THE

GREAT ROCK ISLAND ROUTE.

Take the fast service and elegant equipment offered by this Line between Chicago and Denver and California, either via Omaha or Kansas City.

THE BEST DINING-CAR SERVICE IN THE WORLD.

THE GREAT ROCK ISLAND ROUTE has its magnificent Chicago Station in the heart of the city, close to leading Hotels in business part of the city.

BEST LINE FROM CHICAGO TO THE PACIFIC COAST.

IRELAND AT THE WORLD'S FAIR.

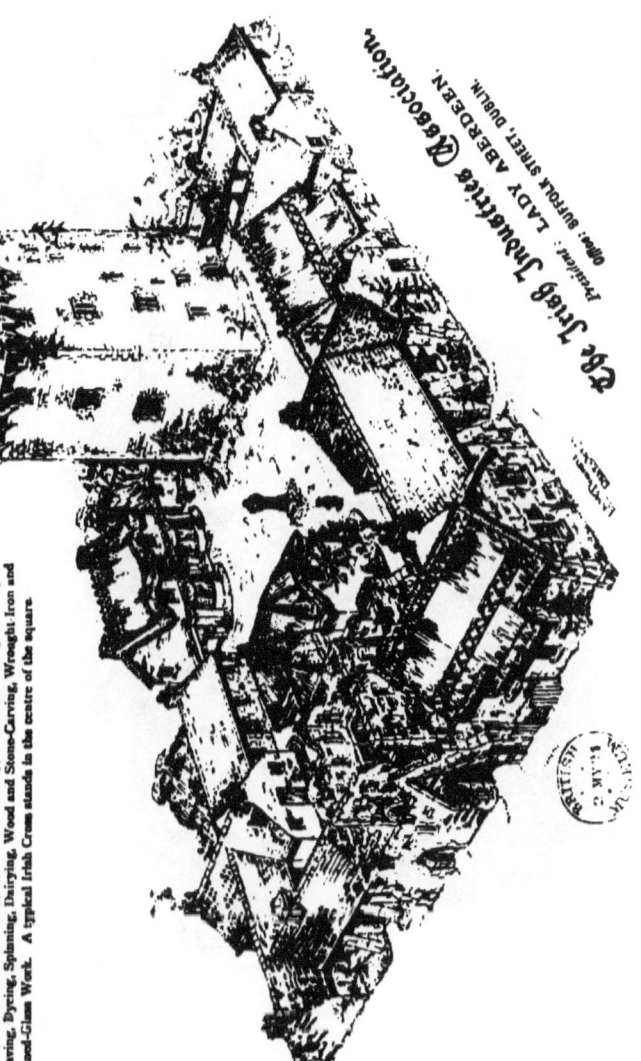

THIS represents a bird's-eye view of the Irish Industrial Village, which is being
erected at the entrance of the Medway Pleasance, World's Fair, Chicago.
The entrance lies through a reproduction of the famous Cloisters of Muckross, and
the castle is a reproduction of Blarney Castle. The Cottages which form the quad-
rangle are typical Irish residences, in which domestic Industries such as Lace-
Making, Shirt-Making, Sprigging and Embroidery, Damask Weaving, Home-spun
Weaving, Dyeing, Spinning, Dairying, Wood and Stone-Carving, Wrought Iron and
Stained-Glass Work. A typical Irish Cross stands in the centre of the square.

The Irish Industries Association

President: LADY ABERDEEN
Office: SUFFOLK STREET, DUBLIN.

(*Reprinted from the* "REVIEW OF REVIEWS," *December*, 1892.)

A REVOLUTION IN PRINTING AND IN JOURNALISM?

AN INTERVIEW WITH THE REVOLUTIONIST.

THIS month THE REVIEW OF REVIEWS is printed by Messrs. Clowes and Sons, one of the highest-class printing establishments in the Kingdom. The first number were printed by the Hansard Union, then the printing was transferred to the Carlyle Press, where it remained until the present number. On the failure of Mr. Burgess, however, it was necessary to seek a fresh printer, and the present number is produced by Messrs. Clowes and Sons. The changes which circumstances have forced upon me have naturally led me to take more interest in printing establishments and printing machines than I have hitherto done. Although it was a foggy night at the end of November, when I was much too busy with the work of getting out the Review to have much time to devote to visits of inspection in any direction, I acceded to the request of Mr. Byers that I should go and see a new printing machine which has just been installed at the works of the English Feister Printing Company, Limited, in Coleman Street, Islington. How we got there I do not exactly know, nor how we got back again, but we trusted ourselves entirely to the pilotage of the driver of our hansom, and certain has that gondola of London been more indispensable in threading the maze that intervenes between Moorgate House and Coleman Street. When we arrived at our destination, we found it was the establishment of the English Feister Printing Company, Limited.

"Now," said Mr. Byers, as we entered, "you will see the machine which is going to revolutionise the printing trade of the world."

The machine for which such lofty claim was made had just been put up, and was doing its first round of printing, using for the experiment some old electrotype-plates which had previously been used for one of the numbers of this Review.

"Explain your revolution," I said to Mr. Byers, who, nothing loth, entered into an enthusiastic description of the machine, which he declared was the latest triumph of the mechanical genius of man.

Mr. Byers is an American, who for the last two years or more has brooded over the idea of this machine; and now that it has been transferred from the domain of the ideal to that of the practical and material, he is as proud as a hen who has hatched her first chicken. Not that this is Mr. Byers' first chicken, for Mr. Byers has had many chickens. He has only hatched it, as the egg was none of his own laying. The machine, to drop metaphor, was originally an American invention, but it has been improved by the genius of two English engineers, Mr. Alexander Gray and Mr. Gibson. The original inventor of the machine was Henry P. Feister, who went to America some years ago, and put up the machine called after his name in the Quaker city. A specimen of this unimproved machine has been at work for some time in London, grinding out pamphlets with an automatic regularity.

Mr. Byers, however, has a soul above pamphlets, and believes that the new improved machine, of which Joseph J. Byers and Co. are the sole agents in England and France, is destined to make a general overturn in the printing trade of the world. But it is best to let Mr. Byers speak for himself.

"This machine," said Mr. Byers enthusiastically, "has solved the problem with which all printing engineers have been grappling in vain for the last twenty years. It will print at newspaper speed from an endless web with the precision of a flat machine. It will not only do this, but it will fold, paste, cut, and deliver at the same time. The machines are adapted to take pamphlets or books varying in width and containing pages which are multiples of four up to thirty-two pages. These sets of thirty-two pages can then be collated, and books of larger sizes made up. The old Feister was no use except for the very longest orders. The cylinder was cased in wood, and the plates were nailed in position. It took six or seven days to prepare for printing, and it was not worth while unless you had an order for at least a million copies. Orders for a million copies are not so plentiful as smaller orders, so it was absolutely necessary for general business to provide a cylinder in which plates could be fixed more rapidly. This object has been attained in the new machine. We can put on a plate with the utmost simplicity, and owing to the perfection with which all the parts have been made and put together, we can undertake to print anything, and we are not without hope that some day we may even print THE REVIEW OF REVIEWS."

"Well," said I, "that will depend upon many things. You certainly will not print it, unless you can print it as well as it is being printed on flat machines."

"We will print it better," said Mr. Byers, with calm assurance. "We will print it better, more rapidly, and more economically. That one machine," said he, pointing to it with pride, "dispenses with the labour of about thirty pair of hands. One man and a boy will supply all the attendance that is required."

"I do not exactly admire that," I said. "Your pasting arrangement, for instance, will destroy the industry of the girls who stitch the magazines."

"All labour-saving apparatus," said Mr. Byers, "in the end, creates a fresh demand for labour. For one of your stitching girls who is thrown out of work as a stitching girl two will be wanted to deal with the increased business which the increased facility of production will inevitably bring into existence."

"Probably," said I, "but in the meantime —— Well, well, go on with your machine."

"No," said Mr. Byers, "I am not going to explain this machine, for I am not a mechanician, I am only the holder of the patents. But here is Mr. Gray: he will explain its true inwardness to you."

I turned to Mr. Gray, who, on being appealed to, gave me a technical account of the machine, and the points which differentiate it from any other machines.

The machine, he said, is designed to print pamphlets of various sizes without the necessity of having rollers of different diameters. It takes paper from the reel, feeds it in, cuts it into sheets of the required length, prints first one side of the sheet and then the other. The sheets are collected together, and as each sheet is collected it is pasted along the middle line, after which the bundle of sheets is thrown down on to the cover placed on the folding-table you see in front of the machine.

The sheets and cover are then folded so as to form a pamphlet or book. The pamphlets thus prepared, being already pasted, require nothing more than to be cut and trimmed. The machine consists of four cylinders; two of them are forme, or printing, cylinders, and the other two hold the paper to be printed. In addition to these cylinders there are the necessary subsidiary machines for cutting, collecting, pasting and folding, all combined in the construction so as to co-operate harmoniously for the end in view. The cylinders are sufficiently wide to take several rows of printing plates side by side, and they are sufficiently large in diameter to be able to print thirty-two pages for each revolution of the cylinder. It is consequently possible to print from two to six or more complete books of thirty-two pages each, side by side, at each revolution. All this is done with the assistance of one man and a boy.

"Now you understand," chimed in Mr. Byers, "these technical details, I do not concern myself about them, I only see the enormous facility which this machine gives for the production of circulars, catalogues and pamphlets of all descriptions, and printing of all kinds."

"Is there much demand for enormous numbers of pamphlets?" I asked.

"Demand, sir," said Mr. Byers. "Why Mother Seigel's Syrup alone requires 120 million copies of a thirty-two paged pamphlet. One hundred and twenty millions every year."

"One hundred and twenty millions," said I, sceptically.

"Yes," said Mr. Byers. "But let me introduce you to Mr. H. K. Packard, from Chicago, who has accepted a seat on the Board of the English Feister Printing Company. Mr. Packard, as Managing Director, has mainly contributed to the enormous success of 'A. J. White, Limited.'"

"Yes," said Mr. Packard, "our annual consumption of pamphlets is 120 millions, and I think this machine will enable us to get them done quicker and better than we have been able to produce them hitherto."

"But," said I, somewhat dazed with the figures, "do you mean to say that you actually disseminate throughout the world 120 million pamphlets about your syrup?"

"That is the figure," said Mr. Packard. "To send them out costs us £100 a day in postage stamps, to say nothing of the cost of private delivery. We produce these pamphlets in twenty different languages at present, and the business is but in its infancy."

"But will you be able to print 120 million pamphlets on this machine?"

"How you talk!" said Mr. Byers. "You see these two machines," pointing to a second improved Feister which was being fitted up opposite to the one which was printing from the old electros. "These two machines will be able to turn out 180 millions of Mother Seigel's Syrup pamphlets in a twelvemonth; but we are having machines built, each of which will be capable of turning out one-third more work than these can do."

"It will take some business to keep them going, and there are not two Mother Seigels."

"No," said Mr. Byers, "but there is no limit to this kind of printing. We are simply choked with orders, and the existing machines cannot turn the work out in time."

"But there is a limit, surely, to the world's consumption of patent medicine pamphlets?"

"No," said Mr. Packard, "there is no limit. We find that the more civilised and highly developed and prosperous a community is the more medicine it takes. In fact," said he, "you can hardly have a better test of

the prosperity and civilisation of a community than the patent medicine it consumes. It is invariably so. The greater the health of the community the more medicine it takes, it is only the downright sickly localities where medicine seems to be at a discount; people lose heart. In prosperous communities, however, such as New Zealand and Australia, the demand for medicine is simply inexhaustible. There is more syrup taken per square mile in New Zealand and Australia than anywhere else on the world's surface."

"But," said Mr. Byers, "we are not going to stick to patent medicines, never you fear. We are going to print all the catalogues, and all the school books, and all the magazines, everything in fact which needs to be quickly produced in enormous quantities."

"Well," said I, "if you really can turn out pamphlets at that rate then there is a chance of the paper which I have dreamed of for many a long year."

"How?" said Mr. Byers.

"How? Why, if you can produce pamphlets as rapidly as newspapers, the newspaper of the future will be in the shape of a pamphlet, and if you can do magazine printing at newspaper speed, illustrations and all, then the revolution which you will make in the newspaper trade, will be greater than the one you propose to make in the printing trade. Just imagine the convenience of having a newspaper which you can read without putting your neighbour's eye out in a crowded railway carriage, and which you can double up and put in your pocket as easily as a magazine. That is the line for your machine if you can really do all that you say you can."

"Sir," said Mr. Byers, "we are going on all lines, newspaper lines as well as other lines. There is nothing that this machine cannot do. The days of the blanket paper are over and ended."

"Well," said I, "we shall see; but I rather doubt the possibility of producing your pamphlets at the speed on which you are reckoning."

"We shall be able to deliver 240,000 copies of a thirty-two paged morning paper with the new machines which we are having built," said Mr. Byers, positively. "Magazine printed, folded, pasted and cut in four hours, using six machines."

"At what price do you sell your machines?"

"At no price," said Mr. Byers; "we would not sell it for its weight in diamonds. The machine is not for sale. No, sir, it is too valuable a patent for the company to part with the machines."

"Then," said I, "Mr. Byers, do you propose to keep the lion's share of the printing of the world in your own hands?"

"Yes," said Mr. Byers, "that is what I reckon we are going to do." From which it will be seen that Mr. Byers is as sanguine as he is audacious.

The machine, as I saw it working, was making from sixteen to eighteen revolutions in a minute. Mr. Gray is confident that the machine will make twenty-four revolutions per minute. He believes it is quite possible to get the speed up to thirty, and even forty revolutions in the minute; but that is, at the present moment, not in the plane of realised fact. The machine, however, was doing better work in printing the illustrations of toned blocks than any other rotary machine that I have ever seen. It was obvious that if this could be done with a scratch set of plates, put on the cylinder without overlay or underlay, much better results could be obtained with proper precautions. I left the building, feeling that the possibility of an improved illustrated English Petit Journal of handy shape was at last brought within the pale of practical possibilities.

Sun Life Office

ALL LOADINGS RETURNED.

For further Particulars write to the Chief Office—

63, THREADNEEDLE ST., LONDON, E.C.

HARRIS C. L. SAUNDERS, General Manager.

Appointed by Special Royal Warrant		Soap Makers to Her Majesty the Queer.

THE WEDDING MORNING.

What happy recollections the above Picture recalls to those who have helped a Bride with her toilet! Friends ask themselves, Has the Bride a thorough knowledge of all the duties of a household, especially of that ever-recurring worry, Washing Day and Spring Cleaning? Does she know what

SUNLIGHT SOAP

can do? Does she know that for a few pence, without boiling or bleaching, she can, by using SUNLIGHT SOAP, have all the household linen washed at home and made to look white as snow and fresh as roses?

Happy is the bride who has been instructed in these matters, because it is on such simple household details as these that the future happiness and comfort of herself and husband must depend!

"I have never tasted Cocoa that I like so well."— Sir C. A. Cameron, M.D., President Royal College of Surgeons, Ireland.

'Tis so nice

FRY'S

'PURE CONCENTRATED COCOA

SIXTY-FOUR PRIZE MEDALS AWARDED TO J. S. FRY & SONS.

☞ Be careful to ask for FRY'S PURE CONCENTRATED COCOA.

Printed by HAZELL, WATSON, & VINEY, LD., 5 and 6, Kirby Street, E.C.; and Published by HORACE MARSHALL & SON, LD., Fleet Street, E.C.

www.ingramcontent.com/pod-product-compliance
Lightning Source LLC
Chambersburg PA
CBHW031113020726
47495CB00007B/2174